GOD KING RISING

FALL OF WIZARDOMS: BOOK 1

JEFFREY L. KOHANEK

FALLBRANDT PRESS

The final approval for this literary material is granted by the author.

First Edition

Paperback ISBN: 978-1-949382-29-7

This is a work of fiction. Names, characters, businesses, places, events and incidents are either the products of the author's imagination or used in a fictitious manner. Any resemblance to actual persons, living or dead, or actual events is purely coincidental.

PUBLISHED BY JEFFREY L. KOHANEK and FALLBRANDT PRESS

www.JeffreyLKohanek.com

ALSO BY JEFFREY L. KOHANEK

Fate of Wizardoms

Book One: Eye of Obscurance

Book Two: Balance of Magic

Book Three: Temple of the Oracle

Book Four: Objects of Power

Book Five: Rise of a Wizard Queen

Book Six: A Contest of Gods

* * *

Warriors, Wizards, & Rogues (Fate of Wizardoms 0)

Fate of Wizardoms Boxed Set: Books 1-3

Fate of Wizardoms Box Set" Books 4-6

Fall of Wizardoms

God King Rising

Legend of the Sky Sword

Curse of the Elf Queen

Shadow of a Dragon Priest - Aug 2021

Book Five: TBD - Oct 2021

Book Six: TBD -Nov 2021

Runes of Issalia

The Buried Symbol: Runes of Issalia 1

The Emblem Throne: Runes of Issalia 2

An Empire in Runes: Runes of Issalia 3

Rogue Legacy: Runes of Issalia Prequel

* * *

Runes of Issalia Bonus Box

Wardens of Issalia

A Warden's Purpose: Wardens of Issalia 1

The Arcane Ward: Wardens of Issalia 2

An Imperial Gambit: Wardens of Issalia 3

A Kingdom Under Siege: Wardens of Issalia 4

ICON: A Wardens of Issalia Companion Tale

* * *

Wardens of Issalia Boxed Set

JOURNAL ENTRY

W hen I look back on my life, I marvel at the things I experienced...and those I survived.

My youth was difficult and troubled, hardening me for what was to come. Later, as a pirate, I fought beside men as apt to stab you in the back as to buy you an ale. Yet, I thrived, eventually rising to captain my own ship.

A woman in a role dominated by men, I chose to venture where only the courageous or foolish might, charting waters previously thought impassable, and earning myself the moniker Queen of the Shoals. Even so, I discovered there was much I had to learn of the world.

Tales of Urvadan, the Dark Lord, prevail throughout the Eight Wizardoms, often told around the fire at night. The source of all evil, his darkspawn stalking the darkness – these tales conjured frightening images and stirred nightmares unfounded in truth. Or so I thought.

In a frantic, horrible clash in the dark of night, my crew and I fought off a goblin squadron led by a shaman wielding unknowable dark magic. My ship was torched. My crew, slaughtered. I would have died as well had a wizard not appeared. Casting fireballs, lightning, and ferocious twisters, he destroyed the darkspawn and saved my life. This man was known simply as Chandan, and it was through him I was recruited to the Order of Sol.

It was a secret society based in a hidden oasis valley amid the desolate deserts of

*Hassakan. But the Order had members strewn throughout the Eight Wizardoms –
tendrils of influence to apply toward their ultimate objective: To end the threat of the
Dark Lord.*

*As a member of the Order, I worked in secret for three years, until, miraculously,
a squad of heroes guided by our hand, vanquished Urvadan. The battle against the
Dark Lord came with a price. It cost our world the other gods as well. Thus, a
vacuum was created, for without gods to worship, without a higher power for spiritual guidance, mortals are doomed.*

*Thus begins my greatest adventure, one that would see a realm destroyed, hope
lost, a world ended...and another reborn. This tale, I now share with you.*

-Harlequin Ahlee
    Queen of the Shoals

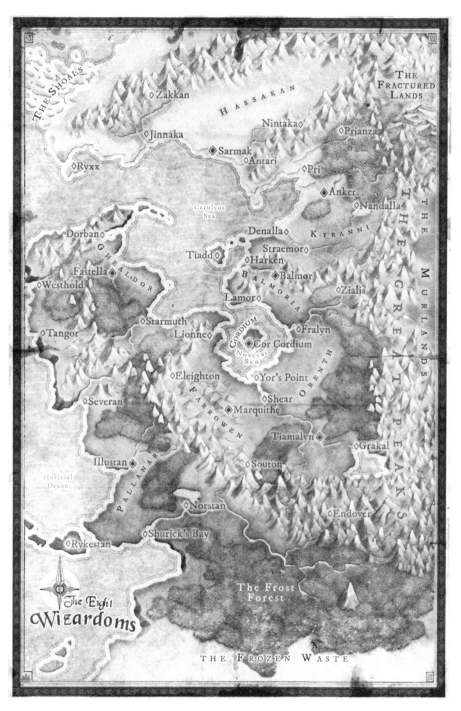

PROLOGUE

G ravel crunched beneath Tranadal's feet as he crested the ridge. Approaching the edge of the cliff, he drew his cloak hood back and stared down into a narrow canyon occupied by a hidden city. A chill clung to the dry night air, welcome after the treacherous journey across the Hassakani desert. During the daylight hours, Tranadal had hidden in the shade of rock outcroppings amid sand dunes and in gorges carved centuries earlier by rivers that no longer existed. As a dark elf, his eyes were attuned to darkness, allowing him to travel at night with little risk of injury. The journey had consumed nine long nights of walking from dusk until dawn, taking him from Domus Argenti, the underground home of his people, to the Valley of Sol. Neither place could be found on any map – one thought lost for millennia, the other unknown to the rest of the world.

The round moon, forever bound to the eastern sky, shone down on the valley and caused the surrounding cliffs to cast dark shadows. Somewhere below him, water ran from a fissure in the cliff wall, spilled over a rocky shelf, and flowed into a narrow lake with a bridge at the far end. White foam bubbled at the bottom of the falls. The reflection of the moon and starry sky wavered in the ripples that drifted across the lake.

Not far from the falls, a massive pyramid loomed over the lake, its crystalline tip shimmering in the moonlight. While the structure's peak stood five hundred feet above the valley floor, it remained a good distance below Tranadal's position.

Along the opposite side of the lake, clustered between the shoreline and the opposing cliffside, were buildings of varied shapes, sizes, and designs – circular and square towers, flat, peaked, and bulbous rooftops, pyramid-shaped buildings, and structures shaped like cubes. The settlement was unique – the result of all civilizations coming together in one tiny Maker-built city. Light came from a handful of village windows, but nothing moved.

He turned and continued along the ridge, circling from the northwest edge of the canyon to the northeast. As always, he carried Ichor in one hand, its smooth black shaft reassuring him, and the soft hum of the souls bound within the weapon constantly singing to him, even while he slept. Should he call upon that song, it would roar like thunder. Many years had passed since he had done so, but that would soon change. While eager to unleash the naginata's power, he could wait. Unlike humans, the Drow were a patient people, their lives spanning centuries rather than decades.

Once above the city, he descended a narrow path along a rock ledge, each step sure and balanced. He knew many humans feared heights, an idea he found ludicrous. Those confident of their footing should discount such fears. Falling was falling. So long as you did not fall, the distance of the fall remained irrelevant.

When the ledge ended, he slid his naginata through loops on his pack and began lowering himself down. The wraps around his feet gripped the jagged rock, while the tips of his fingers found cracks, edges, and lips where none were visible. For hundreds of feet, he descended in a practiced manner, as if born for it.

At the bottom, he followed the cliff wall, careful to remain in the shadows and keep the buildings between him and the shoreline. Soon, he came to a dark tunnel and faded inside. Even with his enhanced vision, the tunnel was nothing more than pale edges of rock amid gloom, the darkest patches leading him deeper into the earth.

A soft light appeared ahead. He rounded a bend and came to a section where striations in the walls glowed with blue light, revealing a door with a sunburst carved into dark-stained wood.

He knocked, the rap of his knuckles echoing in the tunnel.

Noises came from inside, and the door opened to reveal a female. She stood only a few inches shorter than Tranadal, her shaved head revealing tattoos of symbols and spells that ran across her scalp and down her neck. Like him, her skin was ashen in tone, her eyes dark and angled, and her ears pointed. She had long thin fingers with nails painted black. Wearing the golden robes of the Order of Sol, she appeared exactly as she had when Tranadal had last seen her, three seasons earlier.

"Welcome back, brother," she said.

"It is good to return, Dai-Seryn. Is Xavan present?"

"While the humans sleep? Where else would he be at this hour?"

He walked past her. "Good. We have much to discuss."

The doorway led to a domed cavern occupied by furniture – a sitting area consisting of a sofa, loveseat, and low table. A dormant fireplace stood to one side of the room, a long table encircled by chairs to the other. Tranadal crossed the room and ducked into a tunnel, following it to the first room. A bed, a nightstand, and a wardrobe filled the small room. For a hundred years, half of his existence, he had slept in this space. Over that time, he had come to think of it as his own. Of course, it was not truly his, for nothing in the valley belonged to anyone save the Order itself.

He set his pack on the bed, stood Ichor against the wall, and draped his cloak over a hook before following his sister. They soon came to a door at the end of the tunnel, the dark wood pulsing with a malevolent red glow.

Dai-Seryn closed her eyes and placed her hand on a panel beside the door, the ominous light fading. She then knocked.

A musical, lilting voice came from within. "You may enter."

She opened it and led Tranadal inside.

The chamber was as he remembered, perfectly circular in shape, the floor inlaid with thin gold strips forming an eight-pointed star. A desk covered in books stood to one side of the room, where a middle-aged Drow, three centuries old, sat, his finger tracing the pages as he studied a massive tome. Behind the desk was shelving filled with hundreds, if not thousands, of books. Tranadal did not understand how Xavan could be so enthralled by words. *I am a letalis, not a singer.* That very statement said all there was to say on the subject – why Xavan obsessively studied magic of all natures and why Tranadal needed none save for the soul magic of his weapon. Ichor belonged to him, and he to the weapon, bonded for life and paid for in blood. There were times he wondered what it would be like if his own soul had been claimed by the weapon. Sometimes, he wished it had.

Xavan raised his head. Like Tranadal's sister, the singer was covered in ink, but he lacked her natural beauty. With a long face and a slim seven-foot frame, Xavan looked as if he had been stretched by a tool of torture until his proportions were irrevocably distorted.

The singer sat back in his chair, his long elegant fingers flowing as he spoke. "You have returned." As always, Xavan's musical voice lilted when he spoke.

Another female Drow entered the chamber. She stood nearly as tall as Tranadal and, like him, was stout for a dark elf, her frame covered in long lean muscles. As a warrior, few were Arci-Aesha's equal, even without the enchanted naginata at her side.

"Arci." Tranadal gave her a respectful nod. Although unrelated, she had become a sister to him since their exile.

"I am pleased to see you have returned," she said. "I have missed our duels. Humans lack the speed and finesse of a proper warrior. Even Tempest offers little challenge in the sparring yard."

Before Tranadal could reply, Xavan interrupted.

"You two can speak later. First, I would hear of your journey."

Tranadal dipped his head to the singer. "As bidden, I traveled to Domus Argenti and met with the Coven to share what has occurred. When I informed them of the Dark Lord's demise and disappearance of the other gods, they were reluctant to believe. For breaking my penance and returning, they confiscated my weapon and locked me in a cell, holding me until they could prove or disprove my claims, while simultaneously planning my execution.

"Isolated, I remained while they sent scouts south to ferret out the truth. Many weeks passed, causing my hope to dwindle. Finally, those scouts returned, each confirming that the gods of the wizardoms were absent, their towers dark, and their crystal thrones dormant. In the east, Urvadan's tower has turned to solid crystal. It gleams with raw power, a crimson beacon in the dark Murlands. Only then did they free me and truly listen to your plea."

Xavan tented his fingers. "So, they now believe."

"The Coven could no longer deny the truth or ignore the signs. As you requested, they have begun preparing for a return to the surface world.

However, they remain reluctant. Unlike the humans, the Drow remain few in number – their wizards greatly outnumber our singers."

Leaning back, Xavan smirked. "I have foreseen their response and am already taking action. The war last year reduced the human armies and altered the power structure that upheld them for millennia. Pull the right bricks free and the rest will crumble." The singer stood, his height exceeding that of Tranadal. "Without gods to Gift wizards with true power, the wizard lords are no more. Humans are sheep without a shepherd, ripe for slaughter. Our people will soon return to the surface to reclaim our rightful place."

With gliding steps, Xavan floated past, his golden robes swishing like curtains in a soft breeze. Mounted to the wall was a staff, the wooden shaft six feet in length and one end capped by a pointed crystal. Xavan reached up, gripped the staff, and freed it with a pop. He stared into the crystal, his eyes filled with a desire not for flesh but for power. An unfamiliar sensation ran down Tranadal's spine, twisting his innards. Fear.

With a nod, Xavan spun toward the door. "Come."

Tranadal shot a questioning look at his sister and whispered, "Where would we go at this hour?"

Xavan paused at the door and smiled, revealing a mouth with too many teeth. "Is it not obvious? It is time to visit the vaunted leader of the Order."

While Dai-Seryn and Arci-Aesha followed Xavan toward the exit, Tranadal stopped in his room to retrieve his weapon. Unlike the others who wore the golden robes of the Order, he was still dressed in his dark travel clothing. But there was no time to change. They were unlikely to come across any members of the Order at this hour anyway.

As Tranadal emerged, he found Arci-Aesha holding a weapon identical to his own – a naginata with a shiny black shaft, with a metal cap at one end and a razor-sharp blade the length of his forearm at the other. Silver runes marked the shaft. Others etched into the metal. Unlike most letalis weapons, those wielded by Tranadal and Arci-Aesha had been augmented by magic, forever capturing the souls of their victims and giving them abilities far beyond those of other warriors.

Once everyone was outside, Xavan led them down a shadowy path winding between buildings and bordered by palms whose fronds swayed in the soft evening breeze. The path brought them to a road, and the road to a circular tower on the shore of the lake.

9

Xavan opened the door and entered the tower, followed by the two females. Pausing, Tranadal glanced up and down the road but saw nothing moving other than palm fronds. He stepped inside and closed the door before trailing his three fellow Drow up the curved stairwell.

A few levels up, they came to a closed door. Rather than knock, Xavan entered. The rooms on the level were vacant, the light of the moon streaming through east facing windows. So they continued up to the fifth level.

The bedroom was unoccupied; the private study dark and silent. Xavan approached a closed door, his arms extended before him and a soft aria arising from his throat, but while his lips moved, the words were unintelligible. The knob turned, and the door creaked softly until it stood open to reveal another curved stairwell.

Xavan turned toward them. "Do not touch the door. You'll not enjoy what occurs if you do so."

Ascending the stairs, his robes swishing with each step, Xavan led them toward the top floor. Moonlight streamed through an arched window at the midpoint, and another closed door lurked at the top. Again, Xavan sang. This time his tone wavered, rising in pitch until the door clicked and swung open to reveal amber light.

Xavan climbed to the top and entered, the two women close behind, and Tranadal entering last.

A single circular room covered the entire floor with eight arched windows spaced along the wall. The space between windows was occupied by shelves filled with books and pedestals topped by odd contraptions. In the room's center was a table with piles of open books and a flickering lantern on one corner. The lantern's amber light revealed a man with black hair and a black beard.

Rising to his feet, the man demanded, "What is the meaning of this intrusion?"

"I have urgent news, Master Chandan," Xavan said in his musical voice.

Chandan's white robes marked him as the leader of the Order of Sol, a mantle he had earned less than a year ago. More notably, the man was both a passable sorcerer and a skilled wizard. When Arci-Aesha positioned herself at one end of Chandan's table, Tranadal circled to stand opposite her with the butt of Ichor on the floor. Sensing the tension, he called upon the souls trapped in his weapon, bidding them to arise. A hum stirred inside of Ichor, longing to be unleashed.

Narrowing his eyes, Chandan stared at Tranadal. "So, you have returned after your mysterious disappearance. Care to explain?"

Tranadal cast a glance at Xavan, who nodded. "I returned to Domus Argenti to inform my people of what transpired."

"And what did you tell them?"

"The Dark Lord is dead and gone, and the gods of men are no longer of this world."

"To what end? The dark elves have remained apart from the rest of the world for two thousand years. Why would they care about such things?"

Xavan waved his long fingers before his face. "The time nears for the Drow to reclaim their rightful place."

Chandan turned toward the singer. "Which is?"

"We were once the preeminent of beings, destined to rule all...until Urvadan broke the world. The new gods arose in the wake of the Cataclysm, the wizard lords with them, shifting the balance in favor of the humans." The music faded from his voice and he snarled. "But no longer! We will crush the humans and rule the world. And the Order will help us do it."

"Never!" Chandan roared as he launched a lightning bolt, not at Xavan, but at Tranadal.

Ready, Tranadal opened his mouth, the voices of the souls bound to his weapon emerging as Ichor spun in his hands. Chandan's attack struck, the electricity crackling and dissipating.

Chandan spun away and released another spell, blasting the table to shards, pieces of wood spraying toward Dai-Seryn and Xavan. Both gripped Xavan's staff, their mouths opening to release an impossibly high note. The crystal atop the staff flashed with a purple light.

The world froze.

The wizard's face was etched in a snarl, his arms outstretched in preparation to release another spell. Shards of his destroyed table hovered in the air between the wizard and the two singers. The books that had been resting on the table were in disarray, their covers open and pages flaring. The lantern, emitting an amber arc of trailing flame, hovered in a tipped position. It was odd to see fire that did not flicker but maintained a bright streak of solid light.

"Incredible," Tranadal muttered.

Dai-Seryn circled to stand beside him. "The effect will soon fade."

Arci-Aesha prodded Chandan with a blade, its tip stained with the wizard's blood when it was removed. Yet the action elicited no reaction.

Snatching the lantern from the air, Xavan turned it right side up. He then pointed toward Chandan. "Tranadal, strike him in the head before the spell breaks. Do not kill him. Wizard blood has its uses, and I prefer him alive."

Lifting his weapon, Tranadal called on the souls to render the man unconscious. The butt of the staff drove into Chandan's head. Rather than fall, his head and upper body shifted and froze in a tilted position that defied gravity.

The shimmering light of the crystal faded, and the world returned to normal.

Shards of wood struck the wall, shelves, and door, some falling down the open stairwell, others clattering to the floor. Books landed in a series of thuds, pages tearing as they settled. Chandan toppled like a felled tree, his head striking the stone tiles. There, he lay still, his eyes closed and breathing shallow.

"Pick him up," Xavan said as he walked toward the door.

Tranadal squatted, Arci-Aesha helping him drape the unconscious wizard over his shoulder.

Scowling, Xavan glanced back at Tranadal. "Let us return to our quarters. There, we will question the human."

"Then what?" Tranadal asked as the singer drifted toward the stairwell.

"Then we will take his blood," Xavan said. "And I will don the white cloak, for the Order of Sol is ours to control."

1

DUPLICITY

Harlequin Ahlee leaned into the mirror and examined her reflection, tawny skin glistening in the afternoon light streaming through the window. Thin lines branched from her brown eyes and tracked across her forehead – reminders that her thirty-sixth name day had recently passed.

She backed up a few steps, twisted, and ran a hand down her flat stomach. Despite her advancing years, her bare body remained lean and fit, her arms toned from a lifetime of sailing and countless hours of sparring. Yes, her modest breasts had succumbed to gravity, no longer as perky as in her youth, but none of her partners seemed to care, least of all the man in the copper tub behind her.

Three seasons earlier, the reflection staring back at her would have been bereft of hair, not a single strand across her entire body. Now she wished much of that hair had not grown back. The exception was her full head of locks, brown with gentle curls that brushed her shoulders. It would take another year or longer for her mane to reach its full glory. Once, her hair had been a source of pride – long and flowing, readily teased by the ocean breezes. Stories of Captain Harlequin, Queen of the Shoals, often began with her hair. *Eyebrows are also most welcome*, she thought. Somehow, bare brows had seemed odder than a bald head.

From a hook on the wall, she claimed a towel and dried herself starting with her hair. She then moved to her body, from her shoulders to her feet, pausing to examine her shins, desperately due for a shave. Not in the mood, she decided it could wait another day.

Hanging the towel back on the hook, she winced and worked her arm. "My shoulder is sore. You hit me pretty hard today."

From another hook, she grabbed the robes she had worn every day since her arrival in the valley, over a year earlier. She eyed them, rubbing the light golden cloth between two fingers, still damp to the touch. *A few minutes in the desert heat will dry them…but by then, my own sweat will only make them damp again.* Such was life in the Valley of Sol.

Crusser grunted. "You give as well as you get both in the sparring yard and in the bedroom. My cracked ribs will make it difficult to sleep for a while."

Still naked and gripping her robes, she turned toward the Kyranni ex-soldier who remained in the copper tub, his lower body submerged, while white suds gathered around his mocha-skinned torso. Despite approaching forty and having spent the past three years in the valley, he remained fit – his arms thickly muscled, his chest chiseled, and his stomach rippled. While not particularly skilled in the bedroom, his body was among the finest of any man she had known…and she had known many. *With my coaching, his skills have improved.*

Her lips curled in a mischievous grin. "For that hit to my shoulder, you deserved what you got in the yard. As for the bedroom…you seemed to welcome my enthusiasm."

"Must you leave now?" he asked in his deep voice. "You are welcome to remain longer. I could make you dinner, and should the opportunity arise, breakfast tomorrow."

"This visit was just for pleasure." She opened the fabric and pulled the robes over her head.

"Always is," he muttered.

She sighed, the robes bunched at her shoulders. "I told you before. I am not seeking a relationship. In fact, if this new god has any love for me, he or she will appear soon, so I can leave this dreadful, boring valley." Slipping her arms in, the loose robes fell toward the floor, the hem reaching her ankles.

Crusser grumbled, "So you expect me to just bend to your urges when-ever they arise?"

"You have thus far…multiple times a week for weeks on end."

"What about how *I* feel?"

She glared at him. "Don't you dare say it, Cruss!"

"But I love…"

"Stop!" she shoved her palm into his face. "Why must you go there? Can't we just have fun and leave it at that? You know I will eventually leave the valley. When I do, I may never return."

"I could leave with you," he offered.

"That is not how the Order works. If Order business requires you here, you will remain here. If they assign you a role elsewhere, that is where you go. Remember, it is all for the greater good." She frowned. "Which was easier to understand when defeating the Dark Lord was our primary objective. Now…Chandan talks of a new god, destined to rise. But what is time to a god? What if decades or even centuries pass before his or her arrival?"

He rose, water raining off him as he stood in the shin deep water. While Harlequin was tall for a woman, Crusser stood taller and outweighed her by a fair margin.

"Perhaps I can convince him to send me with you?" he suggested.

Sighing again, Harlequin stopped at the edge of the tub and gently raked her nails down his torso, her eyes looking up to meet his as her hand drew lower. "For now, try not to let your feelings or concerns about the future ruin what we have. Focus on the present, and…" She bit her lip, her hand reaching its destination. "Enjoy yourself."

He moaned, reacting to her advances, his hands slipping around her hips, attempting to pull her against him.

Rather than allow it to go further, she backed away and reached for the doorknob. "Do as I ask, and I will be back."

Crusser stepped out of the tub, gesturing toward himself. "So you again raise my flag and leave it to the mercy of the wind?"

She glanced down, grinning. "If the wind does it for you, feel free. However, I must go. I am to meet Chandan for dinner, to discuss my next objective. I am hoping for something other than your body to keep me occu-pied." Stepping into the corridor, she cast him one last glance. "Meet in the sparring yards at sunup?"

He nodded. "I know. You wish to beat me with a stick again."

Chuckling, she nodded. "Better than with my sabre. Still, you know why I practice."

"You don't wish to lose your edge."

"Exactly. See you then."

Exiting the room, Harlequin closed the door and descended the stairs. She passed through Crusser's sitting room and found her sandals beside the door, slipping them on before heading outside.

In the shade of Crusser's cube-shaped abode, she breathed in the warm desert air. Even in the shade, it was hot. Spring had just begun with summer fast approaching. When it arrived, the heat would be intolerable.

She stepped into the blistering sunlight and followed the path from Crusser's home. On one side was a squat tower, six stories tall, with a bridge connecting it to an identical tower next door. A long, narrow, rectangular building with an angled roof stood on her other side, the path winding between palms before connecting to the road that ran through the village. She stopped and drank in the scenery.

Running from north to south, the Valley of Sol was a narrow canyon, its opposing cliffs no more than a half mile apart. A lake ran down the center, its limestone bottom visible through crystal blue, spring-fed waters. Across the lake, water flowed from a fissure in the hillside and over a rocky outcropping before tumbling fifty feet to the water below. The roar of the falls carried across the lake, and sunlight shone on the mist, creating a rainbow above the falls. Also across the lake, down the shore from the falls, was the Temple of Sol – a pyramid hundreds of feet tall, its peak made of shimmering crystal.

A stream flowed from the south end of the lake and meandered down the narrow canyon, the shores thick with trees and shrubs. Over the mouth of the stream was an arching bridge, connecting the village to the pyramid.

A bell rang, echoing throughout the quiet valley. She turned toward the bell tower, a figure in golden robes standing below the narrow spire, tugging on a long rope. She counted; the bell continued until it chimed eight times.

"Oh, no," she muttered.

Since her arrival in the valley, the bell had chimed to a count of eight on only one occasion. On that date, all had gathered to hear Chandan announce the passing of the gods. Now, with the gods dead and gone, she wondered what event had triggered a special meeting.

Dark-skinned and light-skinned humans emerged from the pale stone buildings. Among them were dwarfs and elves, representing every race and wizardom in the world. Most had shaved heads, even the women, and all were dressed in gold robes, walking in pairs as they headed toward the bridge.

Kai Crusser finished drying himself and set the towel aside. He leaned toward the mirror and eyed the stubble on his face. Here and there, shoots of silver hid among the black.

"You are growing old, Cruss," he said to himself. "You survived the Fractured Lands only to grow old from boredom in this forsaken valley."

As a Kyranni soldier, serving in the Murguard had been inevitable. Those were hard, dark years, the kind that left a lasting imprint, dooming him to a lifetime of nightmares. Often, he would wake coated in sweat, his heart racing. The worst of those dreams would lead to violence, and he found himself lashing out toward anything – or anyone – nearby. He suspected it was why Harlequin never spent the entire night in his bed.

He lifted his golden robes off the hook and eyed them briefly before slipping them over his head. He had spent five years working for the Order – four as a private guard for Lord Kelluon, ruler of Kyranni, the last one in the Valley of Sol, waiting for an assignment elsewhere.

Now, Kelluon was dead, and Crusser's entire people had been slaughtered by darkspawn. *Perhaps I should have remained with them. Perhaps I could have done something to save them.* Yet the sentiment, even in his own head, felt hollow. He knew he would be dead as well if he had not responded to Astra's call to leave his home. Only hours after he had left Anker, the wizard lord had died, the city falling with him.

A bell rang, drawing Crusser from his reverie. He counted the chimes while descending the stairs. *Eight. Something has happened.* He slipped into his sandals and hurried outside.

The path led him past clusters of palms, the trees parting to reveal Harlequin at the edge of the road.

"You didn't make it far," he said as he drew near.

She turned toward him. "The bell tolled eight times."

"Yes. We are to gather in the temple." He rubbed the stubble on his head, thinking he would soon need to shave it. "I wonder why."

"While I am starving, I suppose we had better go find out."

Before he could reply, she headed down the road, forcing him to hurry to catch her.

They passed the small crystal pyramid tip that capped Lord Astra's underground domain, a place Crusser had only visited once. He wondered if Astra's quarters would remain empty or if another leader would claim the building. Chandan had told the order members that Astra was no longer of this world. In private, Crusser had asked the wizard if Astra were dead. As usual, Chandan replied in a cryptic manner, stating *"He has moved to an altered state of being,"* Whatever that meant.

They passed beneath an arching bridge, connecting a square tower to a building made of numerous cubic sections, the widest at the bottom, each narrower than the one below, the structure appearing like a six-story tall series of stairs. Beyond it was a single-storied cottage with a peaked roof, the next building capped by a pointed dome. In the gaps between buildings were solitary pillars, obelisks, fountains, and arches. When Crusser first arrived in the valley, the oddly varied architecture of the city had filled him with a sense of wonder. Even after living in the valley for a year, the village remained alien – as if it were a relic from another race, long gone from the world.

By the time Crusser and Harlequin reached the point where the road turned, dozens of Order members were ahead of them and nearly as many trailed behind. They ascended the arching bridge, the air cooling over the flowing water, only to warm again after descending to the other side. The path ran along the shoreline and brought them to the massive pyramid.

Built of pale stone blocks, each taller than a person and twice their length, the Temple of Sol left Crusser wondering how its construction had ever been possible. Even after living a lifetime around Maker-built cities, he often found himself marveling at their skill. His gaze rose higher, settling on the crystal peak, gleaming in the sunlight.

Entering an open doorway at the base, shadows engulfed them, the temperature dropping dramatically. A simple torchlit corridor took them straight forward and past intersecting tunnels which led in both directions.

They came to a stairwell and descended, the temperature dropping further. *Sometimes I wish I could live in the temple and escape the blasted heat.* Then again, he had seen things in the temple – things he would prefer to avoid when trying to sleep. His nightmares were bad enough already.

The stairwell ended at a short corridor leading to an enormous, awe-inspiring chamber.

Walls made of stone blocks encased a square-shaped room hundreds of feet across. A complex mosaic of colored tiles – symbols of power and patterns of magic – covered the floor. The angled ceiling came together at a square section of crystal, sunlight refracting through it in a beam of color, growing continually wider until it reached the floor, hundreds of feet below.

Three of the four Drow who lived in the valley stood within that beam of light. All three had pale ashen-like skin, angled eyes, and pointed ears marking their race. While Crusser knew them by name – Tranadal, Arci-Aesha, and Dai-Seryn – in truth, he did not know them at all. The dark elves kept to themselves, seemingly brooding and rife with secrets. Time and again, he had told himself to stop judging the dark elves by their appearance, but he could not help feeling that there was something amiss. Tranadal's disappearance was a prime example. For the better part of a year, the Drow had not been seen, yet the others repeatedly claimed to know nothing of his whereabouts. *How long was he gone before Chandan noticed and pressed Xavan? The dark elves all live together. How could they not know he was gone? Why did they not report it? Where did he go for all that time?* With Tranadal returned, hair grown back – pure black with a white streak from his temple to his neck – perhaps answers would come. Somehow, Crusser remained doubtful.

Order members continued to filter into the chamber, forming a circle around the dark elves in the center. The temple fell quiet, but Crusser remained unsettled. He wondered why Chandan was not present and thought it odd to see the three Drow without the fourth. *They are rarely apart.*

Harlequin broke the silence, posing a question many had likely been considering. "Does anyone know if Chandan called this meeting?" Without waiting for a reply, she asked the dark elves. "And where is Xavan?"

"He is behind you," sounded a musical male voice.

Everyone turned, their ranks parting to allow the tall dark elf with red eyes to pass through. His skin was even paler than the other three, his body and features long and elegant. Rather than wearing robes of gold like the others, his were white. As Xavan glided past, Crusser wondered, *why is he wearing white?*

Joining his brethren, Xavan turned toward the crowd, held his hands up, and began to sing. The words were unintelligible and foreign, yet they carried a sense of power. The Drow then turned his attention toward the pyramid floor, the eight-pointed star beneath him glowing, pulsing, humming. The beams of colored light began to swirl.

"Behold what has transpired," Xavan announced in his smooth, chanting tone.

The colors coalesced into an image, depicting a circular room with arched windows. Ornate black tables, a desk, bookshelves, and pedestals occupied the room. The floor was marked by an eight-pointed star similar to that in the temple. Chandan, wearing his white robes and looking downcast, stood in the heart of the symbol.

Xavan entered the room and spoke to the wizard, but the vision conveyed no sound. When Chandan lifted his head, he appeared distraught with bags beneath his eyes and tear-streaked cheeks. He said something to Xavan and began to undress. Lifting the robes over his head, he tossed them to the elf, revealing a heavily tattooed body coated in dried blood. Chandan then lifted his head toward the sky and shouted, his body trembling. Xavan walked toward the wizard, his arm outstretched and fingers spread. The wizard thrust a hand toward the elf and blasted him back, his body striking a book-shelf and sinking to the floor. Xavan lifted his head and rubbed his temple, appearing dazed.

Chandan's hands twisted. His lips moved and his body shook as he arched his hands over his head. White-hot flames shot from his hands, obscuring the wizard from view. The table beside him burst into flames, forcing Xavan to shield his face with an upraised arm. Smoke billowed, filling the room. Xavan crawled to the window and threw it open, allowing the smoke out into the night sky. He then turned and began chanting with outstretched arms. When he lowered his arms, the flames dwindled until they were completely snuffed out.

The table was blackened; the books on it destroyed. Beyond them, the unrecognizable remnants of Chandan lay on the scorched floor. Xavan approached the charred corpse and nudged Chandan's leg with his foot. The leg crumbled to dust. The elf backed away with a horrified expression, shaking his head from side to side as if to deny what he had witnessed. Stumbling into a bookshelf, he glanced down at the white robes on the floor. Xavan stared at the robes for a long moment, appearing torn by some internal struggle. Finally, he scooped up the robes and turned to leave.

The image blurred to raw colors and then faded, revealing the four dark elves standing together in the light.

With his musical tone Xavan announced, "As you can see, the Order has come to a crossroads. Chandan, the man in whom Lord Astra placed his faith, has succumbed to despair."

Crusser frowned and looked at Harlequin who stared at the dark elves with narrowed eyes. She had known Chandan for years, describing the wizard as driven and committed to the Order's purpose. Suicide required self-doubt, self-loathing, or overwhelming depression, none of which sounded like him.

"What happened?" Harlequin demanded, breaking the temple code of conduct. "Why would Chandan take his own life?"

Xavan's head tilted toward the floor, his eyes dejected as he shook his head. "Sadly, he is human. Like many humans, particularly those who are most devout, his faith in a higher power was the root of his existence. The passing of his god tore a hole in the man's soul. Although our prophecies foretell the coming of another god – a single true god – to rise and replace those we have lost, he could no longer bear living in a godless world."

Crusser frowned.

Xavan slowly turned as he spoke, his angled eyes meeting the gazes of the surrounding members. "Before he took his life, Chandan bade me to take the mantle of leadership and continue what he, Astra, and prior leaders had done. Certain that humanity would crumble beneath the weight of a godless world, he said, *You have been among us the longest, Xavan. Drow are resilient and have survived many centuries of hardship. Until you came to the Order, you thought the world was doomed to fall to the Dark Lord, yet you did not despair. You must find a way to ensure all peoples find hope while you wait for the coming of the true god.*"

Mutters came from the other members. Crusser noted the grimace on Harlequin's face.

Xavan stopped between his fellow dark elves and placed his hands on their shoulders. "I have not slept since Chandan's death, spending the last two nights and two days meditating and seeking guidance. At noon today, I had an epiphany. I know how to save the peoples." In a friendly gesture, uncommon for the Drow, he put an arm around Tranadal and Dai-Seryn. "We will give them gods to worship."

2

CONSPIRACY

A sea of stars filled the sky. Just to the east, the round moon shone down on the Valley of Sol, bathing the village in a ghostly light. It was nearly midnight and quiet, apart from the falls.

Harlequin slunk through the shadows, avoiding the moonlight until she reached the road. She peered in both directions, saw nobody, and then turned her attention to the six-story tower looming over the lake. Scurrying across, she ducked into the recessed doorway and tested the handle to find it unlocked. She slipped inside, eased the door closed, and went to the window, peering out to ensure nobody had followed. Once satisfied, she headed to the curved stairwell and began her ascent. As she rose past the dark second floor and glimpsed the vacant kitchen and dining areas, she considered the challenge ahead.

Chandan was a wizard and wizards were fond of secrets. To make matters worse, the man also practiced sorcery, doubling the need to protect his secrets from falling into the wrong hands. His reluctance to share information had somehow grown worse after Astra disappeared and left him in charge. As a result, the upper levels of Chandan's tower were protected by a combination of magical wards, one of wizardly magic and another of sorcery. Despite this, he had confided in Harlequin and she knew how to pass each ward in case anything ever happened to him. At the time, she had found it odd that he had placed his faith in her, a pirate. Even her own crew had been reluctant to share secrets, but that reluctance might be particular to pirate life, the only life she had known before Chandan had recruited her to the Order. The faith he had placed in Harlequin made her proud, as though she had turned a corner and made up for some of her past transgressions.

At the fourth level, she passed the guest apartments, crossed Chandan's private sitting room, and entered his study. She rounded the desk, knelt, and felt beneath it until she found a recess. She pressed it and heard a click, as a circular wooden plug came free. She caught the vial that dropped from it. When held to the window, she saw dark liquid inside, sparkling in the moonlight. *Chandan's blood*. It was the key to the first ward.

Harlequin hurried from the room and up the stairs, arriving in Chandan's bedroom. She paused and stared at the empty bed, feeling a pang of loss. The man had often been mysterious and aloof, but he had also been her friend. It hurt to think she might never see him again. *I must know*. With that in mind, she turned to the black door.

She opened the vial and poured the blood on her hand, recorking it and rubbing the dark liquid until it covered her palm and fingers. She held her breath, fearing what might happen, then gripped the knob and opened the door.

A sigh slipped out. "At least that worked."

She ascended the stairwell, illuminated by a window halfway up. Beyond it was a pulsing red glow. At the midpoint, the source of the malevolent light came into view – the door to his secret lair.

She opened the window and leaned out. Fifty feet below, the calm lake waters reflected the moon, Chandan's tower among the few buildings built on the shoreline. Reaching to the right, she felt the stones. When she came across one that felt cool, the others still retaining the absorbed warmth of the sunlight, she pressed it. It clicked and tipped open to reveal a hidden compartment. Blindly, she felt inside the opening, her fingers finding a rounded knob. When pressed, it clicked, the glow from the top of the stairwell fading.

Harlequin closed the window, climbed the stairs, and touched the door. Nothing happened, so she turned the knob and entered Chandan's lair.

It was as she had seen in the vision, except this time the circular room was dark, illuminated only by moonbeams streaming through arched windows. Another difference – the table that had once occupied the middle of the room was destroyed, its shattered remnants strewn about the room amid a handful of books, most lying open, some face down. She turned from the remains of the table, walked to the middle of the symbol on the floor, and knelt. Her hand touched the stone tiles where the vision had shown Chandan's charred corpse. There were no scorch marks and no trace of a fire. What she had seen of the table and the floor confirmed her suspicions. *The vision Xavan shared was a lie.*

She stood, still staring at the floor. *Why did he do it? What happened to Chandan?* Hearing a noise, she spun toward the door.

Xavan crooned in his musical voice, "I suspected our illustrious pirate might know how to access this room."

Tranadal and Dai-Seryn flanked the dark elf as he entered the room .

Harlequin snarled. "You killed him."

"Of course. He would not listen to reason, so he had to be removed." Xavan shook his head. "Have no fear, my friend. You will not miss him for long, for you are about to join him."

Dai-Seryn opened her mouth, emitting a harsh note. A blast of energy surged across the floor, sweeping Harlequin off her feet. She fell hard and rolled aside as Tranadal's blade crashed into the floor, barely missing her. On her other side, a pedestal toppled, the metal contraption atop it crashing to the floor. The object had a tube over a foot in length and a base as big as her head, all made of brass. As she rolled past it to avoid another strike, she scooped it up, stood, and ran. Desperate, she threw the object at the nearest window, shattering the glass in a spray of shards.

Tranadal swung again, aiming to cleave her head from her body. Harlequin dove out of the way, rolled, and came up at the broken window. She vaulted onto the sill and leapt out as a burst of flames came through the opening, setting her robes on fire, the flames chasing her as she plunged toward the lake.

She leaned back slightly, feet together as flames ate at her robes. Her feet broke the surface with her body at an angle. She plunged into the cold water, her trajectory curling until she was horizontal. The limestone bottom scraped her back, and bubbles surrounded her as the momentum ceased.

Surfacing, Harlequin gasped for air. High above, she saw Tranadal peering through the broken window. The soaked robes weighed her down, and she had little time to escape. She ducked beneath the water, and lifted the robes up over her head, kicking her sandals off in the process. Freed from her clothing, she surfaced and swam hard. A sailor and lifelong swimmer, she swam with speed, quickly reaching the shore and climbing the steep bank. Naked, she darted across the road and into the shadow, her mind racing. *I cannot prove their guilt, and even if I could, Xavan controls the Order. I cannot allow them to catch me, or I am as good as dead.* She heard the sounds of a door opening and footsteps darting out.

The dark elves would expect her to return to her home, so she ran straight toward it, reached the front door, and tore it open, darting inside. She went straight for a side window, threw it open, and quickly climbed out. She slunk through the shadows behind two neighboring buildings and arrived at Crusser's hovel, knowing the door would be unlocked. After all, why lock your door in a remote village bereft of crime? *Until Chandan's murder.* The thought aroused her anger and her desire to see Xavan and his brethren punished.

She slipped inside, rushed up the stairs, and spoke in a hushed, yet urgent voice. "Cruss! Wake up!"

When she burst into his room, the man jerked to a sitting position, his naked torso visible in the moonlight as he lay in bed.

"Harley? What wrong?"

"They killed him." She rushed to the trunk at the foot of his bed.

"Who?"

"The dark elves." She opened the lid and began rifling through the trunk. "They murdered Chandan."

Still sitting in bed, he rubbed his eyes and shook his head. "What are you talking about? We all saw the vision."

Harlequin paused and looked at him. "The vision was a lie...manufactured to prevent anyone from asking questions." She turned back to the trunk and dug out a pair of breeches, boots, a tunic, and a vest.

"Is that possible?"

"Apparently it is." She found her hat and pulled that out as well. Last, but most importantly, she found her sabre. "I am *so* glad I agreed to use your chest to hold my things."

As she dressed, he rolled out of bed. "If Xavan killed Chandan, what do we do? Can you prove it?"

Pulling her breeches to her waist, she found herself wishing she had smallclothes. Those were back in her apartment. "Probably not. Now that they are in his private chamber, they can burn the table and the floor to make it appear as it did in the vision. It'll be my word against theirs...unless we can find his body."

"If you challenge them and fail, you will be ousted."

She finished pulling her tunic down and snorted. "Ousted? They will see me dead as soon as possible." Stepping closer to him, she put her hand on his cheek. "Listen, you lunkhead. This is about an agenda. The Drow wish to influence the world of man and intend to use the Order to make it happen. I'll not claim to understand their motives, for they are a secretive lot. Still, if I am right, do you believe they will allow me to leave here alive?"

He blinked and drew back. "You're right. You need to leave before they catch you."

Spinning around, Crusser ran to the wardrobe and began to rifle through it. He dug out clothing, leather armor, metal bracers, and a sword, throwing each item on his bed.

"What are you doing?" she asked.

The man began dressing. "I am coming with you."

An amber light flared in the night. Harlequin ran to the window and peered over the neighboring homes. Just beyond them, a domed single-story building burned, the flames flickering in the night as Order members began to emerge from their homes.

Crusser stood beside her, buckling his sword belt while staring out the window. "You were right."

"My home," she said. "They thought I was inside."

"How are we going to get out of here?"

"We will need food and as much water as we can carry. I know a way out through Astra's underground tunnels. Once in the hills, we will make for Nintaka."

"Then what?"

"Then we head downstream and find me a ship."

"A ship?"

She turned to him with a grin. "I'm a ship's captain, remember? Can't be a captain without a ship."

3

BERSERK

The barge floated downstream, the Rintari River slowly carrying it toward the Ceruleos Sea. Irrigated fields lay just beyond the shrub covered riverfront, fading into distant shadows cast by the hills to the west. Draped above that horizon was the setting sun, painting scattered clouds in pink light, bright against the deep blue sky. Beyond those hills, the dry and desolate Hassakan Desert stretched for hundreds of miles.

Harlequin hated the desert just as she had despised most of the journey she and Crusser had endured since their flight from the Valley of Sol. *Soon, I will return to the sea.* Seven days since their midnight departure, half of which were spent hiking through mountains on foot, the barge rounded a bend and she caught sight of Antari.

Buildings made of hardened mud and pale stone blocks hugged the riverfront where docks jutted into the water, fishing boats moored along them. Farther downstream was the old city, encapsulated by rock walls built to rebuff attackers. Within the old city, Antari Castle stood on a hilltop, its blocky towers rising high above the city walls.

The barge altered course, angling from the middle of the river and easing toward an open dock. They would land within minutes, so Harlequin turned from the rail and ducked into the cabin she shared with Crusser.

"Get up. We are about to dock." She began gathering her things.

Crusser sat up and rubbed his eyes. He wore a sleeveless tunic, which showed off his thick muscular arms. "Thank the gods. I look forward to a real bed and a decent meal."

"Only a meal?"

She buckled her sword belt, the leather resting on the curve of her hips. It felt good to have Talon at her side. She had owned the sabre for over a decade, spending much of the first year training with the highly reputed Hassakani swordsman, Falazon the Black. With it in her hand, she had survived impossible situations more than once.

Hilt in her grip, she lifted it a few inches and let go, the blade dropping back into the scabbard with a satisfying ring. "More than anything, I look forward to a decent drink. The Order makes a passable wine, but give me a nice cold mug of ale or a glass of swoon any day."

Still sitting on the edge of the bed, Crusser pulled his collar to his nose, his face twisting in a grimace. "A week of hot travel has left a funk. My clothing smells of sweat, camels, and other things I'd rather not name."

"You don't smell so great yourself," she noted. "Neither do I."

Rising to his feet, he slipped a metal-plated bracer on his forearm. Wearing only breeches, boots, and his tan tunic, Crusser cast a daunting image. Adding metal bracers to his arms and a longsword on his hip, he appeared every inch a warrior, and he wasn't even wearing armor.

Harlequin lifted her pack. It felt light with her food gone and her water-skins empty. She stuffed her brimmed hat and leather vest inside. Both would go unneeded until she encountered cooler weather. *Once I am on the sea,* she thought. *I just hope Hassaka's Breath is in port.* The ship belonged to the Order, but she had commanded it and its crew for more than a year. Convincing those men to follow her might pose a challenge, but far less so than starting over.

A thump came from the hull, the barge shaking and settling.

"It seems we have landed." Throwing his pack on his shoulder, Crusser nodded. "Let's go."

With Harlequin in the lead, they headed out on deck as the workers secured the lines, the barge hugging the dock. A cart waited as the crew began lifting buckets of ore off the barge floor and dockworkers loaded the buckets onto the cart.

Antari had the best smithies in Hassakan, fed by ore mined in Nintaka, a small city nestled in the mountains along the Kyranni border. She and Crusser had departed from the mining town days earlier. Nintaka was a hot, miserable place. It left her wondering if the miners were criminals sentenced to work there, for she could not fathom why anyone would choose to live in such conditions.

Harlequin approached Jakko the barge captain and placed a gold piece in his hand. "As we agreed." It was five times what they owed for the passage. "Remember. You never saw us."

The man tilted his head, furrowing his brow in feigned confusion. "I am sorry. I do not believe we have met."

Grinning, Harlequin nodded. "Exactly."

As the sun slipped below the horizon, she hopped to the dock and headed toward the buildings on shore.

"Where are we going?" Crusser asked as she led him down the gravel road.

"Into the old city, to an inn called the Dented Cup. It's near the sea harbor, the most likely place to find one of my old shipmates."

"What is this ship you keep mentioning?"

"*Hassaka's Breath*. It belongs to the Order, but I am its captain."

The foot traffic thickened as they drew near the old city walls. She spotted a pair of Hassakani guards in red tunics and loose black trousers tucked into tall boots. Each had a scimitar at his hip and a black turban around his head.

Crusser asked, "If you are the captain, what has this ship and crew been doing for the past year while you were in the valley?"

Harlequin nodded to a dark-eyed guard as she passed through the open gate and entered the old city. Rather than dirt, the narrow winding streets were paved with stones.

She shrugged. "Honestly, I have no idea if the ship is even here. If it is, it may not have a crew. As you said, a year has passed."

They crossed a busy square occupied by a bubbling fountain made of glossy blue tiles. Beside it, brown-skinned Hassakani children played knuck-lebones, the sight reminding Harlequin of a brown-haired orphan girl playing the same game in a similar square on the island of Ryxx. Back then, it had been a way for Harlequin to earn money for food. Quickness and wits had been her allies in those days...until she crossed the wrong pirate and became an unwilling deckhand on the man's ship. That man turned out to be Falazon the Black.

At the next intersection, she took a road that descended toward the harbor. Just before reaching the harbor gate, she turned below a sign depicting a tankard lying on its side, foam-topped liquid spilling out.

"This is it," she said, approaching the inn door, the scent of spiced meat wafting from inside.

He grinned. "A hot meal and a soft bed await."

"And ale." She opened the door and waved him inside. "You mustn't forget the ale."

Stomach full, Crusser sat back, lifted his tankard, and took a drink of his ale. It teased his tongue and soothed his throat, carrying a spiced aftertaste he found to his liking.

The taproom was thick with sailors, most coppery-skinned Hassakani. Some had braided hair, some braided beards, some were bald, and some wore rings in their ears, brows, lips, or noses. All appeared as likely to stab you as to pat you on the back.

A mug in each fist, Harlequin squeezed through the crowd and sat across from him. She arched a brow. "Still not finished? That's your first mug."

"I'm in no rush and prefer to savor the taste."

"I thought you might say something like that, so I ordered two shots of swoon."

She grinned.

He groaned.

"I had some bad experiences with swoon." Memories replayed in his mind, quickly squashed. "Ones I prefer not to revisit."

The barmaid approached, a hefty Hassakani woman, with her hair pulled back in a ponytail and her face drawn in a scowl. "Here's your swoon." She set down two small cups of dark liquid and turned away.

Harlequin picked up a cup. "Thanks for the company. The journey has been dreadful, but it would have been worse if I had been alone." Gesturing toward him, she added, "Now, pick up your cup. It's bad luck to drink alone."

His brow furrowed. "I have never heard that."

"You weren't a pirate."

Despite strong reservations, he lifted the cup and tapped it against the one she held. She downed hers and smacked her lips. He drank, the liquid warm and bitter as it slid down his throat.

"Good," she leaned back with the mug in her hand. "Now, finish that ale before the other gets warm."

Crusser gulped down a long drink, finishing the last third of the mug. It left foam on his lips, which he wiped away with the back of his hand.

She pointed past him. "I see some sailors playing cards. How much coin do we have left?"

"A few silver pieces is all."

"What say you to me earning us some more?"

He shook his head. "I won't let you do it."

"Do what?"

"Sell your body for some coin."

Her relaxed manner changed abruptly, and her face darkened. "You think I am a whore?"

"No...It's just..." He shook his head. "I meant that I would never ask something like that of you."

"You said you would not let me. What makes you think you control me?"

This was going poorly. "I know I don't control you."

She grabbed one breast and lifted it. "I could earn plenty of coin if I wanted to go that route."

He sighed. "Harley...you are a beautiful woman. Of course, you could. I only meant that I do not want you to do it. Not for me." He shook his head again. "No coin is worth it."

Her narrowed eyes stared at him for a moment before relaxing. "Alright. Just so we are clear. I could bed every man in here if I wanted to."

Frowning, he asked, "Do you want to?"

She snorted. "With these filthy men? Never."

Exasperated, he exhaled. "Then why are we arguing about it?"

Rising to her feet, she downed the rest of her tankard, wiped her lips dry, and gave him a grin. "I just wanted to set the record straight." She laid her open palm before him. "Now, give me your remaining coin."

He dug into his coin purse and dumped out the contents, five silvers and four coppers landing in her palm.

"You said we only had five silvers left."

He shrugged. "Close enough."

"These coppers are good for two ales and two more cups of swoon." She turned away before he could tell her no.

With a sigh, he sat back, the room tilting with the movement. Swoon was strong and affected him poorly. "I fear I am going to regret this."

Four men sat at the table with Harlequin, all sailors who spoke Hassakani. Having grown up surrounded by both tongues, she had no issues keeping up with their banter. An hour after she joined their game of Hanapuli, she was down to her last two coppers.

Not long after the game began, she had unlaced her tunic to her breastbone, claiming it was too hot for anything less. From time to time, she would catch the men leering at the exposed portion of her chest. Unfortunately, Crusser loomed over her with arms crossed, a scowl on his face. *We have each had six mugs of ale and half as many cups of swoon. You'd think he would be in a better mood.* She worried he might spoil her plan.

When the next hand was dealt, she glanced at her cards. One depicted a wizard standing on a tower, lightning blasting from outstretched arms. *Finally.*

Her turn came, and she drew from the deck, taking two cards but careful to make them appear as one. She placed them in her hand with the others, looked her cards over, and laid them face down on the table. With one hand resting over the wizard card, the other went to her chest, fingers slowly trailing down the exposed skin. Her opponents' eyes followed the gesture. When the wizard card was hidden in her other palm, she brought the card below the table to join the other she had stowed away a few hands earlier.

The man to her right increased the bid beyond what she had remaining, forcing her to bow out. The hand continued, two other men folding while the last two traded bets. The hand ended, the players revealing their cards. A sailor named Dorvan, who sat to her right, won with one wizard, three knights, and a pair of rubies.

Crusser leaned over her shoulder and whispered, "That's it. You are out of coin. Let's go to bed."

She glanced back at him, her eyes flashing with anger, while her lips formed a fake smile. "You go on without me."

"What? Why?"

"I wish to keep playing."

"How? You have no coin."

Smirking, she turned back to the table. "What say you, men? Can you think of anything I might bet to play another hand?"

The men laughed, Dorvan saying, "Share my bed tonight, and you can keep playing."

"Hmm." She put a finger to her lips. "I might be willing to play for those stakes, but I'll not do it for mere coppers. Anyone who wants a chance must be willing to put in three silvers."

"Three?" another man asked. "I can spend a night with a whore down the street for two."

She leaned over the table. "None of those women are Harlequin Ahlee."

Three of the men arched brows. The fourth furrowed his brow and asked, "Who is she?"

Dorvan punched the man in the shoulder. "You dolt. *The Queen of the Shoals.*"

The sailor nodded. "Oh. *The Bitch Pirate.*"

Harlequin glared at the man. While earned, she had never been fond of the moniker. "Say it again, and you'll leave here missing an appendage. I don't mean a finger or toe, either."

He blanched, as the other three chortled.

One of the men tossed three silvers in the middle. "To spend a night with the Queen of the Shoals is worth an extra silver. I'm in."

Moments later, they all tossed coins in. She grinned, knowing she had just turned five silvers into twelve.

Crusser's head swam from the swoon and ale, but rather than the room spinning, it had turned red.

Arms crossed over his chest, he stewed. It was hot. He was tired. And Harlequin was giving her attention to four sailors she didn't even know. From the moment she had unlaced her tunic, he had fought the urge to lace it back up. Whenever he caught one of the men leering at her, he wanted to break heads.

Now, she had offered to spend the night with one of them if she lost the final hand. Based on the prior rounds, Crusser doubted she was any good at the game. Worse, Harlequin's luck had been poor; she was the only one to not have at least one wizard high hand. *Why is she doing this?*

The cards were dealt, each player peering at them and then drawing another card. Bets were placed, and the pot in the middle rose to sixteen silvers against Harlequin's offer. Crusser clenched his fists at the thought of one of those men touching her.

The hand ended. The males revealed their cards first. The man to Harlequin's right won the hand with one wizard, two archers, and three sapphires. The winning man grinned, his teeth visible amid his bushy black beard. One tooth was missing, another made of silver. He had a gold ring through one nostril, his black hair in braids. Hairy and covered in sweat, Crusser imagined the man with her. As his ire rose, he reached for his sword only to recall he had left it in their room before coming down for dinner.

"This truly is my lucky day," the winning man said.

Harlequin shook her head. "Sorry. It appears my luck has turned."

She spread her cards on the table to reveal three wizards and three knights. A nigh unbeatable hand.

Three of the men gaped, the grin on the fourth's face turning to a scowl.

Harlequin swept the coins toward her and began dropping them into her coin purse. "Thanks for playing, boys. This girl knows when to quit, so I'll take my coin and wish you a good evening."

When she rose from the table, so did Dorvan.

The man grabbed her wrist and snarled, "I say you still owe us some fun. Me first."

Crusser uncrossed his arms, ready to burst.

Harlequin jerked her hand away, and two cards fell from the bottom of her tunic.

"What?" Dorvan's eyes widened. "You cheated us!"

The sailor drew a dagger and lunged but stopped short. Crusser's fist smashed into his face, launching the man onto another occupied table. The other three soldiers reacted, all leaping to their feet, one drawing a dagger.

Roaring, Crusser flipped the table and allowed his buried rage to run blind.

4

INCARCERATED

Thump. Thump. Thump. Crusser's head pounded to the beat of his heart. Opening his eyes in darkness, he sat up and groaned, his shoulder sore and ribs tender. Hand to his face, he felt his lip. It was thick and swollen. Dim light came from the barred window above him, barely enough for him to view his surroundings.

A few strides across and twice the depth, the cell walls were built of stones and mortar. One wall was made of iron bars, and the floor was dirt. Beyond the bars, he glimpsed a dark corridor, but there was nobody in sight. *I am in the city jail,* Crusser realized. The last thing he could recall was Harlequin playing cards with four sailors. Judging by his sore torn knuckles, he had somehow found his way into a fight. *Damn swoon. I shouldn't have let Harlequin talk me into drinking it.*

As if thinking her name had invoked a spirit from beyond, her voice lilted into the cell, calling him. "Cruss!" Her tone was hushed but urgent. "Are you in there?"

He stood and cupped his mouth while staring up at the window. "Harley! It's Crusser. I'm in jail!"

She snorted. "I know, dummy. Back away from the window."

"What are you going to do?"

"Just do it."

He backed up against the bars and heard footsteps approaching. Turning, he saw a pair of guards coming toward him, one holding a torch, the other a cudgel. Both were dressed in long, red tunics with black belts around their waists and puffy black trousers tucked into tall boots. The one with a short pointed beard wore a turban while the other sported a bushy black beard and a bald head.

"I thought I heard something," one man said. "It appears our wild man is awake."

The two men stopped a few strides from the cell door, one tapping his palm with his cudgel. "You caused us a lot of trouble."

"What happened?" Crusser could guess but feared the answer.

Gesturing with the cudgel, the guard said, "You tried to take on a taproom full of sailors. By the time we arrived, three men lay dead, a dozen others unconscious or wounded." He grinned. "Turns out, it only took a few hard cudgel strikes to take you down."

"A few?" the other guard asked. "I think you hit him eight times before he collapsed."

Crusser groaned. *Now I know why my head hurts so badly.* "How much do I owe?"

One guard chuckled. "You aren't getting out. Not tonight. Not ever. High Wizard Ikan is sure to make an example of you. Can't have anyone destroying property and committing murder in Antari."

A tremendous crash came from behind Crusser, causing him to duck on instinct. A chunk of stone struck the bars just above his head and shattered, bits spraying across the two guards. More debris fell around him, some striking him in the legs, a swirling cloud of dust penetrating the area, causing him and the other men to cough.

Crusser turned around to find the upper half of the wall caved in, a boulder leaning against it. He covered his face and scrambled up the rubble, heading toward the moonlight he glimpsed beyond the swirling dust.

"Wait! You are a prisoner!" one guard shouted.

Crusser ignored the man and emerged into a square. A couple hundred feet from the city wall, a catapult sat on the bulwark, but rather than facing the harbor, it had been turned to face the jail. Harlequin stood beside it. Upon seeing him emerge, she ran from the war machine, her sword flashing as she met a guard on the wall. Crusser hesitated in concern and then fled when the guard went over the edge.

He ran across the square into a dark street, fading into the night as cries of alarm rang out behind him.

Ducking a sword strike, Harlequin slashed, her sabre cutting across the guard's abdomen. The man shrieked, stepped backward, and fell from the wall, his cry trailing until he hit the ground three stories below. She cast one glance toward the jail, saw Crusser racing off, and then ran.

The harbor docks stood to her right and the dark city to her left as the gate faded behind her. She glanced backward and saw a cluster of guards giving chase no more than thirty strides behind her. The light faded as she fled, the walls growing darker the further she ran from the docks. Ahead, the wall turned. In the darkness, she doubted that the guards could see her. Unsure if any were coming from the other direction, she made a quick decision, hoping the harbor was as her vague memory recalled.

When she reached the square tower platform at the wall's corner, she leapt into the void, and the night swallowed her.

Arms twirling, she plummeted, praying she had not miscalculated. Her feet plunged into the water as the night sky faded away. She swam beneath the surface. Arrows struck the water and slipped past her in a flurry of bubbles. Only when her lungs were about to burst did she rise.

Harlequin surfaced with a deep gasp, drinking in the sea air. She treaded water while watching the silhouettes on the wall. The guards waved, shouted, and then dispersed, two heading in one direction, while the rest turned toward the harbor gate. As the night fell silent, she swam toward the nearest dock.

Harlequin emerged from the abandoned building. The sky above was a pale blue, the sun yet to crest the castle to the east. A breeze from the ocean cooled her clothing, still damp from her late night swim. Hunched over and covered by a cloak, Crusser walked beside her. She glowered at him, her mood still poor from the trouble he had instigated.

"Before you decided to brawl with an entire taproom of sailors, the innkeeper told me Guta and Korrik visited the inn two nights ago but haven't been seen since."

"It is as much your fault as mine," he said. "I told you, I cannot drink swoon. It...does something to me. Awakens things I'd rather leave buried," Crusser said. "As for the two sailors, what does that mean for us?"

"It means there is a good chance they remain in port. They are likely tight on coin and sleep aboard the ship." She marched down the street toward the harbor gate, and he rushed to catch up.

The street led them to a small square. The city gate was open, the harbor visible beyond it. Harlequin stopped suddenly, gasping before placing her back to the wall. She reached out and pulled him beside her.

"What are you..."

She clamped her hand over his mouth as she gazed across the square.

A familiar form walked by dressed in loose black trousers, wraps on his lower legs and feet, a gray tunic, a black cloak over his shoulders, a raised hood, and a hand gripping his naginata. The dark elf's weapon was distinct – a black staff with a nasty blade at the top. Only one other had such a blade – Arci-Aesha. However, this cloaked figure was male. *Tranadal.*

Four others in black cloaks trailed behind Tranadal, each with the shorn head of the Order. Harlequin recognized each of them – a tattooed Ghealdan named Vex, a tall Pallanese named Temmen, a stoutly built Orenthian named Andar, and a Balmorian woman called Tempest. Whether it was her real name or not, Harlequin was unsure. The woman, a former Black Wasp, was a lethal fighter and had become a rival of sorts during Harlequin's stay in the valley. The two had sparred on four separate occasions, Tempest winning each match handily. Harlequin rubbed her left forearm, having recently healed from the latest fracture Tempest had given her.

"What is Tranadal doing here?" Crusser whispered.

The five figures in black cloaks passed through the gate and faded from view.

"Let's go find out."

She hurried across the square, her hood shadowing her face as she passed the red and black-garbed guards at the gate. None had seen her face in the night earlier, but she was unwilling to take a chance. She glanced at Crusser, still hunched over and walking with a limp. Ragged trousers covered his boots, and the frayed ends dragged across the ground.

Once beyond the city walls, she spotted Tranadal and the others moving along the docks. And at the far end of the second pier was *Hassaka's Breath*. Hope rose in her chest and then crashed when she saw the dark elf lead the others onto the pier, toward the ship. Her ship.

Tranadal and his entourage passed a loaded wagon, the driver waiting for a cart that stood in the way. The cart driver argued with the donkey pulling it, the beast braying noisily while the driver swore profusely.

An idea struck Harlequin, but she had little time. "Follow me."

With long rapid strides, she and Crusser hurried down the pier and ducked behind the wagon. Six wooden barrels occupied the wagon bed, a rumpled gray tarp between them. She lifted the tarp, peering beneath it to find a pile of potatoes. It would be dirty and uncomfortable but only for a short time.

In a hushed voice, she said, "Try not to jostle the wagon."

She crawled over the rear gate and beneath the tarp, waving for Crusser to follow. The man hopped in, curled up beside her, and pulled the tarp over himself as the wagon lurched into motion. The ride to the end of the pier took only a minute, the wagon settling as the driver climbed off. She lifted the tarp and saw Tranadal on the pier speaking with Vex, whose hood was raised to cover his tattooed scalp. Temmen stood beside them, nodding to something Tranadal said. After a brief discussion, Vex and Temmen crossed the plank to an unfamiliar ship, the painted moniker on its hull reading *Gift from Gheald*. At the same time, Tranadal, Andar, and Tempest boarded her old ship.

Once on deck, the dark elf was met by Korrik, one of Harlequin's old crewmembers. The others faded from view. Tranadal and Korrik spoke for a minute before doing the same. Shifting to see beyond the barrels, she spotted another plank behind the wagon, connecting the pier to the ship's open hold. With nobody in sight, she threw the tarp aside.

"Get out! Hurry!" she said with hushed urgency. "We have little time."

They slipped out the rear of the wagon and rushed across the plank into the dark cargo hold. Crates, barrels, and brown sacks lined the hull walls and stood in rows in between. She led him deeper into the hold and squatted behind barrels along the far wall.

Voices came from above, followed by footsteps and grunts as sailors loaded the goods from the wagon into the ship. Minutes later, they closed the cargo door and locked it. The hold fell dark and silent.

"What now?" Crusser asked.

"Now we are stowaways."

"On your own ship?"

She flashed him a scowl, not caring that he could not see it in the gloom. "Facing Tranadal and his dark elf magic would be bad enough. The two with him are among the best fighters in the Order. By now, he controls the ship and has told the crew that you and I have betrayed the Order." She sighed. "Face it. We have no choice."

"So we are just going to live down here for the entire voyage?"

"Do you have a better idea?"

He shrugged. "No."

"Good," she dug through her pack and removed a small disk, the glow from it illuminating his face. "Then let's find someplace comfortable. I fear we will be down here for a while."

5

MUSINGS

On a spring evening, from his fifth-floor palace balcony, Jerrell "Jace" Landish gazed over the city of Marquithe, his home for a quarter of his twenty-nine years. For most of that time, he had lived in a modest apartment over a tavern, but all that changed when he accepted a seemingly innocuous contract a year and a half earlier. Having stolen many items during his illustrious career, he would have never guessed an amulet hidden in the Marquithe Enchanter's Tower would change his life, and the world, forever.

His hand went to his chest, and he squeezed the Eye of Obscurance through his tunic, a habit he had developed since acquiring it. He rarely removed the amulet – comforted by the protection it provided and reminded of the harrowing path he had blazed as a result, leading him to become the second most powerful person in Farrowen.

The sun slid below the horizon, its glow temporarily warding off the purple of dusk. Stars appeared in the east but were blurred by the aura of the full moon. Memories stirred as he stared at the bright globe in the sky.

A year had passed since the fateful journey to Murvaran when, unbelievably, he and his companions had set out to kill a god. *If we only knew the price we would pay*, he thought. The event had changed the world forever... including his own city.

Sprawling out from the palace, Marquithe was a maze of ancient buildings occupied by sixty thousand people. The city had stood for over two millennia, built long ago by the Makers, whose craftsmanship remained unequaled even after all this time. It stood on an expansive hilltop with the palace positioned on the highest point, enabling a view beyond the hundred-foot tall city walls. On a clear day, Jace could almost see everything from the mountains of Northern Pallanar to the distant Novecai Sea. Almost.

After his move from Fastella seven years ago, Jace had undertaken a number of outrageous exploits, his cleverness and flare for the dramatic inflating a reputation unheard of for a thief...until the name Jerrell Landish had grown into something beyond his control. To escape his fame, he was forced to hide behind the name Jace for the better part of two years. Now, his thieving ways behind him, only the people closest to him used the name Jace, the prime example appearing when the balcony door opened.

He turned as a stunning young woman stepped outside, a sapphire-encrusted golden crown nestled on the blonde locks that spilled over her shoulders. Light from the chamber framed her curvy silhouette, her midnight blue dress snug in the midriff and ruffles around her exposed shoulders and her skirts, which flared from her hips to her ankles. As she drew closer, his eyes drank her in, lingering at the exposed bit of cleavage – a hint of the bountiful treasure found within her bodice. He longed to dive into that gap...but that would have to wait.

Narine smiled, her aqua eyes glimmering. "How do I look?"

Jace smiled back. "Ravishing as always."

She cocked her brow. "You say the same thing when I wake in the morning...without makeup and my hair in a twisted mess."

He shrugged. "Perhaps I am not the best to answer such questions." Slipping his hands around her back, he drew her close. "When I look at you, I like what I see. If not, I'd have run off by now, fearful of the shackles you seek to clamp on my wrists."

Concern in her eyes, she asked, "You aren't trying to get out of the wedding..."

His hand went to her cheek and brushed back a stray strand of golden hair. "Nothing of the sort."

"Good. You have made me wait so long already."

"You know why waiting was the right thing to do."

"Yes," she nodded. "I'll admit, you were right. It was best to establish my rule and earn the hearts of my people before taking a husband."

"Especially when the citizens of Farrowen and Marquithe were unfamiliar with you…a princess from a neighboring wizardom. Those who knew you as Taladain's daughter likely feared his seed would be too much like her tyrant father. The stories, even those told here, are not kind to him."

Narine drew herself up, speaking as she led him inside. "I know well how important it is to consider the perceptions of my subjects. If you recall, I grew up in a palace, trained to rule since I was a child." Pausing between the seating and dining areas of her private chamber – a chamber that had become as much his as hers despite their pending vows. "Three different yet equally harsh wizards had occupied my throne in a short span before I claimed it. Time was necessary to establish stability. People find comfort in stability. While the changes I have made are minimal, I hope my subjects view my displayed compassion as a stark contrast to the tyrannical rule of my predecessors."

"Trust me, the people have noticed."

Jace read reports on such talk daily. As chancellor and head of intelligence, monitoring rumors was among his primary duties.

She frowned while staring at his torso.

He looked down at himself. The ruffles of his blue doublet were visible between the open lapels of his long black coat. "What's wrong? Did I spill on myself?"

Her hand went to her hip. "Summer is nearly upon us, the weather fair. Why do you insist on wearing that coat? During winter events, it was perfectly acceptable. Now, it seems out of place. With you among the few not wearing robes tonight…"

"I happen to like this coat. Although, if you prefer, I would happily don my old one."

Narine waved her hands. "No. You may be a rogue, but it is best you don't appear as one when we are at a formal party." She narrowed her eyes. "Why did you insist we attend this one anyway? The Forcas…"

"Yes, I know. You deposed Portia Forca's husband just after he had gained the throne."

She snorted. "He did not earn it but merely seized an opportunity. You know what the man was like. He would have been a terrible ruler."

"Yet you fear Portia may hold a grudge toward you."

Narine nodded, her eyes filled with concern.

What does she suspect? Jace admired Narine's intellect, but sometimes she was too quick for his liking. *Admit it, Jace,* he told himself. *You enjoy the challenge, it is among the reasons you are willing to marry her.*

He gave her an easy smile. "Nevertheless, we were invited, so it would be best if we made an appearance. Even if the attempt does not smooth things over with Portia, it will help to ease your relationship with the Marquithe Wizards Guild."

"I suppose you have a point." She tilted her head, giving him an appraising look. "Are you sure you were never trained in statecraft? You seem to have a talent for it."

He chuckled. "I know *people.* Reading them and anticipating their reactions are among the best skills a thief can hone." His grin widened. "As you know, I am the greatest thief who has ever lived."

Narine rolled her eyes, lifting her palms to her cheeks in a dramatic fashion. "Oh my," she swooned in a high voice. "The great Jerrell Landish! I cannot control myself. Should I just tear my dress off now, oh great one?"

Jace leveled a look at her. "Sarcasm does not suit you."

She smirked. "Oh, I'm sorry. Did I steal your thunder? Based on the frequency you use it, I thought sarcasm was something you enjoyed greatly."

"I prefer to wield a sharp tongue rather than defend against one." He pulled her close, his hands against her lower back. "As for your dress…I'll have you out of it soon enough."

She arched her brow and smirked again. "What if I choose not to grant you access to my palace tonight?"

His voice dropped to a whisper. "I'll finesse a way beyond your defenses. It's what we thieves do."

Their lips met. The kiss started out tender but grew more heated as he pressed her body against his. She pushed him away, breathing heavily as she smoothed down her dress.

"Enough for now." She gave him a look of warning. "It took Shavon an hour to do my hair. If you mess it up before we leave…"

He chuckled and turned to the door. "Fair enough. We can resume after the party."

Jace led her into the corridor where two guards waited. One stood tall and thin with long dark hair and soft clean-shaven cheeks. The other was of medium height and stout, his once muscular body now buried beneath a layer of fat and his face covered in gray stubble. Both wore midnight blue capes over their armor.

The older guard thumped his fist to his chest, directly against the lightning bolt embossed in his armor. The other hurriedly repeated the gesture.

Jace turned to the guards. "Dirk. Kelvin. You two remain here. We will only be a few hours. Nobody enters the queen's chambers while she is away."

"Yes, Chancellor," Dirk responded.

Chancellor. It was an odd term for Jace to hear, but one he had grown accustomed to over the past year. Second only to the queen, others in the palace used the title rather than his first name. Sometimes, they called him sir or Master Landish, which were fine as well. In truth, he did not care if they called him *dung beetle* or *horse's arse*, so long as they listened and obeyed his orders. Regardless of what anyone else thought, Jace made Narine's safety his primary concern; it was a promise he had made to someone special, someone he missed. While it was often said *"There is no honor among thieves,"* protecting Narine was one promise he intended to honor.

The corridor brought the couple to a torchlit stairwell. With Narine at his side, one hand on his arm and her other hand lifting her skirts, they descended to the ground floor.

Four flights down, they followed a corridor to a closed door, opened it, and stepped outside. A tall bald man in a dark blue uniform waited in the courtyard. He had a heavy brow, a grim expression, and one full sleeve, the other sewn shut at the shoulder, giving him a lopsided appearance. Two young guards bracketed the man, both in Midnight Guard armor, helmets tucked beneath their arms. Other than their names, Jace knew little of the two new recruits.

Across the courtyard, a carriage hitched to a pair of chestnut horses waited. A middle-aged driver with a long thick mustache sat at the front. When Jace looked at the man, the driver tipped his short-brimmed cap. *Billings. Good man.* It was reassuring to see one of his own at the reins.

Jace nodded to the bald man in the military uniform. "Good evening, Henton. Are these two our escorts for tonight?"

"Yes. Boris and Hardy have done well with their tests, in combat and in monitoring for signs of trouble. They are raw, but with you as their guide, they should be pliable and capable for tonight's duty."

Jace turned toward the two young men, both of whom stood a head taller than him. Boris had long blond hair and an athletic frame, while Hardy's hair was shorn and his body thickly built. "You wear the capes of the Midnight Guard, so you must be properly trained. What say you? Are you prepared to protect your queen?"

"Yes, sir!" the two young men responded, fists thumping against their breastplates.

Jace gestured toward the carriage waiting twenty feet away. "Have you inspected the carriage for soundness and to ensure no assassin lies in wait?"

The two guards blanched.

"Go on!"

They both scrambled to the carriage, the driver watching with an arched brow and a smirk on his lips.

"If I were the man I once was, I'd escort you myself," Henton grumbled.

Jace shook his head. "Since the Darkspawn War, Farrowen has lacked experienced leadership. You were among the few officers to survive. When you were young, perhaps you needed both arms to fight and to command respect. Now, your keen mind and attention to detail will serve your queen better than your blade."

Henton shot Narine a questioning glance.

She nodded. "What Jerrell says is true. Keep training the new recruits and guide them. They will lean on your experience; you on their strength and weapon skills." Smiling, she added, "If you were bright enough to defeat my brother and my uncle, gaining entrance to two nigh impregnable cities, you are more than man enough for this job."

Jace noticed the man's eyes narrow slightly. *He admits to himself that Garvin was instrumental in those victories and that his role was secondary.* The intelligence gathered by Jace's predecessor had said as much. *Good. I would rather have him uneasy with false praise than claim rightful ownership.*

"All clear, sir," one of the guards shouted from the carriage.

"Good," Jace said. "Join the driver in the front while I ride with the queen. Be sure to open the door for us when we arrive at the Forca estate."

48

6

DINNER PARTY

The carriage wheels rumbled over the brick-paved streets of Marquithe, Farrowen's capital city. Having grown up in Ghealdor, the neighboring wizardom to the west, Narine Killarius was still getting to know the people and the land she now ruled. It had been Jace's idea for her to take the throne, but the idea had required little convincing. She admitted to herself that it had been a unique opportunity, allowing her to rise to queen with little confrontation or backing.

The two previous Farrowen rulers had died in the span of as many seasons, and the bulk of Farrowen's army, the Thundercorps soldiers, had been lost in the process. Conquest, greed, and ambition had claimed one wizard lord, along with much of his army. A horde of darkspawn caused the deaths of most remaining Thundercorps soldiers, madness overtaking the man who had ruled at the time. When the dust settled, Narine merely needed to prove herself a viable candidate by removing another wizard who also saw the vacancy as an opportunity. That wizard was Palkan Forca – husband of the woman hosting tonight's party.

The twenty-five-year-old queen stared out the window, watching the city slip past, some areas dark, others lit by the pale blue aura of enchanted lanterns. The carriage turned down a curving street lined with mansions, each three or more stories tall. Long drives ran between the homes, each estate protected by an iron gate, many with guards on watch. *These are the homes of wizards, people of power and influence. I must find a means to regain their support.* It was a complex issue. Narine not only refused to raise taxes to support the wizards, but lowered them to ease the burden on her citizens. The act had brought her love from the masses and animosity from her former peers.

When the carriage slowed to a stop, Jace gripped Narine's hand, drawing her attention back to him. "I'll step out first. When we go inside, I will escort you until we are greeted by Portia. By then, you will have drawn sufficient attention, and I can slip away."

Narine furrowed her brow. "What are you up to?"

Jace smiled. "I will tell you later. For now, you need to do two things."

"Which are?"

"Do not, under any circumstances, eat or drink anything."

"Why not?"

"You might be a queen, but you don't wield the magic of a god like past rulers. Anyone who realizes this will know you cannot heal yourself if poisoned."

"Poisoned?!"

"Hush," he put his finger to her lips. "It is simply a precaution. You must not appear suspicious or uneasy. Just do as I say, and all will be well."

She pressed her lips together. "Alright. What is the other thing I must do?"

"Remain near your guards. They are here to protect you should anything go awry."

"You suspect something?"

He shrugged. "I heard some rumors that warrant investigation. Nothing more. I cannot dig into them anywhere else. As your companion, I can gain entrance to the party. As the queen, you are sure to attract attention, so I must step away to ferret out the information I seek." He squeezed her hand. "Since I care for you dearly, I also want to make sure you remain safe."

She adjusted the jewelry on her hand – a series of gold chains linking the ruby ring on her middle finger to the ruby-encrusted golden bracelet around her wrist. "You do know I am among the most skilled wizards alive. I can take care of myself."

The carriage stopped. The interior rocked as the two guards climbed down.

He whispered, "I know your abilities well. However, the most lethal magic and the effort required to shield against it both come far more naturally for men than for women."

Pressing her lips together, she remained silent, unable to argue against the truth. Male wizards excelled at battle magic; women with subtler spells such as healing, illusion, and mental manipulation.

"Also," he added, "a knife in the back can kill as readily as a bolt of wizard lightning."

Narine sighed, knowing that he was right.

Jace drew the invitation from his coat and opened it. Golden light shone from the paper, the inscribed words gleaming on his face as Boris held the door open, and Hardy stood ready.

He emerged from the carriage, held the invitation up, and announced in a loud voice. "Presenting Her Majesty, Narine Killarius, queen of Farrowen."

A frown crossed her face, as it often did when she heard her last name. She understood why he announced her name but wished it were not necessary. Her father's reign of Ghealdor was deeply rooted in cruelty and oppression while she preferred a more even-handed approach, balancing justice with compassion.

A pair of guards looked over the invitation and nodded, Jace turning back toward the open door.

Holding his hand out to her, he said, "Come along, my dear. Your adoring subjects are eager to bask in your glory."

"Oh, brother," she muttered.

Narine held her skirts up as she stepped down from the carriage. She peered toward the open torchlit manor entrance while taking Jace by the arm. Chatter and lilting music from inside carried through the open double-door. Lining the path to the front stairs, guards stood at attention, each holding one fist to their chest and grasping a pike in the other, their armor reflecting the orange flames.

The mansion stood four stories tall and extended a good way down the street. Bright flickering light danced along the building's exterior, reflecting off windows and lighting the sculpted shrubs. Even in the great city of

Marquithe, Forca Manor was a thing of beauty. While it lacked the sheer immensity of Marquithe Palace, the home could not be ignored.

With her guards trailing behind her, Narine and Jace ascended the stairs and passed between two sets of fluted columns. A pair of porters waited beside massive double doors, their panels inlaid with gold and silver. One porter bowed while the other opened a door. The couple stepped inside, pausing to gauge the situation.

Marble tiles, dark green with gold and black striations, graced the receiving hall floor. A circular fountain occupied the heart of the room, centered between two curved staircases that rose to an open second-story loft. People filled the loft, holding drinks in their hands, chatting, and laughing.

Narine noticed her reflection in an ornate mirror at the side of the room. Growing up as a princess, her appearance was of the upmost importance. With blonde hair, tawny skin, and more than her fair share of curves, she was blessed with natural beauty, often causing women to cast a scornful eye and men a lustful one.

Father often said that I looked like Mother. I wish I could have seen her face…just once. Narine suspected her mother had been one of her father's concubines, the prettiest women in Ghealdor. The man had claimed to love Narine's mother – a claim she doubted. Having lived through the deaths of numerous wives and children, little humanity remained in him by the time he had come to know her. The man's unnaturally long life, which focused on his own lust for power while watching others age and die, had hardened him until he became something alien. Such was the fate of a wizard lord.

Turning from the mirror, she looked at Jace, drinking in the moment. Narine was average height for a woman, Jace only slightly taller. While not the tall, dashing man she had imagined in her younger years, he cut a handsome figure. With dreamy amber eyes, a carved profile, dark hair, scruff on his cheeks, and an easy smile, it was difficult not to like him…even when his clever tongue strayed too far. And hidden beneath his long dark coat and blue doublet was a lean muscular body that Narine had explored with aplomb.

He looked at her and flashed a smile, which Narine reflected back, her heart stirring.

"Shall we?" he asked.

She nodded. "Yes."

With the two guards a step behind, the couple circled the fountain, passed the staircases, and stopped at the edge of the ballroom to survey the crowd.

Over a hundred guests were already present, the hum of their conversations reverberating off the ceiling two stories above. A myriad of hues, from bright yellow to pure black, greeted her gaze. The women wore capes and shawls over elegant gowns, many with gloves pulled up to their elbows. Per wizard fashion and necessary for the flow of magic, the men were dressed in loose robes secured at the waist by contrasting sashes.

A man in a gray coat approached them, expertly balancing goblets on a silver tray. "Greetings, Your Majesty. Would you care for a drink?"

Narine eyed the glasses on the tray and the carafe of wine in his hand. The liquid was a deep maroon color. "No, thank you." *Best to keep a clear head tonight.* It was frightfully difficult to execute spells when one's head was muddled with alcohol.

"I will take one," Jace grabbed two goblets off the tray. "And I will drink hers as well."

The servant dipped his head and backed away.

Narine arched a brow. "Really? I thought you had business to address tonight."

He took a sip and whispered. "As a reputed rogue and a scoundrel, 'tis best to look the part."

"What about when we are married?"

He shrugged. "I know plenty of married scoundrels." Downing one glass, he set it on a table beside the wall. "Only difference is that my jewels will remain loyal to the crown…even if people suspect otherwise."

"They had better." Narine pinched his arm.

"Ouch. What was that for?"

"Just making sure you remember I can hurt you even if you are wearing that amulet."

He frowned. "I am now rethinking my loyalty…"

She pinched him again. Her guards chuckled in the background.

He rubbed his arm and motioned toward the crowd. "Come along. I would prefer to find Portia before you give me any more bruises."

A wizard in silver robes and a dark blue sash emerged from the crowd, trailed by a pair of armored guards. One of the guards was middle-aged, a scar across one cheek. His eyes were dark and angry, his nose too wide for his face. While a well-built man, his younger companion was much larger with thick arms and a barrel chest.

The wizard appeared to be in in his mid-thirties with dark shoulder-length hair and a lean build, standing a few inches taller than Jace.

The man dipped his head, his squinty eyes lingering on Narine's chest before lifting to meet her gaze, a smirk on his thin lips. "It is a pleasure to meet you, my queen."

Narine arched a brow. "I find myself at a disadvantage. You know who I am, but I do not know…"

Jace glared at the man. "This is Florien Montague, high wizard of Lionne."

Smirk still in place, Montague eyed Jace. "Jerrell Landish. I heard you had weaseled yourself into the queen's good graces."

"Save it, Montague. The queen is aware of my past *and* my reputation."

"Oh, do not worry, Jerrell. I hold no ill will. I have discovered it is best to look forward rather than dwell on grievances from years ago."

Jace glanced at Narine, his expression saying he did not believe the man. Regardless, he gave Montague a smile. "Well said. After all, it was only business…nothing personal."

"Well, I had best congratulate you two now, since I may not make it to your upcoming nuptials."

"Why not?" Narine asked. "Surely you have been invited."

"Oh, yes. I received the invitation weeks ago. However, for the past year, I have been in contact with representatives from Cor Cordium. After many attempts, the enchanters have agreed to hear my proposal. If successful, Lionne would become the primary port of incoming enchanted goods into the southern wizardoms."

"What of the tower here in Marquithe?" Jace asked. "I was under the impression that most of the enchanted goods consumed by Farrowen, Gheal-dor, and Pallanar come from that outpost."

"True," Montague said. "However, the tower is limited in its production capacity, and the enchanters here lack the knowledge and raw materials for more exotic enchantments."

Narine narrowed her eyes. "What are you giving up in order to secure this deal?"

Montague waggled a finger. "Ah. Very shrewd, my queen. No wizardom is likely to give something to another without concessions."

"Such as?" Jace asked.

The wizard shrugged. "The district of Lionne produces the most wine in the world. Turns out, the enchanters are among the prime consumers of our wine. I am promising them fifty tax-free barrels a year in exchange for their guaranteed business. As one of the closest ports to their island, Lionne was already a natural choice. The wine merely helps to seal the deal."

Narine nodded. "Very good. Enchanted items, especially rare ones, sell for premium prices. The added tax income through the Marquithe Bureau of Trading will easily offset the loss from fifty barrels."

Montague smiled. "I am impressed. I had feared our new queen was little more than a beautiful figurehead. To discover a sharp wit accompanies your appearance and reputed skill with the Gift...well, it is no wonder you have claimed the throne and will likely hold it for many years."

Smiling in response, Narine said, "Thank you. I am glad to have your approval and your loyalty."

The high wizard bowed. "Of course, my queen. I pray you will excuse me. I had stopped by to honor Wizardess Forca and her son while I was in the city, but I must be going."

"Leaving the party so early?" Jace asked.

"Yes," Montague sighed. "Something has come up, and I must return to Lionne at once." Stepping aside, he extended a hand toward the ballroom. "Please. Have a wonderful evening."

The high wizard headed outside, the younger of his guards following while the elder stared at Jace with hatred in his eyes.

Jace smirked at the bigger man. "Captain Vordan. I would say it is good to see you, but such sarcasm is beyond your comprehension."

"Someday, Landish..." the man replied in a gravelly voice.

"Sorry, Vordan. It is never going to happen." Jace put his arm around Narine. "I am with the queen now, so you'll have to find another man to love."

Despite the captain's reddening face and flaring nostrils, Narine was forced to cover her mouth, which was nearly bursting as she contained her laughter. His eyes bulged, a vein in his neck appearing ready to burst as he loomed over Jace.

"Vordan!" Montague called out from the front stairs.

Casting one last sneer at Jace, Vordan walked out, following Montague and the other guard toward a waiting carriage.

Jace leaned close, scowling at the retreating wizard and his escorts. "I don't trust him."

"The guard?" she whispered. "He clearly hates you."

The wizard and his guards climbed into the carriage.

"No. Montague."

"He seemed cordial enough."

"Exactly." He narrowed his eyes, watching the carriage pull away. "The man is as arrogant as they come. His type would never forgive a perceived slight against him. He is up to something..."

"Like what?"

Jace shook his head. "I don't know. Yet." He held out his elbow. "Let's go find the mistress of the house."

Florien Montague stared out the carriage window as the wizard estates slipped past. The carriage followed a curved street and then began a slow descent toward the city gate. His visit to Marquithe had been brief but productive. Still musing about the evening, he turned toward the two guards sitting across from him.

Brasco, the younger of the duo, was the most fearsome warrior in Montague's employ. Standing well over six feet and built like an oak tree, the man said little and obeyed orders without question. When told to kill, he did so efficiently and without fail. Such effectiveness had earned him the right to travel with his high wizard. The other man, Brasco's superior, had earned the right for other reasons.

For seven years, Captain Vordan had repeatedly proven his loyalty and worth, sparing Montague from two assassination attempts. Nearly as important, Vordan had helped Montague avoid Malvorian's ill-advised campaign in Ghealdor a year and a half earlier. While the Ghealdans had eventually folded to Farrowen's might, the cost was paid in blood – wizards by the dozens and soldiers by the thousands. While loyal, Vordan's temper was easily stoked, a flaw that had almost cost Montague on numerous occasions, including tonight.

"Did you have to press him, Vordan?" Montague asked. "Can you not contain your anger for one evening?"

Vordan snorted. "Had I not contained it, Landish would have felt the sting of my blade rather than just that of my tongue."

"You forget he is no longer a mere thief. Landish is the chancellor and betrothed to the queen. Killing him now comes with a cost."

The other man grumbled. "Perhaps your gold would be well-spent on him?"

Montague sighed. "Focus." He thought back to his encounter with the new queen and her betrothed. It had been enlightening, although he doubted Vordan had noticed. The man was beyond such subtleties. "Did the boy pay those guards?"

"Yes. I fear our queen's reign will be cut short. If we are lucky, Landish will die as well. At the very least, his star will fall."

While staring out the window, Montague considered the man's statement. His thoughts turned to the queen – young, blonde, and beautiful with the body of a goddess. During their brief conversation, he had been surprised by her ability to reason.

"It's too bad, really. She could have been great had things aligned differently."

Marquithe, the palace, and entire wizards guild would be in an upheaval for the next few days. Accusations would be made, old rivalries reborn, and heads would roll. The carriage ride to Lionne would take two days, but his driver would continue throughout the night.

Montague mused, "Best to be far away come morning."

Her arm around his, Narine and Jace led the two guards into the crowded ballroom. The gazes of the other guests followed them and people whispered. *It is the crown, my position,* Narine thought. *They wonder at my strength and if they might claim the crown for themselves.*

She felt the heat of their gazes, the number growing as she and Jace worked their way across the room. Self-conscious, Narine smiled and nodded to each person she passed, the wizards and wizardesses dipping their heads in response, some taking a knee. To her face, they would fawn and comply, but to her back...

A bell rang, the music stopped, and the hum of conversation trailed off. The bell chimed again, coming from behind her and Jace. As one, they turned, lifting their gazes to the loft at the top of the stairs that overlooked the ballroom.

In a low-cut black gown, a voluptuous middle-aged woman with blonde hair had captured the crowd's attention. To her side was a teenage boy with shoulder-length golden locks, dressed in dark blue robes with a bright yellow sash. A barrel-chested guard in dark studded leathers loomed over the woman's other side.

"That's her," Jace whispered.

The woman leaned against the railing and spoke in a firm voice. "Welcome, friends and colleagues. While much has changed in the world of late, the conflict is behind us, and we can refocus on the future." She put a hand on the young man's shoulder. "Today is my son's seventeenth name day. In addition to reaching this milestone, I am happy to announce he will soon depart for Tiadd to train at the University. It was to happen last year, but like many other plans, his were tossed upside down when war swept across the Eight Wizardoms." She wiped a tear from her eye. "I just wish Palkan were able to share this proud moment."

The crowd clapped and Narine felt their eyes on her. Inside, she wished to recoil and run, but she stood proud, her exterior resolute. *You cannot change the past, Narine.*

By the time the applause eased, Portia had regained her composure. "Please join me in a toast to congratulate Godwin. Tonight, we celebrate."

She raised a glass of wine, and many in the crowd did the same.

"To Godwin," voices echoed from around the room.

After taking a drink, the woman, teenager, and guard turned from the railing.

Narine swallowed the lump in her throat, wishing she were safely in her private chambers rather than in a crowded room filled with wizards and wizardesses who might see her as an enemy.

Jace leaned close. "You and I should head toward the stairs to meet her. It's best to get this behind us, so I can get to work."

She eyed him. "You still haven't told me what this is about."

He shrugged. "It may be nothing. I haven't decided yet."

Tugging her arm, he drew Narine across the room, her guards following. The crowd parted for the crown while Narine steeled herself, fearing the reception she might face from the hostess. Although she had been invited, she worried Portia might twist the party into a platform for public confrontation.

They reached the far end of the crowd as Portia and her bodyguard turned at the foot of the stairs. Her son was nowhere to be seen.

When Portia's gaze met Narine's, her eyes widened in recognition. "My queen." She curtsied, dipping her head. The guard at her side bowed as well. When her blue eyes lifted, they were focused on Jace, her lips turning up at the edges. "You flatter me by accepting my invitation."

She knows him, Narine thought. Although the woman was twenty years Narine's senior, she was attractive. Portia had the curves to draw a man's attention with an added plumpness that Narine lacked.

When he did not react, Narine interjected. "Thank you for the invitation, Wizardess Forca. It is the first I have received since my coronation, despite numerous such events taking place within Marquithe and other Farrowen cities."

The woman's eyes narrowed in thought. "Yes. Perhaps others did not believe you would accept an invite for a private function?"

"Most often, it would be difficult to fit such niceties into my schedule." Narine forced a smile. "In this case, I thought it best if I accepted."

Portia's smile fell away. She moved closer, her voice dropping to a whisper. "You speak of my husband."

Anxiety twisted Narine's stomach. "How is he?"

The woman sighed. "Much the same. Healing does nothing to change his state."

Narine had expected as much. Magic, when wielded by a skilled wizardess, could heal most physical maladies. A broken mind was another matter. *Perhaps I should have killed him.*

Portia took Narine's hand. "In truth, I should thank you."

"Thank me?"

"Yes. Palkan was…consumed by his ambition. It had grown worse every year, him more focused on the wizards guild than our marriage…or our son. When we returned from the campaign in Ghealdor, he immediately assumed Thurvin's place, claiming it was his responsibility while the wizard lord was away. Then, when the tower flames died…" She wiped a tear away. "He moved into the palace, but I refused to follow. I have seen nothing good from wizard lords and did not wish to be married to one. He would never have come home again, and I would never leave this manor. I finally admitted to myself what I should have years ago. Our marriage was over. He did not care for me or for Godwin. He only cared for himself." She wiped another tear away. "Years ago, before Godwin was even born, Palkan had been different – filled with passion for me and his work and compassionate toward others. But the man I loved evolved into something else." Lifting her gaze, she looked up the staircase. "Now he sits in his room and stares into space, an empty shell of a man. I often wonder if you killed the part of him that had become twisted, and by then, this was all that remained."

Narine kept silent, grasping for some appropriate response, the words slipping between her fingers.

Portia turned to Jace. "It is good to see you, Jerrell."

He nodded. "You as well, Portia. You appear as beautiful as ever."

She leaned forward, offering a better view of the generous cleavage nestled in her plunging neckline. "Too bad you are no longer available. Now that Palkan is incapacitated, I no longer need to hide my trysts."

What? Narine arched a brow, bristling.

Jace, focused on Portia, chuckled. "I am flattered, Portia, but I am committed to Narine, and such indiscretions are a thing of the past."

The wizardess sighed. "I suppose I should congratulate you in advance of your upcoming wedding. With your…skills, I am unsurprised at your rise in station…even if it is rare for an Ungifted to marry a wizard."

Hackles raised, Narine pulled him against her side. "As you might have noticed, Ungifted or not, Jace…Jerrell is a rare person. Perhaps it is past time we wizards become more accepting of those who cannot wield magic."

Portia arched a brow. "Careful, Your Majesty. Most of my guests would consider such thoughts heresy."

"Heresy is based on religion," Narine retorted. "Where do such things stand now that the gods are gone?"

Portia's expression shifted to concern. "Are they truly gone?"

Jace replied, "The last two Darkenings have passed without Farrow appearing, the first such occurrences in two thousand years. Does a year's absence not prove the claims that the gods are dead?"

The woman placed a hand against her cheek, her eyes shifting across her surroundings. "I worry. Without wizard lords to protect us and gods to guide us, what of our future?"

Jace said in a confident tone, "Queen Narine is our future, Portia. As for religion...I suspect that will work itself out...somehow." He shrugged. "In truth, I have never been one for gods and such things, preferring to live my life according to my own mantra."

Giving him a sidelong glance, Narine asked, "Which is?"

He grinned. "Follow your heart."

"What does that mean?"

"It means I am to marry you, my queen."

Narine laughed, Portia joining her.

When their laughter calmed, Jace said, "It was good to see you again, Portia. However, you are the host and have many guests to greet. We should let you go so it does not appear the queen is intent on hijacking your party."

"Very well." Portia dipped her head to Narine. "Again, thank you for coming, my queen."

The wizardess and her hulking bodyguard walked into the ballroom, leaving Narine alone with Jace and her two guards.

"Interesting..." Jace muttered, his gaze following Portia before he turned to Narine. "Her attitude toward you seemed sincere and better than expected."

Narine nodded in relief. "Yes. I had feared the meeting would be tense, but she seemed...appreciative."

"I thought so as well."

She narrowed her eyes, recalling another aspect of the conversation. "You and she appear to have a past..."

He held his hand up, stopping her. "Listen. It was the past and meant nothing. It was a business transaction and that is all. Please just forget about it."

Narine nodded. She knew enough of his reputation and personality to realize there were questions better left unasked. "So long as it is in the past."

He gripped her hands, smiling. "Of course. I am still a rogue, but I am *your* rogue."

She smiled. "Terms I accept."

He turned to the two men in Midnight Guard uniforms. "Remain with the queen and watch for anything suspicious. She is not to be alone...even if she must relieve herself."

"Jace!" she blurted.

Grinning, he said, "If you don't like it, don't drink too much."

You told me not to eat or drink anything, she thought and then realized Jace meant to keep his suspicions a secret. "I was going to avoid the wine anyway. Now, I'll have to go thirsty."

"Don't worry. I will not be long. When I have what I need, we can leave."

He turned and ascended the stairs, leaving her alone with the two guards.

She sighed and turned toward them. "Perhaps I will see what waits in the dining room. Would either of you care for a bite?"

7

SCHEMES

A midnight blue carpet ran down the stairs, the edges of each step exposed to reveal darkly stained wood that matched the lacquered railings. Jace ascended to the loft where a group of five teenagers huddled – three girls in dresses and two boys in robes, all wearing varying colors.

When he reached the balcony overlooking the ballroom, he put his hands on the shoulders of two of the males, one his height but more stoutly built, the other standing a head taller. Parting, they turned in his direction.

Smiling, Jace nodded in greeting. "Good evening. I am looking for the young man of the hour. Do you know where Godwin is?"

The tall teen to his left, a boy with shaggy brown hair and dark eyes, asked, "Who are you?"

"I am Godwin's uncle, Jasper."

The lad's face darkened. "He never mentioned an uncle."

Jace widened his eyes in shock. "Seriously? After everything I have done for him?" He shook his head. "If not for me, Godwin might *still* be wetting the bed."

The shorter boy snickered along with one of the girls, while the other two widened their eyes.

The tall one was not so easily duped. "What could *you* do about something like that?"

Jace put his hand to his chest. "I happen to be among the most talented enchanters of my generation. With his problem persisting into his early teens, I set out to make an enchantment to address his issue. I am happy to report, he has not pissed himself for two years."

This time, all three girls joined the shorter boy in a round of laughter.

I fear Godwin is in for a round of teasing. He knew well how cruel teens could be. Their finding humor in the invented malady proved his point.

"I have been Godwin's best friend for ten years," said the taller teen. "I have never heard of such an issue."

Arching a brow, Jace asked, "Would you tell anyone?"

The boy frowned. "No. I guess not."

One of the girls asked, "If you are an enchanter, why aren't you wearing black robes?"

Leaning in, Jace whispered, "There is tension between Cor Cordium and the Marquithe Wizards Guild. Few will speak of it, but we are close to shuttering the doors of the Enchanter's Tower in Marquithe to any wizard as a result."

He paused, expecting and receiving a round of gasps.

"Yes," Jace nodded. "That means no more enchanted lanterns or lifts or any of the other niceties the gentry currently enjoy."

"That is horrible," one girl replied.

"As you might suspect, such a delicate situation requires care. To have an enchanter here, at a wizard's party, would draw undue attention and might place me in an awkward position."

The taller boy said, "That makes sense, I suppose."

"Just be sure to keep this between us. Alright?"

Nods and affirmative replies came from the group.

"Wonderful," Jace said with a grin. "Now, where can I find Godwin?"

The short stout boy pointed up the stairs. "He went up to the tower to see his father. Fourth floor, last door on the right."

"I know it well," Jace said. "Thank you."

Savory scents taunted Narine, her stomach growling angrily while Boris and Hardy ate their fill. The other guests fled the dining room within minutes of her arrival, leaving her alone with her guards. In truth, she found it relieving to be away from the stares – some expressing round-eyed awe, some leering with lust, others displaying narrow-eyed jealousy, and even a few gazes filled with hatred.

Suddenly, Hardy doubled over, gripping his stomach. "Ugh. I don't feel so good."

"What?" Boris asked.

Hardy looked up at him and said, "I think the fish was bad."

"Oh, no. I ate the fish as well." Boris's eyes widened. He groaned and grabbed his stomach. "I think I'm going to be sick."

Narine rolled her eyes. "Do you want me to heal you?"

Palm held toward her, Hardy shook his head. "No need, my queen. I'm sure I'll be fine if I can just throw it up."

Boris nodded. "Same here."

She sighed and turned toward the kitchen door. "Go and find some shrubs in the backyard. I'll tell the hostess she may have some spoiled food." Even as she said it, Jace's warning of poison ran through Narine's head. *Would someone risk poisoning everyone here?*

Shaking his head, Hardy said, "No. We will come with you. We aren't supposed to leave your side." His hand went to his mouth.

Fearing the man might burst, Narine pushed him toward the kitchen door. "I'll go out with you. Now hurry."

As Jace reached the fourth level of Forca Manor, the music faded. The torchlit corridor was quiet save for his own footsteps. Extravagant tapestries and scenic paintings, all lush with color, adorned the walls. He passed closed doors made of heavy wood, a lightning bolt piercing the letter *F* etched in gold on each. Jace recognized the Forca house symbol, one he had long considered ostentatious; it was too close to the lightning bolt through a hollow circle that graced the flag of Farrowen.

Upon reaching the end of the corridor, he opened a door leading to a circular stairwell going up to the right and down to the left. Closing the door gently, he climbed the stairs, focused and alert. Two stories later, he found a closed door and heard a muffled voice coming from the other side.

Carefully, he turned the knob and opened the door a crack, the speaker's words becoming clear.

"...she will be dead, and you will have your justice, Father."

That little bitter brat. He is behind the plot. Jace readied himself and eased the door open.

The circular room had a conical ceiling and was a dozen strides in diameter. A solid moonbeam shone through two of the six arched windows, the silvery light glimmering off the star-shaped symbol inlaid in the floor tiles. Books filled shelves between the windows. In the center of the room, a pen, a capped inkwell, and a scattering of papers rested on a massive table. A middle-aged man in bathrobes sat in a rocking chair beside the table, staring off into space. That man was Palkan Forca, former head of the wizards guild. Godwin stood before the man, his back to Jace.

The light from the stairwell crept into the room and Godwin spun around. Shock crossed his face briefly before it morphed to anger. The teen thrust his arms out, twisting his hands.

The hair on Jace's arms stood on end, the amulet against his chest ice cold, as the magic washed past but left him unaffected. He burst forward, grabbed the teen by the front of his robes, and drove him backward, across the room. Godwin yelped and stumbled, attempting to remain upright until he backed into the wall below an open window. Jace bent the youth backward so his upper body was outside.

Godwin glanced over his shoulder, toward the ground, six stories below. "Please don't kill me," he pleaded in a high voice.

"Why are you trying to kill the queen?"

"I don't know what..."

Jace pushed him farther backward, Godwin gripping his arms in fear.

"Alright. I...wanted her to pay for what she did to my father."

"Your father earned his sentence. It was this or death."

Tears emerged, Godwin sobbing, "He is so...pathetic now."

"Better than scheming, backstabbing, and disobeying orders for his own benefit."

"I wish she had just killed him."

"That I can understand. However, it was in her best interest to keep him alive." Jace pulled Godwin back inside, and spun the teen around, pinning him against a bookshelf, which sent books falling to the floor. "Now tell me about your plot to kill Queen Narine."

"I…" Godwin sobbed. "I paid a pair of guards. They were to get her alone and do it…make it quick so she couldn't use her magic." His sobbing stopped, mouth bending down in a frown. "Why didn't my magic work on you?"

Grinning, Jace said, "You wizards have no power over me. I am immune to magic."

Godwin's eyes widened, "How…"

"Never mind that," Jace insisted. "What are the names of these guards? When is this to happen?"

The teen's brow furrowed. "I can't recall their names, exactly. They are Ungifted nobodies…wait. I remember one. His name rhymed with Horus, the dead Orenthian wizard lord."

"Horus?" Jace said it aloud and began through the alphabet, stopping at *B.* "Is it Boris?"

"Yeah. That's it."

"Is the other named Hardy?"

"You know them?"

Jace raced out the door and down the stairs.

Stepping outside, Narine inhaled deeply. The night air was cool and refreshing, the veranda dark and quiet. Boris and Hardy ran off into the shrubs, and the noise of their retching soon followed. She crossed the paved patio to lean against the railing. Beyond the shrubs, she spotted a cobblestone drive leading to a stone building against the back wall, the Enchanter's Tower looming behind it. *The stables,* she thought, recalling a night not so long ago when she and her companions broke into that very same building and stole horses to aid their flight from the city. Less than a year and a half had passed since that evening, yet the entire world had changed in that span.

As they often did, her thoughts turned to Adyn. The two of them had grown up together, one a princess, the other her protector. But she had been more than a bodyguard. Adyn had been Narine's dearest friend. *I miss her so much.* She sighed, thankful that Jace had entered her life and done his best to fill the vacuum created by Adyn's passing. Still, it was not the same nor would it ever be.

A rustle came from behind as the guards returned. She turned around and a sword flashed, the pommel striking her temple. Pain shot through her brain. The world tilted as she toppled, her head striking the stone tiles.

Head throbbing, she rolled to her back. Everything spun. Her stomach recoiled. And the darkness threatened to close in. She blinked away tears to see Hardy standing over her.

"Hurry up and kill her before she uses her magic," Boris said.

"Relax," Hardy said as he squatted beside her, drawing cloth from his waist. "The wizard said the witch would be helpless if she couldn't think clearly."

Narine tried to draw in her magic but could not. Even if it were possible, she was in no condition to cast a spell.

"Why don't you just kill her?" Boris asked, looking over his shoulder nervously.

"We are supposed to send a message, remember?" A menacing grin crossed Hardy's face. "He wants the others to think twice about claiming the throne."

Hardy stretched the cloth across her eyes, lifting her head to tie the blindfold. Narine tried to resist, her words emerging as a whimper and her weakened arms feebly pushing against his. He pressed another cloth against her mouth, forcing it open to tie the gag. He then wrenched her arms back, shackling her wrists before lifting her off the ground.

"Come on. The wizard said there was a secret exit through the stables."

Draped over the man's shoulder, the pressure on her midriff and his jostling footsteps caused her world to spin.

Boris's voice came from the side, joining his hurried footsteps. "I still don't understand why you won't kill her and be done with it."

The man carrying her grunted. "Have you seen her? If there has ever been a woman I'd wish a piece of, it's this one." Hardy chuckled. "I've often wondered what it might be like to bed a wizardess, not to mention a queen. It is just too good an opportunity to pass up."

Horrified, Narine suddenly missed Adyn more than ever.

8

DESPERATION

S tanding against the railing of the second story loft, Jace swept his gaze across the crowd below. Over a hundred people filled the ballroom, most male and female wizards. None wore a crown on locks of gold.

He spun around, raced down the stairs, and slowed when he spotted a couple at the bottom. Gripping one shoulder, he turned the man toward him. "Have you seen the queen?"

"The queen?" the wizard muttered, his eyes wide.

"I haven't seen her since the toast," the woman said.

Jace turned toward the open doorway to the dining room, rushing in to find a servant entering from the kitchen.

"The queen. Have you seen her?"

The servant gestured toward the swinging door. "She and two guards passed through the kitchen."

"When?"

"A few minutes ago."

Bursting through the door, Jace found a busy kitchen with four cooks in various stages of food preparation. He raced down the narrow aisle between an island counter and shelving, straight toward the door at the far end of the room.

Outside, it was quiet. There was nobody in sight. A cobblestone drive looped around the veranda, leading to the street where her carriage waited. He jumped over the railing and started toward the front, but his feet slowed after a few steps. *They would not wish to be seen.* He turned back and saw the stables at the other end of the drive, the same stables he had broken into over a year prior. In the moonlight, something glittered on the ground beside the drive.

Jace ran toward it, bent, and picked up a gold crown with a sapphire in its center. *Narine!* He tossed it into the shrubs, raced toward the closed stable doors, gripped the handles, and eased them partially open. It was dark inside. A horse shuffled nervously, affirming Jace's intuition. He yanked the doors open wide. The moonlight revealed an empty aisle between the stable bays. Reaching inside his long coat, he withdrew one of the fulgur blades hidden there, its pick-shaped metal crackling with blue sparks shedding additional flickering light into the interior.

Blade ready, he hurried inside and went straight for the far wall. As expected, one section of bricks appeared a lighter color than the rest, marking the doorway the two stone-shaping dwarfs had previously opened at Jace's request. The wall had been repaired since then, but was it as solid as it seemed?

In the flickering light, he noticed one brick recessed from the others. When pressed, the brick sunk into the wall. A click sounded and a door-sized section tilted inward. He pulled it open and peered down the dark hillside street. Below, he spotted a carriage just as the door closed, and the driver snapped the reins.

Jace burst into a run, racing down the hillside as the wagon pulled away. *Narine is in there!* He knew it in his heart. His feet moved as fast as he had ever run before. When the carriage turned at the first intersection, the driver noticed Jace and snapped the reins, urging his team into a gallop. Jace cut the corner, desperate to catch the coach before it reached full speed. He closed the gap and was only a stride from it when the carriage began to pull away.

Reaching beneath his coat, he gripped the other fulgur blade, pulled it out, and leapt. Arms outstretched, he rammed the blades into the back of the carriage, piercing the wood with the blades sliding in to the hilt.

Holding tightly to the hilts, Jace was pulled along the dark street by the speeding carriage, the toes of his boots dragging across the cobblestones. He pulled one blade out, reached up higher, and rammed it into the wood, the magic tip easily cutting into it. A cry came from inside the cab as he pulled himself up, pulled the other blade free, and reached up again. Within moments, he was on the carriage roof.

The door opened, and Boris peered out, his head turning to look at the carriage roof. Jace swung his leg around and kicked. His boot struck the guard in the face, snapping the man's head back. Jace kicked again and again. The guard fell with a cry, his armor clattering as he rolled into a building.

Ignoring the open door as it swung wildly, Jace pulled his blades free and scrambled toward the driver. The man flipped his whip around in a wide arc, the leather flying toward Jace, who leapt over it, driving both his feet into the man's chest. The driver flew from his seat into the horses' harness webbing as Jace landed on the carriage roof. A sword burst through the wood, inches from Jace's head. It withdrew and Jace rolled aside as the blade smashed through right where his head had been. The carriage bounced, causing Jace to slip over the edge and save himself by ramming the fulgur blades into the roof.

Arms straining, Jace pulled himself back onto the roof just as the sword slashed through the open door, narrowly missing his legs. He rose to one knee and turned toward the team, the driver attempting to climb onto one of the horses. Jace dropped quickly to the seat and slashed, severing one of the straps between the coach and the team. He struck again, cutting the strap beneath the driver's boot. The man's feet hit the cobblestones, and he was dragged as the horses raced down the street. Jace slashed one last time, cutting the harnesses from the carriage. When the strap fell, so did the driver. The speeding carriage rocked and bounced when it ran over the downed man. The front wheels turned, angling the carriage toward the side of the street.

Wide-eyed as the wall raced toward him, Jace leapt into the air, his arms extended. He slammed the fulgur blades into the building's brick wall, sparks spraying as the enchanted blades plunged into the stone, raining shards down around him. The carriage struck the wall with a mighty crack, wood splintering as the vehicle deflected off the wall, rolled across the street, and smashed into another wall before falling still.

Jace put his feet to the wall and yanked the blades free, twisting in midair and landing with a crouch, before rushing across the street and yanking the carriage door open.

Hardy thrust his sword out and Jace spun away, the blade slicing through his flaring coat. Jace slashed, the fulgur blade connecting with his attacker's hand, severing several fingers. The man cried out, and his blade fell to the street. Jace lunged and slammed his other blade into the top of Hardy's boot, driving it through the man's foot and pinning it to the carriage floor. Hardy screamed as he fell onto a seat.

Narine lay sprawled on the other seat, her head bloody, her body unmoving. Well aware that emotions clouded the mind, Jace rarely lost his temper. But the sight of Narine blindfolded, gagged, shackled, and incapacitated stirred a rage unlike any he had ever experienced.

He turned toward the guard who was holding his maimed hand in the other, his foot still pinned to the floor. Hardy stood half a head taller than Jace and likely outweighed him by a hundred pounds. That didn't stop Jace from gripping the man's arm, bracing his foot against the carriage wall, and yanking the man out. Hardy screamed as he tumbled to the street, bones cracking as his ankle twisted around his pierced and immobile foot.

Crouching over him, Jace brought his other crackling fulgur blade before the whimpering man's face. "Who hired you?"

"I...I can't say." Hardy's nose and teeth were covered in blood.

"Treason is punishable by death. Tell me, and I'll make it quick. Hold back and…"

"The Forca boy," Hardy choked out. "He paid us each a gold piece."

So, it is true, Jace sighed inwardly. *I had hoped otherwise.* "Do you have anything else to say?"

"I told you what you wanted to hear. Now, just do it."

Jace set his jaw, lifted the blade, and drove it into through the man's helmet, deep into his forehead. Hardy stiffened and fell still. Jace pulled the blade out, wiped it on the guard's cape, and slid it back into the sheath sewn into his coat.

Hearing the rapid beat of approaching footsteps, he turned to see Boris running toward him, the tall guard's eyes wide with fury and his sword drawn and winding back for a killing blow. Jace reacted in a flash, drawing a throwing knife from his sleeve and whipping it as he fell backward. The blade plunged into the guard's open mouth, causing his head to jerk backward. The guard's sword swept over Jace's horizontal body as he tripped over his dead comrade. As soon as his back struck the cobblestone street, Jace rolled aside to get clear. Boris then slammed to the street with a tremendous clatter, his sword skittering away.

Jace's breath came in ragged gasps and his heart raced as he rose to stare down at his attacker who twitched and coughed, blood coating the silver hilt of the throwing knife in his mouth. Turning away, Jace pulled his other fulgur blade from Hardy's foot.

He crawled into the broken carriage, pulled a throwing blade from his other sleeve, and used it to cut Narine's gag and blindfold. Her breathing was shallow, and she was unresponsive. Her yellow hair was matted with dark blood, and her arms were shackled behind her back. He carefully lifted her in his arms and climbed out the door.

While stepping over the two dead guards, he spotted a man in the shadows of a doorway– one of his own. "Styles," Jace said.

The sixteen-year-old thief crossed the street. He had a lean build and was a bit undersized for his age. His brown hair was shoulder length, and his clothing was dark, a simple tunic and breeches. More than anyone he had met, Styles reminded Jace of himself.

The teen nodded. "You have good eyes, Jerrell."

"Never mind that. I need you to get a message to Captain Henton. Tell him to send a squad to clean this up. These two are named Boris and Hardy. I want their bodies brought to the palace and their belongings seized."

"What about you?"

"I have to run."

Jace broke into a sprint, heading back toward the party. He would promise Portia leniency toward Godwin if she could heal Narine. Anything to save Narine.

9

THE CHARLATAN

From a dark corner in a small room on the uppermost floor of the Marquithe Bureau of Trading, Jace laid out the details of a contract for hire.

His face masked by shadows, Jace explained, "The party involved desires to see this man pay dearly. Prove he is dead and it's worth two gold pieces, four if you can recover the stolen items in the process."

Whistler, a tall bounty hunter who doubled as an assassin, grinned back. With three missing teeth to accompany an already-ugly face, the expression most likely stirred fear in those it was aimed toward. In this case, Jace found it reassuring. *Whistler is crude and reckless, but he has proven effective. In these cases, only the results matter.*

The man stood and flexed his hands, as if eager to pull the trigger on the exotic crossbow hanging from his shoulder...or swing the war hammer on his hip. The hammer was narrow in construction, flat on one face with a curved pick on the other. Jace wondered what other weapons Whistler hid in his long leather coat.

"And you sssusspect thisss thief is headed toward Ghealdor?" Each *s* spoken by the man whistled through his missing teeth.

Jace nodded. "I have solid information confirming that was his destination."

Nodding, Whistler tipped his black brimmed hat and turned to the door. "Give me a week. Two at mossst."

"The contract is yours. Good luck."

Grinning, Whistler opened the door. "It'sss Narlik who will need luck when I catch up to him."

The man stepped into the corridor, ignoring the two burly toughs standing at the door. Before the man's footsteps faded, his voice carried from down the hallway, "Howdy, missss."

Alert, Jace watched his two guards, both staring in the same direction. Soft footsteps approached, the two men doing nothing to intercept the person, informing Jace it was an expected visitor.

A familiar voice rang through the corridor. "Easy, boys. I am here to see the Charlatan."

A tall blonde stopped in the doorway and leaned against the frame. She wore a slinky black dress, her legs scandalously exposed below the knee and her plunging neckline competing for attention. Her body was long and lean but with enough curves to prove she was undeniably female.

"Haelynn," Jace growled. "What are you doing here?"

"I heard you had a valuable contract to offer. You didn't already give it to Whistler, did you?"

"I did."

"What?!" Her sultry tone turned to stormy seas in an instant. She entered and slammed the door. The anger slid away, and she plopped into the chair across from him. "Hello, Jerrell. I'm glad to see you are well."

Jace grinned. "Nice performance. Using the contract against Narlik was a brilliant cover."

She shrugged. "You have made it clear others should believe we are at odds." A smirk turned up on her full lips. "In truth, I find it quite fun."

He chuckled. "I suspected you might feel that way."

"You wanted to see me?"

"Yes." He leaned forward, allowing the light to reach his face. She was among the few he trusted with his true identity. "The rumor you brought to me last week came to fruition."

She arched a dark neatly trimmed brow. "When I heard of the mess you left on Jewel Street, I suspected it had to do with Narine."

"Two of her own guards tried to kidnap and kill her."

"Is she alright?"

He ran his hand through his hair. "Yes. Thankfully, she is fully recovered with no ill effects…save for a ruined dress."

"Was Forca's wife behind it?"

"No. His son."

"Huh? The kid? I didn't think he had it in him."

"Me neither. In fact, the entire thing rubs me the wrong way."

"Not surprising. Someone tried to kill your betrothed just weeks before your wedding."

"No. I mean…" His voice trailed off. His mind raced as he stared into space. "This kid, how did he come up with the plan? Why would the guards agree to risk their lives to commit treason for such a small amount?"

"How much did he pay them?"

"One gold piece each."

"While a good amount, it is a pittance for the life of a queen."

"Exactly. Contracts are weighted by risk and reward. In this case, they should have requested at least twenty times that number. Perhaps even fifty gold each."

"I agree." Haelynn crossed her legs, fingers trailing down her smooth shin. "Both the guards and the boy confirmed it was him?"

"Yes."

"So, did you lock the Forca boy up, or did you just kill him?"

"Neither. He remains at Forca Estate, under house arrest until he departs for the University."

"You are allowing him to get away with it?"

"I needed Portia to heal Narine. More importantly, I needed her best effort. In exchange, I promised leniency toward her son, provided he tells me everything he knows."

"And what did you learn?"

"After a brief interrogation, the kid answering in sobs as if I were beating him, I discovered the idea had been brought to him by the two guards."

"Would-be assassins approaching someone to hire them? That's a new one."

"Which is the problem. The men came to Godwin and suggested that they might be able to exact revenge in exchange for payment. When Godwin told them the most he could come up with was one gold coin each, they agreed and left. I guess the boy spent the next three days fretting about what was to happen, but he didn't know how to stop it." Jace squeezed his eyes closed. "I actually felt sorry for him."

Haelynn chuckled. "You are getting soft, Jerrell. Still, what does all this mean?"

Sighing, he sat back. "It means either two stupid guards came up with the idea, thinking to earn a little extra coin...or it means someone else was behind it and intended Godwin Forca to take the fall. If so, this is the beginning of something rather than the end."

"And why didn't the guards just kill her? Why kidnap her?"

Jace frowned, his anger stirring. "Narine heard one say he wanted to bed her before killing her."

Haelynn gasped. "With her bound and against her will?" She shuddered. "That is disgusting."

"I know. However, the man's urges led him to keep her alive long enough for me to catch them."

"True," she nodded. "What is your next step?"

He stood and stretched. "First, I am heading back to the palace to resume my other job."

"You mean as the queen's concubine?"

Grinning, Jace said, "One of the perks for sure. In fact, I might be satisfied with that moniker. However, she would prefer the term 'betrothed'."

"I'm sure."

His smile slid away, her tone becoming serious. "I need you to send out some feelers. Get aggressive if you must. I need to know about any future assassination attempts before they happen."

"Because of me, you knew about *this* one."

Turning away, his shoulders slumped. "And I still almost got her killed. Worse, it was my fault she was placed in harm's way." Sighing, he ran his hand through his hair. "I guess I miss the action and sought to insert myself into the thick of it, not considering Narine's own guards would turn on her while I was away."

Haelynn stood, running her hand up his arm as she spoke over his shoulder. "Don't beat yourself up over what *almost* happened. You have always been a man of action, Jerrell. You are not built for sitting in dark rooms and pulling strings like some spider spinning a web. Caging a wild animal does not make it tame. Deep inside, its nature is to remain wild despite its keeper attempting to teach it otherwise. Based on the man I know, one I have known for years, something like this was bound to happen."

"I suppose you are right."

Surprising even himself, Jace hugged her, something he had never done before. Yes, he had slept with her many times, but emotion had never been involved. Somehow, he now felt closer to her than he did back then. He had few true friends, and while Haelynn had been a rival as often as not, she understood him as few others did. After a moment, he released his embrace.

Her lips curled into a smirk. "Are you trying to bed me?"

He chuckled. "We had some good times, didn't we?"

Leaning close, her hip against his groin and her lips to his ear, she said in a throaty voice, "Yes. We did."

Ignoring his rising pulse, Jace fixed Narine in his mind. "Most are memories I will cherish. However, memories are all that remain. Now, we are friends and business acquaintances."

Shrugging, she turned toward the door. "Suit yourself." Hand on the knob, she looked back at him. "By the way, how much will this pay?"

"I gave you my old apartment. Do this and consider that debt repaid."

"Fair enough." Her smile returned. "Now, throw me out of here, so we give them a show."

"Oh. Yes. Of course." He backed into the shadows, drew a breath, and shouted. "You conniving wench! I want you out of here, now!"

Haelynn tore the door open. "I'll be back, Charlatan. When I return, you had better have a contract for me."

The guards both arched their brows.

Jace used the opportunity to strike back in jest. "When something suitable for a backstabbing wench comes along, I will let you know."

A growl stirred in her throat. "Fine."

With impressive force, she slammed the door. The room fell silent.

Jace waited for her footsteps to fade before crossing the room. In a hushed shout, he called through the door, "Scandrick, Karn, I am leaving for the day. Wait ten minutes, and then you can leave. I'll see you tomorrow."

"Got it, boss," Karn said.

Twisting the lock and throwing the bolt, Jace went to the neighboring room. He gathered up the missives from the previous evening and slid them into his coat. With the lanterns off, he felt along the wall until he found the switch. He pressed it and heard the click of a hidden door swinging open. He entered the dark narrow stairwell, closed the door, and began his descent.

Opening the door to afternoon sunlight, Jace emerged from the nondescript building across the street from the Marquithe Bureau of Trading. He closed the door, locked it, and slid the key into an inside pocket of his leather coat. As foot traffic flowed past the recessed entrance, he slipped behind two men embroiled in a heated argument.

"...telling you, the dragons saved the world. They are akin to gods, so what is the problem?"

The other man snorted. "You would have us worship creatures? What is next? Do we declare Old Man Telliwick's prize winning sow, a god?"

"Don't be ridiculous," the taller man scoffed. "Dragons are unique and extraordinary...creatures of magic and wonder. Telliwick's sow is only a pig that has eaten itself to obscene proportions."

"Still, what comes of worshipping a dragon?" the shorter man asked as they entered a city square.

The Bureau was on one side of the square, and a fountain stood in the center. The area was hundreds of feet across, intersecting with six city streets leading in different directions. Dozens of people occupied the square, the bulk of whom had clustered around a man standing on a wagon. He was impossible to miss. The man was naked above the waist, except for a three-foot-tall headdress made of green feathers that sat on his scalp. The headdress had a spiked crest down the back and eyes made of amber glass with black slits for pupils at the front, making it unmistakably dragon-like.

"There's a dragon priest," said the shorter man in front of Jace. "Let's go listen to him for a bit, and then, you can decide."

The two men walked over to join the crowd surrounding the priest, who waved his arms and preached loudly. "...when the end seemed certain, the city doomed to fall to the Lord of Darkness, the skies parted to reveal a beam of bright light shining down from the night sky. Dragons, massive and majestic, emerged from that beam of light. These gods attacked the darkspawn, tearing the flying creatures from the sky and bathing those on the ground in sheets of flame. In moments, this evil force of darkness – an army of beyond a hundred thousand twisted monsters – collapsed in defeat.

"When the sun rose the next morning, the dragons were gone, as were the darkspawn. Yet the city and its people had survived. Balmoria would rebuild and the wizardoms to the south would be spared from such devastation. The lives of man, our entire race, are owed to our newfound gods." He lifted his arms to the sky. "Praise the dragons!"

The crowd repeated the phrase, shouting and pumping their fists in the air.

Jace walked away, shaking his head as he entered a side street and considered the scene.

The dragon priests had first appeared a few months after the Battle of Balmor, not just in Marquithe, but in many cities across the Eight Wizardoms. The priests were few at first and struggled to draw a crowd. However, without Devotion to connect the people to their gods each evening, something else was bound to meet the need. *The people are conditioned to pray to a higher power. With the gods gone...it is no wonder some have begun to listen to these dragon priests.* It did not matter if the priests had it wrong. People would readily believe, since few had actually witnessed the battle. He suspected that even some who had witnessed the darkspawn attack had begun to believe the dragon priests' twisted version of the truth.

Pushing aside thoughts of gods and dragons, Jace considered all he knew about the attempt on Narine's life...and how close it had come to succeeding. If such a thing were to happen again, he would need to be prepared.

10

LOVE, FEAR, AND COIN

Seated on a sofa in her private chambers, Narine listened while Henton paced.

He paused and looked at her, holding his hand out in a plea. "My queen, only three remain of the Midnight Guard I knew before the campaign in Ghealdor."

The man had remained in motion during most of the conversation. While he paced, she sat, resolute and at ease. Only one outcome could be permitted.

She shook her head. "What happened the other night cannot occur again. I was lucky to survive. If not for Jace…" Between the kidnapping and what Hardy had planned…her stomach recoiled at the memory. Pressing her lips together, she pushed such images from her mind lest she break out in tears. *I must be strong.* "Any guards assigned to protect me must be vetted – reliable enough for you to place your life in their hands. If anything does happen to me, Jace will ensure that you're dead. If you think he won't, just consider what happened to Boris and Hardy, not to mention the driver. The guards were trained to fight, armed, and armored."

Narine had demanded to see the corpses of the kidnappers when they were searched for more clues. The memory of those empty gazes was far less likely to cause her nightmares than hearing what they had planned when they were alive. Still, it had been a mess, particularly the carriage driver, whose head had nearly been removed from his body by the wagon wheels.

Henton tried again. "With only three…"

She held up a hand, stopping him. "Four, including yourself."

He scowled. "I already command the Midnight Guard. I can't afford to spend non-productive hours at your side."

"Until we have a better plan, you will make it work."

A scream came from outside the palace, drawing her attention to the open balcony doors. She rose to her feet and headed out, stepping into the afternoon sunlight. Hands on the rail, she peered down at the gathering crowd. Among them, a woman in white and blue robes lay face-down, her head bent at an awkward angle. Even from five stories up, she could see the blood coming from the woman's nose and ears.

"Another one," she said.

From beside her, Henton grunted. "That's seven in the past three weeks."

They both turned away from the horrific scene, heading back inside.

Narine said, "At this pace, we will be out of clerics by the end of the summer."

"Without a god to worship…they are a rudderless ship on stormy seas."

She gave him a sidelong look. "Really? A sailor metaphor from you?"

He shrugged. "It seemed to fit well enough."

Her thoughts returned to the dead woman below the palace. "I need to do something to stop this. Why now? Why a year after the gods left us?"

"Like the rest of us, they likely didn't believe it to be true."

"I was there, Henton. The gods are gone, destroyed by Urvadan before he came to his own end. I told High Priestess Dianza as much."

Chuckling, he shook his head. "She would rather lie to herself than believe her god, the being she had dedicated her life to, was dead and gone. It wasn't until the recent Darkening that she understood. Yes, Farrow did not appear during the autumn Darkening, but they likely convinced themselves it was a fluke. When he did not appear this spring, it turned from an anomaly to a trend. My guess is that when each priestess comes to grips with the truth, she decides to off herself."

The man's reasoning made sense, but Narine had always been uncomfortable with the clergy. As a child, she had been forced to attend the Immolation rituals in Fastella, her father basking in the dominant magic he shared with his god, not caring that it had cost the lives of an entire family. No matter how hard she tried, she never understood how someone could dedicate their lives to a being who feasted on the souls of the innocent. *If not for the sacrifices…perhaps I would have been closer to Gheald…*closer to the lies only she, Jace, and a handful of others understood. *Losing their god is already causing the most devout to kill themselves. If they knew the full truth…*

Her thoughts turned back to the clerics of Farrow. Rather than attempt to gain their confidence, Narine had largely avoided them, Dianza included. *I know little of their customs or how to ease their concerns.* Another voice in her head countered that thought. *What did you expect, Narine? You are a Ghealdan sitting on the throne of another wizardom.*

Voices, real voices, came from the corridor outside her chamber. Henton spun toward the door. It opened and Jace walked in, waving to Vin and Lykus, the two guards on duty.

"Hello, Henton," Jace closed the door and walked toward the sofa, sitting with a sigh. "Did you two know another cleric jumped off the palace roof?"

"Yes," Narine replied. "We saw her from the balcony."

"I suspect it will get messier before it gets better," Jace noted.

"Henton and I were discussing that very thing. Perhaps I should step in."

"And do what? Unless you can replace their god, they are going to fall apart. Did you know three clerics moved out of the temple last week? Those women now work in a brothel near the south gate."

Henton blinked. "They went from a vow of celibacy to a brothel?"

Narine blanched. "That is horrible."

Jace grinned. "The first guests paid handsomely to bed them. Finding a thirty-year-old virgin whore is akin to discovering your piss turns stone to gold. From the stories I hear, those women are making up for lost time. They are also in high demand, each commanding four times the normal fee for a tickle. While inexperienced, especially for their age, each has shown enough enthusiasm to earn repeat business."

Henton rubbed his jaw. "Which three women?'

"Chartise, Lina, and Sonda."

The man's brows rose. "Chartise is a beautiful woman."

"At this rate, she'll soon be a wealthy one as well."

Standing with her hands on her hips, Narine glowered at the two men. "Will you two stop? You are talking about women who had dedicated themselves to a god and are now defiling their bodies in exchange for coin."

Jace shrugged. "Their bodies are theirs to do as they wish, so long as they aren't hurting anyone. On the contrary, I'd say they are saving some other women from unwanted advances. A man sated is far less likely to cross those lines."

She blinked. "I never thought of that."

A knock came from the door, four quick beats followed by two solid raps.

Jace motioned to the door. "It's a messenger. Can you let them in, Henton?"

The captain walked to the door, opening it to reveal a young man in simple clothing. His eyes widened and he bowed. "Pardon the interruption, my queen."

Rising, Jace approached the door. "What is it, Stephon?"

The messenger glanced over his shoulder.

"You can trust Captain Henton."

Stephon nodded. "I have spent the past twelve weeks in Tiamalyn, most of which as a servant in the palace. When I arrived in the city, Fadi Malone was high wizard. Four weeks ago, there was an uprising against the wizard, one of only a dozen remaining in the city. The rebellion was led by an ex-soldier named Arden Paleo."

Jace nodded. "I know Paleo. He is a hard head with the backing of the military but unsuited to rule."

"Was," Stephon said. "He is dead."

"Already?" Henton asked.

"That's what...four different rulers since Kylar Mor?"

"Five. In just one year." Jace turned back to Stephon. "Who now rules Orenth?"

"A committee of nine, none of whom are wizards."

"I have never heard of a committee ruling a nation," Narine said.

"They call themselves the Forum and claim to be the voice of the people."

"What if they disagree? How do they get anything accomplished?" Jace asked.

"They debate, discuss, and then vote. The majority decides."

Henton snorted. "In this climate with so much upheaval, such weakness seems rife for exploitation."

Stephon nodded. "Already, there are rumors of committee members willing to alter votes in favor of gold."

Jace grinned. "Interesting. Perhaps I misspoke earlier."

Narine nudged him. "You are encouraging corruption. How could you support a government where those with gold get whatever they wish?"

Rubbing his ribs, Jace shrugged. "Whether you like it or not, gold rules the world. I did not make the rules. I merely play the game." He turned to Stephon. "If you have nothing else, you may depart. Get some rest and see me in the morning. I will think on your next assignment."

The messenger bowed and left the room.

Reclaiming his seat on the sofa, Jace sighed. "After what happened last year, despite our heavy recruiting, Farrowen remains short on soldiers and unequipped to deal with turmoil in Orenth."

Narine nodded. "I agree. We must take care of our own issues and allow the Orenthians to deal with this without our involvement...for now."

"Speaking of issues," Jace stared at Narine, his eyes filled with concern. "We must ensure no other Farrowen soldier considers betraying his queen, be it the city watch, Thundercorps, or your own Midnight Guard. I..." His voice cracked. He leaned forward with his elbows on his knees as he stared into the dormant fireplace. "I cannot lose you, Narine. What occurred at the Forca's..." Rubbing his eyes, he shook his head. "It was a near thing and luck alone saved you."

She sat and slid her arm around his back, resting her head on his shoulder. "*You* saved me."

"This time. I was lucky, but my luck is not enough, not when it comes to your life." He looked at her. "You are skilled in magic, and I know you can fend for yourself, but you are not a wizard lord. Most people will not understand the difference, but every wizard knows you do not possess the power of a god. Past rulers could heal themselves at will while able to wield magic far beyond anyone else. Those facts ensured their positions and are among the reasons those men each ruled for a century or longer."

"You have no such assurance, so we must use other means to guarantee your safety."

Narine glanced at Henton who stood a few feet away, listening intently. That very subject had been the reason for his visit. She rubbed Jace's upper arm. "I get the sense you have an idea."

Jace sat back and flashed a grin. "You know me too well...better than anyone I have met, even those I have been friends with for years."

She frowned and jabbed his ribs. "Spit it out, Jace. You know I hate when you do this."

He chuckled. "Sorry. It's an old habit, difficult to break."

After a moment of silence, she rolled her eyes. "Well?"

"Oh, yes." He looked up at Henton. "I want you to gather every soldier you can spare and have them assemble in the palace plaza two hours after sunup tomorrow. Leave only a few at the gates and a handful to guard the palace perimeter."

Rubbing his chin, Henton narrowed his eyes. "I can do that, but then what?"

Grinning, Jace said, "I plan to force fealty upon them."

"Eighty percent of them weren't even soldiers a year ago. How do you plan to do that?"

"As far as I can tell, three things ensure loyalty – love, fear, and coin."

Narine frowned. "While I prefer them to love me, which will work best?'

He touched the side of his nose, a gesture she had seen Salvon use on numerous occasions. "Depends on the individual. Thus, we will give them all three."

11

LOYALTY

Eight hundred armored soldiers stood in ranks fifty men deep, covering the plaza in front of Marquithe Palace. All had the lightning bolt of Farrowen stamped on their breastplate. Seventy of the men also sported the dark blue capes and matching helmet crests of the Midnight Guard.

Dressed in the long blue coat of his office, Jace stood before them, Captain Henton to one side of him and Lieutenant Giralt to the other. Both officers were in full armor, Henton's helmet lined with gold, arrows on his shoulder marking his rank. His one arm was bare from his shoulder to the bracer on his forearm.

"This is all of them?" Jace asked.

"Yes, Chancellor," Henton replied. "All save for four guards manning the north city gate, four posted at the south gate, and ten others posted along the palace perimeter."

"Good. These men will tell the others." Jace turned and waved his arm above his head, drawing a circle in the sky.

A steward standing near the palace corner relayed the signal. Moments later, a horse-drawn wagon rounded the corner. Two burly soldiers bracketed the driver, a middle-aged man with a brimmed hat and brown beard. Clopping hooves and rumbling wheels grew louder as the wagon approached, and all attention was drawn toward it. Amid the crowd, Jace found furrowed brows as some soldiers cast questioning glances at each other, but nobody said a word.

The wagon passed between him and the ranks, turned, and stopped with the horses facing away from the soldiers. The two guards jumped down from the driver's seat, each pulling a thick metal pin free. The wagon bed tipped up, causing the tailgate to slam against the stone plaza tiles.

In the wagon bed were two corpses, both wearing Midnight Guard uniforms. One's mouth was agape, and gobs of dried blood covered his teeth, jaw, neck, and breastplate. The other stared wide-eyed, the dark hole in his forehead appearing like a third frightening eye of another sort. Despite the incline, neither corpse slid to the ground – massive spikes protruding from their palms held them to the wagon bed.

Hands clasped behind his back, Jace approached the wagon and stared at the two men for a long quiet moment, allowing the message to sink in before he even said the words. He turned toward the soldiers, took a deep breath, and spoke in a loud voice.

"Treason." Jace paused a beat to give the word power. He extended his arm toward the wagon. "As these two guards sworn to protect their queen discovered, treason comes at a steep price. Yes, I understand the allure of gold, having chased after wealth many times without pausing to consider how it might affect others. That was before I found something, and someone, to believe in. I speak of Queen Narine. I speak of justice, compassion, and opportunity for every citizen of Farrowen, for those are the things your queen values above all else. However, you must never confuse her gender, or her kindness, with weakness.

"Boris and Hardy made a bad decision, trading honor for gold. Thus, they wound up as corpses. I assure you, any act of treason will yield similar results."

Jace walked toward the crowd, all eyes following him. "There are those who seek power and perceive your queen as nothing but an obstacle between them and the throne. They might offer to bribe you with gold. It will be tempting to be sure, the opportunity to earn ten years of wages for a single act..." He held his hand out and smirked. "Considering such an offer is expected, for you are only human. In your position, I would do the same." He waggled a finger. "Do not accept, for I can make you a better offer.

He walked before the ranks while speaking. "Should anyone come to you with the promise of gold for an act of treason, or if you even catch a whisper or rumor on the streets, gather as much information as you can – contact names, benefactors, descriptions, missives – any proof you can obtain without stirring suspicion. Bring that information to me. Should it help to prove any party guilty, I will pay thrice their offer as a reward for your loyalty." Stopping again, he drew a handful of gold from a pocket, letting it flash in the sunlight. "If you are promised ten gold…a notable sum to be sure…" he pulled a purse out with another hand, lifting the bulging leather pouch and shaking it, so all could hear the coins inside rattling. "I will pay you thirty gold instead."

A shift ran through the ranks. Men shuffled in anticipation, glancing at their fellow guards.

"Yes, betraying the contact who attempts to hire you will place you at risk, but far less risk than trying to kill your queen. Think on it. Talk about it. Tell anyone who joins the city watch, the Thundercorps, or the Midnight Guard. The queen demands your loyalty…and I am willing to pay you handsomely should your actions save her from another attempt on her life."

Jace walked back to stand with Henton and Giralt, all three facing the palace in expectation.

From the shadows inside the open palace door, Narine listened to Jace threaten eight hundred armed men and then offer them incentive should they ferret out any attempt on her life. The idea had been his, and it was a good one – preempting another attack from within her ranks.

She glanced over her shoulder, Shavon giving her a nod. The woman had raised Narine, acting as her nurse and tutor for much of her life. Although her hair had turned white and her skin was wrinkled, Shavon's mind remained as sharp as ever.

With a reassuring smile, Shavon said, "You appear every inch a queen."

Pride swelled in Narine's chest, for Shavon was a miser when it came to compliments. More notably, she was known to speak only truth, often to the point of brutality.

Narine glanced down at her elegant navy and white gown. Her dress was formfitting, and she wore a white stole around her shoulders. She reached up and placed the crown on her head, her golden hair flowing over her shoulders. As Jace finished speaking, he and everyone else turned toward the palace.

"Go on," Shavon said. "You are queen. They already adore you. Make them respect you."

Her jaw set and lips pressed together, Narine emerged, trailed by the two Midnight Guard with the longest tenure – men Henton trusted.

Well over half of those in the guard had joined in the past year, many transferring from the city watch. Some were soldiers who survived the war; others new recruits who had exhibited potential. *The Darkspawn War stripped much from the wizardoms, all but Hassakan and, perhaps, Cordium.* Too many had died, a fact Narine considered often.

Guards shadowing her, she descended the stairs and crossed the plaza to stand between Jace and the wagon. She turned toward it and froze.

Hardy's dead eyes stared at Narine, and her fear returned, stirred by unbidden images of him forcing himself on her. It had never come to pass, but if Jace had not been there... Bound, gagged, and blindfolded, she would have been helpless and unable to use her magic. Rather than recoil from the fear, she embraced it, owned it, and refused to let it make her a victim. Terror turned to anger, raw and unbridled.

Narine drew upon her magic, augmented by the enchanted chain on her hand and anklet around her lower leg. Through a construct of heat, she released the power. Energy constructs were better suited for men and always difficult for women to execute. Yet, with the breadth of her power, it did not matter.

A cone of intense white flames blasted forth and engulfed the wagon. The flames lasted for a few seconds before she released them. By then, the wagon had burned, the guards' armor had melted, and their flesh had wilted. Narine allowed it to continue a few minutes longer, anger still brewing in her gut. Jace had told her to make them fear her power. She would make them fear it times ten.

Narine extended her hand toward the wagon and cast a construct of another nature.

The two burning men suddenly jerked. A gasp ran through the crowd.

Hardy's corpse yanked its hand forward, tearing it free of the spike, the other hand following. The corpse of Boris did the same. Both burning, twisted figures climbed out of the wagon. Although they had been ordered to remain in rank, the soldiers backed away, their eyes wide in horror.

Emerging from the fire, Hardy's mangled burning body shambled toward Narine and stopped ten strides away. Lurching with each step, Boris followed until he stood beside the other corpse, flames still licking their withered remains.

"You have betrayed me," Narine said in a firm voice. "For that, I sentence you to the worst pain, not ending even in death."

She flicked her hand and the men burst in a spray of blood. Both collapsed to the ground, bits of bone and burning flesh visible amid twisted, blood-coated, scorched armor. Gasps came from the soldiers, many backing further away.

Narine turned toward them, still holding her illusion. "You men are the protectors of Marquithe and her ruler. I place my trust in the city watch, the Thundercorps, and the Midnight Guard. In return, I require your loyalty. Should you fail in that regard…" her arm swept in a broad arc, toward the twisted, burning heaps spread across the plaza, "you can expect similar treatment."

Eight hundred men, each bigger and far stronger than her, stared at her wide-eyed. Many of these men had respected her predecessors because of magic gifted to them by a god. Without the backing of a god and the ability to heal herself, Narine had to demonstrate she was anything but powerless. These men now knew that truth. They would tell others, and the rumors were likely to spread throughout the city and surrounding lands like wildfire. She hoped it would give others pause before they attempted anything against her.

Now, it is time to earn their love. She beamed at them with pride. "You men work hard, keeping odd hours, standing, marching, and fighting, and you are rarely shown appreciation. I want you to know that *I* appreciate you. Thus, you will all receive a raise. The city watch and Thundercorps will now earn an extra five coppers per week. The Midnight Guard will receive an extra silver each week. With these added funds, I hope to make your lives easier and make retirement a more achievable goal."

The plaza fell silent, soldiers looking at one another.

She then noticed Jace nudge Henton.

The captain marched forward and thrust his fist into the air. "Long live Queen Narine!"

The men responded with cheers, fists pumping as they chanted her name. Narine beamed, her chest swelling with pride. Still, she maintained the illusion of the destroyed corpses at her feet, using false flames to mask the remains still strapped to the wagon bed.

12

LAST BREATH

From the hold ladder of *Hassaka's Breath*, Harlequin peered through the grates, the purple evening sky visible high above. Thudding footsteps hammered across the deck as sailors scrambled to secure lines to the pier. The voyage had taken a week, the stars informing her that their course had been mostly south, likely landing them somewhere in Ghealdor or Farrowen. It was difficult to tell from below deck. Somehow, she and Crusser had been able to keep their presence a secret. That would end should anyone find them or the waste they had left in a resealed crate. The thought of someone expecting pineapples, opening the crate, and then finding something far less savory made her chuckle.

The sound of footsteps approached, so she leaned to the side for a better angle. Through the grate, she saw Tranadal and Tempest, their voices rising above the lapping water.

"...will be at the castle. If things go as planned, I will remain. Andar is still in his cabin below deck. You are to deliver him and the barrels to Shear, where he will board a barge to Tiamalyn. While at Shear, you can reload with fresh cargo and return to Antari."

"Yes, sir." Harlequin recognized Korrik's gruff voice.

Tranadal turned and walked out of her view, Tempest following.

Korrik shouted, "Settle in! Everyone remains aboard! We depart at first light!"

Harlequin climbed back down the ladder, ducking as she wove her way through the crates and barrels, her hands going to her hips as she stared down at Crusser, still sleeping on his side. She nudged him with her foot, and he stirred.

"What?" he blinked.

"While I am risking my life, you are here sleeping."

He sat up and stretched. "Soldiers know it's best to sleep while they can." Rising to his feet, he worked his shoulder. "You never know when you might go a long stretch without rest."

She frowned, unable to argue with his reasoning. "Tranadal and the others just disembarked. This is our chance."

"Chance for what?"

"To take the ship back."

"Aren't there still sailors on board?"

"Yes. Likely seven or eight. Perhaps more."

"You want to fight them?"

"No. I want to convince them that Tranadal is up to no good." She turned from him, speaking over her shoulder. "I'm going up, but I want you to remain below deck."

He followed her. "Why?"

Harlequin stopped and turned back to him. "To retain the element of surprise should things go poorly."

Nodding, he said, "Sound strategy. Allow your enemy to underestimate you and then strike when their defenses are down."

She put her hand on his shoulder, squeezing. He did not flinch. "Listen. Do *not* do anything to mess this up. If all goes well, I will call you to come up, and you can meet the crew."

"And if it goes poorly?"

"You'll know what to do."

Spinning around, she climbed the ladder, hoping she would not need to use the sabre at her hip. She swung the latch and lifted the grate. It landed on deck with a thud, a half-dozen deck hands spinning in her direction.

She climbed on deck as Korrik and Guta approached, the latter holding a lantern, its shutter open and amber light shining toward her. Korrik's face was covered in dark stubble, his lean torso visible beneath a loose vest. The man was of a similar height, weight, and age to Harlequin. He wore knives at his waist and certainly had more hidden in his boots. She knew well how skilled he was at throwing them.

Guta stood slightly taller than Korrik but was twice his width with thick arms and a broad torso. The red cloth tied around his head matched his loose tunic, and a long scimitar was strapped to his side. While he lacked finesse as a swordsman, he was mean and powerful.

"Harley?" Korrik asked. "What are you doing here?"

Other sailors began to gather, most unfamiliar to her.

As captain, she decided on boldness. "I am here to take my ship back."

Korrik looked at Guta, who wore a frown within his thick black beard. "Tranadal declared you an outlaw. He says you attacked Xavan and betrayed the Order."

She snarled, "He and the other Drow are the traitors. They killed Chandan and lied to the rest of us, tricking them into believing a lie by sharing a false vision."

Guta laughed. "The dark elf said you might say that."

"Why would they kill Chandan?" Korrik asked.

She shrugged, swiveling her head to gauge how the others were reacting. "I don't know exactly. For some reason, they wanted to seize control of the Order."

Guta grimaced. "Where were you for the past year while we wallowed in Antari? We did nothing during that time. Nothing!"

Clamping a hand on Guta's shoulder, Korrik's smile revealed one gold tooth and another one missing. "Perhaps it was time for someone else to take charge. As I see it, Chandan was weak and that's why he took his own life." The sailor's smile slid away, morphing into a sneer. "You see, Harley, we never really worked for you. We worked for the Order of Sol. Xavan now leads the Order. Tranadal brought two writs signed by Xavan himself – one making me captain and the other declaring you an outlaw."

Her mouth turned down in a scowl. "You are no captain."

"Xavan and Tranadal see otherwise. You see, much has changed in the past year. As some stars fall, others rise."

She glanced around, counting the sailors she could see in the light of the lanterns hanging from the masts. Including Korrik and Guta, four sailors stood nearby and three were further away, but all eyes were on her. A stride to her side, the grate lay on the deck, the hole to the hold still open. *I hope you are ready, Crusser.*

"Kiss my arse, Korrik." She drew her sword. "Crusser. Now!"

Lunging, she swiped. Korrik leapt backward. Guta drew his blade just in time to deflect her strike. In a flash, Korrik pulled out a knife and threw it. Ready, Harlequin dove, rolled, and swiped, her sabre biting into the calf of a sailor too slow to react. The man fell with a cry, and she scrambled out of the way. Back against the rail, she held her blade in front of her as Guta and three others stalked toward her, Korrik laughing in the background.

Crusser opened the cargo hold door on the wall of the ship. It was dark outside, the dock eight feet away, the harbor waters lapping against the hull below. Twisting, he clamped a fist around a thick rope running from the ship to the pier and pulled himself up, hand over hand, until he gripped the rail.

Across the deck, Harlequin backed away from three armed sailors, all with swords in their hands. One man lay writhing on deck; another laughed, holding a lamp in one hand and a knife in the other. Three more sailors stood closer to Crusser, their backs to him.

He swung a leg over the rail, careful to remain quiet. A few creeping strides brought him close enough. Spreading his arms wide, he gripped a handful of hair in each fist and smashed the heads of two sailors into one another, emitting a solid *thunk*. The sailors crumpled to the deck as a third man spun toward him. He kicked the sword out of the sailor's hand. His fist followed, striking the man's chin. The sailor stumbled backward and Crusser leapt, thrusting both feet into the man's chest and launching him into the sailor with the lamp. Both men fell hard, the lantern skittering across the deck.

Harlequin spotted Crusser climbing over the rail, just before he knocked out two unsuspecting sailors. When the third spun to attack, she struck.

With a low thrust, she forced Guta backward. The man was too beefy to allow near her. The other two sailors attacked, one with a downward strike she evaded, his blade burrowing into the wooden rail. The other sailor thrust his weapon toward her midriff as she turned, the blade tearing her tunic but missing her flesh. She slashed. Too close to avoid her sabre, it raked across his chest. When he stumbled back a step, she twisted and followed with a heel thrust to his stomach. The sailor fell on his back, his arm striking the lantern, which fell through the open door to the hold.

Guta's eyes widened, and he shrieked, "The naphtha!"

Harlequin froze. "Naphtha?"

The burly man backed toward the rail. "The barrels…" He turned, dove over the railing, and disappeared, splashing into the harbor.

A flickering amber glow came from below as Korrik rose to his feet, drawing a knife.

"Time to end you, wench," Korrik said, ready to throw.

He never got the chance.

The sailor lurched forward, Crusser's longsword emerging from his chest. The knife tumbled from his hand as he fell to his knees. With his boot against Korrik's back, Crusser pushed him off his blade. Wide-eyed, Korrik coughed up blood and fell face first into the fiery hold.

Harlequin sheathed her blade and leapt onto the portside rail. "We have to jump!"

"Why?" Crusser rushed toward her, a bloodied sword in his hand.

"The ship, it's…"

An explosion shook the ship, and she fell toward the dark water. Another far larger blast followed, causing a section of the ship to strike her head. Cold darkness enveloped her.

13

PROPOSAL

"What?!" Montague roared.

Furious, he tapped into his magic, the raw power crackling around his fists. The messenger blanched and began to tremble, twisting his hat in his fists. Unaffected by the tirade, Vordan clasped his hands behind his back and scowled.

Montague thrust his hands out, casting an energy construct. Through it, a bolt of lightning emerged, the thunderous blast striking his sofa and launching it into the fireplace. Fire arose from the hole in the leather, causing feathers to slowly drift toward the floor.

Relinquishing his magic, Montague closed his eyes and took a deep breath. *I swear that thief has the luck of a thousand blessed souls.* Opening his eyes, he turned back toward the messenger.

"Finish your report."

"What do…"

"You said the attempt on the queen's life was foiled by Chancellor Landish. I would hear the details."

The man swallowed, his skin so pale it appeared green. "As you wish, High Wizard." With the back of his hand, he wiped sweat from his head, his eyes flicking about the chamber as though seeking a way to escape. "The carriage was found near Merchant Square, broken. The horses were gone.

Two men in Midnight Guard armor were there as well, both cut up beyond recognition. A witness claims Landish chased after this carriage, running as fast as the horses. He killed the driver, cut the team loose, and proceeded to slay the two guards, both men far larger than him. As..." he wiped his forehead again. "As the witness explained, the two men had no chance, for Landish was a whirling dervish, impossible to track. He suffered not a single cut in the confrontation. The chancellor then lifted the unconscious queen like she weighed nothing and carried her across the city."

Montague listened carefully the entire time, his anger quelled. "The queen lives?"

The messenger nodded. "Yes. She was wounded, but Portia Forca healed her."

"Forca? Wasn't her son behind the attempt on the queen?"

"He admitted his guilt, but Chancellor Landish bargained with his mother, agreeing to spare the boy's life should she save the queen."

Despite the disturbing turn of fate, Montague collapsed in his chair, laughing. The messenger shot a questioning glance toward Vordan, who scowled back in silence.

His laughter subsiding, Montague ran his hand down his face and sighed. "Did the Forca boy find a new home in the palace dungeon?"

"No, sir. He remains at his estate under house arrest until he travels to Tiadd."

Montague frowned. "Landish is allowing Godwin to remain in the luxury of Forca Manor and even to sail off to study at the University? The boy committed treason." He rubbed his chin. "Why would the man...and the queen...agree to allow a confessed traitor to live?"

The messenger did not reply, but that was expected. The question was for Montague to ponder himself. His conclusion caused him more concern.

"He suspects a deeper plot," Montague mused. "He sees the Forca boy as a pawn."

Vordan spoke for the first time since the messenger arrived. "The boy paid the guards in gold."

"Yes, but how much?"

The big man shrugged. "One gold piece each."

"Precisely. A small sum to kill a queen."

"And they didn't even kill her."

"Yes. I wonder why they kidnapped her first. Why not just end it?"

Vordan shook his head. "I do not know."

Twisting the ring on his finger, Montague said to himself, "Landish will take steps to watch for another attempt. His network is extensive – hundreds of ears listening for whispers, thousands of eyes watching for clues. We must take care." In a deadly serious tone, he looked at Vordan. "No witnesses."

The captain nodded, drew his sword, and strode toward the messenger.

Wide-eyed, the man backed away. "No. Please. I won't say anything. Not a word."

"I know," Vordan growled.

With a lunge, Vordan drove his sword through the man's stomach and then pushed him off it, the blade coated in crimson. The messenger fell backward, struck the wall, and slid down. His eyes bulging and his mouth gaping, he fell to his side and lay still.

"Call your men. Have them clean this up." Montague stepped out into the night.

Hands gripping the balcony rail, he gazed out over the city of Lionne – his own by rule. It was a moderate-sized city, barely exceeding ten thousand citizens. The castle stood upon a bluff, overlooking Lionne and the bay that shared its name. In the coming months, the breeze coming off the Novecai Sea would chill the summer heat. When the seasons turned and winter held the lands to the south in its frigid grip, the sea would moderate Lionne's weather, making it a pleasant place to live. Still, it was not Marquithe.

He looked up at the stars and proclaimed the future he had often envisioned. "Someday, Farrowen will be mine."

Montague's star had rapidly risen. He claimed the seat of high wizard younger than thought possible. The early years had been fraught with rivals who thought they possessed the might to defeat him. After killing five ambitious wizards, such attempts ceased, and his reputation was secure. And then, Jerrell Landish appeared and ruined everything. The humiliation caused by the thief was bad enough, but the true damage was in what he stole – the bracelet that had boosted Montague's magic, fueling his rise. With it, Montague had planned to one day challenge Lord Malvorian for the crystal throne.

Montague snorted and said to the night, "Turns out, Landish might have spared my life."

A few years after Landish stole Montague's bracelet for Gurgan, the high wizard of Eleighton, the man tested his might against Malvorian. The wizard lord of Farrowen proved too powerful, even when Gurgan's magic was augmented by the enchanted bracelet. The two halves of Gurgan's body adorned the palace walls for the next few weeks, a reminder to any who might challenge Malvorian.

Those times were now past. Malvorian and his successor, Lord Thurvin, were dead and gone, as were the gods.

"Without the gods to gift men with their magic, toppling a ruler should be a simple thing." He lifted his fist and eyed the ring denoting his station. "I merely need the opportunity…if only Landish were out of the way."

A burst of light lit the harbor, followed by the thump of an explosion. Orange flames and dark smoke billowed into the air.

"What the…"

Vordan rushed out to the balcony and leaned over the rail, peering toward the harbor.

"Are we under attack?" Montague asked.

The captain shook his head. "I don't know. I don't see any ships beyond the pier, but my men will investigate."

Vordan began to turn away when they heard a commotion at the castle gate. Three men dressed in dark cloaks stood in the road, surrounded by castle guards.

"Perhaps you should see about this first," Montague suggested.

Grunting, Vordan spun and charged across the room, slamming the door behind him. Moments later, the captain appeared below, the guards parting as he confronted the intruders. A brief discussion followed, but the voices were too distant for Montague to hear clearly. Vordan then turned and looked up at the balcony, gesturing for Montague to come downstairs.

Eyes narrowed, Montague's gaze flicked back toward the harbor. With the fire gone and no other signs of alarm, an attack was unlikely. He turned his attention back toward the gate as Vordan and a host of guards escorted the three visitors to the castle.

Montague sighed. "I had best go see what this is about."

He went inside, crossed his study, and headed toward the stairwell. Two flights down, he arrived in the grand entrance hall at the base of a circular tower capped by a cone-shaped roof high above. The doors opened, Vordan entering with three newcomers and six castle guards. All three wore black cloaks. Two were tall, one lean, the other broad and bulky. The third, Montague realized, was a woman.

Vordan pointed his thumb at the broader man, whose face remained hidden in the shadows of his hood. He held a glossy black staff in his hand, the bottom end capped with a metal butt, the upper end displaying a gleaming metal blade. *It is a naginata, like those wielded by Kyranni women…at least back before their wizardom was destroyed.*

"High Wizard," Vordan dipped his head dutifully, "this man claims he has traveled across the sea to offer you aid. He has gold and…speaks with an odd accent."

Montague sneered. "How can I trust someone who hides his face?"

The man lowered his hood. Montague gasped.

He had black hair with a white streak over one brow, ashen skin, pointed ears, and dark eyes that seemed sharp as steel. Man or otherwise, Montague had never seen anyone like him.

He muttered, "What are you?"

The visitor smirked. "I am called Tranadal of clan Gris-Ara. I have traveled far in the name of my god, Vol-Taran."

Words came to Montague and fled, again and again, his mouth moving with no sound emitting from it. *Gather yourself. You are high wizard.*

"You claim to offer me aid."

The man, if he was a man, smiled. "If allowed, I will give you the throne of Farrowen."

Stifling his excitement, Montague asked, "To what end?"

Tranadal extended an open hand. "I will do what is needed to ensure you are able to claim and retain the throne. In return, you merely need to turn your people toward my god. Yours is dead and gone, so providing another to fill the vacuum should be of little consequence."

Montague's heart raced, his dream tantalizingly close, yet he had doubts. "How could you ensure the throne? Such things are not trivial."

The stranger turned to his companion who produced a leather sack and a knife. Holding the sack up, he stabbed it and cut. Coins fell to the marble tiles, the gold pieces clinking and clanking as they scattered. There were hundreds of them.

"I have heard your people value gold…" Tranadal said. "Something of which, I have ample supply."

Montague remained skeptical, for such things did not happen without cause. "This is a test. You have been sent by the queen to challenge my loyalty to the crown."

Tranadal nodded. "You are wise to tread with caution. How might I prove my intent?"

The opportunity was ripe and impossible to dismiss, so Montague took a chance. "The queen's betrothed and I have a history. For years, he has eluded me and denied my desires at every turn. Should something happen to him… the queen would become far more vulnerable."

"This man has a name?"

Montague grinned. "Jerrell Landish."

14

CONTRACT

Thick arms crossed over his chest, Crusser dozed in a wooden chair, a blanket draped over his naked body. Sleep came in fits and spurts, making it a long night. When morning light streamed through a gap in the closed curtains, he gave up trying to sleep, deciding rest would come another time.

He sat forward and peered at the bed where Harlequin lay, her head bandaged and a bare arm and leg sticking out from beneath her covers. She remained unconscious but her breathing was steady. He spread his blanket over her and turned to a table and chair, draped with their clothing. He rubbed his fingers over the cloth. His breeches felt cool and moist, still wet from their unplanned swim in the harbor. He sighed, resigning himself to wearing damp clothing.

A female voice came from behind him. "Nice arse."

He spun around. "You're awake."

Harlequin snorted. "Truly? I hadn't noticed." Her hand went to her head, feeling the bandage. "My brain hurts."

He slid a leg into his breeches. "You were knocked out when the ship exploded."

Sitting upright, she groaned. "My ship…"

"Not any longer." He pulled his breeches up and laced them together.

"I notice I am naked."

He grinned. "I wonder how that happened."

She arched a brow. "Sarcasm from you? Perhaps I *am* still asleep."

Crusser shrugged. "You seem so fond of it, I thought I'd give it a try."

She slung her legs over the side of the bed, placed her bare feet on the floor, and unwrapped the bandage. "Where are we?"

"Lionne, at a place called the Feathered Cap Inn."

She finished unwinding the bandage and looked at it, a splotch of dark red staining the otherwise tan cloth. "How'd we get here?"

He gripped his damp tunic and slid it over his head. "After the explosion, I found you floating face-down in the water. I swam the two of us to shore and pumped the water from your lungs. The explosion drew a lot of attention, gathering dozens of guards around the pier. I slipped behind them and into the city with you on my shoulder. Eventually, I found this place and bought us a room." He frowned. "I could only get one with a single bed. Even then, it cost us the last of my coin."

Rising to her feet, Harlequin tossed the blankets on the bed, leaving her completely naked. His eyes drank in her lithe frame, a sight he had enjoyed on numerous occasions. In truth, he doubted he would grow weary of it and was willing to find out.

Stepping close, she gripped his wrist, her normally glib attitude replaced by an earnest expression. "You saved my life, Cruss. Thank you."

The sight of her combined with the physical contact heated his blood. "You know how I feel...I couldn't have done anything less."

Releasing his wrist, she rested her palm on his chest and leaned in for a kiss. Their lips brushed once, twice, three times, each soft and gentle, unlike those when she was in the throes of passion.

Pulling away, Harlequin bit her lip. "That will have to do for now. When I am feeling better, I'll thank you properly."

He felt his pulse racing at the thought. "That is one debt I'll happily collect."

She turned away from him and approached the vanity, the blood-stained bandage still in her hand. A bowl of water sat on the vanity, and she used it to wet the cloth. "I am famished. Once I clean up and get dressed, we can go down for a bite to eat." Lifting the wet rag, she dabbed it against the wound on the back of her head. "Please tell me your coin covered our meals."

He gripped his sword belt and looped it around his waist. "Yes. Through tomorrow."

"Good. That gives us a day to figure out what to do next."

Crusser kept his hand on his hilt as they passed through the harbor gate, ignoring the narrowed-eye stares of the guards posted there. With Harlequin at his side, they descended a short hill to the base of the main pier. Halfway down the pier, a crew of workers busily tore away scorched planks, a stack of fresh ones waiting nearby. The slip beside it was empty, a mast sticking up from the water at an angle.

"My ship," she groaned.

"Belongs to the sea now."

She snorted. "Belongs to the Dark Lord."

He glanced at her. "I thought the Dark Lord was dead."

"So is my ship."

Harlequin turned and followed the shoreline. He trailed behind, wondering what she intended. Waves crashed into dark rocks, broken and blackened sections of wood floating at the water's edge. Ahead smaller docks stood empty, fishermen out chasing the day's catch.

She suddenly gasped and eased down the rocks, positioning her footsteps with care as she neared the water.

"What are you doing?" Crusser asked.

Squatting, Harlequin reached out as a wave came toward her. She gripped something made of black cloth and pulled it into the air, shaking water off while climbing back up the bank. Upon reaching his side, she shook the object again and shot him a grin.

"My hat." She tapped the inner area, unflattening it from the brim. "It survived."

He grunted. "That's nice...but it's only a hat."

"It is not *only* a hat. This is the hat of Captain Harlequin, Queen of the Shoals."

Crusser had heard of the Shoals – a shallow sea north of the continent, consisting of hundreds if not thousands of small land formations, most of them just below the surface.

"Queen of the Shoals?"

She headed back toward the gate. "It's a title I earned years ago."

Crusser caught up to her. "What comes with the title?"

"Mostly pride…and a bit of respect among pirates."

"Pirates are ruthless killers who target honest, hard-working people."

Stopping, she turned toward him and arched her brow. "*I* am a pirate."

"You?"

"How did you think I learned to fight? How to sail? How to handle myself amid brutes like you?"

He scratched his head. "I'll admit you are a bit rough around the edges, but you hardly seem like a ruthless pirate."

"That's just it. Pirates are not ruthless. We are businessmen, no different than any others. Even pirates have rules. Unlike the stories you hear, we don't just kill and destroy for no reason." She drew herself up, proudly. "Most often, we take only a portion of a ship's wealth and send them on their way in return for their compliance. Think of it as a tax one must pay to sail in our waters."

"What about raiding cities and villages?'

She snorted. "Never happened. Those are nothing but fanciful stories intended to scare, entertain, or manipulate others."

They passed through the gate and into the city, navigating the busy streets until they reached an inn called the Torn Bodice. The image on the sign above the door drew a grin on Harlequin's face.

She pointed toward it. "I'm surprised you didn't choose this one."

"I thought about it but decided it was too close to the docks. After our ship exploded, I figured it might be best to avoid places the city watch was most likely to search."

"I am impressed, Cruss. That was solid reasoning. Are you sure you haven't…"

Her voice trailed off. She suddenly came at him, her lips locking with his and her hands pressed against his chest, forcing him backwards into the shadowy doorway across from the inn. Despite his surprise, he responded to her kiss, enjoying the moment. Just when it became most intense, she pulled away and looked over her shoulder. His eyes followed hers, spotting a tall thin man with a black cloak entering the building. He gripped a glossy black staff, a silver blade at one end.

"Tranadal," she said softly. "Let's see what he is doing."

"You want to go inside?'

"How else are we going to spy on him?' She pulled the hat over her head, bending one side brim up. "I'll go in first and settle in a quiet corner. You follow and find a spot on the other side."

He shook his head. "I'm a soldier, not a spy."

Patting his cheek, she smiled. "We all make sacrifices, so put on your big boy breeches and do it."

Without another word, she crossed the street and disappeared into the Torn Bodice. He took a breath, wishing he had a cloak or something similar to hide his appearance. People with his skin tone were not common in the southern wizardoms and he feared bringing attention to himself.

A wagon rolled past, a gray tarp covering what lay beneath. Inspired, he grabbed the tarp and pulled it free, exposing bushels of carrots and green beans. The cloth was dirty, but it would have to do. He wrapped the gray sheet around himself so it covered his head. Bending his back and limping with one leg dragging behind him, he crossed the street. People tended to look past beggars rather than at them. He just hoped Tranadal would do the same.

Crusser entered the dark inn, pausing at the door while his eyes adjusted to the dim light. Three tables were occupied, neither Tranadal nor Harlequin visible.

"Out with you!" came a rough voice.

He turned and saw a heavyset man in an apron standing nearby. "We don't need beggars in here, scaring away payin' customers. If you ain't got coin, you need to leave."

"I won't be any trouble." Crusser whined, "Please..."

The man gripped the back of the tarp, dragged Crusser back outside, and shoved him away. Still playing the part of a beggar, he stumbled along the building and fell into the mouth of a narrow alley beside it, landing hard on his side. When he looked back, the brawny bouncer dusted his hands off and stepped back inside.

Crusser lay back and sighed. *So much for my spying.* He then heard low voices talking and rolled over. In the shadows of the alley, he saw two silhouettes, one with a hood up and staff in his hand. Hurriedly, he rolled against the side of the inn and fell still, the tarp over him as he pretended to sleep, his breath calming as he listened.

"…need this man eliminated," Tranadal said.

The other man replied, "You wisss me to kill Landisss?"

"Do you know of him?"

"Of coursss. Better yet, I know hisss sssecret, a weaknesss."

"Good. Track him down and take care of it."

"What of the queen?"

"We will take care of the queen once Landish is out of the way."

"What you requessst…it carriesss risssk."

"I gave you ten gold pieces already. Once this thief is dead, return, and you will receive the rest."

"One hundred in total?"

Crusser's eyes widened. *One hundred gold?!*

"As agreed," Tranadal said.

The other man chuckled. "I will sssee you sssoon."

The crunch of footsteps approached, joined by the periodic thud of the staff striking the ground. Lying still, Crusser feigned he was passed out from a long night of drinking. Through the narrow gap in the tarp, he saw the staff hit the ground just inches from his face and then, Tranadal was past him.

Unsure if the other man remained in the alley watching, he did not move. Minutes passed before he lifted his head and found the alley empty. He threw the tarp aside and stood as Harlequin rounded the rear corner of the inn. She strode down the alley, continued past him, and waved for him to follow.

He caught up to her, speaking in a hushed voice. "Tranadal hired a man to kill someone."

"I know."

"Where are you going?"

"We have little time."

"To do what?"

She paused and pulled him aside, her gaze flicking up and down the street before speaking. "This man will leave the city soon. We need to get some food from the inn, steal horses, and wait outside the inland gate before he leaves the city."

"Why?"

"So, we can follow him, of course."

"Where do you think he is heading?"

"My guess? One of the southern capitals since a queen was mentioned."

"This is all to stop whatever Tranadal has planned?"

"Yes, but there is more." She gave him a sidelong smirk. "The man they intend to kill is Jerrell Landish, someone I know. Frankly, I like him and would rather not see him dead. Besides, he can help us stop whatever Xavan and Tranadal have planned."

He shook his head. "I don't understand. Why is this man so important? Isn't he just a thief?"

"When Chandan and I arrived in the valley a year ago, we had four heroes with us."

"Yes. I recall them. A dwarf warrior, a woman of metal, a pretty blonde wizard, and a short arrogant man with a sharp tongue."

She laughed. "The last was Jerrell Landish, and to call him *just a thief* is akin to calling the sun *just a star*."

15

INEQUALITY

An eager crowd filled the Fastella Palace throne room. Occupying the seats were merchants and artisans waiting their turn to appeal to their queen, each with their own complaint, many about the recent rise in taxes. However, those citizens were relegated to the rear benches, the seats in the fore filled by wizards in shimmering silk robes and wizardesses in florid-colored dresses. The personal bodyguards for those gifted with magic stood along the outer walls – men trained to fight, dressed in leather, and armed. At the four corners of the massive chamber, guards in gold-plated armor stood ready. Their dog-shaped helms and purple cloaks marked them as Indigo Hounds, the elite force personally assigned to protect the queen of Ghealdor.

The towering arched ceiling and stone walls gave the room booming acoustics, while the midday sunlight streaming through stained glass windows high upon the walls painted the room in a myriad of colors. Most impressive was the dais at the front, with stone steps rising to a wooden throne at the top. Long purple pennants covered the wall behind the dais, and a chandelier hung above.

A woman, blonde, petite, and middle-aged, sat on the throne. She wore a black and purple gown accompanied by an ornate gold necklace and matching bracelets. Upon her head sat a golden crown, a purple amethyst at the front. A stern and steady expression remained on Queen Dalia's face as she listened to the proceedings.

Halfway up the stairs stood an imposing man, heavy plated armor covering his robust frame. A metal helm rested beneath one arm, and a massive spiked mace at his hip. He had dark hair, a heavy brow, and wore a hard scowl. The sight of him alone would be enough to strike fear into the heart of most anyone.

Lang was not anyone. Defiant, as if the scowl were a personal challenge to him, Lang stared at the man, both of them unblinking.

Arms crossed over his chest, Lang stood beside his employer, Wizardess Malene Willola, and listened to both sides argue their cases. Compared to her peers, the wizardess lacked magic talent, yet had used her appearance, charm, and cunning to her advantage, carving out a position of influence within Fastella.

Wizardess Willola stood tall for a woman, no more than a half-head shorter than Lang, who was taller than most men. Brown hair with golden highlights tumbled over her tawny bare shoulders. The angle of her green eyes gave her an exotic appearance, one most would term as beautiful. Her long, lean frame made her curves pronounced and impossible to miss. Men often ogled at the sight of her, while women eyed her with envy. Lang did neither, for he knew what lay behind the mask.

"As you can see, Your Grace," Willola said. "This man failed to deliver on his promises."

The man in question was artisan Miles Ferrock who owned a smithy in the Dregs, the least savory quarter of the city. At six-feet tall, his thick arms and barrel chest made him look the part of a man who swung a hammer for a living. His head was bald and his beard thick, yet his eyes were soft as he held his hands out in appeal. "I beg you, my queen. It was not my fault. Taxes were collected before I could purchase additional ingots. Three other wizards owe me for services rendered, and I had no coin remaining. If not for the recent tax increase…"

Queen Dalia leaned forward and arched a brow. "Are you placing the blame on me, blacksmith?"

The man shook his head. "No. It's just…I would have finished on time had I been paid by the other two wizards."

"So you blame the wizards for your troubles."

The man's mouth moved, but no sound emerged as he struggled to reply.

The queen continued, "Regarding these other two wizards, what were your payment terms?"

"Payment upon delivery," Ferrock replied.

"And did you deliver said goods?"

"I finished both items last week, but the wizards did not come to claim them."

"Why not bring the goods to the wizards then?"

"The axle on my cart is broken. I can't afford to have it fixed."

The queen sat back and smiled. "So, you were to get paid upon delivery, yet you never delivered the goods to these wizards? How exactly do you expect to be paid?"

"I...I asked them to send a wagon to pick up their items."

"Why not carry them?"

He shook his head. "I cannot. I build statues made of metal. One was a dragon, the other a unicorn. Both are too large to carry. It would take two or more men to place either onto a wagon bed."

Queen Dalia tapped her chin in thought. The room was silent, tension filling the air until she looked at Willola. "I find your claim valid. A contract with a wizard must be honored. If he agreed to produce a statue for you and did not deliver, he is guilty. The rest of his argument is irrelevant."

Willola beamed. "Thank you, Your Majesty."

The smith shook his head. "There was nothing I could..."

"Silence!" The queen clapped her hands together, the throne room shaking from the thunderclap that followed. As the echo of the boom faded, she glared at the man. "I demand order in my court. My decision has been made. It is final. Only the punishment remains." Each sentence snapped like the crack of a whip. She turned to Willola. "In this case, I will leave the penance up to the victim."

Victim? Lang thought. *She did not get a fancy new bauble for her lawn. How does that make her a victim?*

Willola tapped her fingers together while eyeing the blacksmith. "You appear to be a strong, fit man. I should think a trial by arms would be entertaining. Should you win, you will pay nothing and this entire issue will be forgiven."

Lang's head spun toward her. *She wants me to fight this man?* As her bodyguard, it was within her rights to force him to do so, but he wanted no part of it.

"If I lose?" the blacksmith asked.

She shrugged. "It might be painful. You might die. We shall see. Either way, you will have paid for your transgression."

He glanced at Lang. "I am to fight him?"

"No." Willola pointed toward the hulking armored man standing on the dais stairs. "Him."

The blacksmith blanched.

"Herrod?" Queen Dalia laughed and clapped. "Oh, *this* will be fun." She stood. "I would witness it for myself." She shooed the crowd. "Everyone, out to the plaza. We shall conduct this trial immediately. Court is adjourned until this matter is settled."

The crowd arose and began filtering out of the room, the bodyguards melding with their masters, and the Indigo Hounds bringing up the rear.

Dalia summoned four guards and pointed toward the blacksmith. "Get this man a helm, a shield, and his choice of weapons. Once armed, escort him to the plaza. Be quick about it, for we have an audience waiting."

Two guards gripped the man by his arms and rushed him through a side door, two others trailing with weapons drawn.

Still standing at the foot of the dais, Lang turned to Willola and found her mouth turned up in a smirk. "This seems extreme, even for you."

Her eyes narrowed, as she pressed her lips together. "You are paid to protect me, not lecture me about some moral code." She frowned. "Besides, don't you Orenthians do this sort of thing daily? You know, those grand gladiators battling in the Bowl of Oren all in the name of your god?"

Mention of the famous arena drew a scowl on Lang's face. "Perhaps I left Orenth to escape such twisted justice."

The queen descended the dais and stopped a step away from Willola, the queen's massive bodyguard looming behind the petite woman. "Since this was a judgement in your favor, Willola, you will stand on top of the stairs beside me to bear witness."

Dalia swept past. Herrod grimaced at Lang before following. The hulking man bumped into Lang as he pushed past, causing him to stumble a step. He glared at Herrod's back as the behemoth lumbered behind his tiny, yet powerful, mistress.

"My, my, Lang," Willola said in a taunting tone. "You do have some back-bone behind that handsome exterior, don't you?"

His scowl remained fixed on Herrod. "Regardless of what you believe of me, I would have died long ago if I were stupid. Taking bait from a bully like Herrod would be stupid."

Her hand rested on his chest and slowly trailed down, drawing his attention. "Restraint. Good. Much better than cowardice."

"I am no coward."

"The way you talk to me, a wizardess of note, proves you are not. Just remember, I pay you to protect me."

"How could I forget? You remind me all the time."

"That is because, unlike my other servants, you have a backbone. Like any good watchdog, I must remind you of who is master, but I do not wish to break you. What good are you if you bend to the will of others?"

She turned and walked down the center aisle, following the strip of purple carpet leading to the open doors. After a few strides, she paused and looked over her shoulder. "Come, dog. I wish to witness this man's death."

Lang took a deep breath and followed the wizardess out of the room.

16

PENANCE

The palace receiving hall, a space large enough for a thousand people, was surprisingly empty. A grid of heavy beams supported a ceiling three stories above, the front wall graced with tall arched windows. At all four corners were corridors fading into darkness, the walls in between graced by closed doors leading to courtrooms where lesser trials were held. The queen would only oversee those deemed most important, beginning with any issue involving a wizard.

Following the queen and her retinue, their footsteps echoing in the cavernous space, Lang and Willola crossed the marble tiled hall and passed through the massive double doors that led outside.

The front stoop was ten strides deep and ran the width of the façade, an awning above supported by a pair of massive fluted columns. A flight of stairs descended to the palace plaza, paved in stone tiles and bordered on each side by a tall hedgerow. At the far end, the plaza terminated at the three story tall palace wall, patrolled by archers holding their bows ready. The central palace gate stood open with a host of armored guards watching the gathering crowd.

Queen Dalia stopped at the top of the stairs, Willola and Lang standing beside her. Guards stood along the stairs to either side, and the crowd formed a half circle. Those furthest away backed up to the fountain in the heart of the plaza. Herrod descended the stairs, the noisy clanking of his armor lending an ominous weight to each step. The behemoth strode into the middle of the circle, slid his helmet over his head, and waited.

A door on the side of the main entrance opened, and guards emerged along with the blacksmith. The man wore a cuirass strapped to his torso and a helmet. He carried a shield on one arm and grasped a heavy hammer in his other hand. They followed the path and emerged from a gap in the hedges, the crowd parting as the man was escorted to the duel circle.

The blacksmith slowed as he emerged from the crowd, his gaze going from Herrod to the queen. "Please, your majesty. There must be some other way. I'll work for free and give the good wizardess the best sculpture I've ever made."

Dalia gave Willola a questioning look, but the other woman shook her head. "Sorry, Master Ferrock. It appears we have passed the point of negotiation." The queen raised her arm. "When I drop my hand, you will fight until one of you is incapable of continuing. Displease me and you will both die. If either of you attempt to flee, the wizards and guards will ensure you don't make it far." She waited a beat and then dropped her arm. "Fight!"

Herrod stalked toward the man, the blacksmith sidling sideways in a circle. Apparently annoyed, Herrod roared and charged. The mace came toward the blacksmith who raised his shield to block. A loud clang echoed, the impact sending the smith stumbling sideways and denting his shield. He righted himself and swung around, his hammer flying toward the charging bodyguard. Herrod reacted with a backhand swing, the mace crashing into the hammer's handle, knocking it backward. Herrod then lifted his foot and kicked, driving his heel into the smith's cuirass. The smith staggered backward but caught himself before falling, his face becoming a sneer.

Ferrock charged, his hammer sweeping around. Rather than reel back, the bodyguard lunged forward, lifting his free arm. The heavy plating on his forearm caught the hammer's handle, blocking the swing, while his mace swept upward beneath the smith's shield. The impact was devastating.

The mace struck the man's cuirass and launched him through the air to land three strides away, his hammer skidding across the plaza tiles. He lay sprawled out, his cuirass dented, attempting but unable to breathe.

The bodyguard stomped over to Ferrock and looked down at him before lifting his gaze to Queen Dalia. She waved at him to back away.

The blacksmith coughed, and bloody spittle ran from his mouth. His hands fumbled for the straps on his sides, his feet kicking at the ground. He gave up and gripped the edges of the armor, straining to pull it free as his eyes bulged and his lips turned blue. Then he fell still.

Lang had seen a crushed ribcage before. It was a hard way to die, those final moments filled with terror and helplessness.

"Well," Willola said, "that settles things." She turned to the queen. "Thank you for your time, Your Majesty. I wish you a good day. I am off to see a man about a new dining room table."

The queen tilted her head. "Are you coming to the Trumble Troupe performance tomorrow evening? They are reputed to be among the best in the southern wizardoms."

Grinning, Willola nodded. "Of course. I am looking forward to it."

"I shall see you then. Good day, Wizardess. May you have better fortune with your next merchant." The queen then turned back to the palace.

Willola descended the stairs, stopped at the bottom, and turned back toward Lang. "Why are you standing there? I am paying you to protect me, so keep up."

He hurried down the stairs and slowed as he neared the smith, his dead eyes staring at the heavens. *Poor guy. At least you no longer need endure this madness.* The crowd parted, most heading back into the building, while he and Willola headed toward the front gate.

She grimaced. "I can't believe I have to walk today in this heat."

"Heat?" he muttered. Even with his sleeveless leather jerkin and breeches, he did not feel hot, not like he would when summer arrived. And her dress left her shoulders bare and upper chest exposed – she certainly wore less than he did. "I'm sure Isaac will have your carriage fixed when we return to the manor."

She slowed at the gate and flashed him a frown. "He had better. I am too important to be forced to walk about the city like some *Ungifted.*"

Although Lang wanted to lash out, he let it drop, rolling his eyes instead.

As they crossed the square outside the palace walls, an old woman stumbled into him, her hand gripping his arm as she fell to her knees.

Lang helped her to her feet. "I am sorry. I should watch where I am going."

She shook her head. "You are too kind. I am the one at fault," her voice croaked. "My eyes aren't so good any longer. I miss the beauty of sunsets and friendly smiles. Everything now is but a blur."

The woman's wistful tone made him smile.

Ten strides away, Willola stopped with her fists on her hips. "Come along, Lang. I am not paying you to woo old hags to your bed."

His smile slipped away, and he looked back at the old woman. "I'm sorry, but I must be going."

"Yes. You are with someone important, far more so than the likes of me. Have a good day."

He turned and hurried to catch Willola, unaware of the note the woman had slipped into his belt.

17

ROYALTY

The carriage drew to a stop and Lang stepped out, his hand on the hilt of his sword, a habit formed many years earlier. The carriage was one of many lining the circular drive of the palace side entrance. Some drivers sat in carriages; others stood in clusters quietly talking. There was no threat nearby, but none was expected within the confines of the palace wall.

"All clear, Wizardess," Lang held his hand to the open door.

Willola took his hand and stepped down from the carriage. Her hair was piled high, and she wore a silver tiara that matched the silver trim on her black gown. She stood tall, her chest thrust out as she shimmied her tight skirts down to hide her calves. Lang wondered why she bothered.

"Walk me to the door," she said. "Don't say a word. I'll not have you embarrass me."

Grunting in reply, he fell in beside her.

They followed a curving path of inlaid bricks, passing sculpted hedges illuminated by eight-foot torches, their flames flickering in the evening sea breeze. With each step, the woman's heels tapped noisily, a sound Lang found irritating. In truth, everything about the woman had become irritating, even the body she shamelessly flaunted.

An outdoor theater came into view, built into a massive alcove beside Fastella Palace. In the center was a low area shaped like a semicircle. Stairs led up each side, giving it the illusion of a bowl, except for the ten-foot plat-form standing at the far end with a throne at its center. At the top, chairs had been placed in a half circle, allowing each an excellent view of the perform-ers. Between the chairs and the palace stood a ring of tall fluted columns, one of which was broken off a third of the way up.

Palace guards were posted along the area perimeter, from the garden path where Lang stood to the palace itself. Each guard was in full armor, the metal tinted gold, purple capes draped down their backs. Some held spears, others a sword and shield. To one side, wizards in long flowing robes and wizardesses in elegant gowns had gathered, chatting and laughing, many with drinks in their hands.

All the other guests were already present as expected, for Willola adored arriving late. It gave her the chance to make an entrance that guaranteed all eyes on her, sating the woman's constant craving for attention.

Willola turned toward Lang. "You are dismissed. Remain with the carriage. It will be a couple of hours. When the performance is finished, I will be along. I expect you to be alert and ready."

The woman crossed the tiled floor and began climbing the stairs, her hips swaying overtly with each step, a fake smile plastered on her face.

"Loathsome woman," Lang grumbled beneath his breath.

Before he could turn away, a gong sounded, the palace door opening. From it, Herrod emerged, dressed in full armor and holding a mace in one hand, the image stirring memories of the bodyguard's one-sided duel against the blacksmith.

Wearing a white dress, her bodice sparkling in the torchlight, the queen of Ghealdor walked past her bodyguard, a smug smile on her face as she nodded to those in attendance. The crowd parted to receive their queen, greeting her with applause, compliments, and broad grins. Even at a distance, the fawning made Lang ill. *She was one of the least important wizards in the city when Parsec ruled. How did she ever rise to power?* As the fifth wizard to rule in little over a year, tracking the turns that brought each the crown had been difficult at best.

He turned and followed the path, scowling as he thought about the wizard class. *They care nothing for anyone save themselves and the next social event. At least Parsec had ambition and sought to extricate Fastella from beneath Farrowen's thumb.* Lang had never loved his former employer, but he had respected him. That was more than he could say for any other wizard in the city.

As he drew close to the carriages, he heard a commotion.

"...are the performers," a man exclaimed. "These are not real weapons."

Lang emerged from the path, the hedges falling away and a group of guards coming into view, surrounding some others. A woman stood among five men, two in garish armor, one with antlers mounted to his helmet, and one with white feathers fanning out of his helmet. The fifth man wore black robes, his face painted red, a ridiculous, garish eight-foot staff in his grip. The woman had long black hair and a bright orange dress, her chest and arse as full as anything Lang had ever seen...and he had seen a lot.

A palace guard grabbed the woman and squeezed her breasts, frowning.

"I told you before," the woman said in a deep voice. "Those are grapefruit. They aren't real."

Lang snorted, shaking his head as he walked past. "A man dressed as a woman. Now I have seen everything."

He approached Willola's carriage as Isaac, her private driver, jumped down. The man turned toward him, adjusted his black brimmed hat, and straightened his matching coat. "So now we sit and wait."

Lang grunted. "While Willola and the others entertain themselves."

Isaac rubbed his broad bearded chin. "At least she pays us."

"Yeah. I guess." Lang peered toward the gate the performers had passed, heading down the path to the theater. "It will be a couple of hours. After what happened here yesterday, I'd rather not remain and dwell on it." He looked back at Isaac. "I plan to go find a taproom and down a few ales. You interested?" While the man might wish otherwise, Lang knew he would not leave the carriage.

"No," Isaac shook his head. "The carriage is my responsibility. I will sit here while you catch a respite. Don't worry, I'll not tell Willola."

Lang clapped his hand on the shorter man's shoulder. "You're a good man, Isaac. Too bad you drew a short straw with the wizard you serve."

"From what I have seen, few of their lot are better anyway."

"True." Lang walked off, waving. "I'll be back in about an hour."

"See you then."

Leaving the carriage and driver behind, Lang left the palace grounds, crossed the wide plaza surrounding the palace, and headed toward a narrow street. At the street entrance, he passed an enchanted lantern, its pale azure light fading behind him, similar lanterns waiting ahead, lighting each intersection. The streets were quiet, scattered foot traffic passing by as he wandered away from the palace.

The farther he roamed, the smaller the surrounding buildings became. Soon beggars appeared at corners, crates and refuse clogging the alleys. Turning, he followed a narrow, winding street, noise coming from ahead. He passed two taverns, the hum of conversation emitting from each, and arrived at the one he sought.

Upon entering the Silver Tooth, he was met at the door by two armed guards.

One, a heavyset man with a shaved head and brown goatee, pressed his palm against Lang's chest. "Sorry. The inn is closed for a private event tonight. Go down two buildings. The Copper Crow would be happy to serve you."

Lang frowned. "I was asked to come here."

"Sorry. Like I said, we are closed."

His gaze flicked to the other man, tall and lean with a loaded crossbow in his hand. Beyond him, the inn was quiet and empty. He then recalled the note in his pocket. Fishing it out, he read it in the flickering light.

If you desire freedom, ditch the performance in favor of the Silver Tooth. When asked, say, "A new god comes."

The man with the crossbow lifted it. "Leave. Now."

Lang said, "A new god comes."

The man lowered his crossbow and snorted. "You should have said that first. I was about to put a hole through you."

The hefty guard moved aside and pointed toward the corridor ahead. "First door on the left. Watch your step."

Lang walked past the men, entered the dark corridor, and stopped beside a closed door. Opening it, he found a steep stairwell descending into darkness, voices coming from below. He stepped inside, closed the door, and began his descent, his boots thudding with each step.

Men dressed in leather armor filled the cellar, all facing the far end where two lanterns hung from the ceiling, a flame flickering in each. Many turned to look at him, most of their faces familiar. *Why is this place filled with guards hired to protect wizards?* The question nagged at him as he wove his way through the crowd, seeking an open space. He settled at the end of a shelf filled with barrels, leaning against the wall with his arms folded over his chest. Questions flitted through his head, aching to be answered. *Who called this meeting? What is the agenda? Why involve the wizard's bodyguards?* He opened his hand and frowned at the crumpled paper, again pondering how it had come into his possession. *It must have been that old woman.* He wouldn't have given his brief encounter a second thought had he not discovered the note while undressing for bed. The paper had twirled to the floor when he unbuckled his belt.

The door atop the stairs opened again and footsteps descended. Two men appeared. The tall, athletic one wore leather armor. The other was thin, his hood covering his head, and his dark cloak clutched to his chest. With the warrior in the lead, the two crossed the crowded room, heading toward the two lanterns.

The cloaked man climbed on a crate, lowered his hood, and threw his cloak back. He was shirtless, and his entire body, from his bald head to his waist, was covered in strange symbols.

"Welcome, all. My name is Paetro Vex. I am pleased to have you here. You will be the vanguard against tyranny, ushering a new age into existence.

"The gods who placed wizards above the rest of mankind, those who gifted rulers with magic beyond reason, are gone. With them, wizard lords are no more. The people are no longer saddled with a single, self-serving, authoritarian ruler for centuries on end. Yes, a wizard currently sits upon the throne of Ghealdor, but unlike Taladain and those before him, her magic is not endless nor can she heal herself. I assure you, when cut, she will bleed. When poisoned, she will choke. When set ablaze, she will burn.

"Yet, the citizens of Fastella and the rest of Ghealdor continue to pay taxes that fund the lavish lives of wizards. The Gifted waste our money on their mansions, elegant clothing, extravagant jewelry, and pointless social events, focused not on the welfare of the people, but on their own status and advancing their own agenda.

"Fastella is primed for a revolution. We Ungifted greatly outnumber the wizards. The mantle of power looms before us. We must merely seize it."

Lang had listened carefully, the strange man making good points. However, he had seen others attempt to rise, only to fail. He had witnessed a ruler deposed only to be replaced by one who was worse.

Unable to hold his tongue, he shouted, "And if we overthrow the wizards, how long will that last? They would come for us, wielding magic we barely understand and cannot defend against."

Vex grinned. "How will they wield magic if they are dead?"

"You plan to kill them all?"

"They are a scourge. There is no reason to allow them to live."

Lang frowned. "Even the children?"

The man nodded. "I am afraid so. It is the only way."

The statement caused a round of mutters, some spurring arguments. The guard who had accompanied Vex blew a horn, the noise shaking the floor joists above them and quieting the crowd.

"Tell me," Vex stared at Lang. "What is your name?"

Lang frowned, not wanting to be implicated in talks of rebellion should someone talk. "Never mind my name."

Vex arched a tattooed brow. "Well, *Mister Nameless*. There is a price to pay for freedom. It often costs lives. Will it be yours or theirs?"

His frown becoming a hard grimace, Lang sought to turn the question back on the man. "Should we eliminate the wizards and depose Queen Dalia, what then? Who would lead? You?"

Loud, maniacal laughter burst from the man. When it subsided, he shook his head. "I knew it would be you who spoke up...*Lang*."

He knows my name.

"Or, should I say, GaLang Reagor?"

Gasps and mutters followed. It was a name Lang had not heard for years.

"Yes." Vex jumped off the crate and began across the room. "Here stands the greatest gladiator in the history of Orenth. How long has he hidden in your midst, guarding the lives of wizards while masking his own identity?"

"Not long enough," Lang said.

The man stopped a stride from Lang, his dark eyes staring up at him. "Tiamalyn might be two wizardoms away, but the Bowl of Oren is a fount for stories across the world. Even in Fastella, citizens know your name, Reagor. It is the name of a hero, a name to inspire ordinary people, instilling a belief that they might become extraordinary. With you to lead them, these men might follow. What say you?"

All eyes focused on Lang, who scowled in return. He had won his freedom and had paid in blood. Each foe had entered the arena on two feet. Every single one left as a corpse.

"I am already free," he said. "I do not wish to rule. I only wish to be left alone."

The man produced a vial of crimson liquid, sparkling in the amber light. *Wizard's blood*, Lang thought. He had seen it enough to know.

Vex popped the stopper. "Even after you see this?" He poured some on his chest, the viscus liquid sparkling as it ran down his torso. He rubbed it across his skin and began to chant.

A fog arose, swirling through the air, twisting and snaking as if alive. It twisted around Lang, who stood still, afraid any movement might anger it. The mist curled around his chest and up toward his face. It smelled sweet – of flowers and sunlight and the sea. His blood began to rush, his head buzzed, and a longing stirred in his gut.

Years ago, Lang had been a leader among men – a hero who quenched a rebellion in eastern Orenth. He soon found himself back in the capital city of Tiamalyn, raised to the rank of captain at the young age of twenty-seven.

Charged with the protection of Lord Horus, ruler of Orenth, with over a hundred elite guards under his command, he was revered and respected. Proud and confident, tall and handsome, women longed to be with him, and men aspired to be like him...until his arrogance led him astray.

Somehow, Lang had survived the impossible. When he left Tiamalyn, he left his old life and his identity behind, choosing to bury the past and start anew. In Fastella, he was nothing more than another bodyguard. Nobody expected anything more of him than any other hired sword.

Now, three years later, a feeling awoke inside him, something he had thought lost forever. Pride.

Lang drew his sword, the sound echoing. He leveled his blade at Vex's throat.

"Give me a reason why I shouldn't kill you and drag your corpse to the palace as a traitor."

Vex smiled. "There it is."

Frowning, Lang said, "What?"

"The fire in your eyes. It is the fire of a leader, the flame of someone who wishes to fight rather than bend to the whims of others."

"So?"

"So I am not a traitor." Vex knelt. "I am loyal to the cause, dedicated to seeing mankind free of wizard rule." He gazed up at Lang, jaw set. "If you will lead these men, I will plead fealty to you here and now. With my support, you will soon sit upon the Ghealdan Throne."

Lang looked around, all eyes on him. Thirty-some men, all trained to fight, stared at him with a sense of expectation. In those eyes, he saw something important, another thing he had thought gone from his life. Hope.

Finally, he sheathed his blade and nodded. "Fine."

Vex leapt to his feet and pumped his fist into the air. "Reagor! Reagor! Reagor!"

By the time he said it three times, others had joined in. Soon, everyone was shouting his name, the pride in his gut growing stronger with each cry. Years had passed since he last heard the chant. His mind drifted back to that day.

18

GLADIATOR

Three Years Earlier

S itting on a bench with his elbows on his knees, Lang stared at his cell wall three strides away. Absently, he twisted the metal-plated bracers on his forearms. Other than boots and a skirt made of leather strips, he wore nothing else. He was not allowed to wear more, for the spectators wished to see his tall muscular frame as much as the blood he was sure to spill.

The door behind him opened, noise from the crowd coming through, thousands chanting in unison, "Reagor! Reagor! Reagor!"

Someone stepped into the cell, a familiar voice saying, "Leave us."

The door closed, the cell quieting.

Lang took a deep breath, rose, and turned to face the man.

Lord Horus stood Lang's height, his shoulders broad for a wizard. He had angled eyes, a hooked nose, and a crown of golden leaves resting upon his bald head. An emerald the size of a large grape graced the front of the crown. His robes were shimmery gold, his sash and lapel emerald green. While he appeared no more than forty years old, Horus was a wizard lord and had aged little since claiming the throne many decades ago.

Dutifully, Lang bowed. "Your Majesty."

"You remind me of your grandfather."

"As you have said before."

Rubbing his chin, Horus slowly circled the room. "KaLang was the best of his generation – intelligent, unequaled in combat, a leader among men. Something burned inside him, and others, like moths, were drawn to his flame. I cried the day he and I were poisoned. Of course, I healed myself, burning the taint from my blood as only a wizard lord can. By the time I recovered, he was too far gone. I sometimes wished I had passed with him."

Lang had heard the story before but chose to remain silent, wondering why Horus had graced him with a visit.

"Yes, you are much like him." Horus stopped before him and stared into his eyes. "I had once thought you would lead my private guard for decades, filling the vacuum left by KaLang."

"I wish it were so, sire."

Horus closed his eyes and grimaced. When he opened them, they were filled with sadness. "I do not blame you for what happened. In truth, I never did. I know my wife well…enough to realize loyalty is not among her best traits. Worse, she has…insatiable appetites. When we married, I thought her lust a boon, but unlike my prior wives, I grew weary of it. I fear I overlooked the ugliness inside her."

He placed a hand on Lang's shoulder. "If your affair had not been exposed in such a public manner, I would have forgiven you and let it pass. Unfortunately, that was not meant to be."

Lang's chin dropped. "I never meant to betray you, Horus."

The wizard sighed and turned away. "I know. Yet, I could not allow it to pass unpunished. Even for a wizard lord, the throne is a precarious place to sit with others seeking to topple you in their quest for power. Any perceived weakness becomes an open wound with wolves circling, drawn to the exposed flesh." Horus turned back with a smile. "After three years in the arena, facing countless foes, you will be free."

Not countless – the faces of four hundred sixty-five men haunt my dreams. "It is not assured." Lang shrugged. "I have one last gladiator to face."

Laughter came from Horus. "Oh, you cannot lose to this man. You will be freed from your sentence, and I will be glad to see it happen. In truth, I had always hoped you might survive. If anyone could do it, I believed it would be you."

The wizard walked back to the door, pausing before it to speak over his shoulder. "Today, you will be free, but I cannot allow you to remain in Orenth. Too many love you, and I cannot blame them for it. My private barge departs from the lower landing this afternoon, bound for Shear. You will be on it. Have a good life, my friend."

Horus opened the door, and the noise of the chanting crowd again rushed through it.

"Reagor! Reagor! Reagor!"

Two guards entered his cell, separating at the door. One waved his sword toward Lang. "Come on, Reagor. Time to give them a show."

He walked past the men and down the corridor, stepping into the small dark waiting cell he had visited so many times during the past three years. The door closed behind him, the darkness complete. Moments later, the opposite wall tipped up, another door rising to reveal the sunlit Bowl of Oren, home of the gladiators.

Marching across the dirt arena floor, Lang raised his fist in the air, and the chanting rose to a crescendo. Thousands filled the oval ring of seats surrounding the battlefield. He strode toward the middle of the ring as another door opened, revealing his opponent.

An overweight man waddled out and squinted in the sunlight. His torso consisted of soft pasty rolls, his thick arms pinched by the leather bracers strapped on them. He spun around, a hand shielding his eyes as he stared at the crowd, mouth agape.

Lang turned toward the end of the bowl, his gaze settling on the throne. As always, Lord Horus sat there, ready to watch Lang fight. Beside the wizard was a woman of rare beauty with long dark hair, tawny skin, and enchanting eyes. Her voluptuous curves were barely contained by her tight yellow dress. Grenda smiled when she met his gaze, as she had done every time he fought. It had not taken long for Lang to determine she received satisfaction at his plight. More so, he suspected she reveled in being the cause of his predicament.

Horus rose to his feet, spread his arms, and slapped his hands together. A thunderclap shook the stadium, Lang nearly staggering from the wave washing past him. It left his ears ringing and the reverberation humming in his chest. The crowd fell silent.

"Welcome citizens of Tiamalyn!" Horus's voice boomed, boosted by his magic. "Today is one without precedence. As you know, our longest tenured gladiator faces his final foe. GaLang Reagor, three years past, your life was placed in Oren's hands – per Orenthian tradition, your innocence proven or disproven on the field of battle. Should our god will it and you survive this challenger, you will leave the Bowl a free man." He raised his hand high. "When my arm falls, you shall begin."

Standing three strides away, the other man stared at Lang with wide eyes, kneading his hands. Beads of sweat emerged from beneath his helmet, tracking down his face. When Horus dropped his hand, the crowd roared. Rather than leap into action as usual, Lang stood still and waited for his opponent to react. The man did not move.

Lang shouted over the crowd noise. "You are supposed to fight me."

The man lifted his fists. "Just a fist fight?"

"Have you not watched a fight in the Bowl?"

Shaking his head, the man said, "No. I live in Grakel...never been to Tiamalyn before this week."

"Why are you here? What crime did you commit?"

"I...I was drunk. I did not hear Devotion. Two guards found me sleeping in an alley while it was happening. They threw me in a dungeon cell. When they woke me this morning, I was hauled here and told to fight or die."

Lang sighed. *I am supposed to kill this fat slob because he slept through a prayer?* Yes, Devotion was required for all citizens, but the penalty was typically a night in a cell, at least for the first offense.

"Well, we will have to fight. If we don't, it'll go badly for both of us." Pointing toward a dark red spot a few feet away, Lang asked, "See that? This marks where the last battle ended."

The man gaped at the bloodstain. "What happened?"

"A man died."

"From a fist fight?"

"No." Lang pointed toward one of the bays beneath the stands, weapons visible beyond a grid of metal bars. "Those gates will soon open. When they do, arm yourself, for we will not avoid a fight at that point."

"What if...what if you just knock me out right now. You know, a good punch to the jaw?'

Lang shook his head. "That would never satisfy the wizard lord, nor this crowd. Anyone who does not battle with actual weapons is executed. Your only chance is to put up a good fight."

A horn blew, echoing through the arena. The gates barring the three weapon bays began to rise.

"This is it." Lang gestured across the arena. "Run and arm yourself."

Wide-eyed, the man hurriedly waddled off. Lang turned and jogged toward a weapon bay in the opposite direction. Once inside, he chose a round shield and a club, hoping he might spare the man's life.

While hidden in the shadows of the bay, he stared at the weapons in the rack, thinking of the lives claimed by those instruments of death and wishing he could burn every weapon in the rack, destroying the entire arena in the process.

He shook his head to clear it. *You have killed hundreds of men in this arena. Why are you letting this one get to you? Win this and you are free.* As he turned away, the other man emerged from a bay across the arena. In one hand, the man hoisted a shield almost as tall as his own body, in the other, a spear at least a foot longer than ideal for his height. The man made it only a few strides before his foot caught on the tail of the spear. He tripped, his other foot kicking the bottom of the shield, the top end smacking him in the face. He went down, landing flat on his back. The crowd burst out in howling laughter.

Lang walked out of the bay and looked up at the blue sky. "Why, Oren? Why must you make this so difficult?"

As he continued toward the middle of the floor, the other man sat up, his nose bloodied and his eyes watering. With great effort, he rose to one knee and then stood, leaning on the spear, adjusting the tall shield. His eyes narrowed and he set his jaw before marching toward Lang.

The two opponents stopped a few strides apart, the bloodstained dirt between them.

"Are you ready?" Lang asked.

The man nodded. "Just do it."

With a roar, Lang burst forward, club striking his opponent's shield with a mighty blow, the metal ringing like a gong. He swung again and again, each attack denting the shield and driving the other man backward. When he paused, the fat man made to jab with his spear, but Lang smacked it aside with his shield and followed with a tremendous underhand swing, striking the bottom of the tall shield and knocking it back. It smashed into the other man's shin, sweeping his feet out from beneath him. He crashed to the ground, landing face first on top of his shield, his spear flying to the side and rolling away.

The fat man rolled over on his back, his face bloody and eyes teary as he gasped for air. "Please. Just end it," he pleaded.

Lang placed a boot on the man's chest. The crowd fell silent as he peered up at Lord Horus.

Rising from his throne, Horus held his fist high. Lang waited for the signal.

Please, Horus. Please, let this one live.

The wizard lord swung his arm in a flourish and then slowly dragged two fingers across his throat.

By the gods…why?

Lang stepped back and stared down at his opponent, a man whose name he did not know…did not wish to know. Still, he memorized the face. It was the least he could do.

"May the gods have mercy on you," Lang said, raising his club.

"And you as well," the man replied.

With all his might, Lang drove the club into the man's face, caving it in. He died instantly – the only gift of mercy within Lang's power.

The crowd went wild, the applause deafening.

Disgusted, Lang tossed the bloodied club and shield to the ground and walked across the floor, heading toward the exit before it even opened.

A chant arose, one he never thought he'd hear again.

"Reagor! Reagor! Reagor!"

19

MISSIVE

Willola Manor was nestled in the middle of Wizard Hills, the district of Fastella dominated by walled estates, sprawling lawns, and enormous mansions. The building housed the wizardess and her staff – two maids, two stewards, two guards, a driver, and Lang, her personal bodyguard. Despite the woman's lavish abode, the servant's quarters consisted of small rooms, barely large enough for a bed, a nightstand, and a wardrobe. Over the past year, Lang had grown used to it, but he often longed for his former room at the palace, accommodations he had briefly enjoyed until the mysterious disappearance of his prior employer, Van Parsec.

He left his coworkers at the front gate and ascended the dark drive that led to the stables, musing about Parsec's rise to the station of high wizard. The wizard had ruled Fastella while attempting to extricate Ghealdor from beneath Farrowen's rule. *Funny,* Lang thought. *The problem sorted itself out. If Parsec had simply waited...* He sighed. Whatever had happened, Parsec was certainly dead; nothing else could have prevented the man from fighting to keep the throne. When Queen Dalia took over, Lang blamed the woman, for there was no other explanation.

Circling the rear of the manor, he melded into shadow, the moon blocked by the large three story building. He reached the rear door and ducked into the kitchen, pulling the door closed quietly behind him. There was nobody in sight. The door to the great room stood open, Willola's laughter carrying from the dining room beyond. Lang recognized her artificial laugh. Little of the woman was genuine, other than her single-minded manipulation of others toward her own ends. Her dinner guest, Jalen Harbin, was not much better. As head of the Fastella Wizards Guild, he was in a position of power – reason enough for Willola to invite him for dinner. The man was also a widower, a fact Willola was sure to use to her advantage.

Lang heard footsteps as Olban rushed into the room. Roughly Lang's age, Olban had been working for Willola for nearly a decade and had recently been raised to the position of head steward. Tonight, he wore a navy coat over a white doublet, his trousers matching the coat. His dark hair was oiled back, giving him the extra air of polish that Willola demanded when guests were present.

Olban jerked with a start, placing a hand to his chest, the other hand balancing a silver platter. "You startled me, Lang. What are you doing in here?"

Lang thumbed toward the door. "Pendry and Nolan asked me to grab them some bread if there is any left."

"Dinner has been served, and the cooks have gone to their rooms." Olban pointed toward a pan beside the brick oven. "There should be half a loaf left." He grabbed a carafe from a cabinet and turned to the wine barrel on the counter, filling it in moments. "Now, you had better get out of here before she catches you."

Lang grabbed the bread, finding it still warm. "I'll see you once Wizard Harbin departs."

"Yeah. I just hope he doesn't stay the night." Olban scurried out of the room with the carafe in his hands, the kitchen door swinging closed.

Alone, Lang crossed the kitchen, bent, and dug a jug from a low shelf, sniffing it to ensure it was clean. He stuck the jug beneath the barrel spigot, opened the spigot, and watched as crimson liquid began to pour out. Once the jug was full, he closed the spigot and hurried out the door, bread in one hand, a jug of wine in the other.

He followed the path along the building to the moonlit drive and walked down the hill. As he drew close to the gate, he heard Isaac talking to the estate guards, Nolan and Pendry. The three men turned toward him.

Isaac's round face was shadowed by his wide-brimmed hat, his ever-present suspenders dark against his pale tunic. The man had a full belly but thin legs, his trousers ready to fall to his ankles should the suspenders fail. The two guards were in their mid-twenties, neither particularly skilled with a weapon, but both big enough to cause someone to think twice before sneaking into the estate.

Flashing a grin, Lang held the jug up. "Got it. Should be enough for all of us. Half a loaf of bread as well."

Pendry rubbed his hands together eagerly, showing white teeth amid his trimmed brown beard. "You are my hero, Lang."

"Like a knight of legend, come to save the day," Nolan added.

The three men laughed heartily.

Lang stopped a stride away and held the bread toward Isaac. With Balmorian blood, Isaac had tawny skin and a dark bushy beard, the curly hair on his head thinning should anyone catch him without his hat – but that was a rare occurrence.

"Thank you, sir." Isaac broke off a chunk and handed the rest to Nolan.

Lang tipped the jug up and took a deep drink. The wine was sweet but dry, tickling his tongue and warming his throat. "Farrowen red." He smacked his lips and passed the jug to Pendry. "Willola might be a pain in the arse, but she has great taste in wine."

Pendry took a drink and passed the jug to Nolan. "Just don't let her hear you say that. For a woman so pretty, you'd think her heart would be less black."

"What do you think she would do if she found us stealing her wine?" Isaac asked.

Lang shrugged. "She might own this estate, but we live here, too. We work long hours with little praise. The way I see it, we deserve a jug of wine now and then. It's not like she is low on funds."

Wiping his lips dry, Nolan passed the jug to Isaac. "You always see the right of things, Lang. For a bodyguard, you are not a bad sort."

"Not bad?" Pendry jabbed Nolan. "I'd say he is a downright savior right now. Here, he gives us fresh baked bread and high class wine along with a bit of company on a night where we'd be fighting not to doze off while waiting for the wizardess to woo that unsuspecting dupe of a wizard."

Nolan then went on to tell stories of Willola's diligent pursuit of Prince Eldalain, one that started mere weeks after her husband's suspicious death.

On eight different occasions, each including a rather noisy visit to the woman's bedroom, Eldalain had visited the estate. Despite being fifteen years younger than the prince and as beautiful as they come, her efforts to woo him into marriage had failed. When the prince died, her plans to rise had been dashed. All that had been before Parsec's odd disappearance, forcing Lang to find a new employer. Now, Willola was at it again, attempting to hitch her carriage to the head of the wizards guild, the man most likely to assume the throne should something happen to Queen Dalia. *Unless wizards no longer ruled the Ungifted.* Thoughts of Vex's speech resurfaced, as they had repeatedly for the past two days.

Lang considered telling Pendry, Nolan, and Isaac about the rebellion, but Vex had insisted that nobody who had attended his meeting tell others. *"Surprise is our greatest asset,"* the man had said. *"The wizards will never suspect their own guards would betray them."* Lang could not disagree with the assessment. The wizard class had ruled unchallenged for two thousand years. Only a wizard would dare challenge another wizard. It was the way of things. *It is time the way changed.*

A cloaked form came down the dark street and approached the gate, stoking Lang's suspicion.

The man stopped a stride beyond the bars. "I am seeking a man named Lang."

Lang peered at the man, but his hooded face was draped in shadow, his voice unfamiliar. All three of Lang's companions turned toward him, the two guards arching their brows.

Isaac thumbed in Lang's direction. "You have found him."

The man extended a hand through the gate, a folded piece of paper between two fingers. "I have a missive for you."

"A missive? Who would send me a letter?" Lang asked.

"An admirer."

Pendry snorted and jabbed Lang in the shoulder. "Looks like you caught the eye of some woman."

"Maybe the widow of a wealthy merchant," Nolan added with a chuckle.

Reaching out, Lang snatched the folded paper. The man turned and walked away, footsteps fading into the night.

"That was strange," Isaac noted.

Curious, Lang lifted the paper and noted a sunburst pressed into the wax seal. He broke the seal, unfolded it, and read in the moonlight.

Meet me tomorrow, two hours after nightfall. Moarbear Smithy in the Dregs.
-V

Doubt and a tinge of regret gripped Lang by the throat. *Have I made a mistake?* He worried what Vex had planned and where it might lead. His concern was not for himself but how his actions might impact others. Lang had faced death many times and had come to terms with it. His end would likely come soon, but how many men would fall with him?

Pendry peered over his shoulder, "What's it say?"

Lang turned toward the man, recalling his inability to read. "It says I am to meet this woman tomorrow night."

The other three men laughed, Isaac passing the jug to Lang, who drank deeply. It would be a long night, and he would rather not spend it sifting through troubled thoughts.

20

ENSORCELLED

It was late, the streets quiet, as Lang made his way toward the outer edge of Fastella. Fog hung in the cool evening air, obscuring anything beyond a block away. The full moon above appeared blurred by the mist. He passed through the Merch, the city's primary business district, and entered the Dregs, marked by worn buildings, refuse, and far less reputable inns than those found elsewhere in Fastella.

Upon reaching the street nearest to the city wall, he turned and followed it, peering at the signs he passed as he searched for the building where he was to meet Vex.

Two men in cloaks stepped out from a recessed doorway and blocked the road. One, tall and lean, brandished a short sword. The other was short, standing little over five feet, holding a loaded crossbow.

The one with the sword said, "We will be taking your coin purse."

Stopping, Lang arched a brow. "Do you even know how to use a sword?" From his stance, it was obvious the man did not.

"Yeah. I stick you with the pointy end and you bleed."

Scowling, Lang said, "I am not an easy mark. Find someone else to rob."

Footsteps came from behind, a deep voice booming, "Easy or not, you'll give up your coin, or blood will spill."

Moving slowly, Lang glanced back to find a burly man holding a cudgel.

He stood Lang's height but easily outweighed him. The man had a black cap on his head, his face too shadowed to determine his age.

Lang shrugged, "It's your blood. If you no longer have need of it, test me. Otherwise, be on your way."

"You've a tongue on you," said the thief with the crossbow. "Perhaps we should cut it off as a tithe for making this difficult."

Laughter burst from Lang's mouth, not forced or nervous, but mocking. "If you think this is difficult, test me. You'll find the price higher than you wish to pay."

"Enough," said the tall one with the sword. "Give up your coin or we will take it."

Lang sighed. "Alright."

He looked down, holding the coin purse at his hip with one hand, the other gripping the four-point razoreth blade from his belt. In a sudden motion, he whipped the razoreth and ducked. The spinning blade struck the bowman in his chest. He lurched and pulled the trigger, which sent the bolt sailing over Lang, narrowly missing the brawny thief with the cudgel.

Drawing his sword, Lang swung at the burly man's head. As expected, the brute raised his cudgel just in time to prevent decapitation. Kicking with all his might, Lang drove his boot into the man's crotch. The tough released a strangled grunt and doubled over. Lang smashed him across the head with the hilt of his sword and immediately leapt aside, sensing an attack from behind. The thief with the sword lunged, his blade finding empty air. With a downward chop, Lang's sword struck the other man's weapon near the hilt, the impact knocking the blade to the ground.

The thief yipped and backed away, Lang leveling his sword at the disarmed man's chest. He glanced to the side to see the small thief leaning against a wall, his face etched in pain, the razoreth blade sticking from his chest and the crossbow in his hand empty.

"I know how it is," Lang said in a friendly tone. "You three are guild members and are doing your job. Attempting to rob someone like me is a mistake few would make twice. Although that's difficult to do when you are worm fodder. If you go now, I'll give you the chance to try again, although I don't suggest it."

The tall man's eyes flicked to Lang's sword tip, inches from his chest. "You'll let us go?"

"Yes, so long as you never come after me again."

He nodded. "Sounds fair." Glancing toward his companion against the wall, he asked, "Are you alright, Drek?"

"I think so."

Lang stalked toward the smaller man and pinched the blade still stuck in his chest. "It hurts, I know. However, the blades are clean and are not buried deep."

With a yank, he pulled the razoreth blade free. The man cried out, his hand clutching his chest.

"Good." Lang wiped the blood on the man's cloak. "Keep pressure on the wound. Clean it, bandage it, and you'll be fine in a week or so."

"I won't die?"

Lang chuckled as he slid the blade back into the slot in his belt. "If I had wanted you dead, I would have aimed for your throat."

The big man on the ground stirred, his hand going to his bloody head as his friends circled around him. The tall one helped him to his feet. The small man with the chest wound led the stumbling trio into the fog.

Lang turned away and continued down the street. After crossing another intersection, he spotted a sign in the moonlight, depicting the image of a moarbear, the word *smithy* beneath it. The shop was dark, and its door closed, so he slipped into the alley beside the building. It brought him to a courtyard against the outer wall of the city. The smithy's back doors stood open, leaving an opening four strides wide, dim light coming from inside. In the middle of the yard, coals burned in a forge, their bright orange glow illuminating a nearby anvil. Made of black iron, the anvil was solid and immovable and reached Lang's waist.

Vex emerged from the building. "You are late." He wore a black cloak over his clothes, the tattoos on his head blurred lines in the hazy moonlight.

Lang considered mentioning the run in with the thieves but thought better of it. "I had to wait for Willola's leave. Told her I needed a drink. As you might suspect, time for myself comes second to her needs."

The man nodded. "I assumed as much." He pointed toward the open smithy door. "Meet my associate, Bonn."

A man with broad shoulders and a barrel chest appeared from the shadows to stand beside Vex. With stubble for hair, a heavy brow, and a wide nose, Bonn had a rough appearance, the white scar on his chin adding to the image. He raised his thick, meaty fingers to rub his cleft chin. "This is him?"

"It is," Vex replied.

Bonn grunted. "Doesn't seem as impressive as the stories."

"He doesn't need to be." Vex strode into the moonlight, his arms spread wide. "The stories have created the perception we need. Commoners see him as a hero – the man who defied a wizard lord and defeated a thousand men to earn his freedom."

Lang corrected him. "It was only four hundred sixty-six men."

Vex chortled. "A thousand sounds much better, don't you think?"

Face lit by the glow of the forge, the grin he flashed sent a shiver down Lang's spine. Made of stronger things and having faced death countless times, Lang refused to be intimidated.

He set his jaw. "I am here as you requested. What is this about?"

"This," Vex headed toward the workshop, "is the next step in our plan. Come inside."

The two men entered the smithy, Lang following them from the dirt yard to a floor made of dark stone. His gaze swept the room, noting tools and weapons hanging on the walls and a pair of workbenches in the middle. Just beyond the benches, the floor was marked by an emblem in the shape of an eye, the lines glowing a pale blue. Within the white of the eye was a complex pattern, differing from the swirling lines that made the iris. The pupil was blank and oddly dark compared to the rest.

"What is this?" Lang asked. "Some sort of enchantment?" He turned to Vex. "Are you a wizard?"

Vex laughed. "Quite the opposite. My power comes from sorcery, and with it, I can help you defeat the wizards." He pointed again. "Stand in the center but avoid stepping on the lines."

A sorcerer? *This man uses magic I do not understand. In truth, I understand little of wizard magic either.* He found himself again questioning his path and wondered if he should turn back. *I could just walk away and return to my life.* It was not a bad life, better than most, in fact. However, another part of him refused to accept the mediocrity. Some voice from within cried his name, *Reagor, Reagor, Reagor.* The chant stirred something inside him, a spirit he had bound and gagged but refused to remain silent. *You must be brave. You must persevere. If this man's magic can give us a chance for freedom, you must take it.*

Resigned but apprehensive, Lang stepped carefully past the outer portions of the pattern before settling in the pupil of the eye.

Vex removed his cloak and tossed it to the floor, exposing his heavily tattooed torso. The sorcerer pulled a vial from the pouch at his waist, unstoppered the cork, and tipped it over the symbol. Drops of blood dripped to the floor, sparkling in the firelight. *Wizard's blood.*

Vex dribbled the blood on his chest, the crimson liquid running in streaks as he corked the vial and slid it into his pouch. He then rubbed the blood across his torso, coating the symbols inscribed there.

The entire time, Lang watched with a furrowed brow. Blood magic was forbidden in every wizardom he had visited. The priests of Oren, Farrow, and Gheald all proclaimed it evil. Again, his apprehension about his new allegiance swelled, and he worried that he had made a mistake. Just as he reached the decision to leave, Vex began to chant in a foreign language, his arms outstretched.

A new sensation caused Lang to freeze, making his muscles tense. Glowing sparks of light floated up from the symbol on the floor, shimmering with energy. The sparks began to swirl around Lang, faster and faster, as though he were in the eye of the storm. The sparks suddenly stopped, hovered motionless for a moment, and then collapsed toward the center, plunging into Lang's body.

Extreme heat filled him, his heart hammered in his chest, and sweat formed beads on his forehead. The room twisted and tilted, spots dancing before his eyes. He fell to one knee, both palms pressed against the cool stone as he fought to remain conscious. The heat faded, his vision clearing and his pulse slowing.

Lang lifted his head to find Vex standing a few feet away. The sorcerer used a wet towel to wash the blood from his body.

Still panting from his ordeal, Lang asked, "What did you do to me?"

The sorcerer grinned. "I gave you a gift. You and I are now bonded. With the added power of our connection, you will rise to rule Ghealdor…and perhaps more."

Rising to his feet, Lang frowned. "I don't feel any different."

"We are not finished. One last step remains, one that means the difference between success and failure…between life and death." Vex tossed the towel on a bench and waved for Lang to follow.

From a workbench, Bonn hefted a metal rod as long as Lang's arm, one end made of thin metal shaped into a complex symbol. Frowning, Lang recognized it as a brand, one far more elaborate than he had seen on livestock. When the smith headed outside, Lang followed, watching closely. Without a pause, Bonn approached the forge and thrust the brand into the coals.

Vex turned to Lang. "Remove your jerkin."

Picturing his skin burning, Lang shook his head. "You aren't branding me with that thing."

Again, Vex produced his vial, this time dripping blood on his fingers. He rubbed the blood on his lips, coating them with crimson. When the wizard spoke his voice took on a musical quality.

The sorcerer's voice rang in Lang's skull, overwhelming all other thought. "You will be king. You are the one. This is but a stop on your journey to the throne. Strip to the waist, step forward, and accept your birthright."

Enthralled, Lang unlaced his collar and pulled the jerkin over his head.

"Tunic as well," the sorcerer added.

Lang removed his tunic, leaving him naked above the waist other than the bracers on his forearms.

Bonn pulled the rod from the forge and turned toward Lang. "This is going to hurt. A lot."

Somewhere deep inside, Lang screamed to flee, but his body remained resolutely in place.

The smith extended the glowing brand toward Lang and pressed it against his chest. It seared with intense pain, but Lang remained still. After a few seconds, Bonn drew back, removing the hot metal.

Lang glanced down, smoke rising from his still-burning flesh. Vex moved close to him and pressed the vial against Lang's collarbone, tipping it up until sparkling blood ran down. When the blood reached the burn, it sizzled and steamed. But the pain receded as the angry red of the burn faded to white. Suddenly, it no longer hurt and the haze that had captured his mind faded. Amazed, Lang touched it. His flesh had raised to a scar in the shape of a sunburst with an eye in the center.

"It is done," Vex said. "Now, you and I have much to discuss. Taking the throne will not be easy. It will be bloody and will require sacrifice."

21

PREY

I t was past the dinner hour when Jace emerged from the building across from the Marquithe Bureau of Trading. From the shadowy doorway, he peered up and down the street to see if anyone was watching. The air was cool and damp for late spring, the cloud-covered sky darkening with the threat of rain, a common evening occurrence this time of year. Jace despised being caught in the rain and longed to hurry back to the palace for a night before a warm fire with Narine in his arms. However, the missive in his pocket outweighed such longings, drowning them not in rainwater but concern.

He pulled the slip of paper from his coat, unfolded it, and reread it for the third time. Having an exceptional memory, he recalled the words perfectly, but chose to stare at it again, seeking a hidden message.

Jerrell,

I have discovered the party behind the contract in question. Beware, for another exists. Your bride is in grave danger. Come sundown, meet me at your old haunt.

-H

· · ·

Tappy, a beggar with a wooden leg, had delivered the note to Jace an hour earlier. When asked, the man claimed someone passing by had dropped it in his collection tin. He had only caught a glimpse of a cloaked figure fading into the passing foot traffic. If Haelynn had not sent the note, it had been someone who knew the beggar was part of Jace's intelligence network. Either way, he could not ignore it, not if another killer were after Narine.

Only a few days remained before the wedding – an event rife with opportunity for a would-be assassin. Narine insisted it proceed as planned – a ceremony before a thousand guests ranging from wealthy merchants to high wizards from other cities, and every wizard in Farrowen. Worse, after the ceremony, Narine demanded she and Jace make an appearance in Merchant Square to present themselves to the citizens of Marquithe. She was convinced that the ordinary people would be inspired at the sight of a royal marriage – a sign of stability and prosperity for years to come. Considering the upheaval within the church after the loss of Farrow, she felt it was critical to give her subjects something upon which they could place their faith. That something would be a strong but compassionate queen and her new husband, the chancellor of Marquithe. While Jace agreed on her points, he dreaded exposing Narine to public danger, especially after the recent kidnapping and assassination attempt.

Once married, I will be called Prince Jerrell, he mused. The two words sounded bizarre beside one another. His mouth twisted at the thought of being considered royalty. For most of his life, royalty had often been the subject of his disdain…or the target of a contract he had been paid to execute. The latter had earned him some powerful enemies, at least those who knew or suspected his involvement. Ironically, many of those enemies were now dead.

With the sky darkening and no sign of anyone following him, he pocketed the note and slipped behind a well-dressed couple walking arm-in-arm. They reached the square and crossed it, heading toward the heart of the city while he turned in the opposite direction. He slowed while passing a crew busily securing posts and beams together.

The structure was to become a platform upon which he and Narine would stand before what he expected to be a crowded square. While he was no carpenter, he trusted the crew would finish the stage on time. He had certainly paid them well to do so. The rumble of thunder shook the city, a streak of lightning flashing across the northwest sky. One of the crew called out, the others immediately gathering their tools. Night was upon them anyway, so Jace was not surprised.

Turning, he left the square and entered a narrow street, an enchanted lantern illuminating the next intersection, creating an island of pale blue light amid the darkening surroundings. He passed two similar intersections, the foot traffic growing steadily lighter. Upon reaching a taproom called the Blue Hen, he ducked into a dark alley and pressed his back against the wall, his hand gripping the fulgur blade hidden beneath his coat.

A full minute passed before he moved deeper into the alley, satisfied nobody had followed him. He circled around two broken crates, his eyes sweeping the shadowy darkness beneath the stairwell ahead. Rather than climb the stairs, he looked up. Lines with drying clothing connected buildings on opposite sides of the alley, one of those lines broken and dangling with the end hanging nine feet off the ground.

Jace backed up, ran toward the wall, and leapt, his feet scrambling up as he gripped the dangling rope. Hand over hand, he climbed, his feet braced against the brick wall. Once he was high enough, he raised his feet, crouched, and pushed off, swinging and scrambling to a second story window, where he hooked his boots on a ledge to keep from swinging outward. Gripping the rope with one hand, he drew a throwing knife and slipped it between the upper and lower windowpane, flipping the latch open. He lifted it and whipped a leg over the windowsill before releasing the rope and sliding inside, careful to step to the side and avoid the bear trap beneath the window. Despite the darkness, he navigated the room easily, its furniture and layout unchanged from when he lived there.

Across the apartment, light seeped from beneath the closed door at the end of the hallway. He hesitated, wondering if Haelynn might try to seduce him, and he worried she might hold information hostage to get what she wanted. Jace had made a personal pact he would never cheat on Narine, but what if it were required to save her life?

He then noticed the crossbows pointing toward the apartment door. Neither was loaded, the lines connecting the triggers to the door cut. His worry turned to alarm. Haelynn would never disarm the traps on his account, not when they were of his own making. Certainly, she would not cut the lines to the door.

Jace drew a fulgur blade, the flickering sparks illuminating the immediate area. With the blade ready, he eased down the corridor and pressed his ear to the bedroom door. Silence. He rested his hand on the knob, turned it, and threw the door open while pinning his back to the wall. No attack came.

He peered around the doorframe and gasped. "No."

Naked, Haelynn was nailed to the wall above the bed, a crossbow bolt through each of her wrists. Her head drooped to the side, streaks of crimson down her torso, eyes staring into nothing.

He put his back to the wall and listened but heard no movement. With caution, he entered her room. It was a mess, clothing, shoes, makeup, and other items strewn about. Sheathing his blade, he hopped on the bed, gripped one of the bolts, and pulled hard. It came free, her body falling against his. Holding her with one arm, he yanked the other bolt free and then gently laid her on the bed.

The side of her head was badly wounded, her golden hair matted with dark blood. He grabbed the lantern from the nightstand and held it close, examining the deep puncture in her skull. The injury was distinctive, square in shape. He only knew one person who carried a weapon likely to cause such a wound. He pulled the covers over her body and turned away from the bed, angry as he walked down the corridor. *Whistler will pay for this.*

Rather than go out the window, he made for the exterior door. Opening it, he stepped out onto the landing.

Something flashed in the darkness and Jace dodged aside, catching himself on the railing. A war hammer struck the wood rail with a crack. His weight against it, Jace fell with the broken railing and landed on the crates below with a mighty crash, striking his head in the process.

Darkness invaded. He floundered, trying to dig himself out, his ears ringing and head pounding. He rose to his knees and saw Whistler standing only a few strides away. The bounty hunter held his hammer in one hand, its pick end slick with Haelynn's blood. In his other hand, he held his exotic crossbow. Jace knew the weapon could release six bolts in rapid succession. Even if he ran and the man missed the first few shots, he would not miss them all. Once slowed, the hammer would finish him.

A wave of dizziness struck, and Jace fell sideways. He caught himself on a crate, the man before him splitting into multiple images.

Whistler laughed. "Looksss like you rattled your brainsss in the fall."

Jace readied himself, hoping he might get a lucky knife throw before the man impaled him with a bolt.

"Sssorry I had to kill Haelynn."

"Why?" Jace cried.

"It wasss only busssinesss." Whistler's smile melted into a hardened scowl. "Important people want you dead, Jerrell."

"How important?"

"A contract worth a hundred gold."

Jace groaned inwardly. For that sum, Whistler would not stop short of killing him.

"Time to die, Jerrell." Whistler extended his arm and took aim, unaware of the shadow approaching from behind.

A blade crashed down, severing Whistler's arm as Jerrell dove to the side, two bolts passing between his arm and torso before striking the crates. He made it to his hands and knees in time to see Whistler swing his hammer at someone. The attacker dodged the wild blow and thrust, driving a longsword through the bounty hunter's midriff. The man yanked the blade free and pulled back, his face still masked by shadow. Whistler fell to his knees, wobbled, and collapsed to his side, his stomach and bloodied stump of an arm bleeding profusely.

The man approached Jace, looming over him. Lightning flashed across the sky, giving Jace a brief glimpse of his benefactor. He had dark skin and darker eyes with a shaved head and a body as muscular as any warrior Jace had seen. This mysterious savior left Jace worried about his motives.

"Who are you?" Jace asked, rising and backing away.

Rather than reply, the man shouted. "Harley! I found him!"

Still reeling from dizziness, Jace placed a hand on the wall. Footsteps came from the street, a woman running into the alley.

She slowed, the disk of light she gripped illuminating her face. It was a face he recognized.

"Harlequin?" Jace asked.

The woman grinned. "Jerrell Landish. You are a hard man to find."

The sky opened and it began to pour.

Jace rushed through the rain, around the corner, and toward the door of the Blue Hen with Harlequin and her dark-skinned companion close behind. His shoulder sore and head still throbbing, he ducked into the dry interior and scanned the dining room. Roughly half the tables were occupied, the patrons eating, drinking, and laughing. The air smelled of roasted chicken. The building was dimly lit by the enchanted lanterns Jace had given to the owner years earlier.

A few patrons turned to watch as he entered the room, but he decided that they were staring at his wet, disheveled state rather than viewing him as a target. Holding his hand to the wound on his head, he approached the bar where a husky middle-aged woman stood with her back to him. She turned around, her gaze sweeping the bar before landing on him.

"Hello, Frella," he said.

Rather than smile as expected, she arched a brow. "Jerrell. I thought my taproom was now beneath you."

He removed his hand, his palm covered in blood.

Frella's plentiful chest expanded as she inhaled, her eyes widening. "You're bleeding."

"Yes. I noticed." He glanced at the couple beside him. "We need a place to discuss something in private."

The barkeep nodded. "The back room is vacant."

"Perfect."

She raised her voice, "Shar!"

A young woman in a gray dress and stained apron spun toward the bar. She had a pair of empty tankards in each hand, her eyes the same green as the barkeep. "Yes, Mother?"

"Watch the bar. I'll be back in a few minutes."

"Alright," Shar then smiled, her tone becoming smooth and sultry. "Hello, Jerrell."

He forced a smile in return. "Good to see you, Shar. You are as pretty as ever."

Her grin widened. She appeared ready to say more, but a patron caught her attention and Jace turned away.

Frella arched a brow. "You know to stay away from her…"

He held his hands up. "I know. I know. Besides, I am betrothed. My wedding is just days away."

"Exactly," Frella said. "Keep it in your pants. As much as I like you, Shar is too young and you too much a rogue for anyone so sweet to handle."

Harlequin burst out laughing and thumped Jace on the back, eliciting a grunt from him. "She knows you well, Jerrell."

He sighed. "Let's go to the back room."

Nodding, Frella headed to the end of the bar and led them down a corridor. They passed the kitchen, where a young man was pulling a whole chicken off a spit. It was Gar, Frella's son and Shar's twin brother. When he was younger, Gar used to follow Jace around, wishing to become a thief. Frella would not have it, demanding he make an honest life for himself. One day, Frella would die or retire and the Blue Hen would go to the twins. It was not a life Jace would choose, but he could think of far worse.

Frella opened the door to a small room, the walls lined with shelving stocked with supplies. There was a round table and four chairs in the middle. "Take a seat. I'll get something for that knob on your head."

"Thanks," Jace said as he collapsed into a chair.

"Would you three care for food?" Frella's gaze swept them, landing on Jace. "And ale?"

Crusser responded first. "Food sounds good."

"Ale sounds better," Harlequin noted.

"Alright. Food and drinks for everyone," the barkeep said. "I'll be right back."

She closed the door as they all sat. Jace released another grunt from the pain in his shoulder. With a noisy thud, Crusser set Whistler's brass crossbow on the table.

"Careful with that thing," Jace said. "As I understand, it's always loaded and will fire a bolt if you trip the trigger."

Harlequin stared at Jace. "You knew the man who tried to kill you."

He nodded. "I did. His name was Whistler. A bounty hunter. I've hired him for a few contracts, one just a week ago."

She frowned. "I wonder how Tranadal found him so quickly. We had only just arrived in Lionne."

Jace held his palm toward her. "Please. Start at the beginning. Where have you been for the past year?" He glanced at Crusser. "And how do I know I can trust you two?"

She went on to explain the situation and how it had led her to Farrowen. Jace listened closely, seeking any sign of falsehoods, the motive behind her actions, and Crusser's role in the entire thing. When she finished, he frowned in thought.

"You followed Whistler from Lionne, which is where you last saw this dark elf. You also said you overheard him stating he was going to the castle."

She nodded. "That's right."

He sat back and rubbed his jaw. "Montague is high wizard in Lionne. He is an arrogant, ambitious wizard who has reason to hate me. I saw him not long ago, and he claimed to have gotten over our past, even expressing his best wishes toward both me and Narine." His mouth twisted in a grimace. "I doubted every word at the time, and now, it appears he might play a role in all this. It all seems too coincidental.

"However, what concerns me most is Tranadal telling Whistler that plans to deal with the queen were in motion. Undoubtedly, he means Narine. I need to get back to the palace, so I can take the necessary precautions."

The door opened, Frella appearing with a trio of foam-topped mugs in one hand, a bowl of water in the other, a small white towel draped over her arm. She set the tankards, bowl, and towel on the table. They each grabbed an ale and took a deep drink, Jace setting his tankard down and wiping foam from his lips with the back of his hand. Frella dipped the towel in the water and lifted it to the side of his head, patting the wound. He winced at the pain but allowed her to clean it. There was no arguing with Frella.

When she finished, Jace dug into his coat, fished out a coin purse, and set it on the table, sliding it toward Frella.

"What's this?" she asked.

"You'll find eleven gold pieces and a handful of silver inside."

She arched a brow. "That is a large sum."

"Consider it payment."

"For what?"

He sighed. "Haelynn is dead."

Frella pulled the towel back and stared at him. "Are you serious?"

"Yes."

Her eyes softened. "What happened?"

"A man killed her to get to me."

Sadness turned to anger. "What man?' she growled.

"The dead one in the alley outside."

"Good," she nodded. "Did you do it?"

Jace pointed at Crusser. "That pile of muscle over there did it before I got the chance."

The bruising warrior set down a chicken leg stripped of meat. "Seems he was about to kill you when I arrived."

"I've been in worse situations."

Crusser chuckled. "If you say so."

Jace looked back at Frella. "Haelynn is in her room. She was naked when I found her. Please see that she is treated well and receives a proper funeral."

Frella nodded. "You know I will."

"I knew I could trust you, Frella. The coin will pay for it and more. Keep the apartment empty for now. I need to decide what to do with it."

The woman rinsed the rag, turning the water in the bowl crimson. "I'll give you a year."

When she reached for his head again, Jace pushed her hand away. "I need to leave. Narine might be in danger." He took another deep drink and stood. "Are you coming to the wedding?"

Frella smiled. "Nothing could stop me. Even if it were not the most talked of event in Marquithe in decades, I must be there to wish my friend a good and happy life."

He put his hand on her cheek. "You are a good woman. Stay well, and I will see you in a few days."

When he opened the door, Harlequin slammed her empty tankard on the table. "We are coming with you."

Crusser, whose face and hands were covered in chicken grease, paused. "We are?"

"Fine," Jace said. "So long as you don't mind staying at a palace."

Harlequin tilted her head in thought. "Are the beds soft?"

"So soft, you'll think you're sleeping on a cloud."

Crusser asked, "The food is good?"

"You'll wonder how you ever survived without it."

They glanced at each other, Harlequin saying, "We don't really have anywhere else to go, so…why not?"

Tired, head throbbing, and stomach twisting over anxiety for Narine's safety, Jace suddenly found himself in the company of someone as fond of snarky comments as himself.

He sighed. "I suddenly understand why others get so annoyed with me."

22

TAINTED

The balcony outside Narine's chamber was cool, the palace obscuring the morning sun and coating the balcony in shade. Narine wrapped a shawl over her exposed shoulders for warmth as she sat at the table, the maid having already dried the furniture after a rainy evening. Peering over the railing, she gazed over the city of Marquithe.

In the bright sunlight, the pale buildings shone brightly, the streets dotted by puddles, another reminder of the storm. A squad of Thundercorps soldiers marched down the street beyond the palace walls, heading toward the palace square, its gates still unopened.

She sighed, still concerned about finding the other side of her bed empty when she woke. There were times when Jace would quietly slip out of the room while she slept, but not without leaving a note or telling her of his plans beforehand.

A knock came from the door to her chamber, and she called out, "Come in."

Two servants, a man in a dark blue coat and trousers and a woman in a navy and white dress, entered the room. Each carried a large tray as they crossed through the chamber and emerged on the balcony.

"Your breakfast, Your Majesty," the man said as he gave a shallow bow.

"On the table will be fine, Lindley."

He set down three plates, silverware, and goblets, filling the latter with grape juice. The woman unloaded her tray, placing fresh fruit, steaming sausages, and a basket of warm bread on the table. Lastly, she set a plate before Narine, the contents hidden beneath a metal dome. The servants then bowed and turned to leave. From inside the chamber, the corridor door opened.

Lindley's voice carried from inside. "Good morning, Captain."

The door closed. Narine heard the tap of approaching footsteps as Captain Henton materialized on the balcony.

The tall man bowed. "Hello, my queen. I hope you are well on this fine morning."

"Yes," she muttered half-heartedly. More urgently, she added, "Have you seen Jace?"

"I'm sorry." He shook his head. "The chancellor was not in his office. Perhaps he already left for the day?"

Henton knew Jace ran the intelligence network, but he was not aware of the role Jace played as the Charlatan. The captain occasionally asked where Jace went during the day, but the thief always proved adept at avoiding such questions. There were times when his slippery nature irked Narine, but in this, she could hardly fault him. *Henton is in charge of the city watch and is too pragmatic to find humor or irony from learning that Jace, the man who gave him orders, was in charge of the thieves as well.*

She sighed. "I was afraid you might say that."

"Is something amiss?"

Yes. Someone tried to kill him last night. However, even as Narine healed Jace, he had made her promise to keep the information a secret. Thus, she used a far more mundane excuse. "Jace was to dine with me this morning. He has been busy of late, and with the wedding just two days away, I wish to ensure everything has been addressed."

Henton nodded as he slid two sausages onto his plate. "I understand."

Curious, Narine lifted the metal cover from her plate. The sweet aroma made her smile. Covered in a red sauce, two hot pastries filled with berries sat on the plate. She did not eat such things often, but the kitchen staff knew how much she loved the dish, as did Jace, causing her to wonder which had decided to gift her with such a delicious treat. *I should not eat all of this, or it will go to my hips.* She had lost weight during her adventures a year prior, some of which had returned since she took the throne. While busy, the life of a queen did not include much physical activity, requiring her to take care with her diet. With the ceremony looming, her wedding dress was already tight, and she was determined to wear it without need of alterations.

"Would you like one?" She held her plate toward Henton.

"You don't want them?"

"One will do. Go on. I know you like this dish as well."

"Yes, I do. Thank you." He used his fork to slide a pastry from her plate to his, taking a third of the sauce before handing her the bowl of sausages in exchange.

With a sausage on her plate next to the pastry, Narine lifted her knife and began to cut.

The door to the chamber opened, and Jace entered with two others close behind. He crossed the room to the balcony.

"Sorry I'm late," he said.

A muscular Kyranni man in a leather jerkin stood to one side of him. To the other was a tall woman with dark hair and a black wide-brimmed hat. Anger stirring, Narine squeezed her fork rather than reach for her magic.

"Hello, Narine," Harlequin said with a smirk.

Rather than reply, Narine turned to Jace. "What is *she* doing here?"

Jace rolled his eyes. "Harlequin and her friend are staying at the palace at my request."

"Right before our wedding?"

He sighed. "You and I need to have a discussion. In private."

Narine stood, lips pressed together. "Yes. We do."

She stormed past him, Harlequin backing inside to clear the path. Narine crossed the living area and headed toward the bedroom. Once inside, she spun around and glared at Jace.

The moment he closed the door, she asked, "Why is *she* here?"

"Your life is in danger."

Her anger faltered. "What do you mean?"

"My head injury from last night was the result of a contract out on my life. Apparently, the intent was to get me out of the way so you would be easier to assassinate."

"Are you sure? How could you know…"

"Narine." He moved closer and rested his hands on her hips. "You know me. I would never tell you such a thing unless I believed it to be true."

"What should we do about it?"

"I am working on that."

As she considered the situation and the timing, concerns she had buried resurfaced. "Please tell me you won't cancel the wedding." For most of the last year, she had secretly feared he might scheme a way out of the betrothal.

Jace touched her face and gave her a sad smile. "Never."

She then recalled their new guests. "What of that wench and her companion?"

"Harley and Crusser? Well, in truth, they rescued me from a bad spot last night. Afterward, they shared useful and interesting information that points toward a larger scheme."

"And must they stay here?"

"Don't worry. Last night, I set them up in two vacant quarters connected to the Palace Temple."

"Rooms that were used by the dead clerics?"

"Yes. These two can cause little trouble from there and would be challenged should they attempt to enter the palace without a proper escort."

She nodded, accepting it as a reasonable compromise.

"I also wanted you to know I received a missive from Illustan today."

"Priella?"

"Yes."

"How is she?"

"Very pregnant."

"She still has not had the child?"

"No. As a result, she is currently bedridden. She and Kollin will not be coming to the wedding."

Narine sighed. "That's too bad. We haven't seen them in a year, and I was looking forward to them visiting." Another thought arose and she smirked. "You know, I could just..."

"No," he said firmly. "We agreed to keep that particular magic secret. As it stands, too many know of it, even if they cannot replicate it. Yet."

She sighed. "Alright, I..."

"Jerrell!" Harlequin's shout carried through the closed door. "Come quick!"

He spun, threw the door open, and rushed out with Narine close behind.

Harlequin stood near the balcony door. Outside, her companion squatted near the table, his broad back to them. The man looked over his shoulder, revealing Henton lying on the balcony floor, his eyes swollen, foam from his mouth running down his face.

Narine gasped and raced out, falling to her knees beside Henton. She drew in her magic, the raw power of life filling her, lifting her soul into a state of euphoria. Casting a construct of repair, a complex pattern appearing around her open palm, she rested her hand on his head and poured magic through it, attempting to heal his poison-ravaged body.

Nothing happened. It was too late. Even she could not heal the dead.

Crestfallen, she released the spell and dismissed her magic. The world turned back to normal. A tear traced down her face as her hand rested on the dead man's forehead.

Jace squatted and pulled the fork from Henton's grip. It was coated in red sauce. He sniffed it, frowning. Tongue extended, he gave the fork a tentative lick. A moment later, he turned his head and spat.

He said, "Sylbane powder. Deadly, but it leaves a metallic aftertaste. Someone added it to the berry sauce."

Eyes widening, Narine gasped. "Berry sauce?"

He looked at her, nodding. "Someone knew how much you enjoy the sauce and pastry. This was meant for you, Henton merely collateral damage. Had things gone differently…"

She looked down at the dead man, his bulging eyes staring toward the morning sky. It had been a near thing, Narine ready to take her first bite when Jace arrived. If she had not become angry about Harlequin being with him, she would be dead as well.

Jace stood, grimacing down at Henton's body. "The wedding is off."

Narine burst to a stance. "What?!"

He pointed toward the corpse at his feet, angry. "Someone is trying to kill you, Narine! Twice, they have failed, and we have no way of knowing when the next attempt might come. Henton was an obstacle, and he is now dead. They paid a large contract to kill me and rid themselves of another. Whoever is behind this…they have the coin, contacts, and ambition to see it through."

Feeding off his anger, she drew herself up, her volume rising above his. "Would you have me succumb to fear? Should I hole myself up in my palace, never to emerge, never to live freely? If I bend to fear imposed by others, they win." She shook her head, setting her jaw in determination. "As queen, I cannot bend to acts of terror. I will marry you in public, as planned, and will use it as a platform to prove I am stronger than my enemies."

Jace opened his mouth to retort, the anger in his eyes softening. He took her hand in his, tone pleading, "I fear I cannot protect you in such a public event."

Narine yanked her hand away, forming it into a fist as she closed on him, nostrils flaring. "Admit it. You don't wish to marry me."

He jerked back as if she had slapped him. "Narine, how can you think that?"

"You delayed the date twice and until convincing me to set it a year out from the day the gods died, stating you wished to give the public cause to see it as a day of celebration rather than one of loss. Now, after all your promises, you wish to cancel."

Jace put his hand on her arm. "Come now, Narine. Be reasonable."

She shouted, "I don't want to be reasonable! I want to be your wife! I want you to give me your heart with thousands to witness it. You claim you love me, yet you persist with secrets and excuses, constantly stirring doubts I thought quelled." Lips pressed together, she glared at him. "If you love me, you will find a way to make this work."

Looking toward the city, he stared into space for a few breaths and nodded. "Very well." He turned back toward her. "We will proceed as planned, but I have much to do and little time to see it done."

Still gripping Narine's arm, he pulled her past Harlequin and Crusser and opened the door to the hallway. The two guards in the corridor both turned toward him.

Jace said, "There has been an attempt on the queen's life."

The guards' eyes widened.

"Do not worry. She is fine, but Captain Henton was not so lucky." He backed away and gestured toward the balcony, the man's corpse visible through the open door. "He was poisoned. I need you to remove his body."

Dirk, the elder of the two guards, asked, "What should we do with him?"

"Bring his body to Lieutenant Giralt. He is now in charge of the palace guards and is to immediately sequester the kitchen and serving staff for questioning. Hold them in Henton's office. I will be down shortly to conduct the investigation personally."

With Dirk in the lead, the two men approached Henton. One gripped his arms, the other, his legs.

As they headed toward the corridor, Dirk stopped and looked at Narine. "Who is going to guard your door?'

Jace pointed to Harlequin and her muscular companion. "These two will take your post until you return."

The guards nodded and faded into the corridor with Henton's corpse drooping between them.

Harlequin arched a brow. "So, we are now guards?"

"Try to keep an open mind. You will likely find yourself playing many different roles before this is finished."

Crusser shrugged. "Doesn't bother me."

She snorted. "Of course, it doesn't. Nothing bothers you." She led him into the corridor, crossed her arms, and leaned against the wall. "This had better pay well."

Crusser snorted. "For guarding a door?"

"You wanted my help," Jace said. "Give me time to plan. I'll be of no help to you if I'm dead, so guard the door well."

"Fine," she sighed. "And when the guards return?"

"Go back to your rooms. I'll come find you later. Don't worry. I'll keep you busy. There is much to do and few I can trust." Pushing the door closed, he turned to Narine. "Follow me."

He led her into the bedroom, closed the door, and turned to her. "If you are determined to hold the wedding as scheduled, I need something first."

Narine smiled, sensing her victory. "What would you have of me?"

"I wish to borrow your anklet."

She gasped. "Why?"

He gave her a sad smile. "I am aware of how much you value it. It will return to your ankle prior to the wedding, but for now, I need it."

She looked down at her skirts, the enchanted anklet hiding beneath them. Since acquiring it over a year earlier, she had not removed the item. Not once. Not to bathe, not during sex...not ever. Taking a deep breath, she told herself, *You will still have the added magic of the hand chains.* She raised her leg and placed her slippered foot on the bed, lifting her skirts.

He gently rubbed his hand up her exposed calf, the action sending quivers up Narine's leg, causing her pulse to quicken.

His eyes filled with emotion as he said, "While your beauty had me smitten from the start, you are among the brightest and bravest women I know. Few would proceed as you intend and fewer would do so by placing blind faith in their mate." His hand roamed over her knee, back down her calf, and to the golden bracelet.

Heart racing, she gave him a coy smile. "You are far too smooth, Mister Landish. One might think you wish to seduce the item off me."

Pressing the hidden release, the bracelet popped open and into his hand. "I just realized that we are alone." He set the bracelet on a table beside the door and slid his arms around her waist. "With what we face, such opportunities might be rare and infrequent." Their lips met, the kiss light and tentative. He leaned closer, his breath tickling her ear. "Perhaps we should seize the moment?"

His lips brushed her neck, again and again, rising to her ear. Breath coming in gasps and heart racing, Narine melted into his embrace, her victory complete.

23

MACHINATIONS

Rolling hills, covered by crops or grazing cattle, passed by as Montague stared out the window, his thoughts lost in the steady noise of his private carriage rumbling over the paved roadway. While louder than gravel, the reliable state of Farrowen roads made for faster travel. Legend said it took a thousand men two decades to complete the roads, building them brick by brick, from border to border. *At least Pherelyn left some legacy other than tales of horror.* Farrowen's lone female wizard lord had died many centuries earlier, her rule tainted by a misuse of her magic. Afterward, women had been forbidden to rise to a crystal throne until Priella Ueordlin became queen of Pallanar. Just as Pherelyn had, Priella misused her magic in an attempt to conquer the world. *I wonder if she might have succeeded had the gods not died, her power contracting to a fraction of a wizard lord.* Such musings had become irrelevant. Without the gods, there could be no wizard lords. Montague grinned at the opportunity before him.

His new advisor, Tranadal, sat across from him. He was an odd sort, quiet and brooding. With his strange eyes, pointed ears, and pallid complexion, Montague understood why Tranadal preferred to keep his hood raised. *I would as well.*

The carriage slowed to a stop, the rumble ceased, and the clopping of approaching hooves rose above the din.

Montague turned to Vordan who sat beside him. "Go and see why we are stopped."

The man grunted, stepped out, and closed the carriage door behind him. His muffled voice rose, another replying, the words unintelligible although the voice was clearly female.

When Vordan opened the carriage door, he backed away. A woman stood beside him, tall and lean, dressed in breeches and a brown vest over a tunic and a gray cloak over her shoulders. She pulled the hood back to reveal cropped hair and oversized facial features – large eyes and an even bigger nose. Montague recognized her as the scout sent to follow the assassin hired by Tranadal.

Vordan turned toward the open door. "Go on, Dionna. Tell the high wizard what you told me."

The woman pursed her full lips and nodded. "As commanded, I followed Whistler to Marquithe. On the day he arrived, he broke into an apartment. I heard screams from inside, apparently from the woman who lived there. An hour later, the bounty hunter emerged. I followed him to a nearby square where he dropped something into a beggar's cup and then sped off."

"The man returned to the same area as before, climbed to a rooftop, and watched the alley leading to the stairs of the woman's apartment. When it grew dark, another man showed up. I believe he was the target of the contract. This man entered that same building by climbing a rope and sliding in through a window. While the target was inside, Whistler reappeared on the stairs to the woman's apartment, and waited outside the door until the man came out. In a surprise attack, Whistler knocked the man off the stairs and then went after him. The target was sure to die until a warrior entered the alley and chopped Whistler's arm right off. A moment later, the bounty hunter was dead."

"A woman dressed in breeches with a black hat entered the alley. Judging by the snippets I heard, she knew the target and the big warrior was her companion. It began to pour, so the three of them ducked into a neighboring taproom. A while later, they emerged. The rain had died down to a sprinkle, but they were difficult to follow."

The messenger frowned. "After two streets, I lost them. I made for the palace, thinking it might be their destination, but was unable to find any trace of them again. Since it was dark, the city gates sealed, and still raining, I purchased a room for the night and rode north at sunup. That was five hours ago."

Montague listened to every word with care, keeping his emotions in check. He had heard the stories and knew the truth of it. The thief's luck was beyond comprehension, so Montague had placed little hope in Whistler's success. As a result, he was disappointed but not discouraged.

"Thank you, Dionna," Montague said.

"What of the missive I sent with you?" Tranadal asked.

The woman replied, "As instructed, I gave it to the palace guards, who were instructed to see it delivered to the serving maid."

"Did they read it?"

Dionna nodded. "Yes. The sergeant on duty even offered his condolences, but only after asking how the man mentioned in the note had come across sylbane poison. I told him I did not know, but the family was reputed to have been in a squabble against a neighboring vineyard. I suggested that the other family planned to kill off their competition and an investigation was underway."

"What a wonderful tale, Dionna," Montague said with a grin. "You have a knack for this. You may return to Lionne to rest. We may need your services again soon."

The woman bowed, "Yes, High Wizard."

As she turned toward her horse, Vordan called up to the driver. "Continue to Marquithe. We must arrive before they close the gates."

The captain climbed back into the carriage, closed the door, and settled on the seat beside Montague. With a lurch, the carriage sprang forward and continued the uphill drive to Marquithe.

Finger to his cheek, Montague arched a brow at Tranadal. "It appears your bounty hunter has met his match."

The Drow suggested, "Perhaps his reputation was not justified."

"Oh, I am sure it was justified. However, not all bounties are the same. Landish has proven time and again difficult to kill." Montague smirked. "Did you know he is rumored to have killed four wizard lords?"

Tranadal's eyes narrowed. "Wizard lords are reputedly invincible...or they were before the gods died."

"Yes, they were. Still, many died leading up to the Battle of Balmor. How this one man, this conniving thief, could have had a hand in so many deaths,

I do not know. However, even if he killed only one, it was an achievement few throughout history could claim."

Tranadal grimaced. "If you doubted this bounty hunter's ability, why did I pay him?"

"Simple." Montague smiled. "It was a test to ensure your intentions. If you intended to turn me in to the queen, you never would have paid to have her betrothed killed. Even now, I have witnesses ready to declare you the mastermind behind the attempt...including Dionna, who witnessed the hired hand attack Landish."

The Drow nodded. "Astute and commendable. However, that brings you no closer to the throne." A smirk turned his lips up at the corners. "Perhaps my contact within the palace will have more success. If so, the throne might already be empty by the time we reach Marquithe."

"You never told me, how do you know this maid? What makes you believe she will understand your message and follow through with the poisoning?"

Tranadal gazed out the window with narrowed eyes. Finally, he said, "I am a representative of a secret organization, one with agents throughout the world." He turned toward Montague. "Our leaders would like to see you upon the throne, the rule and future of Farrowen resting in your hands. This maid is an agent, oft used as a source of information from within the palace. This missive, mentioning her father, Astra, would have meaning to her, as would the suggestion that sylbane poison had claimed his life. She knew she might one day have to poison the ruler of Farrowen, likely believing it would be a wizard lord like Malvorian or even Thurvin. This woman will do as she must."

"What if she is captured? Landish is clever and likely to track down anyone with access to the queen's food."

"Do not worry," Tranadal's gaze returned to the rolling hills slipping past. "It is impossible to garner any useful information from the dead."

"This woman will kill herself?"

"As she knew she must should this come to pass." Tranadal shrugged. "Sacrifices must be made to ensure the future. All who join the Order know this."

The statement was a revelation to Montague, leaving him wondering what, exactly, the Order was and why they sought to see him upon the throne. *Should I be concerned?* he wondered. *Still, Tranadal has proven he has both gold and contacts I do not possess. I would be a fool to turn down such assistance and can worry about his motives when the throne is mine.*

Montague asked, "What if this poisoning fails and the queen still lives?"

"Then," Tranadal said, "We will find another means to eliminate the woman and her betrothed. It seems to me, this wedding might present an ideal opportunity. When we arrive in Marquithe, I will have my people investigate the event. Be it the schedule, venue, or planned protection, there will be a weak point rife for exploitation. Once identified, we will focus our efforts toward that end." The man smiled. "Do not worry, High Wizard. The throne will soon be yours."

24

SUBTLE SORCERY

A loud crack echoed in the Willola Manor great room, the impact jarring Lang's hands.

"What was that?" Willola's voice called from upstairs.

"Set it down," Lang said softly, hesitating to reply to the wizardess's question and hoping Olban might. Instead, the steward stared at the splintered doorframe, his eyes round with fear. Sighing, Lang took a deep breath and bellowed. "The table struck the door frame to the dining hall."

Willola's voice came from above, and she peered over the railing. "Is the frame damaged?"

"Yes. Badly." Lang said. Olban backed away until his back was pinned against the wall.

The wizardess came down the stairs in a rush, slowing when she reached the bottom and scowling at them. "My party is tomorrow." Her voice raised two octaves. "Tomorrow!" Fists at her sides, she spun toward Lang, her lips white and eyes glaring. "How did this happen?"

How did I ever think this woman was beautiful? The ugliness inside her taints anything on the exterior. He patted his own chest. "It was my fault. I stumbled while backing through the doorway."

She twisted her lip and stared at him with narrowed eyes.

He spoke before she could reply. "I know a carpenter. He is skilled and works fast. I am sure he could replace the frame in a day."

The wizardess raised her brow. "An arched doorframe in one day?"

He nodded. "I believe so."

"Go get him. I want it done, and it had better be perfect, whatever the cost." Her scowl went from one man to the other, then to the furniture between them. "You two are lucky it was the old table. If it had been the new one, you'd be wishing you were dead." She spun away and climbed the stairs.

When she was gone, Lang gestured toward the table. "Pick it up. We still need to get it out of here. Once the new one is inside, I'll go find that carpenter."

Olban wiped sweat from his forehead while glancing upstairs. In a hushed voice, he said, "I thought she might destroy you. How did you stumble anyway?"

Shrugging, Lang said, "It just happened. It's not like anyone stumbles on purpose." *Except this one time.*

They each grabbed one end of the table and lugged it past the stairwell and toward the front entrance of the manor.

The doorframe pulsed as if alive. It was odd to see a frame standing by itself in the center of the workshop, odder to see the crimson glow emitting from it. The glow faded, dimming the shop.

Vex backed away from it, his tattoo-covered torso glistening with sweat. "It is done."

Trepidation thrummed in Lang's gut. "What will happen when we touch it?"

Laughing, Vex picked up his black cloak. "Nothing at all."

"If I walk through it?"

"Still nothing."

Lang rubbed his jaw. "So it only works on wizards?"

"In a way, yes." The sorcerer pulled his cloak around his shoulders. "The gateway is subtle in nature, one of the most difficult spells to detect, regardless of a wizard or sorcerer's skill."

Narrowing his eyes, Lang glared at the man. "You are overly fond of speaking in riddles."

The man chuckled again. "When wine passes through this gateway, it alters in nature, ever so slightly. Alcohol affects one's blood, wizards as much as anyone. Wizard's blood has far more metal than the Ungifted. The altered wine will coat the metal and reduce its conductivity."

Fixing the man with a grimace, Lang shook his head. "Somehow, your explanation is worse than the riddle."

Vex rolled his eyes. "They will have a difficult time wielding magic."

Arms spread wide, Lang blurted, "Why didn't you say so in the first place?"

The sorcerer turned and opened the door, waving to the man standing outside. "Merrick. Come in and help this man load the frame into the wagon."

The carpenter peered inside, appearing nervous. "What were you doing in here anyway?"

"I told you." Vex patted the frame. "I was to bless the door in the name of Gheald. It is for good luck, to bestow a blessing over anyone who passes through."

Merrick's brow furrowed as he approached the frame. "I have never heard that one before."

Lang replied, "Wizardess Willola is most devout to her god. Best not to question her. In fact, I suggest you never broach the subject with her. At best, you'll get an earful. At worst...you don't want to know."

The man snorted. "Other than taking their gold, the less I have to do with wizards, the better."

They picked up the frame, the temporary brace across the bottom holding it together as they carried it out and set it in the wagon bed. In the sunlight, it became clear that the brown stain on the door was noticeably darker than the wagon bed.

"Are you sure the stain is the same as the door?" he asked.

Merrick nodded. "Yeah. I paid close attention when I measured the doorway."

The man's visit to the estate had occurred two days earlier, while Willola was in bed and the servants were busy in the kitchen. At the time, the carpenter had asked why Willola wanted to replace a perfectly good frame.

In response, Lang told him it was poor form to question the actions of a wizard. Appearing satisfied, Merrick focused on the project and the gold he was offered for the job.

Lang climbed onto the wagon and sat beside Merrick, casting one last glance at Vex, who stood in the shadowed recess of the doorway. The sorcerer gave him a nod, lips moving, his voice whispering in Lang's ear as if he were inches away. "Harbin must die tonight."

The weight of the statement sent a chill down Lang's spine. He had killed men in battle and in duels before a crowd of thousands, but what Vex asked of him now was murder.

The wagon eased forward, drawn by the carpenter's old workhorse.

After the wagon turned at the next intersection, Merrick said, "I still don't understand. Why does the wizardess need a new doorframe? The other one was flawless."

Still haunted by Vex's voice in his head, Lang gave the man beside him a sidelong look. "Do not tell anyone, but Willola is also a witch – able to predict the future. She foresaw the frame getting damaged and demanded a new one made before her gala."

Merrick's eyes widened. "Truly?"

"When we arrive at the estate, you will see for yourself."

25

MURDER

It was a dark night, a thick layer of clouds obscuring the stars and the ever-present full moon. Scowling, Lang squatted on the stable roof, a dagger in his hand and a sword on his hip. *I hate this. I am no thief and am not meant to be creeping about in the dark.* More so, he despised waiting. It often seemed his entire life had been spent waiting for something – a woman, a job, his next fight, his employer...his own death. *And here I am... waiting...again.*

The clopping of hooves arose, joined by the rumble of wheels on cobble-stone. A horse-drawn carriage stopped at the estate gate. Lang heard distant voices, the words unintelligible. Two guards opened the gate, a low creak echoing in the night.

I can't do this...it's wrong. He started to turn away when a voice whispered in his ear and he saw an image of Vex shimmering in his mind's eye.

"You will be a hero to the people, praised as a liberator, the one who shattered the shackles crafted by the wizards." Vex made a fist, fire-filled eyes boring into Lang's soul. *"Kill the wizard and his driver. It must appear like a robbery."*

Once Lang's resolve solidified, the image faded, all other thoughts drowned by the clopping hooves and rumbling wheels as the carriage ascended the curved cobblestone drive that ran past Harbin Manor. When the carriage drew near the stables, the driver pulled the reins, the horses slowing to a stop.

Lang crept to the roof's edge, gripped his knife, and leapt. He landed on the seat, his momentum driving the dagger downward, into the driver's chest. The man's mouth opened in a silent scream, but Lang held him still as he died. *I'm sorry.*

A man's voice came from inside the wagon. "What was that?"

Another said, "Get out there and do your job!"

The carriage door opened, a big guard diving out, rolling, and drawing his sword as he rose to his feet. Lang's longsword sang as he yanked it from its scabbard. He jumped with a downward strike. The other guard blocked it, a mighty clang ringing in the night. His opponent kicked, forcing Lang backward. He eyed the man, gauging his balance, and waited for the next attack. With a roar, the man swung. Lang blocked a strike from the right and another from the left. He then feigned a swing but pulled his blade back, bent, and swept his leg around, hooking the other man's ankle. With a cry, the guard fell on his backside. Lang raised his blade for the killing blow, but it never landed.

Something invisible tightened around his waist and lifted him off the ground. He swung wildly, trying to cut anything within range, but he was helpless. Five feet off the ground, his body spun around to find a man in dark robes standing beside the carriage, one hand extended toward Lang, the other on his hip.

It was the wizard, Harbin.

With the flick of Harbin's wrist, Lang's sword twisted, forcing him to release it lest the force break his arm. The sword clattered to the cobblestone drive as the two guards from the gate ran in holding weapons.

The wizard turned toward them. "I have this under control. Mycka, Devin, inspect the manor for any other intruders." As the men ran toward the building, the wizard turned back toward Lang. "Which are you?" the man asked. "Foolish or suicidal?"

Lang frowned. "What?"

"I ask because only a man lacking good sense or one who wishes to die would attack a wizard of my caliber."

With a shaky voice Lang pleaded, "Please. I...I did not know. I needed gold to save my wife. She is sick, and I can't afford to pay a wizardess to heal her…"

"Enough!" The wizard roared. "I care nothing for you or your wife." He strode closer and sneered. "Now, I must make an example out of you. I cannot allow anyone to believe they can cross Jalen Harbin, head of the Fastella Wizards Guild."

Focused on Lang, Harbin did not notice his own bodyguard slipping behind him. As the wizard raised his arms, ready to unleash some deadly spell, the guard struck. A foot of steel emerged from Harbin's chest. Harbin clutched at the blade, his eyes bulging in shock. His magic faltered, dropping Lang to the ground, where he stumbled before righting himself. The guard put a boot against the wizard's back and yanked his sword free. Harbin fell to his knees, wobbled as blood gurgled from his mouth, and fell over. Dead.

"Good timing, Balcor," Lang said to the guard.

"A moment later, and it would have been too late for you." Balcor turned toward the manor. "In addition to the two guards, four servants are inside the house. Should we kill them?"

Lang bent and claimed his sword. "No. It was bad enough that I had to kill the driver."

The other man looked down at the blade in his hand. "Should I clean the blood?"

"No. Claim you were unconscious and woke to find your sword covered in blood and me gone. Tell them that I must have used it to kill Harbin."

"Unconscious?"

"Yes. Sorry. This is going to hurt." Lang drove his hilt into the side of Balcor's head.

The man crumpled to the ground, just a stride from his former master.

Lang slid his own sword into the scabbard, picked up Balcor's sword, and drove it through the wizard a second time, just to make sure he was dead. Harbin lay still, his head turned to the side and his chin covered in sparkling blood.

Squatting, Lang gripped the pouch secured to the wizard's sash, and tore it free. The contents clanked, undoubtedly gold and silver. His attention shifted to the carriage driver, who lay dead beside the front wheel. The man, whose name Lang did not know, stared into infinity.

Lang felt no remorse for killing Harbin. The wizard was arrogant, selfish, and had regularly beaten his own wife until she committed suicide two seasons earlier. No, it would be the carriage driver's face that would haunt Lang's dreams…just another in an army who waited for him every night.

Turning from the gruesome scene, Lang ran down the drive, opened the gate, and slipped out. With calm confidence, he walked along a road bordered by brick walls and wrought-iron gates, slowing when he heard cries coming from the guild hall up ahead. An orange glow flickered in the night, shadows eclipsing a burning building. It was a building he knew well and had visited many times, first while escorting Parsec, later with Willola.

He headed toward the fire as shouts and cries echoed in the night, men calling for a bucket line. It was too late, for the fire had taken hold, the flames licking stone and the doors and interior already burning.

Starting the fire, an act executed by two fellow rebels, had been a key part of the plan, creating additional chaos while offering Lang an excuse to have left the Willola estate. Rushing ahead, he joined the bucket line that was forming, linking the building to a fountain two intersections away.

Two men ran past – one a young wizard with long yellow hair and dark robes, the other an armed guard wearing leather armor and a metal helm. Both were men Lang knew by sight. Wizard Roderan, a recent graduate from the University, was already among the most respected in Fastella. Despite Roderan's youth, Lang considered him most likely to run the guild once Harbin's death was discovered, for many of the most skilled wizards had died during the Farrowen invasion and subsequent Darkspawn War, leaving weak competition for positions of influence.

As Lang waited for the first bucket to arrive, he watched the wizard and his bodyguard.

Slowing as he drew near the fire, Roderan spread his arms and released a spell. The billowing smoke from the burning building was suddenly cut off, trapped inside a massive invisible cube that encompassed the entire structure. The flames died down, their glow fading until only smoke filled the cube. The wizard dropped his arms, the cube disappeared, and the smoke rose in a giant puff. Roderan leaned against his guard, Fencig, and panted from exertion.

Lang narrowed his eyes, considering what he had just witnessed. *The wizard smothered the flames by removing the air inside the building.* If a single wizard can do that… Roderan would pose a risk. Also troubling, his bodyguard, Fencig, was among the few who had not been recruited to the rebellion.

With the fire snuffed out , the bucket line fell apart before it had even begun, some members gathering near the burned building, others drifting off into the night. Lang turned away and continued down the road toward the Willola Estate, his mind consumed by worry.

The plan he and Vex had hatched was dangerous, but everyone knew facing wizards would come with risk. When the time came, they had to be ready. They would only get one chance.

Lang jerked awake as Willola opened the door and stormed into his room. A narrow strip of morning sunlight streamed through a gap in his curtains. The wizardess strode into the light and stared down at Lang, who was still in bed.

"Get up," she demanded. "I need you dressed and off to the harbor as soon as possible."

He sat up, dropping his feet to the floor, his torso exposed, and the covers still over his lap. "Why the rush?"

She pressed her fists against her hips. "I just got word…Harbin was murdered last night."

So, word travels fast. He rubbed his eyes. "A wizard murdered?" He frowned. "Didn't he become the guild leader after Parsec took the position of high wizard?"

"He did. While not quite Parsec's equal, he was strong with the Gift." She ran her hand though her long locks. "It is frightening to think a wizard of his stature could be murdered in cold blood."

"Did you hear how it happened?" Lang was genuinely curious to hear the story, knowing how easily details got twisted from one person to the next.

She crossed the room and pulled the curtains open, allowing bright sunlight to invade. "His guards claim a team of men, at least a dozen, attacked his carriage as it was pulling into his estate. They slaughtered Harbin and a few others. His personal guard, Balcor, was left for dead, but he survived. It was a miracle, they say."

Lang grunted. "Hard to believe anyone would risk attacking a wizard."

"Indeed...and on the same night the guild hall was set on fire."

Frowning, Lang tilted his head. "I had not considered that. Still, the hall did not burn down completely. Roderan spared the structure with his magic, although it will take time to clean it and replace what was burned."

Willola nodded. "That is precisely why I need you and Isaac down at the harbor as soon as possible. My party tomorrow night has become more than just another social gathering." A smile teased the corners of her lips. "With Harbin's death comes opportunity. The wizards council must have a leader. Thus, we will hold a vote for his replacement as soon as possible, but the guild hall cannot be used. With my event already in motion and many of the wizards already planning to attend, the Willola Estate becomes the venue of choice." Arms crossing over her chest, she smiled. "Everyone will be here. Everyone!" She laughed and clapped her hands, facing the ceiling as she slowly spun around. "The most important event of the year will be held here, at my estate. Praise Gheald for this opportunity."

By the gods, she is self-absorbed even for a wizard. "I am happy for you." Just saying the lie was painful. "But what does that have to do with me going to the harbor?"

She turned back to look at him, her smile replaced by her usual stern demeanor. "Olban just checked. We have but one wine barrel in the cellar. I had two more on order, due to arrive today, but that will not be enough with the expanded guest list."

She tossed a pouch at him. He snatched it inches from his face, the motion causing his covers to fall to the floor, leaving him exposed.

The woman arched a brow, her eyes on his nether region. "Too bad you are not a wizard or someone of means. You and I could have..." Her smile fell away as he knew it would. "It does not matter. There are two gold and a handful of silver pieces in there. Purchase as many barrels as you can. Farrowen's finest, mind you." She turned and walked back to the door, casting one last leer in his direction. "Yes...too bad."

Her padding footsteps faded down the corridor.

"Yes," he muttered. "Too bad a horrible person hides behind such beauty."

He glanced down at the pouch in his hands as Vex's voice whispered in his mind. *"Soon, she will be dead, along with all the others."*

26

RED BANDS

"Careful," Lang warned. "You break one of those barrels, I break your head."

The two dockworkers slid the barrel onto the wagon bed, each casting a scowl in his direction before turning back toward the ship. Since they said nothing, he let it slip. Better not to draw undue attention.

Another pair of men emerged from the hull, struggling beneath the weight of the barrel as they crossed the plank and stepped on the pier. Like the others, the barrel stood waist-high, the wooden slats held in place by rings of black metal. When the men reached the wagon, they tipped the barrel upright and slid it beside the others.

"That's five," Lang said. "One more to go."

The ship's captain approached with a sheet of paper, handing it to Lang. "There you are. Six barrels of Farrowen's finest."

Lang read the paper over, noting the total at the bottom. He opened his coin purse and fished out three gold pieces.

Flashing a grin, the captain tipped his hat. "Thank you, sir. I pray Wizardess Willola is pleased and will consider placing another order, for I will return to Fastella with another shipment in four weeks."

Grunting, Lang said, "We shall see."

The captain and Lang turned away from each other as the last barrel was loaded into the wagon. Holding the paper, he walked to the front of the wagon.

"All loaded, Isaac," he said to the driver. "I'll meet you at the harbormaster's office."

Isaac nodded, tipping his hat. "See you there, Lang."

Continuing past the wagon, Lang marched down the pier, glancing at the towering city walls looming above.

Fastella was built on an island where a river of the same name met the sea. In the distance, to both sides of the city, bridges arched over the waterway, connecting the island to the mainland. Crossing those bridges was the only land passage across the river within twenty miles.

With walls a hundred feet tall, a defensible harbor, and limited ability to reach the city by land, it was a wonder that an enemy army had successfully broken into Fastella a year ago. Prince Eldalain, a wizard of infamous power, had died during that battle. Very few knew the truth of Eldalain's death. Lang was among them, for his former master, Van Parsec, had a hand in the prince's demise. *I wonder if Parsec's thirst for vengeance is what gave the invaders the edge.*

Ironically, Farrowen had held the city for only a season before removing their forces and ceding control to the latest ruler, Queen Dalia. *So many twists and turns...why would I pursue the burden of kingship?* The answer was in his heart despite the doubts in his mind. He did not know if the rebellion would succeed, but he knew he had to try. All he had seen from the wizards was a selfish desire for power and money, without any regard for who they hurt to achieve it.

Upon reaching the shore, Lang glanced back to find the wagon rolling down the dock, drawn by two workhorses moving at a lazy walk. Following the waterfront road, he headed up a small hill to the harbormaster's office. There, a gray-haired man with a weathered, unshaven face and permanent scowl waited, elbows resting on a wooden counter beneath an open window.

"Six barrels of wine," Lang said as he slid the paper on the counter. "All shipped in from Farrowen, bound for the Willola Estate."

The man picked up the paper, eyes narrowing as he read it over. He handed it back to Lang. "Two silvers for loading the wagon, six more for import tax."

"A silver each?" *For doing nothing. This is why smugglers exist.* He dug out eight silver and slammed them on the counter.

The man produced a purple candle, tipping it so the wax dripped down. He then pressed a ring into the wax, marking it with the seal of his office.

Lang grabbed the paper and sneered. "I hope you choke on that silver."

As he turned away, the man said, "I ain't the one who makes the laws. I just hold to 'em."

One more reason why things need to change. He knew taxes existed to pay for soldiers, street repairs, and other necessities, but how much was wasted on nonsense?

Lang hopped on the wagon seat and flashed the paper at Isaac. "All paid. Let's go."

The wagon lurched into motion, climbing the road up to the city gate where Isaac drew it to a stop, waiting while the city guards inspected the barrels and the paperwork. Once satisfied, they were allowed into the city.

They rode through a busy square occupied by women and children beside a flowing fountain, carts filled with fish, crabs, lobsters, grain, and produce, citizens procuring goods, guards on patrol, and even a pair of beggars on the corner. All were things found in every city across the world. Yet Lang saw no smiles. Even the children appeared forlorn, the younger ones clinging to their mothers' legs.

The wagon entered an uphill street, bracketed by a building made of the same gray stone as the city walls. Two intersections later, Lang patted Isaac on the arm, drawing his attention.

"Do me a favor." Lang pointed toward a sign showing a sea creature with a long snout, a mug of ale in its mouth. "Pull in behind the Drunken Dolphin."

The driver's brow furrowed. "The wizardess said we were to return straight away."

Lang sighed. "Yes, I know. However, that woman is relentless, working her staff day and night. We are barely allowed time for a drink." He flashed Isaac a grin. "Come on. I'll buy a round. We can have a nice chat and enjoy life for a moment. Then we'll be off. Besides, tonight's event is at her estate, so you won't be driving her carriage."

Isaac lifted his hat and scratched his head, messing his thinning dark hair. "I guess we have time for a drink."

Clapping the man on the back, Lang pointed down the alley. "We will leave the wagon behind the building, so we are out of the way. Besides, nobody will look for us here."

"True and true," the man said as he steered the wagon down the narrow alley.

Once in the yard, a bulky man with a goatee and a scar on his face emerged from the stables.

Lang hopped down and met the man. "No need to feed or water our team." He slid the man two coppers. "Just watch our wagon for a bit. We are going in for a drink and will then be on our way."

The man grunted. "Alright."

Isaac climbed down and headed toward the inn's back door, Lang following along. Once Isaac was inside, Lang glanced over his shoulder and made a gesture, mouthing the word *hurry*.

When he saw another man emerge from the stables, he gave a nod and followed Isaac inside.

Downing the last of his mug, Lang continued his story as he and Isaac turned away from the bar. "Then, Parsec took the stage and stood before the entire wizards guild. He raised his hands to draw everyone's attention. When the room quieted and all eyes were on him, the man's robes shimmered. He glanced down, frowning. His eyes widened as his gaze shifted to the side of the dais. There, Eldalain stood with a smirk on his face. In a flash, Parsec's robes shrank, the hem lifting to expose his shins, his thighs, and then his manhood. The fabric tightened around his torso until it was a fraction of its original size. It was so tight, his pale flesh bulged at the hems. Before every wizard in Fastella, he stood naked from the waist down, his arms sticking straight out and unable to bend."

"That did *not* happen," Isaac said with a grin.

"Oh, it did. Worse, it was a cold winter day – a bad day to forego wearing smallclothes." Lang shook his head. "If Parsec hadn't already been guild leader, he might have had a difficult time after that, for whispers of his frightened turtle went on for a long time." Both laughing aloud, the two men emerged from the inn, Lang's hand on the driver's shoulder. "You should have seen his face. If wizards could explode from anger alone, he would have blown the entire building to bits." The irony that the guild hall was now a charred mess was not lost on Lang.

When Isaac's laughter cooled, he shook his head. "I bet Parsec was livid."

"Oh, you have no idea. He disliked Eldalain before that prank. Afterward...he hated the prince!"

The man who had agreed to watch the wagon was leaning against the stables, arms crossed over his chest. When Lang's eyes met his, the man nodded, mouthing, *it is done.*

Lang's mirth fled in an instant, replaced by resignation. Still, he forced himself to continue, not wanting to alert Isaac. It was not that he did not trust the driver, far from it. Rather, he hoped to protect him. *I like Isaac and do not wish to implicate him should anything go awry.*

Stopping beside the wagon, Lang rubbed his jaw. "You know, I only saw Parsec that angry one other time."

The two men sat on the driver's seat, Isaac gathering the reigns and snapping them. The wagon rolled slowly, the horses turning in a tight circle in the small dirt yard.

Isaac asked, "What else could have caused such anger?"

"In truth, it was half anger, half sorrow." Images flashed in Lang's head, disturbing and unbidden – two female cooks covered in blood, a beautiful woman stripped naked and hanging from the chandelier over her own bed... the same bed she shared with Parsec. In a saddened tone, Lang said, "It was when we found his wife murdered."

"Oh, my," Isaac's smile melted as they rode down the alley. They emerged into the street and continued the uphill drive, about to leave Dockside en route to Wizard Hills. "That's horrible."

Lang could not argue the point. While he had remained loyal to Parsec during his employ, he had never loved the man. His wife was another matter. Weak in magic, the woman made up for it in every way possible. Lang often thought to himself that Parsec was blessed to have her in his life. The woman's death had stricken him nearly as badly as it had her own husband. The quest to find her killer had been personal to Lang, yet when he found the assassin, Parsec chose to allow him to live. The wizard's decision had been difficult to swallow at the time, but Parsec had seen the truth of it. Rather than kill the hired hand, he chose to destroy the man behind the contract for murder. In that, Parsec had, indeed, extracted his revenge.

"You know," Isaac said in a musing tone. "I was working for Wizardess Willola when she found her husband dead."

Happy to have something else to think about, Lang arched a brow. "Really? I heard that he died while pleasuring himself."

The driver shrugged. "Could be, but it seemed odd at the time. Yes, his sash was around his throat, and he was otherwise naked, but the wizardess did not appear distraught…not as one might expect. Sure, she shed tears and said words of sorrow, but the next day she behaved as if nothing had changed."

"Perhaps she loves herself too much."

Isaac chuckled. "She does at that." He shook his head. "Sad how someone so beautiful could turn so ugly when you get to know her."

Lang grunted. "Why work for her, then?"

Shrugging, Isaac said, "I needed a job and this one pays well. If not for her, I'd likely be driving wagons and carriages for some other wizard, perhaps one who is worse. It is the way of things."

Pendry and Nolan held the gates open so the wagon could enter Willola Estate. It rolled up the cobblestone drive and rounded the manor, stopping near the cellar entrance at the rear. Lang hopped off and opened the cellar doors while Isaac ducked into the manor's kitchen entrance to get help.

With both doors lifted open, Lang descended the stairs, leaving the sunlight behind. With each step, the air cooled as expected. His boots scuffed along the dirt floor, his hands fumbling in the shadows until he located a brass object on the end of a shelf. He flipped the lever, the enchanted lantern humming as it came to life, a soft blue glow emanating from it and giving shape to the room.

Shelves ran along the exterior walls, which were filled with sacks and crates. At the far end of the room was another set of stairs, leading to the kitchen. In the center of the room was a five-foot tall cylinder, coated in a layer of frost. White crystals on the surface obscured the silvery lines of enchantment he knew were present. *This chilling core must have cost a fortune,* he thought. *It will be a shame to destroy it.* A half-dozen crates surrounded the chilling core, along with a single wine barrel.

He turned, climbed the stairs, and emerged into the sunlight as Isaac, Olban, and Lowell exited the manor.

Olban eyed the wagon load. "The mistress wants four barrels in the kitchen, and the others in the cellar as backup should we need more."

"There is one in the cellar now. Isaac and I will bring that one up to the kitchen and carry the remaining ones down." Pulling the pins out, Lang removed the wagon's rear gate. "You and Lowell can begin by grabbing a barrel from the wagon."

The two stewards reached for a barrel with red metal bands.

Lang's hand shot out and gripped Olban's wrist. "Not that one."

The man frowned. "Why not?"

"Um..." He searched for a viable excuse. "The dockworkers dropped that one. It needs time to settle." He tapped one with black bands. "Take this one instead."

Olban shrugged. "Makes no difference to me." He and Lowell tipped the barrel up, lifted it with a grunt, and headed toward the house.

Isaac leaned close to Lang and said in a soft voice, "I don't recall them dropping any barrels."

"Don't worry about it. Let's just get these in the cellar before they get any warmer." Lang tipped the barrel up, noting the other two with red bands, all of which had to go in the cellar. He could not risk anyone tapping one such barrel and discovering the truth.

27

ANXIETY

In her bedchamber, Narine paced, the layered skirts of her wedding gown swishing with each step. "Where is he?"

Shavon sighed. Finished with Narine's hair and makeup after having to pause numerous times while Narine fretted, the royal attendant tried to ease Narine's anxiety. Instead, her efforts and each passing minute seemed to increase Narine's ire.

Not to be dissuaded, the stubborn old woman tried again. "I am sure he will appear soon."

"Soon?!" Narine's voice rose an octave. "The ceremony is scheduled to begin in less than an hour!"

Shavon drew a scowl, crossing her arms over her thin torso. "Watch your tone, young lady."

Queen or not, Narine bit her lip, her anger cooling. The woman had a way of making her feel like she were twelve years old again. "I'm sorry. He just..."

"Nearly half a year has passed since I moved from Fastella. In that time, I have come to know your betrothed." Shavon's lips drew into a flat line. "For him, disappearing is a regular occurrence. Running late is also not out of character. He can be manipulative and is constantly scheming. His comments are inappropriate, his nature brash and unrefined, and the man is a hopeless cheat when it comes to dice or cards." Her expression softened, and she rested her hand on Narine's bare shoulder. "Despite all this, I *do* like him. It is difficult not to, for he is dedicated to you heart and soul. Jerrell knows this is important to you, and he would never let you down of his own volition."

Narine sighed, nodding. "I hope you are right."

The woman snorted. "I am always right."

Laughing, Narine's anxiety relaxed. She turned to the mirror and examined herself.

Her golden hair was tightly braided along her scalp and secured at the back of her head, brushed locks falling to her upper back. Blue highlights on her eyelids emboldened the aqua of her irises, lightly applied rouge sharpened her cheekbones, and a layer of soft gloss enhanced her full lips. Her shoulders exposed, the white dress was cut low enough to make her blush, white ruffles wrapping around her upper arms, and glittering crystals running along the neckline, narrowing to a point at her midriff. The ruffled white skirts puffed out broadly, held by a hidden hoop. She turned and eyed her profile, her voluptuous frame accentuated by the gown.

"Yes," Shavon said, peering over Narine's shoulder. "You are a vision." The woman lifted a crown and gently placed it on Narine's head, the sapphire-encrusted peak at the front. "None would deny you look the part of a queen today."

The door to the adjacent room burst open. Narine spun around to see Jace approaching through the open bedroom door. He stopped in the doorway and stared, his gaze running from her skirts to her face.

"Where have you been?" Narine asked, her anger returning.

He drew closer, his hands slipping around her waist. "You look gorgeous."

The spark in his eyes sent her heart fluttering, quelling her anger.

"Oh, no, you don't." Shavon gripped his arm and pulled him away. "It took three hours to achieve perfection, and I'll not allow you to muss her up now."

Jace gave the woman a sidelong look. "Alright. I can wait until later...but she will be getting mussed. Multiple times I suspect."

Narine blushed.

Shavon snorted.

Jace grinned.

He pulled his sleeve up, exposing his wrist, an enchanted bracelet around it. "Here. As promised."

Pressure applied to just the right points resulted in a click. He placed it in Narine's palm. She clenched it, happy to have it back, relieved to again be among the most powerful of wizards in a world without wizard lords.

Recalling the looming ceremony, Narine said, "You never answered my question, Jace. Why are you late?"

Spinning away, Jace crossed the room and eyed the formal outfit hanging from the rack near the window. "I was making final preparations."

"For what?"

He unbuttoned his doublet and turned toward her. "Did you forget? Someone is trying to kill you."

She pressed her lips together. "Of course, I didn't forget."

"While those coming into the palace will be searched and stripped of weapons, other risks remain." He pulled the doublet off and tossed it on a chair, exposing his lean muscular torso. His chest bare, she saw that the Eye of Obscurance was noticeably absent. Narine frowned. *He almost never removes the amulet.*

Jace sat, lifted his foot, and gripped his boot. "If I only had to worry about the ceremony in the throne room, I would feel better. However, you insist on appearing before the populace and that leaves you exposed to far more threats." Pulling his boot off, he set it aside. "I have gone over everything personally – the guards, the carriage, the driver, the route, the barricades around the dais in the square…everything."

With the other boot off, he stood and pulled his breeches down. He was not wearing smallclothes.

Narine glanced at Shavon, the woman arching a brow as she stared at Jace, who was completely naked. "Um…Jace…did you forget Shavon was here?"

He turned away, Narine's attention going to his tight pale buttocks.

"No." Holding up black formal trousers, he slipped one leg inside. "I figure we are in a hurry and she has likely seen a naked man before."

Shavon smiled. "Yes, but it has been a while." She leaned close to Narine and whispered, "Yes. I see why you are so smitten with him."

Impossibly, Narine's cheeks grew even hotter.

With Jace on her arm, Narine entered the side entrance to the throne room. The unmistakable noise of a crowd came through the closed double-doors at the rear of the chamber. Wizard royalty, wealthy merchants, and guests from across the southern wizardoms waited in the receiving hall, eager to witness the ceremony and anticipating the party that was scheduled to take place in the palace gardens after the ceremony.

Four guards stood inside the doors, thrice that number likely posted outside. The only other person in the room was Dianza, High Priestess of Farrow. Dressed in blue robes streaked by silver lightning around the neckline, down the seams, and on the cuffs, she rose from the front bench, her hands clasped at her waist.

Sighting Dianza caused Narine to recall a conversation they had shared in the woman's private chamber three days earlier.

While Narine had entered the room intent on restoring Dianza's faith in herself, she soon found herself walking a thin line between resolve and compassion, fearing the wrong word would send the woman over the edge.

"I am sorry, but it is true." Narine replied softly while staring at the high priestess in concern.

The woman appeared far older than her thirty-eight years, her blue robes wrinkled and stained, her dark hair a twisted mess, and bags beneath her eyes.

Slumped in her chair, Dianza shook her head. "I still don't understand. How could Farrow...how could all the gods be dead? They are gods! Are they not immortal?" Her voice croaked, on the edge of tears.

"It was the Dark Lord," Narine explained. "Backed by the same demon lord that attacked Balmor, the two of them destroyed the new gods."

It was a lie. Although hurtful to someone like Dianza, it was better than the truth. Farrow had not appeared during the past two Darkenings nor had the previously persistent flames returned to the Tower of Devotion above the palace. Those facts were certainly not lost on Dianza and Narine offered an explanation...although one the woman was loath to accept.

In a sad voice, Narine added, "Afterward, Vandasal and Urvadan left this world as well."

Dianza raked her nails down her face, appearing distraught. "What will we do? How can we endure without the guidance of gods and the protection of wizard lords?"

Narine sat forward and took the woman's hand in her own. "We will persevere. We must prevail. If we can no longer hold faith in the gods, we must place our faith in ourselves."

The woman nodded. "Yes. The populace still needs spiritual guidance."

"Many do. In that, you can still be of service. In time, perhaps another god will emerge to fill the vacuum."

Dianza grimaced. "Like those who claim the dragons are our new gods?"

Narine had been aware of the issue for the better part of a year. At first, she had considered the dragon priests a small handful of radicals armed with the crazy notion that the creatures were deities. Now their followers ranged in the hundreds in Marquithe alone, thousands in total. *Dianza is right. People need something to believe in.* Narine admitted the sight of a dragon was majestic and awe-inspiring, their magic extraordinary and impressive. *Yet, dragons are creatures, not gods.*

Still, I must calm Dianza, not stir her ire. "Is that so wrong?" Narine asked. "If some find hope or comfort in worshiping dragons, is that not better than giving in to despair?"

They both knew Narine was referring to the recent suicides. It had been the reason for her visit.

Dianza sighed. "Yes. It is a preferable path than relenting to darkness. Regardless, you have given me something to consider."

Narine stood. "Good. Just remember, my wedding is in two days. I am counting on you to preside."

The woman nodded. "I will do my best."

That conversation was the last time Narine had seen Dianza until now, moments before her wedding.

The priestess ascended the dais stairs and met them before Narine's throne. Her hair was tied back, covered by a silver headdress engraved with lightning bolts. Her eyes were alert and her expression stoic. She seemed to be in far better condition and appeared years younger than she had two days earlier.

"Welcome, my queen." Dianza dipped her head and turned to Jace. "Chancellor. Are you ready to begin?"

"Yes," Jace replied. "As we discussed, Narine and I will wait in the antechamber. Inform the guards that it is time to begin seating our guests."

Narine frowned. "The antechamber? That was not what we rehearsed."

"Precisely. I changed the plan, as I have changed others. Best to keep our enemies guessing should they seek to take advantage." He turned toward Shavon. "You are welcome to sit in the front row. For raising someone as wonderful as Narine, you deserve the best seat we have to offer."

Shavon smiled as broadly as Narine had ever seen. "How kind of you, Jerrell."

Jace took Narine by the arm and led her across the dais, descended the short staircase and approached a closed door. Entering the chamber, Jace moved aside and held the door as she swept past him.

Narine stopped and scowled across the room. They were not alone.

"It's about time," Harlequin said from the divan, her leg draped over the arm as she ate an apple.

Jace shrugged. "Arranging a performance of this scale takes time. There is much that could go wrong, so precautions must be taken."

Crusser sat at Jace's desk chair, his ankles crossed and his feet up on the desk, asleep. He stirred, blinking his eyes open. "Oh. You two are here."

Facing Crusser, Jace arched a brow. "I'm glad you made yourself comfortable."

Lowering his feet, Crusser stretched, spreading his muscular arms and thrusting out his barrel chest. "Best to sleep when possible. Who knows when the next opportunity will come along?"

Harlequin snorted. "It's disgusting how easily you can fall asleep."

"Handy talent for a soldier," Jace commented.

"That's what I keep telling her," Crusser said.

Narine could not take it any longer. She reached out and gripped Jace by the wrist, speaking when he turned toward her. "Why are these two in here? You're not planning on marrying them as well?"

He smirked and slid a hand to her waist. "Harley and Cruss are here at my request. Should anything happen, they are close by as extra swords… swords I trust."

She arched a brow. "You trust her over my own guards?"

"After what has occurred recently, do you blame me?"

Narine released a sigh. "I suppose not."

"Good. Now, no more questions. I need you to concentrate." He swept his arm in a broad gesture. "Look at this room closely. Memorize it in detail. I want you to know it well enough to cast it in an accurate illusion."

"What are you…"

His finger against her lip, he shook his head. "No time. Just do it. For me."

Narine nodded and turned her focus on the room.

The chamber was square in shape, ten strides across. A bookshelf covered one wall from the floor to the high ceiling, filled with thick tomes, a ladder leaning against one end. Before it was a desk made of dark cherry, the legs ornately carved, each adorned by a twisting dragon, the top lacquered and polished to cast a reflection. The wall opposite the door was made of stone blocks, a massive stone fireplace in the middle, the arched opening as tall as Narine's five-and-a-half-foot frame. The other two walls were adorned with tapestries, the one to her left depicting Farrow blessing some wizard lord from centuries past, the other showing a battle with wizards on horses and surrounded by ranks of soldiers in plated armor. Covering half the floor was a midnight blue rug, the divan before the fireplace tailored in tan suede. From a chain and ring secured to the ceiling hung a chandelier, the eight enchanted lanterns mounted to an octagon of dark stained wood, illuminating the room in soft blue light.

As Narine drank in every detail, filing the imagery away as she had practiced for half her life, the noise coming from the throne room grew increasingly louder. Minutes passed before Jace put his hand on her arm, drawing her attention.

"Are you ready?"

"What?" She blinked.

He smiled. "I wish to make you my wife…if you will have me."

A smile stretched across her face and she fought the urge to kiss him. *Best to not muss myself or Shavon will have my hide.* "Yes. Of course."

Music began to play from the throne room. He went to the door, placing his hand on the knob. "As we practiced. Only this time, you will approach the dais from the opposite side of the room. I'll be waiting for you."

He opened the door and stepped out, walking toward the dais where Dianza stood waiting.

Narine's heart raced, and her stomach twisted as if she were on the seas. Having fallen sick on every ship she had sailed on, she suddenly feared she might vomit. *You can do this, Narine. You are queen and these are your subjects. This is your day. Enjoy it.*

In her own head, the conversation continued, one voice trying to settle her nerves and give her confidence, another voice shrieking. Gradually, the first voice calmed the latter, her pulse slowing to a moderate rate.

When the music stopped, Dianza greeted the crowd, and Narine's anxiety returned with a vengeance.

"Everyone, please rise," bade the high priestess. All stood in expectation, the room falling silent. "Before me stands Chancellor Jerrell Landish, a man many of you know by name." She smirked. "Or, perhaps by his legendary reputation."

A chuckle ran through the crowd.

"Regardless of Jerrell's past, he has proven over the past year that he is ready and equipped to hold this office, doing so with efficiency and earning the respect of those around him. I have come to know him during this time, and I am honored to stand here and present this man to his betrothed.

"Four individuals have ruled in Farrowen during my lifetime, each with strengths and weaknesses. None, until now, has proven both boldness and compassion coupled with the innate ability to seek justice for all rather than the benefit of the few. This woman I speak of is your queen, Her Majesty, Narine Killarius. Please, greet her with the love she deserves."

Applause arose, loud enough to make Narine's ears ring, numbing her senses. Steeling herself, she headed out the door, her skirts trailing behind her. She glanced toward the audience, thickly packed with people. Sweat ran down her ribs, her breath now coming in gasps. She stopped at the edge of the dais and her eyes widened in alarm. She held a hand to her stomach and trembled, her tongue watering.

Suddenly, she turned away from the crowd and vomited.

The applause faded, and smatterings of nervous laughter filtered through the room, turning her anxiety into anger. Still facing away from the crowd, she wiped her mouth with the back of her hand. *You are their queen. Show them a queen.* She stood tall and felt a hand on her shoulder. Turning, she saw Jace standing beside her, a caring smile on his face.

"I'm here, Narine." He spoke in a soft, reassuring tone. "It's just you and me and Dianza. Come. Join me now and forever."

Again, she wiped her mouth and flashed an uneasy grin. "So much for avoiding a muss."

He shrugged. "I was going to muss you soon, anyway."

Taking his hand, she followed him onto the dais. Side by side, her hand in his, Narine and Jace faced the high priestess as the rest of the world faded away.

28

TREACHERY

W edding guests filled the Marquithe Palace gardens, the air mild and comfortable on a beautiful late spring afternoon. Amber sunlight shone upon the high reaches of the surrounding trees, the foliage and palace walls casting much of the grounds in shadow. At the edge of the lawn, Montague and Vordan watched an extravagant dark blue and silver carriage roll down the paved drive, prepared to carry the queen and her new husband away. A complement of Midnight Guard soldiers rode before the carriage, the retinue passing through the gates and into the city.

For the occasion, Montague had selected his finest robes – shimmering silver with a midnight blue sash. In his dark blue uniform, stripes on one shoulder, even Vordan looked refined and deserving of his rank.

A thousand people – chatting, drinking, and laughing – were spread across the lawn, many standing in clusters, some seated at tables. For weeks, Queen Narine's wedding had been declared the event of the century, outstripping even her own coronation the year before. Of course, Montague had not attended that coronation, for he had not yet come to terms with his new reality. How could anyone claim rule of Farrowen without the Gift of Farrow? Worse, how could a foreign princess do so? As Montague discovered, time can alter perceptions, and he eventually came to understand the changing reality.

Somehow, this upstart queen had taken the throne and had done so in a stunning manner, thwarting Palkan Forca, a reputable wizard, with superior magic. A woman displaying such power could only mean one thing: her magic must be augmented by an enchanted object. He should know, for he had once possessed such an item. Until the bracelet had come into his possession, he had not been aware such a thing was possible – a secret well-kept by the enchanters, one they would kill to protect.

Time and well-spent coin confirmed that the very same bracelet he had once owned, a bracelet stolen from him by Jerrell Landish, now belonged to the queen who kept it hidden beneath her skirts and wore it constantly. Thus, his plan had begun to form. *It is ironic for this to come to fruition on the queen's wedding day.*

A young pretty brunette with full lips and large brown eyes approached him, hips swaying overtly. She had a narrow waist, accentuating the curves beneath her sleek black gown. Beside her was a hooded woman dressed in tight leathers. A pair of short swords with odd hilts and narrow blades rested on her hips.

"High Wizard Montague," said the woman in the dress. "It has been many years."

Montague arched a brow. "Ydith Gurgan?"

"You remember." Already attractive, her smile made her strikingly so. "However, the proper term is *High Wizardess* Gurgan."

"Yes," he nodded. "You assumed the role after your father's ill-fated confrontation with Malvorian."

Ydith's smile slid away, her eyes narrowing. "I am a graduate from Tiadd, same as you. I was among the most talented females in the school during my eight years there, with only the queen's strength surpassing mine. I earned my title as well as you did."

"I won't deny you hold a title, but would you if challenged to a duel by an accomplished male wizard?"

She tightened her lips, narrowed her eyes, and glared at him. "Regardless of how you feel about it, we are equals, Montague."

He smirked. "Yes. How is your little mining city? Are there even any other wizards in Eleighton besides yourself? How many have challenged you for the title of high wizard?" His eyes widened in feigned surprise. "Oh. None?" Shaking his head, he said, "You and I are anything but equals, Ydith.

I soundly defeated six challengers in my first five years as high wizard, proving my superiority. Lionne is the busiest port in Farrowen, the surrounding lands home of the most prized vineyards in the Eight Wizardoms. I rule a city more than twice the size of Eleighton, my castle cooled by the ocean breeze each summer, warmed by the sea and sun each winter. Others long to take my position while yours remains unchallenged because nobody wishes to claim it."

The entire time he spoke, her face grew redder and redder until she turned on her heel and stomped off, her bodyguard casting Montague a questioning look before following her mistress.

Montague laughed and said to Vordan, "That was fun."

Vordan grunted. "I hear she is quite vain about her appearance and her position. She is likely to hold a grudge."

"Let her," Montague said. "She lacks the power, experience, and connections to do anything about it. Now, had she also inherited the bracelet her father possessed when he died..." *It will soon be mine.*

A porter approached, balancing a silver platter with six goblets filled with red liquid. "Would you care for wine, sir?"

Montague smiled. "Yes." He took a goblet while Vordan waved the porter off.

Glass to his lips, Montague sipped the wine. It was smooth and flavorful, soothing his tongue and warming his throat as it slid down. "Ahh," he breathed, eyeing the goblet. "Farrowen red. Nothing else is the like of it."

A woman's voice came from behind him. "High Wizard Montague."

He spun to find Portia Forca approaching. Flashing a smile, he dipped his head. "Wizardess Forca. It is good to see you again."

Leaning close, Portia spoke above the din of chatter, "It was a beautiful ceremony, don't you think?"

Her hand rested on Montague's arm in a familiar fashion, his eyes flicking to her ample cleavage, which stirred more than curiosity. She was pretty enough but ten years his senior and had a thicker build than he preferred. Still, her husband was now a useless lump and Portia remained quite healthy...

He smiled, not about the wedding, but about what he pictured doing to her when they were alone. "Yes, it was grand, perhaps the most moving wedding I have ever attended."

With a wine glass in his hand, he pretended to enjoy a conversation with Portia Forca as the woman droned on, but he only half listened while his mind remained elsewhere, waiting for some sort of alarm. Forcing himself, he refocused on Portia, catching her in mid-sentence.

"...commend the queen for presenting herself and her new husband to the people of Marquithe. I hope she does not keep us waiting for long." Leaning close, her chest pressing against his arm, Portia whispered, "After dinner, I hear we are to move to the palace plaza for dancing. Do you dance, Montague?"

He opened his mouth to reply when horns blew. The crowd turned toward the sound as a squad of Midnight Guard raced toward the gates.

"I wonder where they are going," Portia mused. "The queen and her new prince departed fifteen minutes ago, so it is far too late for additional escorts."

Montague saw his opportunity. Wide-eyed, he feigned worry. "What if something has happened to the queen? If there is trouble, I must go and offer my assistance, for I am her liege lord of Lionne." He drained the remainder of his glass, the wine soothing his throat, and handed the goblet to Portia. "Please excuse me."

He rushed off, waving for Vordan to follow.

Her call came from behind him. "Hurry back!"

Dismissing thoughts of Wizardess Forca, his attention turned to the circular drive where his carriage waited, the driver sitting ready.

Moving at a brisk walk, Montague waved to the man. "Driver! Follow those soldiers!" He opened the door and ducked into the carriage while Vordan sat with the driver.

The carriage sped out through the palace gates and turned, racing along a curved street while Montague peered out the window in anticipation. Down-hill they went, the carriage steadily drawing closer to the running squadron. A few intersections later, they came to a wall of stacked barrels and crates barricading the street. Just before it, the guards turned into a narrow alley. The carriage slowed to a stop, just short of the barricade; Montague's door faced the alley.

It was filled with smoke.

Heart pounding in anticipation, Montague emerged from the carriage as his captain jumped down. Vordan scowled as he drew his blade and fell in beside Montague as they advanced into the swirling black smoke. Shards of burnt wood crunched beneath their feet, and they heard the sounds of coughing, cries, and shouts coming from the gloom. The smoke cleared, revealing dead guards with armor scorched, some missing limbs. The guards they had followed from the palace stood in an arc, blocking the scene ahead.

"Move aside," Vordan commanded. "The high wizard of Lionne is here to help."

The guards parted to reveal a horrifying scene.

Shattered, splintered, and charred wood lay everywhere, the spokes and rim sections of wagon wheels among the debris. Some sections still burned, although a line of citizens stood beyond the wreckage, passing buckets from one to the next. The big man who stood nearest to the fires dumped each bucket before passing it to a child who would run off to refill it.

Montague took in the entire scene in an instant, yet his focus remained fixed on two burned bodies amid the rubble. One was a female with sparse remnants of blonde hair and a once white dress, now torn and badly burned. The other was likely male, but it was difficult to be sure with his face destroyed and his black clothing shredded.

Our plan worked. He closed his eyes for a beat and said a prayer to the dead gods. Opening them, he strode forward and snarled, "Back away!"

Hands extended, he called upon his magic and crafted a dome-shaped shield over the wreckage. With another construct, he sucked out the air inside and snuffed out the fires, causing the smoke trapped in the dome to thicken. He then released the spells, a thick puff of black swirling up into the late afternoon sky.

Montague then navigated the hot smoldering debris and knelt beside the dead woman. Dangling from a ring on her charred finger was a melted, twisted chain with a ruby inset, the item familiar to anyone who had ever been in her presence. His attention turned to her exposed leg and the remnants of the gold bracelet clamped around her ankle. The metal was melted, twisted, destroyed. Surely the enchantment had been lost in the blaze. His heart sank, despite all else. *Such a waste. It would have given me an edge, my magic outstripping all others.* He sighed and rubbed his eyes at the loss of something so wonderful.

A hand clamped down on his shoulder. He looked up and saw one of the

Midnight Guard standing over him. The man had an arrow emblazoned on his shoulder plate, marking him as an officer.

The guard shook his head while gazing at the woman's dead body. "Thank you for your help, High Wizard, but it was too late. She was a fine queen for one so young. We are all saddened by her loss."

He believes I am sad about Narine's death. Montague had to cover his mouth lest someone see his grin.

The guard turned, cupped his hands to his mouth, and shouted. "The queen was murdered! Queen Narine is dead!"

Gasps from the guards near the wreckage and the citizens beyond echoed in the alley. Montague rose to his feet but kept his eyes downcast, his shoulders slumped as he walked through the guards and lumbered to the mouth of the alley. A glance revealed guards moving the last of the barricade aside, leaving the street clear. He ducked into his carriage. Vordan joined him. The carriage lurched into motion and they left the grim scene behind.

Only then did Montague allow his grin to return. "It worked. Tranadal's plan worked."

"You will become king."

"King," Montague tested the word and found it to his liking.

The doorway he had sought for so long had revealed itself and stood open. He merely needed to walk through it. *Soon, Farrowen will be mine.*

29

NO ESCAPE

An hour earlier

The wedding ceremony passed in a hazy blur until, somehow, Narine found herself in the receiving hall, greeting and thanking an endless stream of guests, most whom she did not know. After congratulating her and Jace, the guests slowly filtered out to convene in the gardens. No expense had been spared on the reception and the party was expected to last many hours after nightfall.

When the last guest had passed by, Jace took Narine by the arm, and the newlywed couple trailed an escort of guards down a corridor and through a side entrance to a courtyard occupied by a single carriage. Painted midnight blue with silver trim, even the spokes of the wheels sporting a coat of silver, the carriage was unique and difficult to miss. Two white horses stood before the carriage, the driver similarly dressed in all white. It was one of the most beautiful things Narine had ever seen.

She smiled at Jace. "It is wonderful."

He grinned back. "I am glad you feel that way. Commissioning it, down to the silver plating, cost me a fortune and a fair bit of personal attention." Opening the door, he peered inside before extending a hand to her. "Allow me to help you in. I'm sure those skirts make it difficult to navigate tight spaces."

Narine looked down at her dress, still feeling lightheaded from her whirlwind day. "Yes. I hadn't considered the carriage ride."

"Just remember, it was your idea to address the populace. We can't very well reach Merchant's Square without a carriage...unless you prefer to walk."

She snorted. "Don't be absurd. The square is over a mile away. It's already been a long day, and I'm not traipsing through the streets of Marquithe dressed like this, even if I were not fearful of the risk."

Taking his hand, she climbed up, the hoops of her skirts wedging against the doorframe. His palms gripped her backside and pushed her through. Narine looked back to find him grinning.

"Did you enjoy yourself?" she asked as she sat on a bench, the hoop puffing up in the air.

"As a matter of fact, I did." Jace turned to Captain Giralt. "Is everything ready at the square?"

Giralt nodded. "Yes. A dozen Midnight Guard already hold the platform, ensuring all is safe when you arrive."

"Good. I want you and four guards riding ahead of us. Four more will stay with the carriage, two on the front with driver, two standing on the back rail. Be ready for anything."

Giralt thumped his fist to his breastplate and slid his helmet into place.

Jace added, "You remember the route we planned?"

Giralt nodded. "Yes, my prince."

"Prince?" Jace gave Narine a sidelong glance. "That will take some getting used to."

She laughed. "We all must make sacrifices."

Giralt turned toward a waiting horse and climbed into the saddle, joining the four other mounted guards.

Seemingly satisfied, Jace looked up at the driver. "Do not stop until you reach the square, regardless of what happens. Follow Giralt. He is prepared to deal with anything should it arise."

The driver tipped his cap. "Yes, Your Highness."

"Highness?" Jace shook his head as he climbed in and sat beside her. "That also sounds odd."

A guard closed the door. Giralt called out and the first group of horses trotted off. The driver called out and snapped the reigns, the carriage lurching into motion. As they rode toward the palace gates, Jace closed the curtains, the interior falling dark.

Narine noticed a familiar look on his face, the expression he wore when scheming. "What are you planning?"

He feigned surprise. "Who said I was planning anything?"

Her eyes narrowed. "Why close the curtains? You don't expect to muss me any further prior to speaking in the square, do you?"

He chuckled. "Hardly."

They rode through the gate and began a downhill trek, following a curving road that led past Wizard Estates.

A bad odor caused her to pinch her nose. "What is that smell?"

Gripping her hand, his grin changed to an intense expression. "You need to trust me."

While an alarm flared in her mind, she remained calm and nodded. "Always."

"Good. Now restrain yourself. This will be startling."

Narine knew Jace well. Little startled him, and the two of them had been through much together, experiencing things few others could comprehend. His warning set her on edge.

Jace leaned forward and gripped the seat across from them, lifting it open. A stench wafted out, ten times worse than before. Inside the compartment was a male dressed in dark clothing. Gripping the man by the coat, Jace lifted him out, the man's dead eyes staring at Narine.

Hand over her mouth, she stifled a scream. Once removed from the seat compartment, Jace set the man on the floor.

Through clenched teeth, she asked, "Why is there a dead man in our carriage?"

"There is more." He replaced the seat on the bench.

"What?"

"I need you to sit on the other bench."

She glared at him, prepared to snap back, and then recalled her promise. "Fine."

With an effort, she swung herself to the opposite bench, the hoops of her skirts nearly knocking Jace out the side door. He followed and opened the seat to reveal another body. It was a woman, blonde and curvy, dressed in a wedding gown identical to Narine's.

Her eyes wide, Narine placed a hand over her mouth and stared in horror. It felt eerily like peering at her own corpse. "Why, Jace?"

He pulled the woman out. Her head drooped over his shoulder and her arms flopped as he fell back on the bench beside Narine.

Grunting, he asked, "Would you be a dear and close the other bench for me?"

Caught amid a storm of conflicting emotions, Narine stared at him, the tempest flowing from horror to disgust, sadness to anger, shock to bewilderment. Finally, she did as requested, the seat dropping back on the bench.

He shoved the dead woman, causing her head to smack against the carriage wall. Her body slumped to one side. Again, he lifted the dead man by the coat and placed him beside the other corpse before sitting back with a sigh.

"That was more difficult than I expected." He panted and wiped his brow. "It's stuffy in here."

She turned back to the dead couple. It felt like peering into a grotesque mirror, the reflections alarmingly close to their own likenesses. Except their doppelgangers were dead.

"Please explain what is happening." Narine pleaded.

The carriage turned a sharp corner, tossing her against the wall. The two corpses tipped over, and the woman lay on top of the man, her eyes staring through Narine.

Jace peered through the curtain. "We are almost there."

"Where?"

He turned toward her. "There is little time, so please do as I say, and all will be explained."

She nodded numbly.

"When we stop, things will happen. I will need you to scream and cry for help, but you must not lose control. Find your center. You are strong, and I believe in you."

Again, she nodded. Shouts came from outside.

"Good. Now, it is almost time to use the secret spell."

The carriage turned sharply, the two corpses flying across the bench, placing the man atop the woman. Jace held Narine steady, her mind racing.

She frowned. "Spatial transference?"

"Yes."

The carriage stopped. Cries of alarm preceded the twangs of arrows fired, the thuds of bolts striking, and the clangs of swords ringing.

As the carriage rocked, Jace shouted. "Guards? What's happening?"

"We are under attack!" A man shouted, followed by a cry of pain.

Jace tried to open the door, but less than a foot away was a brick wall. He turned the other side and tried again. That door opened even less. They were in a narrow alley, trapped.

It took no effort for Narine to scream. It burst from the throat, loud and shrill.

"Help!" Jace shouted. "We're trapped!" He then said to her. "Nice scream. Can you do it again?"

She did, tears blurring her vision.

Something crashed on top of the carriage. Liquid, thick and dark, dripped down the window.

He took her by the cheeks and turned her face toward his. "Alright, Narine. Make a gateway."

Right. Remain calm. "To where?"

"The throne room antechamber. You just memorized it. Hurry."

She drew in her magic, the enchanted anklet and hand chain boosting her power to thrice its normal capacity. Extending her hand, a construct formed around it, one not used for millennia until she had rediscovered it a year earlier. The magic flowed through the pattern as she pictured the throne room antechamber, forming the image in detail. A gateway materialized to reveal the arch of a large fireplace. The bottom of the opening appeared just above the carriage floor, the top near the ceiling.

His arm around her back, Jace pulled her off the seat and through the opening. They landed on the floor and rolled into the fireplace.

"Close it!" he said.

A loud rush came from beyond the portal as the carriage burst into flames. She released the gateway and it snapped shut as a blazing swirl of fire and smoke shot at them. He covered her, protecting her from the intense heat.

Jace cried out and rolled away, his fine coat on fire. He rolled back and forth on the dark blue carpet, snuffing out the flames before lying flat on his back, panting.

"Now, *that* was an entrance," Crusser said from behind the desk.

From the divan, now moved against the far wall, Harlequin chuckled. "I told you. The thief has a flare for these things."

Narine crawled out of the fireplace and stood. Her beautiful wedding dress – a gown she had dreamed of for half her life – was ruined, covered in soot, torn, and streaked with blood. Lifting her hand, she frowned at the cut across her palm. "How did that happen?"

Jace rose to his feet, dusted himself off, and flashed her a smile. "You were wonderful."

Anger rising, Narine growled. "You had better explain and fast."

"Yes. Of course." He walked over to one of the tapestries and pulled it aside. "I will do so as we head down. Should anyone find us in here, it would ruin everything."

Jace probed the wall until he found the right spot and pressed, three small sections of stone giving way. A click sounded and a door swung open.

Narine recognized the door but had forgotten about its existence. The night she had last passed through it had been frenetic and traumatic. "It is the same door Algoron used to get us out after our fight with Malvorian."

He shot her a grin. "Exactly. It took me hours to find it. If you recall, I was unconscious at the time and only learned of it after hearing the story from you. As it stands, very few know about this tunnel, and I thought it best to keep it that way."

Stepping into the dark opening, he felt around, and soft blue light bloomed, revealing an enchanted lantern in his grip. He extended his hand toward Narine, beckoning for her to follow. "Come along. Quickly, now."

She took his hand and followed him into the gloom, Harlequin and Crusser close behind.

"Push the door closed, Cruss," Jace said. "Be sure it latches."

The man closed the door, which clicked in place, the tunnel falling dark save for Jace's lantern. Just before him, a stairwell descended into blackness.

Leading them downward, Jace began telling his tale.

"Over recent weeks, two attempts have been made on your life, Narine, and another on mine. Something significant was occurring. With Henton's death, which happened right on your own private balcony, it became clear that I could not keep you safe – not until those behind the curtains were exposed and eliminated." He paused. "You see, while I admire your willing-ness to lead the citizens of Farrowen, I am too selfish to allow assassins to kill you for such a sacrifice. It was not power you sought when you claimed the throne, but others do not hold such pure motives. For many, power is the ultimate drug, and their thirst for it is insatiable."

He resumed his descent, the other three following. "Accordingly, I hatched a plan to make those behind the assassination attempts believe they have won. When the carriage fire is doused, they will find our dead bodies within the wreckage."

Narine gasped. "That's why we were riding with a pair of corpses." Another thought occurred to her. "Please tell me you did not kill that poor woman."

Jace looked back at her and smiled. "So compassionate. These people do not deserve you, Narine. You are among the best of us."

She frowned. "You didn't answer me."

He shook his head. "I did not kill her. A patron too cheap to pay for her services drove a knife through her chest...and such a fine chest it was. Pity, for she was among the most talented whores in Marquithe. In the end, the man paid...dearly. He may survive, but I suspect he will wish he had not."

Narine released a sigh. "Thank the gods it was not you."

Pulling her along, they reached the bottom of the stairs. A tunnel led to the left and the right. Without pausing, he took the right path.

"What of the dead man?" she asked.

"He was the target of a contract killing. Turns out, he embezzled from the wrong merchant in Tiamalyn and thought he could hide in Marquithe. Contract fulfilled, I kept the body, thinking it close enough...although the man was not as fit as I am." He shrugged. "Sometimes, you must just make do. With the naphtha, the fire will burn hot and cause extensive damage, leaving the fake us difficult to distinguish from the real thing."

Narine frowned. "So you set up your own assassination?"

"Yes." He stopped and grinned again. "The best part, I got paid ten gold as a down payment to accept the contract."

Harlequin laughed. "You were paid to kill yourself?"

"Poetic, isn't it? Styles is to meet the contract broker tonight to collect the remaining ninety gold. That should set him and the thieves' guild up for a long time."

"The boy is taking your place?" Narine asked.

"He is bright and deserves a chance. Besides, he remains loyal to me, and I paid a number of team leaders well to support him." Jace sighed. "The Charlatan's rule is over. Long live the Sly."

They came to a cavern with smooth walls. Shelves were carved into some of the walls. A bed stood in one corner, piled with stuffed brown sacks. In the middle of the room were a table and chairs.

Jace set the lantern on the table and walked toward the bed. "While working for Malvorian, this was Algoron's room." He ruffled through the sacks. "I thought it a good place to store our things."

Narine put her hand to her forehead. It was all happening so fast – the wedding, the carriage ride, the explosion, their escape…

She frowned, holding her fists to her hips. "Why didn't you tell me?"

He looked at her, his eyes sad. "I wanted to, even felt I owed it to you. However, I care more about your welfare than what you think of me. Thus, I hid the truth, not to deceive you, but to deceive others. It was the best means to ensure you behaved as if we were getting married and you would go on as queen. I dared not allow anyone to guess we might fake our own deaths."

His explanation made sense but did not resolve her concerns. "So you expect me to abandon my responsibility as queen? Who will sit on the throne?"

"Exactly. Whoever takes the throne is either behind this scheme or a pawn in a larger conspiracy." He approached her, placing his hands on her upper arms as he gazed into her eyes. "We are dead, Narine. With that death, we have shed the shackles of fame and authority and are free to go wherever we wish, do as we please. This is important, trust me. Whatever is happening…it is more critical we pursue the truth than continue to rule Farrowen. I fear what is happening will impact far more than one wizardom."

Harlequin chimed in, "Jerrell is right. The Order has unlimited funds and agents planted throughout the world. Those who have usurped control seek to influence these events. To what ends, I do not know, but they were willing to murder Chandan and tried to kill me when I discovered their lies. We must stop them."

"Chandan is dead?" Narine recalled the man fondly, despite their mixed past.

Harlequin nodded, the gravity of the situation suddenly taking shape. And thus, Narine's world changed. Her rule as queen had lasted for only one year, her future again cast in doubt. Amid this realization was another that brought a smile to her face.

"What?" Jace asked.

"You waited until after the wedding."

"Of course I did."

She gripped his cheeks, pulled his face to hers, and kissed him, pouring her soul into the moment. Her head swam with the heat of their contact and her heart swelled with emotion.

Pulse racing, she released him and smiled. "You are my husband. There is no escaping me, now, Jerrell Landish."

30

FAR AWAY

The light disk in her palm casting a pale blue light, Harlequin led Crusser into a neighboring cavern to give Narine and Jace some privacy while they changed their clothes. She ran her hand along the walls, which were smooth and obviously the work of a stone-shaper. While she had met a few dwarfs, none possessed the rare ability to form stone with their bare hands. *It would be a wondrous thing to wield such magic.* Entire cities, Marquithe among them, had been crafted by stone-shapers, but those cities were built long, long ago. The idea left her wondering if stone-shaping had been a more common skill back when Makers roamed the world, living among men and elves.

"That was a time of legends," she muttered.

"What?" Crusser asked.

She shook her head. "Never mind. I was just marveling at how this cavern was crafted, which had me thinking of the Makers."

He grunted, his gaze sweeping the room as she passed him, walking toward three recesses carved in the opposite wall. Oddities made of brass, gold, and other materials filled those cavities. Among them, she spotted a tight coil of leather, a wrapped grip sticking from the loop.

The sight of a whip stirred memories of her years as a pirate, the best years of her life. Back then, she had only cared for herself, her ship, and her crew, living each day as if it could be her last. It had been a time of freedom and adventure that had eventually left her longing for something more, something meaningful. That was when she met Chandan, the man who introduced her to the Order and gave her a sense of purpose. The Order would save the world and see the Dark Lord dead. *In that, we succeeded. But somehow, solving one problem led to others.*

Still staring at the whip, she bit her lip and reached for the wrapped grip. Her hand brushed against the coil, and she pulled back, her fingertips tingling from the brief touch. She tried again, wrapping her hand around it, the tingles teasing her palm as she lifted the whip and held the light disk close to it, noting the curling silver script of an enchantment.

"What do you have there?" Crusser stopped beside her.

"It's a whip. Enchanted as well."

"Why enchant a whip?"

"I don't know." Harlequin raised the whip, holding it ready.

"Careful," he warned. "You'll hurt yourself if you don't know what you are doing."

She shot him a grin. "Few alive are better with a whip."

Years had passed since she had last wielded a whip, yet it felt comfortable to hold one again. She turned, took aim, and lashed out, snapping her wrist. The whip extended. The popper crackled as it wrapped around the chair leg, and the leather began to glow. The whip contracted on its own, drawing the chair toward her. When she flicked her wrist, it extended and released from the chair. It then withdrew, self-winding toward Harlequin until it was, again, a coil.

"Neat," she said.

Crusser walked past her, examining the other items occupying the cavities on the wall.

"Try using it on a person," Jace said from the cavern entrance, holding a coat in one hand and a leather strap and sheath in the other.

She turned toward Crusser, who stood with his back to her as he lifted a coil of gold from the shelf and peered at it closely. With a sideways swipe, she flung the whip toward him, the end wrapping around his knee, just above his boot. He stiffened, his body convulsing and arms flailing. The coil of gold fell to the cavern floor, clanking and rolling away.

"What's wrong with him?" Harlequin asked.

Jace chuckled. "His muscles are contracting into knots. If you keep it on him for much longer, he'll collapse and curl into a ball like a newborn babe."

She flicked her wrist, and the whip unwrapped. As it coiled back toward her, Crusser fell against the wall, sinking to one knee.

Breathing heavily, he grumbled, "Keep that thing off of me!"

Harlequin arched a brow. "It seems I found a new toy."

"You seem to know how to use it," Jace noted.

"I owned a whip for nearly a decade. It was useful, and I always meant to replace it."

"You can have that one."

"Me? You don't want it?"

"I have enough toys to entertain me already. Besides, last time I tried to use it, I lashed my own face and had a scar for two weeks."

Crusser crossed the room, squatted, and picked up the golden coil.

"Careful, Cruss," Jace said. "Once you put that thing on, it will never come off."

The man held it in his palm, furrowing his brow. "What is it?"

Jerrell slipped an arm into his black leather coat. "It's called the Band of Amalgamation. Like the whip, it's an enchanted object."

"I recognize it," Harlequin said. "Adyn wore it on her arm."

He nodded while pulling his coat over his other shoulder. "Yes. It's what turned her flesh to metal."

Crusser's eyes widened as he peered at the object in his palm. "I remember when you four arrived in the valley. The metal woman drew my curiosity. It was as if her own skin had become armor. I wondered how that was possible."

"Slip that thing on your arm, and you'll find out." Jace strapped a sheath to his thigh, the leather blending with his black breeches. "Just remember, the effect is permanent. It made Adyn nearly invincible, boosting her strength and stamina in addition to all else. Even magic had a limited effect and only a few spells really caused her trouble." He sighed. "I miss her."

"What happened to her anyway?" Harlequin asked.

He smiled. "Adyn saved us all by sacrificing herself during our confrontation with the Dark Lord. When she died, the enchantment faded, her body returning to normal. I grabbed the band a moment before Narine and I returned from Murvaran."

Narine walked in from the other cavern, wearing a purple and blue dress, simple yet elegant. "Leaving Adyn behind was among the most difficult things I have ever had to do."

Jerrell put his arm around his bride. "Had we stayed any longer, we would have died as well."

She leaned her head against his shoulder. "I know."

Harlequin's smirk melted, the moment becoming somber. Eyes filled with pain, Narine stared into space for a quiet moment until Jace cleared his throat.

"With our clothing changed, all is ready," he said. "Let's gather our things and be off."

"What of this?" Crusser asked, the armband still in his hand.

Jace eyed it for a moment and then shrugged. "Stuff it into your bag. We may need it, and I have no idea if or when we'll be back." He turned away. "Perhaps we will find ourselves in need of its power again."

They followed Jace to the neighboring cavern, where he began handing out packs.

Peering inside her pack, Harlequin found a water skin, trail food, and a change of clothing. "What is all this, Jace? Are you planning on a long journey?"

"We cannot remain in Marquithe...not until things settle down."

Narine asked, "Where will we go?"

"Somewhere safe, yet where nobody would expect us or be able to find us. Many of our acquaintances live in palaces, which are all doubtlessly occupied by spies and traitors, so those locations are out of the question. We cannot go to the Valley of Sol, for Harlequin is considered an outlaw by the Order, whose motives we must question until we know more. Where does that leave us?"

Fists on her hips, Narine glared at him. "Spit it out, Jace."

"I thought we might spend a few days, far, far away. I suggest we return to Kelmar."

"The Seers?"

"Some call them witches," Harlequin noted.

Chuckling, Jace shook his head. "I don't suggest you use that term in their presence...or while around their protectors." He turned to Narine. "Kelmar is ideal. Extremely isolated. The Seers do not have visitors nor are they likely to have spies. Even if the Order has infiltrated Kelmar, it is so remote and so far removed from the Valley of Sol, we could stay there for a week without word reaching anyone of import."

Crusser shouldered his pack with ease, his strength making it seem far lighter than it was. "Isn't Kelmar somewhere in the distant southeast?"

"Yes."

Harlequin frowned. "You expect us to travel to a distant corner of the world just to avoid notice? How are we ever going to figure out what is happening from there?"

"Oh, how easily you forget." Jace slid his arm around his new bride. "We have Narine. Her spell can transport us a thousand miles as easily as walking through a doorway."

Narine narrowed her eyes at Jace. "I just realized why you weren't wearing the Eye of Obscurance today."

"While wearing it, I could not have escaped that carriage, nor could I travel to Kelmar...at least not through a gateway. That is, assuming you recall something of the city well enough to get us there."

She nodded. "Our last visit lasted close to two weeks, and much of our time was spent in my room, which I remember well. It should not be an issue."

"Wonderful. Perhaps we will even surprise Xionne." Jace rubbed his palms together. "It would be satisfying to catch the Seers unaware for once. Maybe it would wipe the haughty expressions from their smug faces."

"Jace..." Narine's tone carried a warning.

"Don't worry." He held a palm toward her. "I won't cause any trouble."

Narine turned and gazed into space, her lips pressed together and her eyes narrowing in concentration. Extending one arm, she spread her fingers. The air shimmered as a hole opened, expanding until it was six feet in diameter. Through it was a room with a bed, a side table, and a curtainless window above another table with two chairs. The walls and ceiling sparkled with tiny points of light, reminding Harlequin of a starry sky, something she used to enjoy during nights at sea.

Jace stepped through the portal and extended his hand to Narine who took it and also stepped through.

"Go on," Harlequin said.

Crusser ducked his head, going through after them. Harlequin followed, holding her hat and dipping her head as she traveled many hundreds of miles in a single step. When she turned, the gateway snapped shut with a pop.

The room was bare other than the sparse furniture. Crusser, Narine, and Jace all walked toward the window. Harlequin joined them and peered out, feeling a sense of awe at the sight.

They were in a small city built inside a massive circular cavern, easily a half mile in diameter. High above the city, the cavern ceiling was shaped like a dome speckled with a million sparkling purple lights. Likewise, dots of purple light shone from the city itself – the walls, rooftops, and even the streets. The building they were in was circular in shape, their position four stories above the city.

"Where are we?" Crusser asked.

"We stand in the Temple of the Oracle, home of the Seers of Kelmar," Narine replied. "As you can see, the city was built inside a mountain.

Drawn to motion below, Harlequin spotted a pair of armored dwarfs sparring in a triangular-shaped yard. Similarly dressed dwarfs emerged from a building near the yards.

"Those are the barracks," Jace said. "The dwarfs are guardians for the Seers, as was Hadnoddon."

At mention of his name, Harlequin recalled the gruff dwarf. He had seemed ornery and unlikable at first, but the more time she had spent around him, the more she realized it had been a false impression, likely one he had created on purpose.

"He died during your battle against the Dark Lord?" she asked.

"Yes." Narine said in a sorrowful tone.

Harlequin longed to ask more about the confrontation but sensed Narine's mood and decided to wait.

Jace turned from the window and crossed the room. With his hand on the doorknob, he shot them a grin. "This will be fun."

He opened the door and jerked backward. "What?"

A young woman, little more than a girl, stood in the corridor. She was petite, her eyes blindfolded, and had wavy black hair draped over her shoulders. Two other women flanked her – one tall and pretty, the other old with a sour expression. All three wore simple white sleeveless dresses.

"We have been expecting you, Jerrell," said the blindfolded one.

"Xionne," Jace sighed in obvious disappointment. "I thought I had you this time."

Flashing a smile, Xionne said, "Not yet, but I suspect you will soon surprise us."

31

SLAUGHTER

A silent sentinel, Lang stood beside the staircase, his arms crossed over his sleeveless leather jerkin. Wizards and their bodyguards filled the Willola Manor great room. Plainly dressed, some wearing light armor, the bodyguards stood out amid the fine robes and elegant gowns. Many of the guards acknowledged him in passing, some with a subtle wave, others with a nod, even a few with a smile, as if they found joy in what was to come. Lang's response was muted, his nod nearly imperceptible. He wished to avoid suspicion. Worse, he worried that one of the guards would turn against the rebellion, betraying him and throwing the entire plan into disarray. A piece of him wished it would happen.

Across the entry hall, Isaac stood on the front step with a ledger, recording the name of each arriving guest. A trail of tall torches lit the path from the stairs to the estate gate where carriages dropped off the guests.

As expected, Willola was all smiles, her brown locks arranged in a pile atop her head and held in place by a simple silver tiara. Her dress was lavender, the material shimmering in the flickering light of the great room chandelier. Once again, the wizardess displayed her ability to transform into the most engaging and gregarious woman in Ghealdor. This was her night to shine, and she greeted every guest like he or she were the most important person in Fastella. The single men, regardless of age or appearance, received familiar touches on their arm, shoulder, or hip as she bestowed them with glowing smiles and flirtatious laughter. To the women and married men, she was attentive and complimentary, often gifting the wives with compliments on their hair, jewelry, or gowns. Lang found her performance simultaneously impressive and revolting.

Cleared of furniture, the great room was an octagon shape, large enough to hold hundreds of people. Two stories above, a mural of wizards kneeling before Gheald graced the ceiling, a massive chandelier hanging from the center. A colossal stone fireplace acted as the focal point of the great room, encompassing the middle wall opposite from where Lang stood. The two angled walls to each side of the fireplace featured tall windows, arched at the top, wooden strips securing each diamond-shaped pane. A harpist sat beside the fireplace, fingers flowing over the strings in smooth, elegant strokes. Lang found it ironic to have such a sweet aria as a precursor for the screams sure to follow.

As the manor filled, Lang felt something building inside him – a form of anticipation he used to experience before every gladiator battle. Death was coming, the sense of it lingering in every shadow, every movement around him. *Is this the day it comes for me?* He had whispered the thought times beyond counting.

In the dining hall to Lang's left, Lowell stood beside a long table that held four tapped wine barrels. As guests approached, the man filled glasses with the dark red liquid. Beside him was Marta, one of the maids, pouring cups of wine. The new table, twelve feet long and made of heavy oak, occupied the middle of the room. The table held enough food to feed twice the guest list.

People trickled in and out of the dining room, carrying drinks and laughing as they chewed on some tasty treat. Not all had wine, yet Lang watched with curious trepidation each time a wizard passed through the newly replaced doorframe, seeking some sign of warning – a flash of light, bubbles in the wine, or a wizard lurching with a start as an unknowable internal alarm went off. None ever came. The more he watched and saw nothing of note, the more he worried that the spell had failed or had been a hoax.

As Lang had expected, Willola decided to open all four of the wine barrels brought up from the cellar. Also as expected, the estate staff members were all forced to taste the wine, even Lang. While she suggested they should consider themselves lucky to sample fine Farrowen red, her true motives had little to do with generosity. When none of her staff fell ill or died, the wizardess was satisfied, but she warned them all to watch the stock. Should anyone poison it, they would all be blamed. Surprisingly, she did not iterate the penalty for attempting to kill a wizard. There was little need to do so. Everyone in Fastella had seen severed heads mounted to the palace wall.

And, thus, the party continued for over an hour with guests mingling, chatting, laughing, and drinking – Lang watching in still silence the entire time. He counted over sixty wizards and believed every adult other than the queen herself was in attendance. Along the walls stood thirty-three guards, most waiting as he was, knowing what was to come.

An hour passed before Willola disappeared into the kitchen. When she returned, Olban was at her side, the two of them stopping in the center of the great room. The steward raised a triangle made of iron and rang it, the metal rod in his other hand clanging off the three sides. The harpist dropped her hand, the guests' attention on Willola as the room quieted.

"Welcome! I am honored to have you here," she bellowed. "While I hope you will stay long into the evening and enjoy yourself, we have business to discuss first. Guild business. Two heinous acts were committed two nights ago, one of which leaves us without a hall to conduct formal meetings. As a result, we will hold a special meeting here and now. Per guild rules, I ask all servants and guards to step outside. Only wizards may remain."

The bodyguards began filtering out the front door, Lang watching as they marched past. Isaac, Olban, Lowell, and the two maids, Gretchen and Marta, joined them.

Lang cast one last glance toward the crowd in the great room. Men and women, from those in their mid-twenties to the elderly, stood in clusters. Some whispered and pointed in his direction, smiles becoming frowns. Rather than respond, he glared at them, unmoving until Willola stormed toward him.

"What are you doing?" Her teeth were clenched, her hushed voice thick with vitriol. "You are embarrassing me. Get out or I will have you flogged in the palace square!"

He grunted. "I knew the real you hid in there somewhere."

Her mouth opened to reply, but he turned away and strode out, resolute in what he must do next.

The door closed behind him as he descended the front stairs. He reached out and tore the nearest torch from the ground, the flame at the end of the six-foot rod flickering as he marched across the lawn. Like a mother goose leading her young, the other bodyguards gathered behind him, some asking where he was going. He did not stop until he reached the cobblestone drive. There, away from the household staff and the smattering of guards unaware of the rebellion, Lang faced the men he had agreed to lead.

"We have one chance. This must end quickly, or we will fail." He examined the men's faces, some new, others he had known for years. All appeared hardened and familiar with a fight, whether on the battlefield or in the streets. "You must be ruthless. We give no quarter, for any wizard who survives this night becomes a vengeful enemy tomorrow."

Determined gazes and nods were the only response.

"Good. Now, I need those with blunt weapons to grab a torch from the front path, choose a window to the great room, and get ready. When the assault starts, smash the glass. Once broken, toss your torch inside and back away."

"I noticed some of you carrying crossbows. You will target any wizard who attempts to climb out the windows." He pointed toward two men on his right, both of whom he knew. "Fram, Glennon, you two will come with me to guard the back door. The rest of you, take the front entrance. Do not kill any of the palace staff unless you have no choice. They are not the enemy, nor are the other guards, not unless they choose the wrong side. When it all starts, they are to join us or die. We outnumber them six to one, so they should see the right of it." He held his finger up. "Be ready, but don't act until you hear the signal."

"What signal?" Balcor asked.

"Oh, you will know it."

Lang turned and followed the drive past the stables, circling behind the manor, the two guards on his heels. He went straight for the cellar doors, lifted one, and flipped it open to reveal stairs receding into darkness.

He pointed toward the door to the kitchen. "You two, guard the back door. Kill anyone who comes out. I will be right back."

As the two men walked away, he began his descent, careful not to bump his head, the pole in his hand held horizontal with the flaming end in front.

As always, the cellar was damp, smelling of must and dirt. He was thankful it smelled of nothing else.

When he reached the bottom, he stared at the wine barrels clustered near the chilling rod. *Best to keep fire away from them.* He wedged the torch against a shelf and approached one of the red-banded barrels. Gripping the sides, he rocked it back and forth, shifting it across the floor and away from the others. When it was against the wall and could move no further, he squatted and gripped the tap sticking from the barrel. Opening it caused thick dark liquid to ooze onto the dirt floor. The pool spread until he tightened the spigot and the flow ceased. Hoping it would be enough and fearing he had released too much, Lang retrieved the torch. Backing to the bottom step, he extended the pole, the flame flickering as it drew near the spill.

The naphtha on the ground lit in a whoosh, launching a wall of flame five feet high.

Lang tossed the torch aside, raced up the stairs, and burst into the back yard.

"Run!" he shouted.

The two guards watching the back door hesitated for a breath, staring at the amber light coming from the cellar. Lang slowed as he neared the stables, and turned to find the men racing toward him.

An explosion came from beneath the manor, a tongue of flame thrusting out the cellar stairwell and toward the night sky. The cellar door Lang had left closed flew across the yard, straight at him. He dropped to the ground just in time. The door struck the stables in a spray of splinters. The two guards dove to the ground as the other two naphtha barrels ignited.

The ground shook with a thunderous boom, shattering the rear wall of the manor and sending a spray of debris across the yard. A flaming inferno raged in the kitchen, fed by the barrels of naphtha below it. The door was destroyed, the fire far too intense for anyone to pass through the rear of the manor.

Lang leapt to his feet, both guards doing the same. "Are you alright?"

They nodded numbly.

"Good. Let's go help the others."

He ran back down the drive, slowing as he reached the front lawn.

Windows were broken, fires burning inside, people screaming.

Swords were drawn as a fight ensued between his men and those who had not been recruited.

Suddenly, all the great room windows shattered, glass spraying across the lawn. Thick black smoke billowed out the window. Male and female wizards coughed and flailed, many attempting to use magic to no avail.

Out of the black smoke, Roderan emerged at one window. Bolts of lightning lashed out from his arms, arcing from guard to guard and catching their hair on fire. When the attack stopped, ten guards lay dead.

"Crossbows!" Lang shouted, racing toward them. "Kill that wizard!"

Bows were lifted and bolts loosed, but Roderan was ready. Every bolt stopped a stride short of the man, shattering as though against an invisible shield.

We cannot afford to lose more guards, Lang thought as he leapt into action.

Roderan climbed on the windowsill and launched another assault, lightning again striking numerous guards. With Roderan focused on the guards between him and the front door, he did not see Lang running along the manor wall, approaching from his backside.

As Lang reached the window, Roderan spun toward him. With a desperate backhand strike, Lang swung his blade into the wizard's shins. The blow knocked Roderan's feet from beneath him and he fell face first on a broken windowpane, shards of glass slicing into his chest. The wizard convulsed, coughed blood, and fell still.

Screams and cries came from inside, panicked people stumbling over one another. Those who made it out the front door were swiftly cut down, and those attempting to climb through the window were stopped by crossbow bolts. It was a slaughter, no more than a handful even making it out of the house before they died.

When the screams ceased, Lang backed away and stared at the burning manor. While he had agreed to lead these men and knew most wizards were beyond redemption, many innocents had died in the process. Roderan's face would join the growing army in his nightmares.

A familiar voice came from behind him. "Why are you just standing there?"

Lang turned toward the sorcerer. "You got what you wanted, Vex. The wizards are gone."

Vex shook his head. "Not what *I* wanted, but what the citizens of Fastella wanted." He pointed at Lang. "What you wanted."

"I never said I wanted this."

"Yet here you are."

It was a statement Lang could not argue with. He glanced away to see others drawing closer. No more than fifteen had survived.

"However," Vex continued, "your work is not finished. The queen still lives, and until she has been ousted, the people of Fastella remain under wizard rule."

Running a hand down his face, Lang said wearily, "Tomorrow, we can…"

"No!" the sorcerer shouted. "It must be tonight. If given time, she will fortify her position, and it will be impossible to get near her. Surprise is our ally, the only one we need."

Lang looked over his fellow conspirators. "Barely more than a dozen of us remain. How can we take the palace?"

In the light of the burning manor, a smile spread across the sorcerer's face, a humorless smile. "I have ensured a way to get you inside. Once in the palace, the rest is up to you."

32

A GOOD DAY TO DIE

With Lang in the lead and Vex at his side, the rebels marched down the dark streets of Fastella. They passed an inn, the hum of conversation and raucous laughter coming from within. The sound was a stark contrast to the grim mood gripping Lang and his men.

Each intersection was illuminated by the pale blue light of an enchanted lantern mounted to a pole. From time to time, they passed other citizens – a man in a dark cloak, another man with a woman under his arm, two unsavory characters who narrowed their eyes in suspicious glares – but did not encounter the city watch or any soldiers.

At the end of the street, they came to the massive square surrounding Fastella Palace. Torches burned on the walls and beside the front gate where four palace guards stood ready. The palace itself was visible beyond the wall, a complex made of blocky buildings and dark towers. At the far end of the square stood the Temple of Gheald, a massive dome-shaped building connected to the palace.

Lang and his companions waited in the shadows as a pair of guards patrolled the palace perimeter. Both men were dressed in gold tinted armor and purple capes, wearing doglike helms. The guards turned the corner and stopped to chat with the guards posted at the main palace gate.

Waving them forward, Vex headed away from the gate, remaining close to the buildings across from the palace until they reached the side entrance. It was an entrance Lang knew well, giving access to a circular drive and the palace stables where the horses and carriages were stored.

The sorcerer led them across the square to the gate. It was closed, two men standing inside, two more posted atop the wall, each holding a bow.

"Greetings," Vex said, raising a hand.

One of the guards, a middle-aged man with a scarred cheek, placed a hand on the hilt of his sword. "What do you want?"

"We have grave news for the queen. Is she available?"

The man snorted. "She is the queen, a wizard of great importance. She has no time for the likes of you. If you have a message, give it now, and I will have it relayed to her should I determine it worthy."

Vex frowned. "I will only speak with the queen. Does she have no time for her people?"

The other guard drew his sword. "I suggest you move along. One shout and the men above will begin loosing arrows."

The first guard scowled at the younger man. "You are not in charge here, Norri."

"Go ahead," Vex challenged. "Have the guards loose upon us. We are ready."

"As you wish," Norri's free arm wrapped around the older guard's head, tipping it back as his sword sliced across the man's throat. He then shouted, "Loose!"

One of the archers turned on his companion, his arrow flying into the other man's chest. The impaled archer toppled off the wall, forcing some of Lang's men to scatter clear. He struck the ground hard, his neck bent at a grotesque angle.

"Hurry, Norri. Open the gate," Vex commanded.

As the guard made for the winch, the sorcerer gestured toward the dead archer. "Two of you, pick him up. We need to hide him inside before the guards come around again."

The gate began to rise. Once it was at chest height, Lang ducked beneath it, the others following. He bent, gripped the dead guard by the arm, and dragged the corpse off to the side, hiding it behind the hedgerow. A moment later, two of his men dumped the dead archer beside the first corpse. With everyone inside, the gate closed and Vex led them down the drive toward the palace side entrance. Just outside the door, he stopped, Lang standing beside him. They both turned toward the other rebels, counting eighteen men in total after Nolan and Pendry joined them.

Vex placed a hand on Lang's shoulder as he addressed the other rebels. "Reagor lived here while Parsec held the throne. He knows it well and will lead you. Beware, for the queen's magic is dangerous. Also, beware her bodyguard, Herrod. The man is as strong as an ox and as mean as a badger."

"What about you?" Lang asked.

Vex bit his own lip, drawing blood. He licked it and it turned his tongue crimson. He then spoke, his voice humming, enthralling, and undeniable. "This is *your* rebellion. In the name of liberty and justice, the queen must die. You will lead these men or die trying."

The sorcerer's words called to Lang. His heart suddenly raced, his vision turning red, as he was overcome by a compelling, urgent need to see the queen dead.

Pulling the door open, Vex waved them inside. Lang drew his sword and led the charge.

They raced up the stairwell, no longer concerned with stealth. Lang and his followers charged up four flights and burst into the fifth level corridor. Two guards stood ready, swords drawn, dog-shaped helms on their heads, purple capes on their backs. They were Indigo Hounds. Through the haze in Lang's head, the thought barely registered.

He roared and prepared to charge but two of his companions pushed him aside and met the guards, swords clashing briefly before they died. A crossbow bolt sailed past, impaling one of the Indigo Hounds and causing the man to spin around from the impact to his shoulder. Lang followed with a high swing, forcing the other guard to raise his blade. Another rebel lunged, plunging a steel boot into the guard's exposed ribs.

Lang turned to the door leading to the queen's chamber – the same chamber Parsec had used during his brief rule. He tested the knob and found it locked, so he backed up a step and drove his heel into the door, cracking it. Balcor joined in, the two of them thrusting their boots into the door at the same time. It blasted open with a loud crack, the room's interior falling silent. Only darkness waited beyond the corridor.

"Careful," Lang grabbed the torch from the sconce near the door.

Torch in hand, he dove into the room, rolled, and came to a stance, his blade in front of him. No attack came. Moonlight shone through the glass balcony doors, the sitting room vacant and the long dining table empty except for a golden candelabra.

"Spread out," he said as he headed toward the study.

The room was empty other than a desk with scattered papers, a chair, and shelves filled with books. As he walked back to the middle of the central chamber, two men came from the bedroom and two more from the balcony.

"Nobody is in there," Balcor said.

Another added, "Nor on the balcony."

Scowling, Lang marched past them into the corridor where six of the rebels remained, two holding swords over the guard with the bolt in his shoulder. Lang sheathed his blade, squatted, and gripped the guard's cuirass, lifting him by it. The man winced in pain.

"Where is the queen?" Lang demanded.

The guard shook his head. "She would kill me."

"She will be dead."

"Don't you see?" The guard pleaded. "Another wizard will take her place, and then I will die all the same."

"Not this time. We are not here just to place a new ruler on the throne. We are removing *all* wizards from rule. As it stands, Dalia might be the only wizard remaining in Fastella."

"What...what of the guild?"

Balcor laughed. "Dead. All of them."

"What is your name?" Lang asked.

The guard blinked, considering his response before saying, "Iben."

"You have a chance to join us, Iben. In the process, you could retain your job, but rather than protecting the life of a wizardess who sees you as nothing more than a pawn, you can serve a king who cares about you and understands the difficult life of a guard."

Iben's eyes narrowed. "Who would this king be?"

"Have you heard of GaLang Reagor?"

"Of course."

"*I* am Reagor."

The man looked at Balcor, who nodded. Eyes widening, Iben said, "She is in the throne room, meeting with Chancellor Perlock."

Lang stood and gave the guard a nod. "Good man. That bolt hurts, but it will not be a fatal wound if properly dressed. If I survive the night, I will see you again."

"Watch out," Iben said. "That beast Herrod is with her."

"As I expected." Lang turned and strode down the corridor, the others falling in behind him.

Hidden in the corridor shadows, Lang peered around the corner into the palace receiving hall. Four armed guards stood before the closed throne room doors, but the hall was otherwise empty. He slid back to where his men waited, determination in their eyes.

Whispering, he pointed toward Balcor. "Four soldiers guard the door. You take seven others and confront them. Draw them away from the throne room. The rest of us will race past while they are engaged and busy trying not to die."

Balcor nodded. "We shall do our best. Even if things go poorly, we fight for freedom. Today is a good day to die, for I'd rather give my life for a chance at liberty than continue as we have."

The man tapped seven other rebels on the shoulder, gesturing for them to follow him. They crept down the corridor and then raced out into the receiving hall.

"Alarm!" a palace guard shouted. "We are under attack!"

The clang of swords rang out, joined by grunts, boots scraping on tile, and a man crying out in pain.

Facing the remaining eight rebels, Lang said, "We are going after the queen. I will take her bodyguard, the rest of you spread out and attack her at the same time. She can't stop all of you at once." Without waiting for them to respond, Lang spun and rushed down the corridor.

The rebels and palace guards fought furiously. Two men from each side were already down, shifting the odds three to one in the rebels' favor. Lang darted for the throne room doors, knowing timing was critical. The rapid thuds of rushing footsteps came from another corridor, but he ignored them as he threw the door open and led his team into the throne room.

At the head of the room, Queen Dalia sat in her throne. Herrod stood beside her in full armor, a helmet beneath one arm. The only other person in the room turned toward Lang. He was a middle-aged man, a ring of brown hair surrounding his otherwise bald pate. The man stood, a white ruffled doublet stretched tightly across his abundant stomach. His eyes filled with fear, and he backed toward the side of the room.

"What is the meaning of this interruption?" the queen demanded.

Lang strode down the center aisle while the other eight rebels split into two groups, four approaching along each outer wall. "This is a rebellion, Dalia." He purposely omitted her title. "The citizens of Ghealdor can no longer live under the weight of wizard oppression."

She arched a brow. "Is that so? What of Gheald's laws?"

"Gheald is no more. He and the other gods are gone, along with the wizard lords, making Devotion a thing of the past. It is time for wizard rule to end and for liberty to claim the crown."

She sneered. "Even if you killed me, another wizard would take my place."

"Not so," Lang, now halfway to the front of the room, held his sword at his side. "The other wizards are dead, killed in a fire at the Willola Estate."

The queen frowned. "I see." She glanced toward Herrod, the imposing man slipping his helmet over his head. "Is there nothing I can do to change your mind?"

"Abdicate the throne and leave Ghealdor for good," Lang demanded. "Anything less is unacceptable."

"I thought you might feel that way." She stood, head shifting to the left and right, taking note of the other rebels. "We appear to have reached an impasse. Too bad for you." Pointing at Lang, she snarled, "Kill him."

Herrod launched himself off the dais with a roar and charged at Lang with a mighty sweep of his mace. Lang raised his sword to block it, but the force of the blow knocked his sword aside and sent him stumbling back, hands stinging from the hard blow. Spinning away, Lang retreated, giving Herrod room as he prepared for another attack.

The queen spun and thrust her arms toward the attackers on her left, blasting them with a cone of flames. Two men were set ablaze. The other two dove over the benches to escape her deadly magic. She spun in the other direction and released another spell, blasting lightning from her hands. It struck the man in front and sent arcs of electricity at the three men behind him. The first target fell to his knees, his body convulsing. The attack ended quickly, the man and his companions all collapsing to the floor.

The queen's bodyguard attacked again, Lang twisting as he knocked the mace aside with his sword, doing his best to avoid taking the full force of another blow. Herrod's face turned up in a snarl as he swung again and again, Lang dodged and knocked the blows aside while seeking an opening.

Herrod swung again but missed when Lang leapt back, the mace smashing into a bench in a spray of wooden shards. When the hulking warrior raised his mace for a downward strike, Lang twisted his body and lunged. The mace came down in a flash, spikes grazing Lang's jerkin as his sword tip sank into Herrod's thigh. The big man grunted and stumbled back, Lang following with a slash that tore through a strap beneath Herrod's arm and left a shallow gash. Again, Herrod grunted in pain.

Suddenly, Herrod tried to race past Lang toward the exit. Lang thrust his sword aimed at the man's exposed ribs but found no resistance. Overbalanced, he stumbled forward, he and his blade somehow passing right through the man. Herrod continued down the aisle as the entrance doors opened. Balcor and three other rebels burst inside, but rather than collide with Balcor, Herrod passed right through him.

Dumbstruck, everyone froze.

An illusion, Lang thought, the realization filling him with alarm.

He spun back toward the dais as Herrod, the real Herrod, swung his mace. The heavy spiked weapon struck Lang in the chest. The thunderous blow lifted him off his feet and launched him through the air. He landed on his back, dropping his sword. His vision blurred in a haze of pain.

Lang writhed while blood bubbled through holes in his jerkin where mace spikes had impaled him. His chest was crushed, his ribs shattered, and he was unable to fill his lungs. The agony was overwhelming, far beyond anything he had ever experienced.

Herrod strode closer and gazed down at him, one hand held against his wounded side, the other still gripping the bloodied mace.

Like a tunnel sealing, darkness closed in, and Lang fell still.

The pain receded and Lang felt nothing.

Light burst through the darkness as he floated upward. When he looked down, he saw himself lying on the floor, his chest bloodied and his eyes staring into infinity. The colossal bodyguard loomed over him. Balcor and the other remaining rebels stood frozen in the doorway, transfixed in a state of shock. At the fore of the room, the queen stood before her throne, corpses on the floor to either side of her, some still burning.

I am dead, Lang realized. *I have failed. It is over.*

"No," a familiar voice whispered. *"This is not over."*

Vex?

"Yes. I am with you. Now breathe."

Breathe? How?

The sorcerer entered the room, followed by a host of palace guards who surrounded the remaining rebels, all eyes on Lang's corpse in the center of the room.

A glow rose from Lang's chest, rays of light emitting from each wound and twisting to form a column of swirling amber light. Sparks of similar light emerged from the chests of each person in the room – Herrod, Queen Dalia, Balcor and the other rebels, Vex and the palace guards. The sparks floated toward the light above Lang's body, merging with the spinning column and causing it to brighten tenfold.

Vex spread his arms and said aloud, "Breathe, GaLang Reagor. Accept your destiny."

Lang opened his mouth and saw his own body do the same. He inhaled. The column of swirling light bent toward his mouth and was drawn inside.

Reagor opened his eyes with a gasp. He lay on his back, Herrod still staring down at him. He rolled over, gripped his sword, and climbed to his feet.

Herrod stumbled backward with widened eyes, shaking his head. "It cannot be."

"You cannot deny destiny, Herrod," Reagor said.

He launched himself toward the man, his sword flashing with incredible speed. Herrod swung a roundabout blow, but Reagor expected it, stopping his momentum just shy of the big man's reach. The mace flew past and Reagor followed it with another swing of his own. This time, the tip of his blade tore Herrod's throat open. The bodyguard staggered, dropping his mace to the floor as he reached to touch his bloody gash. He fell to his knees and collapsed against a bench with a mighty clatter.

Turning toward the dais, Reagor met Queen Dalia's gaping eyes. "Your use of illusion was well-played, drawing my attention away from the true threat until it was too late."

The woman's surprise turned to anger, her hands twirling as she wove a spell. A ball of fire bloomed between her palms, smoking and hovering in midair.

She sneered, "You should be dead."

Calm and confident, Reagor shook his head. "It was not my destiny to die at his hand. Nor at yours."

He tossed his sword to the carpet, watching her eyes follow it. The momentary distraction was all he needed. In one motion, he drew the four-pointed blade at his hip and gave it a sideways fling, the razoreth spinning until it struck her stomach. Dalia bent with a lurch, dropping her jaw for a quick breath before snarling at him.

The fireball burst forward.

Ready, Reagor dove sideways between two benches, feeling the heat of the magic missile as it slipped past him and struck a wooden bench, blasting it backward. Bits of flame scattered across the room. On his knees, he peered over the bench. The queen yanked the blade from her flesh, and gazed at it. Two tips were wet with her blood, the others blackened. She staggered back and fell into the throne, dropping the throwing blade to the floor.

Reagor rose to his feet, the flames burning behind him a reflection of the fire in his gut. "Yes. The blades were poisoned." Stepping back into the aisle, he strode toward her. "Unlike wizard lords of the past, you lack the magic of Gheald and cannot heal yourself." He shook his head, voice sad. "Soon, you will be dead."

She convulsed, blood running from her nose. "Why?"

"We are done having our taxes spent on wizard estates and lavish parties." He climbed the dais stairs. "After thousands of years of bending to the whims of the Gifted, the people of Ghealdor will be free."

Shaking with sharp jerks, her mouth began to foam. Blood ran from her nose, ears, and eyes. She slumped in the throne, her head drooping to the side as she fell still.

Reagor turned toward the room.

An arc of Indigo Hounds surrounded Balcor and the last remaining rebels, all with weapons in their hands, all staring at him in wide-eyed shock. Vex broke away from the group and strode down the center aisle, passing burning benches, Herrod's corpse, and, finally, the bodies of slain rebels.

The sorcerer ascended the dais to stand beside Reagor before addressing the room. "The queen is dead. Wizards will no longer rule the people of Ghealdor, for our savior has risen. You have witnessed proof of his immortality." He gripped Reagor's wrist and lifted his arm high. "This is no mere man. This is GaLang Reagor, the god king and champion of Ghealdor." Raising his voice, he bellowed, "Long live King Reagor."

A beat of silence followed.

Then Balcor marched forward, pumped his fist in the air, and chanted, "Reagor! Reagor! Reagor!"

The other rebels repeated the chant while Reagor waited for the palace guards to react. Amazingly, they sheathed their swords and joined in.

33

KELMAR

The water rolled down Harlequin's throat, taking the last of the boiled leaves with it. She wiped her lips, her face twisted in disgust. "The food here is worse than in the Valley of Sol. It might be the worst I have ever had, and I have lived half my life on a ship."

Last night's meal had been just as difficult to choke down. *Last night...* She chuckled to herself, considering the oddity of the statement.

Following dinner, Harlequin had been led to her own room. After hours of fitful sleep, she had risen to stare out the window, watching dwarfs in the streets below as she wondered what time it was. Day and night were difficult to distinguish, the sky somewhere above the rock dome that emcompassed the city of Kelmar. At all times, her surroundings remained constant – the city's only source of light coming from thousands of tiny sparkling purple lights embedded in the walls, ceiling, and cavern dome. The concepts of night and day suddenly seemed irrelevant and left her wondering if the citizens of Kelmar bothered with any sort of schedule synchronization or if each merely slept when they were tired and worked when they were alert. After an hour of peering through the window, she lay back down, more from boredom than anything else.

A knock at the door stirred unexpected eagerness, and she leapt out of bed to answer it. A pair of Seers waited in the corridor, ready to escort her and her companions to breakfast.

Now, less than an hour later, her stomach was sated, but that eagerness was dead and buried, destroyed by the bland, soggy meal.

Jace chuckled at her comment. "While you will get used to the food over time, meals here are a means to remain alive rather than a source of pleasure."

He and Narine sat across the table from her and Crusser. The other six seats remained empty. Two Seers stood at the end of the room watching them as they had watched them during their previous meal. She wondered if they would have an escort every time they left their rooms.

Scowling, Harlequin used her fork to slide the remaining food across her plate. The meal included strange vegetables and a piece of tasteless cake made of rice. Only the fish was completely eaten. "It would help if we had wine or ale to wash it down."

Narine arched a brow. "You want ale with your breakfast?"

Harlequin shrugged. "It wouldn't be the first time."

"This food isn't so bad," Crusser said. "Spend a year or two in the Murguard and then tell me this is disgusting. One of the cooks at my outpost even attempted to make a meal out of goblin meat. Turns out, darkspawn flesh turns rancid when cooked."

"That sounds disgusting." Narine soured her face.

"It was...or so I was told."

The two Seers approached the table, one asking, "Are you finished with your meal?"

"Yes, Jionna," Narine said.

The other Seer clapped her hands. Two young men rushed in, both stripped to the waist. Each had long dark hair, dark eyes, and lean muscular frames. Harlequin eyed them with a smile, watching as the men collected their plates and then rushed off.

Still grinning, she turned toward Jionna. "I commend you on the help. It is refreshing to see male servers forced to flaunt their bodies for once. Too often, it is women in such positions."

Jionna gasped. "Women...they would serve meals with their bodies bared? That is unthinkable."

"Well, not bared exactly...but close."

She shook her head. "The Thrall serve here. It is the way it has always been." Leaning close, she whispered, "If you are in need of pleasure or wish to birth a child, Kip, the taller of the two who just left, has a particularly impressive…"

Narine blurted, "No need, Jionna. We will be gone soon, and Harlequin does not need, um, pleasure."

"Hold on," Harlequin leaned over the table, eyeing the Seer. "Just how impressive?"

"He is among the favorites for those who are selected to bear children. I have not seen it for myself, but I have heard…"

Jionna stopped mid-sentence as an older Seer entered the room – the same woman Harlequin had seen with Xionne the night before.

The woman fixed Jionna with a stern glare, and the younger Seer appeared ashamed. "That will be enough, Jionna."

Dropping her chin to her chest, Jionna replied, "Yes, Zhialta."

Zhialta then turned toward the table. "Come along. Mother will see you now."

Jace stood and took Narine's hand, the queen rising as well. Curious, Harlequin and Crusser followed as the old woman led them out of the dining room and down a long curved corridor, the two younger Seers trailing behind them. They descended a stairwell illuminated by glowing purple flecks within its stone walls. After crossing a large open hall, the old woman took them along a curved corridor, turning down a hallway and past a dark stairwell that led below ground. Just beyond the stairwell was a closed door. The old woman stopped at the door to look back at Jace.

"You are to be respectful, thief." She turned toward Harlequin. "You as well, pirate."

Harlequin blinked in surprise. "Pirate?" *How could she know that?*

Zhialta smirked. "The Seers know all."

Jace snorted. "Not quite."

The old woman's scowl returned. "Respect."

He said, "We have been in the Oracle before, remember?"

"Then you should know. The Oracle is a place of power, a holy place blessed by Vandasal himself, long, long ago."

As the old woman opened the door, Jace shot Narine a look of concern.

Harlequin's brow furrowed. *The Seers do not realize Vandasal is gone from this world.*

The door led to an outdoor circular theater. A single row of seating surrounding the theater, and the seats filled with Seers of all ages dressed in white. High above, the domed cavern ceiling sparkled with tiny purple lights

The floor of the theater was rounded like a bowl, a circular dais in the center. A crystal throne sat upon the platform with an odd frame built over it. A massive octahedron-shaped diamond was mounted in the frame, ten feet above the dais. Xionne sat patiently on the throne, blindfolded, hands folded on her lap.

Zhialta led the visitors down the ramp to the bottom of the bowl, stopping a few strides before the dais. Jace and Narine stopped on one side of the Seer, Harlequin and Crusser settling on the other.

The old woman bowed. "Blessed Mother, I have retrieved our guests as bidden."

"Thank you, Zhialta." Xionne turned her blindfolded face toward Jace and Narine. "Welcome back to the Oracle. When you last visited, the future was in doubt, the fate of the world teetering, and we were blinded to prophecy. A year ago yesterday, prophecy opened to us once again and gave us a vision of a new future. It was an enthralling vision, distinct and unique, the first ever depicting events beyond the confrontation with the Dark Lord."

Jace crossed his arms over his chest and frowned. "While Narine and I appreciate your hospitality, we did not return to Kelmar to become pawns to your prophecies. We and our companions followed that road once. Those of us who survived were beyond lucky to do so, for a fair number died to fulfill your little prophecy. While we were successful, the victory felt hollow and unrewarding. Looking back, I'm not sure if our actions made things better or worse."

Xionne lowered her gaze and sat in silence for a time. Harlequin wondered if the girl was sad or lost in thought.

The Seer lifted her head, opening her mouth, but no words emerged. Again, she tried, her voice hushed as if she lacked the will to speak with more energy. "Tell me. What happened in Murvaran? What of the gods?"

Jace looked at Narine before replying. "The gods are gone, Xionne. The Dark Lord with them."

"And...what of Vandasal?"

Pressing his lips together, Jace seemed reluctant to answer. Finally, he said, "Gone…" He shrugged. "Dead, I guess."

A collective gasp came from the ring of Seers surrounding the Oracle. Many women burst into tears, some falling from their seats to lie prone on the floor, sobbing hysterically.

Gesturing toward the diamond above her, Xionne said, "A year ago, after our final prophecy, the light in the gem faded. In my heart, I knew it was connected to Vandasal. I feared the cause, and as each week passed without any form of vision and the Oracle powerless, my hope waned. If Vandasal is truly gone, our ability to prophesy is gone with it." She raised her hands to the blindfold and lifted it from her face, exposing overly large eyes with purple irises.

Another gasp echoed in the Oracle. Most of the women present were now openly weeping. Even the stern, stoic Zhialta was visibly disturbed.

Xionne stood and raised her voice. "For two millennia, the Seers have remained loyal to Vandasal, dedicated to our craft, and committed to our cause. The Dark Lord is no more. Our mission is complete." She spun around slowly, all eyes on her. "Your obligation has been fulfilled. You are free to leave Kelmar, for the Seers are no more."

34

UNCERTAINTY

An air of melancholy clung to the Oracle as Seers filtered back into the building, their expressions ranging from vacant bewilderment to excruciating sorrow. Some could barely walk, requiring one or two other women to support them as they stumbled toward the exit. It was as if all hope had fled from their lives, leaving Narine near tears.

In her head, she fumbled for a sentiment that might offer comfort but came up wanting. The truth had been revealed, a truth many had known deep inside. *Sometimes it is easier to lie to yourself than to face a frightening reality.* There had been moments when Narine wished she could have shied from a dark truth rather than face it. The support of others, particularly Adyn or Jace, had kept her from such denial. *These women know nothing of the world beyond Kelmar. Worse, they have been groomed since birth for this one thing. To have it taken away in this manner... I pray none turn to despair.* Narine had already seen too many of her own Farrowen clergy resort to suicide.

The last of the women passed through the doorway and faded from view, leaving only Zhialta and Xionne in the company of Narine, Jace, Harlequin, and Crusser.

Xionne descended from the dais and stood beside the taller, much older Seer. It was odd to see the young woman without a blindfold, her oversized eyes making her appear to be in her mid-teens. Yet, the others had called her

Mother, and she had displayed wisdom, patience, and maturity well beyond such a young age. *I wonder…maybe she is much older than we first believed.*

Jace's eyes flicked from Narine to Xionne, his hand running through his hair. "I now realize that my response to your question was abrupt. I had not considered…did not expect such a dramatic reaction from the Seers."

Xionne arched a brow. "Is that an apology? From the Charlatan of Ages?"

His face darkened. "I have apologized to others before."

The girl moved closer and patted his cheek. "To Narine, yes. Name one other who has caused you to swallow your pride."

He frowned. "I'd rather not."

"Never mind," she smirked. "The difficult part is behind us. While their world and all they have known has been shattered, the Seers will recover, for they are stronger than they know. They require time to come to grips with a new reality. When they are ready to listen, we will give them another purpose to fill the vacuum." Turning away, she headed toward the door, Zhialta at her side. "Come along. We have much to discuss."

Narine, Jace, Harlequin, and Crusser trailed behind the two Seers, climbing the upslope of the bowl and reentering the building. Rather than follow the corridor, Zhialta and Xionne descended a long dark stairwell, which stirred more memories for Narine. During their last visit to Kelmar, she and her companions had spent many hours at the basement level.

At the bottom, a curved corridor ran in both directions, but rather than glowing dots providing light, sconces lined the outer wall, each holding a glowing purple orb. The corridor was bordered by smooth stone walls until they came to a door on the inside wall of the circle. The door was ornately carved and black as night.

Zhialta lifted the nearest orb off its sconce and opened the door. With the orb held up, she led them inside, the dim light revealing the tall shelving that bracketed the entrance. The old woman approached one shelf and placed the orb into an empty sconce beside it. A hum arose and light bloomed from similar orbs throughout the sprawling circular room. As Narine recalled from her previous visits, row upon row of bookshelves filled the space, the end of each shelf illuminated by a glowing orb of light, somehow triggered by the orb placed in the first empty sconce. A smaller walled chamber, also circular in shape, stood in the center of the chamber. The space between the shelving and the room at the center was encircled by tables.

"Where are the books?" Narine asked.

A scratchy wizened voice came from behind her. "Destroyed."

She turned to find two women dressed in white, recalling them in an instant - the librarians, Tabitha and Margarete.

Tabitha was even older than Zhialta. Her hair was white wisps and her body was bent and gnarled. In contrast, Margarete's tall frame made her look like a giant beside Tabitha. They each wore their hair in a braid and were among the most severe of Seers. The younger woman's eyes were haunted, her face even paler than Narine remembered.

"Why destroyed?" Narine asked.

Both librarians glanced toward Xionne. "All will soon be revealed."

With Margarete's help, Tabitha shuffled past, following Xionne and Zhialta toward the center of the library.

Jace leaned close to Narine and whispered, "They have not lost their love of secrets, nor of frustrating anyone bold enough to ask questions. Would it kill them to answer directly?"

Narine hastily raised her hand to cover her smile.

Harlequin snorted. "It feels like I am back among members of the Order."

Crusser grunted, apparently in agreement.

They advanced deeper into the room, joining the four Seers to gather near the closed door leading to the center chamber. The door was red with three concentric rings and four recesses in the center.

From beneath the neckline of her dress, Xionne withdrew a diamond-shaped pendant attached to a cord. She pulled it over her head and held it toward the two librarians, the pendant with its sparkling white gem dangling from her hand. Mirroring her action, Tabitha, Zhialta, and Margarete produced similar pendants, each with a different colored stone – purple, gold, and black. Margarete collected all four and turned toward the foreboding red door. One at a time, she held each pendant up to the lock and snapped it into a diamond-shaped opening.

When the final pendant clicked into place, all four began to glow with pulsing light and the center door panel began to rotate. Simultaneously, the runes surrounding the pendants turned in the opposite direction, the third outer ring spinning in the same direction as the center panel. The three panels all stopped with a lurch, a solid thud echoing in the library. The door creaked open to reveal a dark interior.

Margarete grabbed a glowing orb and entered the chamber.

"Come," Xionne bid them to follow.

Once inside, Narine surveyed the circular room. The walls were lined with shelves, all empty. In the center of the room were four tables pushed together in the shape of a diamond, a single circular column in the center of the diamond. Small stacks of books rested on the tables, as well as inkwells and quills.

Margarete approached the column and placed the orb in a sconce. The column came to life, the stone illuminating with thousands of dots of light and chasing the shadows away.

Xionne spoke, her tone serious. "The prophecies, both true and false, led to a singular event with two possible outcomes. That event was a confrontation with the Dark Lord, the outcomes either his victory or his defeat. With that event now in our past, those prophecies have been proven false and can no longer guide us." She turned to the tables. "Only these remain."

Narine blinked. "There were thousands of books."

"Yes. Now there are fewer than twenty."

Tabitha hobbled to a chair and sat with a sigh. "Two seasons ago, Mother suspected that Seers were approaching the end of our existence. She forbade all from visiting the library while Margarete and I led a small group of women, sorting through the prophecies. Any that ended before or with the confrontation against the Dark Lord have now been destroyed."

Narine narrowed her eyes and turned toward Xionne. "You knew. You knew about the gods. You knew Urvadan was dead, Vandasal with him. You knew why the gem had gone dark."

The diminutive Seer nodded. "I did."

"Why wait until we returned then?"

Jace said, "So I would be the one to break their hearts."

Zhialta grimaced. "Thief…" Her tone carried a warning.

Xionne put her hand on the old woman's arm, quieting her. "The news had to come from someone who had been there when the gods died. While I am pleased to know you care, Jerrell, it was best it came from you, someone those women have grown to revere."

He blinked in surprise.

Xionne allowed a small smile. "As you recall, we follow the prophecies. As we determined which were true, word of your exploits spread, including the role you played leading up to the final conflict." She turned to Narine. "To answer your question, yes, I knew why the light in the gem had died. It was quite a jolt at first, but the final prophecy offered the guidance required. Thus, Zhialta and I used much of the past year to prepare, for the Seers will soon depart from Kelmar. It will be the first time any of them have ever ventured outside of Paehl Lanor."

"Paehl Lanor?" Crusser asked.

"It's the name of the mountain above us." Jace turned to Xionne. "This conversation could have occurred in the Oracle or in your chambers, yet you brought us down here." He spread his arms. "This might be the most secret, most protected room in the entire temple. You would not have done so unless there was something else you needed to share." He crossed his arms. "So say it. What do you want from us?"

"Direct as usual, I see." Xionne sighed. "As you said, there is more. Please, sit. Zhialta will read the prophecy, our final prophecy, aloud."

They all found chairs and sat while the old woman lifted a heavy tome with a dark red cover.

Zhialta opened the book to a page marked with a narrow ribbon, cleared her throat, and began to read.

"The gods of man are gone, never to return. With them, the Dark Lord's shadow no longer darkens the world, just as Vandasal's light faded long ago. A year of calm comes in the wake of their passing, but beware, for it precipitates a time of great turmoil.

"Inherent magic forever altered, the races of old begin to fade. Pushed to the edge of extinction, these embattled races refuse to succumb to the darkness. Their resistance is futile.

"A shadow stretches across the land, cast by an ancient enemy from the distant north. The fall of rulers leads to the rise of false gods as war, chaos, and strife wrack the realm, weakening the foundation of society. Vulnerable, mankind is unprepared for the true threat.

"Shed in a contest of gods, a single drop of blood doomed the world. A festering infection, this wound alters all. Monsters rise, their fury unmatched, the destruction they render unprecedented. Opposition, led by valiant heroes from across the realm, merely delays the inevitable. The end approaches – an endless night draped in crimson light. The only means to survive is to flee. Even then, the end of all things has begun.

"Upon the anniversary of the Dark Lord's death, She Who Bends Magic Until it Breaks and the Charlatan of Ages will reappear in Kelmar, joined by the Sun Pirate and the Gray Warrior. Their return marks the end of the Seers. As their light fades, the world darkens and the apocalypse draws near.

"Seek out the Cultivators, for with them lies the first sign of hope."

Zhialta closed the book and gazed at Xionne in concern.

Jace sighed. "Typical prophecy mumbo jumbo. What does this have to do with us?"

Xionne arched a brow. "You do acknowledge your mention in the script?"

"Yeah." He shrugged. "So what? The rest is all just vague doom and gloom. Why even read this if we can't do anything about it?"

"Yes, Mother," Zhialta said, "without further guidance, how can we proceed?"

Xionne shook her head. "I do not know. The gift of sight has fled me, forever obscuring the future. I do know we must leave Kelmar, at least for a time."

Narine asked, "Where will you go?"

"We will travel to Silvacris to seek out the Cultivators. What occurs next...I do not know."

"Elves?" Jace asked. "You believe the elves have answers?"

"I do not know what assistance the elves might offer. I only know that we must try."

35

RAGE

The encounter with the Seers left Crusser unsettled. Long ago, he had joined the Order to fight against darkness, to wage war on a higher scale than he had as a Murguard soldier, and to do good beyond the concerns of any single wizardom. In the Seers of Kelmar, he saw a similar cause. Their collapse, coupled with an ominous prophecy, left him worried about the future. Worse, the Order remained firmly in the control of traitors. He was now in Kelmar, half a world away from the Valley of Sol, but he still had no idea how to stop whatever Xavan and his followers had planned.

After climbing the stairs from the basement library, Jace led them along a curved corridor and into the spacious receiving hall, which stood empty.

The thief stopped and arched a brow at Narine. "For once, we have no escort. Perhaps the Seers are too preoccupied?"

Narine snorted. "You mean distraught…or hysterical?"

"Same result," he shrugged. "Since we are free to do so, I believe an outing in the city is in order."

Harlequin grinned. "I could use a diversion."

"Agreed," Crusser added.

Rather than heading into the corridor leading to their rooms, Jace led them toward the tall double doors at the far end of the hall. Once outside, they descended the stairs and followed a path between empty sparring yards. The path wound between two Guardian barracks, then opened to a square. Across the square, they entered a narrow street between buildings made of interlocking black stone blocks, each embedded with the sparkling purple specks. The structures varied in shape and size, some simple and blocky, others with curved walls, ornate pillars, and cantilevered overhangs that appeared to defy gravity. *The work of Makers,* Crusser realized. Dwarf craftsmanship was undeniably distinct.

The activity in Kelmar was not so different than the cities of man except for the citizens themselves. Dwarven men and women dressed in drab gray walked the streets, worked in shops, and filled jugs at a bubbling fountain. Dwarven children played in the square, tossing glowing orbs to one another. Here and there, Crusser spotted shoddily dressed human men with vacant eyes carrying armfuls of goods or pulling carts. Each had one or more supervising dwarfs, barking out orders or prodding them along with a rod.

At the sight of Crusser and his companions, some citizens stopped and stared, their expressions unreadable. Every one of them had black hair, dwarf and human.

A pair of female dwarfs in simple gray dresses passed by, staring at them the entire time. Once beyond the group of humans, the women began to whisper to each other, glancing backward again and again.

Jace stopped and pointed up at a sign that read the Cup of Life. "This is it."

Harlequin said, "Sounds like a taproom."

"Exactly," the thief said. "However, you'll find neither ale nor wine served here."

"What then?" Crusser asked, "Brandy?"

Narine shook her head. "Something far sneakier."

Jace laughed, took her arm, and led her into a long room made of angled walls, the layout akin to three interlocking diamonds. The building was lined with stone tables and benches, the space large enough for a hundred patrons. Only a handful of the tables were occupied.

In the center was a circular bar, a female dwarf standing behind it and serving a pair of dwarven guards. The men's helmets rested on the bar, and each held a dark cup in their hand.

Jace and Narine headed toward the bar where the bartender greeted him.

"Our human guests. You have returned." The bartender had dark eyes and a round face, her black hair tied back in a braid. "How long has it been?"

"Over a year," Jace said.

She arched a thick brow. "Already? Time passes so quickly."

"It is good to see you, Arletta. Four mugs of ludicol, please."

The dwarf nodded. "As you wish." She turned and crossed the bar to an oven with an open flame and an odd funnel-shaped structure above it.

Crusser recalled a problem. "I left my coin purse in my room."

"No need," Narine said. "They don't use coins here."

"How do they pay for goods?"

Jace grimaced. "They don't pay at all. Somehow, this society exists without the use of money."

Harlequin's eyes grew wide. "That is appalling."

"I know," the thief agreed. "Without coin to keep score, how do you know if you are winning?"

Crusser laughed. "You act like wealth is part of some elaborate game."

"It is. Most others simply don't realize they are playing."

Arletta approached with four steaming mugs. Jace handed one to Crusser and another to Harlequin before retrieving the last two.

"Let's find a seat," he said as he headed deeper into the room.

Jace sat with Narine beside him. Crusser and Harlequin claimed the other two chairs. The table and chairs were hard and cold to the touch, both made of stone rather than wood.

When Jace slid a mug in front of Narine, she stared down at it with a furrowed brow. "I had better not. Remember what happened last time?"

"You *did* enjoy it," Jace noted. "Perhaps too much. However, one should be safe enough."

Crusser lifted his cup and sniffed the steaming liquid. His senses were greeted by a sweet and spicy aroma. He took a sip, the hot liquid burning his tongue and warming his throat as it slipped down. The aftertaste carried a hint of the spice he had noted in the aroma. "Seems harmless enough to me."

"Oh, just wait," Jace warned. "This stuff is smooth, but it'll catch you unaware if you don't pace yourself." He smirked. "Narine never drinks, yet she rapidly downed three mugs during our last visit. She was lucky to make it back to her room."

Harlequin grinned. "I wish I could have seen our uptight princess when she was drunk."

Jace laughed. "It was funny...until she vomited on Hadnoddon."

"She did what?" Crusser chuckled.

Grimacing, Narine crossed her arms over her chest. "I didn't know it was alcohol. You know why I don't drink."

"Yes, yes," Jace patted her arm. "It muddles your brain and affects your use of magic. However, you are in Kelmar, a city hidden inside a mountain. What could happen?"

She gave him a heavy glare. "Did you forget about the darkspawn attack?"

He shrugged. "No. I just figured...with the Dark Lord gone, darkspawn are unlikely to have such guidance. In the past year, have you heard of anything more than random attacks in the wild?"

"No. I guess not."

Jace took a sip of his drink and smacked his lips. "That is good," he said in a breathy voice. "Come on, Narine. You know you want some. Just one mug."

She sighed. "Fine." Lifting the mug to her lips, she took a sip.

Taking another drink, Crusser realized his head had already begun to buzz.

The four engaged in friendly conversation, one subject leading to another. Another round was ordered, each drink slipping down his throat easier than the last. As additional patrons entered the building, dwarfs began to gather around them and ask questions. It soon became evident that Jace and Narine were famous in the city of Kelmar.

As round after round of ludicol was delivered to the table, Jace continued telling stories to the growing crowd while Crusser drank and listened. As time went on, his mood darkened, leaving him glaring at Jace who seemed to thrive on the attention. *The arrogant thief needs a lesson on humility.* The thought fumed in the back of Crusser's mind.

When the stories turned to a visit upon the pirate island of Ryxx, Jace and Harlequin acted out the daring and outrageous rescue of a captured princess. The crowd of dwarfs seemed to hang on every word, often laughing, guffawing, or hooting as the story turned from humor to wild action to a frightening crash. All the while, Crusser's anger built, the room slowly changing from purple to red, until he could stand it no longer.

Filled with rage, he rose from his chair, strode toward Jace, and attacked.

36

BEST LAID PLANS

Alone with Jace in their assigned room, Narine sat on the edge of her bed while attempting to picture the underground chamber he had asked her to memorize just days earlier.

"Can you believe Crusser?" Jace asked. "Sure, there have been plenty times where I deserved to get punched, but last night was not one of them."

"Hush," she snapped, slapping his leg. "I need to concentrate."

He grunted but otherwise remained quiet.

The image firm in her mind, she drew upon her magic.

Power flooded in, making her soul sing. As always, her senses felt heightened, colors seemed brighter, noises sounded more pleasant, and odors smelled sweeter. She imagined the construct of spatial transference – a disc of light containing a complex pattern only those with the Gift could see. The pattern was akin to one of illusion but with a few key differences, differences that enabled the next step. She bent the disc, making it three dimensional. The center bulged on both sides while the outer edges remained connected, thin lines linking both surfaces. Through the pattern, she released her magic – like light streaming through a lens – and a portal materialized on the other side of the construct. The dim purple light in her room shone through that shimmering gateway, giving faint illumination to a wooden table and chairs in a dark chamber, just as she pictured them in her mind's eye. A dormant enchanted lantern rested on the table, its brass, cylindrical shape distinct.

Jace stepped through, approached the table, and activated the lantern. Pale azure light bloomed to reveal the cavern beyond. Lifting her skirts, Narine followed him through the portal before releasing her magic. The gateway snapped shut with a pop.

"Here we are…back in Marquithe. This is just too easy." He rubbed his jaw. "Again, I realize just how advantageous gateways could be for a thief. One visit to any place with items of value would open the door for a late night return – just slip in, take what you want, and slip back out." Grinning, he added, "We could become the richest couple in history."

Narine shook her head. "I doubt that was what Barsequa had in mind when he shared his secret construct with me."

Jace chuckled as he turned to the bed and picked up the two cloaks lying on it, one black, one dark blue. He handed her the latter. She draped the cloak over her shoulders and secured it.

When they were both cloaked and ready, Jace raised the lantern and headed toward the dark cavern exit. "Come along. We have work to do."

With Jace in the lead, they followed a tunnel past the dark stairwell leading to the throne room antechamber. A few hundred feet and a few bends later, the tunnel terminated at another set of stairs, rising up into shadow. Jace ascended, holding the lantern high, Narine only a few steps behind. Three full flights later, Narine's breaths were coming in gasps, but the stairs ended at a small landing with a brick wall straight ahead. Jace reached into a gap in the bricks and pulled a release. A section of the wall pivoted inward to reveal the back of a woven tapestry.

Finger to his lips, he doused the lantern. They were plunged into darkness except for a horizontal sliver of dim light along the floor ahead. There was a soft clink as Jace set the lantern down. He then took her hand and pulled her past the open door. Slowly, he drew the tapestry aside to reveal a room cluttered with junk – old furniture, barrels, crates, and shelves, all covered in dust. Sunlight shone through a narrow window high up on one wall. They entered the room, the tapestry falling back to hide the doorway.

"Aren't you going to close the door?" she whispered.

"I don't think so. We may need to leave quickly." He pointed. "Look at this junk. Nobody comes in here other than to stash a piece of old furniture.

Sometime long ago, it turned into a storage room and that is all anyone knows of it."

"Where are we, exactly?"

"This room is below the palace temple. As you know, the temple is outside the palace walls, so it provides easy access to the city."

Her eyes widened in realization. "This is the route we took with Algoron. It was night at the time and too dark to see, so I didn't recognize it."

"Yes. It's a bit convoluted, but I sometimes go this way to get in and out of the palace, just in case someone is following me. I try to avoid patterns, constantly changing my schedule and routes for that very reason." He went to the door and unlocked it. "Quiet now."

Opening the door a crack, Jace peered out before motioning for her to follow. A dark corridor led them to a stairwell. They ascended and stopped at the top as Jace lifted the hood of his cloak.

"As much as I prefer to look upon your face...and other parts," he grinned, "I need you to cover up. We do not wish to be recognized."

She pulled her hood forward and followed him out.

The outer wall to the palace grounds stood to one side of the door, a hedgerow just a few feet from it, running parallel to the wall. To the other side was a side entrance to the temple. A brick path led to it, bracketed by another row of hedges and another wall. A guard in city watch armor stood halfway down the path, his back to them, feet a shoulder width apart and arms crossed over his breastplate.

Wrapping his arm around her shoulders, Jace walked her down the path while whispering. "You are sad...crying...distraught over the death of your queen, a woman you loved and admired."

"What?" she asked.

"Just do it. Be convincing."

The guard spun around to their approaching footsteps. Arms uncrossing, his hand went to the sword at his hip. "Who are you? Where did you come from?"

Jace replied, "We were in the temple, praying."

"The temple is closed today. They are preparing it for tomorrow's coronation."

Narine gasped. *Coronation?*

"As we found out," Jace said angrily. "They kicked us out. We only came to pray to Farrow."

"Farrow?"

"Yes," Jace held an angry edge in his voice. "Can't you see my wife is upset? She loved Queen Narine and mourns her death."

"The queen…they held her funeral yesterday, right here in the temple."

Jace blurted, "I know, you idiot! We were there. In fact, we never left." He held Narine close. She took the cue and leaned her head against his shoulder, sobbing. He kissed the top of her hooded head, his tone softening, thick with sorrow, as though he were also on the edge of tears. "All night, we remained and prayed for the queen, hoping Farrow might somehow spare her."

A bubble of laughter rose, forcing Narine to sob noisily to cover for it.

"Well…" the guard seemed confused. "We all are saddened by the queen's death, but you must leave."

Jace snapped, "We were trying to leave when you stopped us!"

The man, who stood a full head taller than Jace, jerked back and then stepped aside. "May Farrow be with you."

With Jace still holding her against him, he and Narine passed the guard and headed toward the nearest street, where they faded into the foot traffic. Releasing her, he circled a line for a bakery and was beyond the crowd. She caught up to him, keeping her head down to hide her face as she walked at his side. The guard's words had made her angry.

In a near growl, she said, "I can't believe they are holding a coronation just two days after my funeral."

He chuckled.

Narine lifted her head and glared at him, as they continued walking. "I don't see how this is funny."

Giving her a sidelong grin, he asked, "How often are people able to complain about events following their own funeral?"

"Hmm," she grunted. "I suppose that does sound a bit odd. Still, who is taking the crown?"

"That should be easy to determine."

"Where are you heading?"

"To the Bureau of Trading."

He took her hand and slipped around the wagon stopped in the middle of the road, foot traffic squeezing past the narrow gaps on each side. Turning at the next intersection, they followed the road to a square, crossed it, and took another long street. Minutes later, the street opened to another square, this one familiar, the massive Bureau of Trading looming across the open space. In the heart of the square, a platform made of wood remained, people, wagons, carts, and horses moving past it without pausing.

Narine stopped, and Jace turned toward her.

"What's wrong?" he asked.

A wave of sadness came over her, as tears, real tears, began streaming down her cheeks. "That is where we were to present ourselves to the public. It was a moment I dreamt of for so long...but it was not meant to be." She wiped her cheeks. "Now, it will never happen."

His hand went to her chin, easing her face toward him. "I understand. You imagined this perfect moment, something you had anticipated for so long, it became almost real. However, the world does not work like that. Perfect moments, the ones you end up cherishing the most, cannot be manufactured. The reason they matter so much, years later, is that they were unexpected." Leaning in, he kissed her. "Forget what could have been. Focus on what we have. Each other."

She smiled. "How do you always remain so positive?"

Shrugging, he stepped back. "I'm lucky, remember? I just figure as long as I keep trying, things will work out well enough. Come on. Let's go see how we can ruin someone *else's* special day."

Smiling, her moment of sadness forgotten, Narine followed him across the square and into a street beside the bureau. He took her hand and backed into a nondescript recessed doorway before an abandoned building.

"At last," she whispered, "I get a glimpse into your secret life."

Jace produced three lock picks from an inner pocket and flashed them in front of her. "You had *better* feel honored. Only one other person alive knows what you are about to see."

After peering up and down the street, he turned, knelt, and began picking the lock on the door. Moments later, the door opened. Jace pulled Narine inside, locked the door, and pocketed the pick.

The building was dark. Pale light came through the cracks between the boarded windows. The interior was a mess, a dusty counter at the front and rows of bare shelves behind it. She followed him around the counter, all the way to the last row of shelves, before heading deeper into the building.

"Never walk down the other rows," he warned in a hushed voice. "It won't turn out well."

"Traps?"

"Yes. Harsh ones."

At the rear of the store, he turned and followed the wall, passing an open doorway and heading to a closed door. Rather than turn the knob, he simply pressed his palms to the door and slid it sideways. It disappeared into a pocket in the brick wall, stopping just short of the knob. Beyond it was a stairwell descending into darkness.

"Also, never touch the door handle." He grabbed an enchanted lantern from a shelf over the stairwell, activated it, and led her below ground. "Just a warning, the smell gets quite pungent down here."

Descending the narrow stairwell with care, she asked "Where are we going, exactly?"

"The sewers. Through them, we can reach the secret stairwell to my office."

Jace slid through the door, Narine a step behind. The small room was as he had left it, a handful of missives sitting on the desktop. He set the lantern on the table and put his finger to his lips, warning her to remain quiet.

Pressing his ear against the door to the neighboring room, he listened. Voices came from the other side, one belonging to Styles, as expected. The other was Jonnel, the man in charge of smuggling goods in and out of the city. Less than a minute later, the conversation ended, the outer door opening and clicking closed. Jace waited a beat, listening to ensure Styles was alone. Only then did he open the door.

A knife flashed toward his throat. Jace twisted, gripping the assailant's wrist and ramming it against the doorframe. A male voice cried out, a dagger dropping to the floor with a clatter.

"It's me, Styles," Jace said as he pushed the thief backward.

Holding his wrist, Styles stumbled. "Jerrell!" Although alarmed, he kept his voice a whisper. "What are you doing sneaking up on me like that?"

"I brought somebody." He waved for Narine to come in.

She stepped into the light and lowered her hood.

Eyes widening, Styles stuttered, "Oh...um...my queen." He dipped his head.

"No need for any of that. I am queen no longer."

Styles ran his hand though his dark hair, the motion reminding Narine of Jace. "Yeah. I even attended your funeral. The temple was packed. Lots of tears at that one."

Narine smiled. "So the people did care for me?"

"I should say so. Even now, angry talk over your death darkens the streets of Marquithe. The citizens are outraged that their queen was attacked in her own city and that the culprit escaped." Styles made a fist. "That bastard holding his coronation so soon afterward does not sit well either."

"Which bastard?" Jace asked.

Styles arched his brows. "You haven't heard? High Wizard Montague is to be crowned tomorrow." He shook his head. "I hear the citizens of Lionne don't even like him, but what are we to do?"

Nostrils flaring, Jace scowled at Narine. "I told you he was a slime ball."

"Yes. It appears so, but now what?"

His grimace slipped away, replaced by a grin. "Now, we ruin his day." He turned to Styles. "Get the word out. I want every person in the network talking about Montague, and not in a good way. Tell them that those who were involved in the queen's assassination have been captured and they have proof that Montague paid them."

Styles nodded. "Alright, but what can our people do?"

"Let's tell the citizens to boycott the coronation. I want that temple as empty as possible."

"What of the wizards?"

Jace rubbed his jaw, thinking aloud. "The wizards are self-serving, so we will use that to our advantage. Have the citizens gather outside the temple to protest the coronation. Any wizard who wishes to attend will have to carve their path through the crowd. I doubt any love Montague enough to upset the populace, especially if they believe his rule will be short lived."

Once again, Narine found herself grinning at one of Jace's plans, happy to have his scheming mind on her side.

37

CRUSHER

Harlequin knocked, her knuckles rapping against the door. While waiting, she glanced behind her at the Temple of the Oracle looming nearby. The door opened and she turned to find a male dwarf with a bald pate his long black beard peppered with gray. He had a heavy brow and bulbous nose.

His gaze climbed from her boots to her face, a smile nestled in his beard. "How can I help you?" he asked in a gravelly voice.

"I am looking for my friend."

"Would your friend happen to be the size of a small mountain?"

"Yes," she laughed. "His name is Crusser."

The dwarf stroked his beard while peering over his shoulder. "Your friend remains asleep."

"Passed out."

He shrugged. "Could be from the ludicol. Could be from the blows to his head. The result is the same either way."

"I spoke with Xionne," Harlequin said, "She told me to see the jailor. Are you him?"

"I am. The name is Loggadon."

"She also said you would release him once he woke."

"Also true."

"Do you mind if I wait? It can't be long....I think." The lack of sunlight as an indicator left her unsure of the time. She had slept and awoken well-rested, but her head remained a little fuzzy from the strong drink.

The dwarf grinned broadly. "Let it never be said that Loggadon would reject the presence of a beautiful woman." He stepped back and swept his arm. "Welcome, my dear."

Harlequin stepped inside what appeared to be a study, three of the four walls covered in books. She sat on a pillowed-sofa while Loggadon walked into a neighboring room. Noise followed and he returned with two cups, both steaming.

He held one toward her. "For you, my dear."

"What is it?" She asked while reaching for the cup.

"Ferrin-root tea."

Harlequin sniffed the steam, a spiced aroma teasing her senses. "The smell reminds me of ludicol." She cocked a brow. "You aren't trying to get me drunk, are you?"

Loggadon chortled. "Nothing of the sort." He sat on a padded chair made of wrought iron. It rocked back as he settled in. "The tea helps to whittle away the aftereffects of alcohol. Judging by your friend, and after hearing the tales told by the guards who hauled him in, you likely drank near as much as he did."

"How astute of you," she said with a smile.

Tentatively, she took a sip. The liquid was hot and warmed her throat. "Mmm. This is good."

"I am glad you like it."

She craned her neck and peered down the corridor. At the far end was an empty room, the door made of iron bars visible. "Is he back there?'

"He is. Do not worry. It is not so bad. The cells are clean, the pallet's not too hard, and the blankets are cleaned regularly."

She glanced at the books, brow furrowed. "I must say this is nothing like any jail I have seen, and I have seen more than most folks could say. Why do you have so many books?"

"Ah," he grinned. "I was wondering when you might ask. You see, I get very few visitors. When I do, they spend a night in a cell and are then on their way. Thus, I have a great deal of free time. I use that time to read."

"You have read all these books?"

Loggadon nodded. "These and thousands more, borrowed from the Seers."

"And you don't find all this reading…boring?"

He snorted. "Not in the least. Books are many things, but rarely boring. From them, I can learn facts and expand my knowledge of history, politics, races, wars, and faraway lands. Oftentimes, I choose to read outlandish tales featuring dashing heroes and damsels in distress, allowing my mind to venture far beyond the confines of Kelmar."

Harlequin shook her head. "Not all women are damsels in distress. Many save themselves. Some can fight as fiercely as any man."

The dwarf leaned forward in his chair, a grin on his face. "I sense a story."

She smirked. "I might have a few tales to share."

"As do I," Loggadon said. "What say you, we trade yarns?"

"Alright," Harlequin figured she had nothing else to do and it would help the time pass. "You go first."

The dwarf took a long sip of his tea, set it on the table beside him, and sat back, the chair rocking slowly while he stroked his beard. When he spoke, his voice was altered, taking on the lilting quality of a storyteller.

"This is a tale from long, long ago, a tale of High King Fandaric Buurom. Fandaric, a Maker of renown, was bound heart and soul to a dragon."

Harlequin arched a brow.

Loggadon grinned. "Yes, a dragon. A creature to fear. A creature of power. A creature of magic. This legendary monster was stunning to gaze upon with scales of gold and green. You see, Zyordican was the wisest of dragons and had foreseen a future where man might one day wield magic. In this act, man would claim the world and change it forever. Despite her size and power, the dragon feared this future, for this magic was the energy at the core of all things – a power never meant to be tamed.

"And so, Zyordican watched and waited with the patience only a being who had lived for many centuries could comprehend. Men and kings came and went until she learned of Fandaric's plan to hunt a rock troll that had attacked a hold within his kingdom.

"It was a clear autumn evening; the trees were covered in leaves of gold, amber, and crimson, while the leaves that had lost their battle against the seasons covered the forest floor. The king and his men entered this forest armed with axes, swords, bows, and spears. A horn blew, announcing the sighting of a troll. Fandaric's men broke into three groups, one sweeping to each side while Fandaric led the group in the middle. The king's steed raced through the woods in search of the monster until he reached a clearing and stopped dead.

"At the heart of the meadow was a towering dragon, large enough to eat Fandaric in a single bite. The king's steed reared up in terror and bucked him off. He crashed to the ground, his crown rolling away until it was stopped by a massive talon, which hooked it like a ring. The dragon picked up the crown, her slitted eyes shifting from it to the fallen king, while the king's men froze in fear.

"'It seems,' the dragon said, 'that you and I should talk.'"

Harlequin grinned throughout Loggadon's telling, enjoying the dwarf's energy and flair for the dramatic. When his tale ended, she went on to recite a tale from her early days as a pirate, the dwarf hanging on every word. Oddly, she found as much joy in his interest of her story as she had in listening to his. Thus, they swapped stories again and again. And time passed without her notice.

Crusser woke to a pounding headache. He rolled over and gasped, wincing from the stabbing pain in his ribs. Blinking his eyes open, he found himself in a small cell, the walls and ceiling sparkling with purple dots of light. When he raised his hand to rub his eyes, a chain clinked, and he felt a metal shackle cut into his skin. He pushed himself up on his elbows, gasping as a knifing pain shot through his side. *My ribs are broken.* It was a familiar injury, one that would make sleep difficult for weeks.

He lay on a pallet just above the floor, his wrists and ankles shackled with heavy chains securing him to the iron rings that protruded from the stone floor. Across from him was a door made of iron bars.

"Help!" he shouted. "Get me out of here!"

He heard approaching footsteps, and a broad-shouldered, barrel-chested dwarf appeared. Standing less than five feet tall, he had a bald head and a black and gray peppered beard, the braided end reaching his thick black belt. The dwarf wore a dark gray tunic, loose black trousers, and brown boots. A nasty, four-pointed mace hung from a loop on his hip.

Standing with his fists on his hips, the dwarf grunted. "Seems the wild man is awake."

A taller figure sidled up beside the dwarf, a black hat on her head. "It's about time. That blow to the head must have rattled his brains plenty," Harlequin smirked. "Not to mention all the ludicol he drank."

Crusser lay back and groaned, his hand instinctively going to his ribs but stopping short when the chain drew taut. "My head is killing me. Ribs as well."

She snorted. "Good. You deserve it."

He turned his head, looking down his nose to see her and the dwarf. "What happened? Why am I chained up?"

Harlequin put a hand on the dwarf's shoulder. "The wild man appears tamed, Loggadon. Can you release him so we can head back to the temple?"

Arching a bushy brow, Loggadon seemed doubtful. "You sure? The story I heard…"

"Don't worry. I will keep him in line. Besides, you read the announcement. We are to depart from Kelmar in two days. I suspect you have better things to do than play nursemaid to this lummox."

The dwarf snorted. "You have the truth of it, Miss Harlequin." He removed his keys, unlocked the door, and swung it open, the iron hinges squeaking. Stepping inside, he held the keys up and eyed Crusser. "You had better behave or you'll be in twice the pain when you wake next."

Crusser groaned. "I have no wish to cause trouble. I only wish out of here…and perhaps a gallon of water. My mouth tastes like a goose nested in it and left droppings behind."

Chuckling, Loggadon proceeded to unlock his wrists and ankles. Crusser gingerly sat up and rubbed his wrists, Harlequin smirking at him the entire time. The dwarf helped Crusser to his feet and he lumbered out of the cell. Harlequin fell in beside him, the pair of them following a short corridor to a room with a sitting area in the center, the walls covered in books. In the corner was a bucket of water and a cup. Crusser headed straight for the water and began drinking heartily.

While waiting for him to quench his thirst, Harlequin faced the dwarf. "Thank you again, Loggadon. It was nice to chat while I waited for him to wake up."

The dwarf snorted. "The life a jailor can be quite dull, and when it's not dull, it's usually too dangerous to appreciate. It was nice to have a visitor, not to mention one so pretty. Thanks for trading stories with me. Someday, I would like to look upon these endless seas you speak of."

She clapped him on the shoulder. "Perhaps that day will come sooner than you think."

After five cups, his thirst was finally sated by the water. Crusser wiped his mouth and set the cup aside. Harlequin then led him out the door. They followed a narrow path between the barracks and the temple, climbing the stairs, and entering the temple.

Crusser groaned numerous times during the journey back to his chamber. He did not ask questions, nor did she offer him any answers. Instead, he fought an internal battle between curiosity and dread, fearful of what he had done. Alcohol had again left him with blank spots in his memory. He wondered if he subconsciously pushed the events, whatever they were, from his mind because his actions were so deplorable.

Once they reached the upper floor, she led him down the corridor. Rather than go to her room or his, she knocked on another door.

"Yes?" Jace called from inside.

"It's Harley. I have Cruss with me." She grinned at him. "He's grumpy and sore, but otherwise, back to normal."

The door swung open. Jace was standing just inside, Narine seated on the edge of the bed.

"Come in." Jace crossed the room and sat beside Narine, folding his arms across his chest while glaring at Crusser.

Groaning inwardly, Crusser walked past Harlequin and she shut the door.

"Have a seat," Jace said, pointing toward the small table and two chairs.

The other two sat, Harlequin still wearing a grin, while Crusser groaned from the pain in his ribs and a pounding head.

Jace stared at him for a few seconds and then said, "Well?"

"Well, what?" Crusser asked.

"Aren't you going to apologize?"

Crusser frowned. "Yes, I...I am sorry for whatever I did."

Narine arched a brow. "You don't remember?"

Jace suggested, "Must be from when Harley smashed him to the floor with that chair."

"No," Harlequin said. "I don't think so. As I told you last night, I saw him like this once before. We had swoon that night. Ludicol is nearly as strong. He seems to have issues when he drinks."

Crusser's gaze went to the floor, one hand twisting the other. He longed to bolt from the room and hide. *I have faced darkspawn in the dead of night and fought goblins by the hundreds with towering rock trolls to back them. Why is this so difficult?* Closing his eyes, he held fast to the courage he had displayed in those moments, refusing to give in to fear.

With a sigh, Crusser opened his eyes, lifted his head, and bared his soul. "My Murguard squad mates used to say that drink turns me from Crusser to *Crusher*. It was not a term I embraced." He held his hands out in appeal. "Something happens to me when I drink. With a glass of wine or a couple ales, there is no issue. However, when it goes too far...I change. Bad things happen. From deep inside me, something dark is unleashed, a thing of anger, hatred, and violence. I go wild, berserk even, breaking anything in my path just because it is nearby. Often, people get hurt. Sometimes, they die." He shook his head. "Try as I might, I can never recall what happened. None of it. Instead, I remember only...seeing red, and the red turning to black."

Harlequin leaned forward and put her hand on his arm. "That is what happened in Antari."

Numbly, he nodded.

"And, again, last night."

"Huh," Jace grunted. "So you don't remember punching me in the eye?"

Crusser shook his head.

"Or fighting six dwarfs at once?"

Again, he recalled nothing.

Jace grinned. "You threw one of the dwarf guardians across the bar. I half thought he might fly right out the door."

Narine added, "After Harlequin snuck up behind you and smashed you over the back with a chair, you fell to the floor. Dwarfs piled on top of you and held you in place until the jailor arrived. Using a little magic, I put you to sleep. They then hauled you away to sleep it off."

Harlequin nodded to Narine. "Whatever you did to him worked." She turned to Crusser. "You slept for a full day, at least twice as long as any of us slept last night."

He blinked at the realization. It did not help that time was difficult to gage in Kelmar. Turning to Jace and Narine, Crusser said, "Again, I am sorry for my behavior." Frowning, he added, "However, I am a bit disappointed. You appear no worse for wear, Jace. I would like to believe I am a better fighter than that."

Jace laughed. "Oh, you did just fine. I was lucky to escape with as little damage as I did." He slid his arm around Narine. "I also happen to be married to an amazing wizardess, who was kind enough to heal my wounds."

"I could heal yours as well, Cruss," Narine suggested.

He nodded. "I would appreciate it."

"Hold off," Harlequin said. "Let him suffer a bit longer. Best if he remembers something of last night. You can heal him before bed. At least, then he can sleep. I know how it is to have broken ribs."

Flashing her a crooked smile, Crusser nodded. "Fair enough."

She smiled in return and then turned to the other couple. "Now that is finished, what did you discover today?"

"While disguised, Narine and I returned to Marquithe and visited the palace. Turns out, there is to be a coronation tomorrow, placing a new ruler upon the throne of Farrowen."

"Who is it?" Harlequin asked.

Scowling, Narine said, "Montague, the high wizard of Lionne."

Jace smirked. "I knew that man was a snake."

"Lionne," Crusser looked at Harlequin. "That's why Tranadal landed there."

"Indeed." She turned to Jace. "What are you going to do?"

The thief stood and grinned. "The four of us are going to be there to welcome our new king. Unfortunately, his rule is doomed before it even begins."

38

GOD KING

S imilar to the extravagant bedchamber in which Reagor stood, the image in the mirror was familiar, yet foreign. Somehow, his brown hair had turned white during his rebirth, creating a stark contrast to his tanned Orenthian skin and dark eyes. A form-fitting black leather jerkin covered his torso, gold plates protected his chest and shoulders, and a shimmering purple cape hung down his back. When coupled with the thick golden belt at his waist, golden-tinted bracers, black breeches, and tall riding boots, his appearance was striking.

"You truly look like a king," Vex said from the doorway.

Reagor turned toward Vex whose dark eyes seemed to always be watching him. Sometimes, he swore he felt Vex in his own mind, although those moments passed swiftly. "While a bit ostentatious, I'll admit that this outfit is impressive." He rapped his knuckles against his chest, the metal ringing loudly. "It's even functional, except for the cape. I could do without the cape."

The sorcerer entered the room. "Keep the cape. It reminds others of the Indigo Hounds, known for their skill in combat and their close ties to the throne. Remember, you are a man of the people, not some wizard raised in luxury. You must maintain a piece of that despite the awe you are sure to inspire. Tales of your return from the dead have spread like wildfire." He gestured toward the window. "Listen to the citizens gathering in the palace square. They ache to see their new god and king."

God? Reagor did not feel like a god, but a man confused by magic he did not understand.

A knock came from the other room. Turning from Vex, Reagor entered the central room of his royal chambers. The door to the corridor stood open, still broken from the events two days earlier. A man stood in the doorway, waiting to be addressed.

"Balcor," Reagor said. "What news do you bring?"

The guard stepped inside. "You should get that door fixed."

"The carpenter was here this morning, taking measurements. It'll take him a couple days to build and install a new one. Until then, I'll get by some-how." Reagor glanced around. "I know this is not quite a hovel in the Dregs, but I think I'll manage."

Balcor grinned. "Yes. I can see how you suffer for us."

The statement made Reagor frown. He glanced around the room. "Per-haps I will donate the furniture to a needy family. I am a warrior and have little need of all this finery."

"A fine thought, Your Majesty," Vex said. "Anything you do to endear the people to you will solidify their loyalty."

Scowling, Reagor shook his head. "Don't call me that. I am not crowned yet. Even if I were, I don't need such titles in private settings. My name will do just fine." He turned back toward Balcor. "How many did you find?"

The man's smile fell away. "Twenty-seven children in all. They are currently in the temple, under guard as you requested."

"Good," Reagor said. "We must get them out of the city soon, before some vigilante mob goes after them.

Vex warned, "They may be children now, but they will grow into their abilities. Today's orphans could become tomorrow's most powerful enemies."

"I don't care," Reagor snapped. "I already told you, I'll not allow inno-cent children to be murdered just because of the blood coursing through their veins." He turned back toward Balcor. "I have another mission I wish you to lead."

"Anything," Balcor said.

"Track down Isaac and the other drivers who no longer have a job after…the rebellion." It was a preferable term to murder or genocide. "They are to bring their carriages to the temple tomorrow morning. Those carriages will convey the wizard children to Marquithe. Deliver them to the palace. They are Queen Narine's problem, now. When you're finished, return here. As for the drivers, pay them each one gold piece for the trip. They can keep the carriages and horses, and hopefully, that will help them find new employment, whether they choose to return to Fastella or find a home elsewhere."

"Yes, sire," Balcor said with a bow.

Reagor growled. "I told you, no titles…"

Balcor's grin stopped him short. "Got you, Reagor." He chuckled. "I will do as you say and return in two weeks."

Chuckling, Reagor nodded. "Fair enough. Give the queen my best." Mentioning her again gave him an idea. "Hold on a moment before you leave." He entered his new bed chamber and scooped a gold ring off the vanity, eyeing the black onyx mounted to it as he walked back. He held the ring out to Balcor. "Take this. Keep it safe, for it holds significant value. When you arrive in Marquithe, give it to Queen Narine as a gift from me."

The man arched a brow. "You are gifting a wizard queen some old ring?"

"Yes. It was Dalia's and Parsec's before that. In fact, at one point, it belonged to Eldalain."

"Why give her a gift?"

"In truth, I have no need for the ring, but I also wish to avoid a war against Farrowen. We must focus on securing Ghealdor under our new laws, and we are in no position to deal with external aggression. She will surely appreciate this gesture. It is a small price to secure our relations and our border."

"What of Pallanar?" Vex asked.

Reagor shrugged. "I'll deal with Pallanar later."

Holding the ring in his hand, Balcor bowed and left the room, his footsteps fading while another set of footsteps approached. An elderly gentleman stood in the doorway, his heels together and hand at his waist as he bowed. He was dressed in a black coat and trousers, his collar pressed, and his white hair slicked back.

"Your Majesty," Ruthers said in a nasally tone. "The square is filled with citizens. It is time for the ceremony."

"Thank you, Ruthers," he said with a firm nod. "But you may call me Reagor when we're alone."

"We are not alone, sire."

He glanced at Vex. "This is my advisor. He will frequently be around me. I consider that alone."

"Even if Master Vex were not present, you would not be alone, for both you and I are present."

Reagor rolled his eyes. "Never mind." The man was old and likely set in his ways. Better to wait for him to die than try and change him. "Let's go downstairs and get this over with."

The clamor of the crowd came through the open front doors of Fastella Palace, echoing from the walls and ceiling of the empty receiving hall. Only Reagor, Vex, Ruthers, and a handful of Indigo Hounds stood in the hall. Shouts arose outside. Someone started a chant, and others quickly joined in.

"Reagor. Reagor. Reagor…"

It was as if he again stood in the Bowl of Oren. *This time, I will not be forced to shed blood…at least, not today.*

"They call your name," said Vex. "It is time you greet them."

Reagor took a deep breath, "There are so many. How will they hear me?"

Vex produced a vial, unstoppered it, and dribbled sparkling blood on his fingertips. He then brought his fingers to Reagor's lips, muttering something beneath his breath as he wet them. The entire time, Ruthers watched with an arched brow, but he said nothing and maintained his position. As head of the palace staff for decades, the man had likely witnessed many strange things.

"There." The sorcerer stepped back. "All will hear your words. In fact, they will be drawn by them, for you give them what they wish."

"Which is?"

"Liberty, of course."

The sorcerer moved aside. "Go on, my King. Your people await."

Placing his palm on the pommel of the sword at his hip, Reagor marched toward the open door, an escort of guards ahead as he stepped out into bright daylight. As they neared the top of the stairs, the guards spread out, four on each side of Reagor as he stopped and stared over the plaza.

Thousands had gathered, men, women, and children of all ages, all chanting his name. In him, they saw the hope of a new future. He longed to reward them for such belief.

Vex appeared beside him, the sorcerer tipping his hood back and facing the crowd. "Welcome!" His voice boomed and the crowd fell silent. "You are all here to witness something unprecedented. In the past, you have been ruled by wizard lords. Near-immortal, those men often ruled for centuries, gifted with the unmatched power of your god, Gheald. This can no longer happen, for Gheald and the other gods are dead and gone along with the wizard lords."

The crowd stirred. Many had not yet come to terms with the disappearance of Gheald and the other gods.

"However," Vex continued, "humanity was not meant to exist without a shepherd to guide and protect the flock. To fill this gap in your lives, another god has risen. You likely have already heard stories told in the streets, at taprooms, and by firesides. These tales speak of a man who dared to challenge our oppressors. He led a small group of rebels against the might of their magic, exterminating the entire wizards guild before taking the fight here, to the palace, where he faced the witch, Queen Dalia, herself.

"As queen, of course she was well protected, both by soldiers held fast by a sense of duty to the crown and by her massive, terrifying bodyguard, Herrod the Terrible. This man…a champion of the people, fought against Herrod in a duel to the death. Tricked by the queen's dark magic, our champion died.

"Unfortunately for Queen Dalia, not even death can prevent true justice.

"As witnessed by a dozen palace guards, along with the meager remnants of the rebellion, the man standing beside me rose from the dead, for he is no mere mortal." A stir ran through the crowd. "Yes, this sounds incredible, but I am here to tell you, it is true." He gestured toward Reagor. "Already a legend in his native wizardom of Orenth, GaLang Reagor is no mere man. He is a gift from beyond, blessed and immortal."

Gripping Reagor's wrist, Vex lifted his arm up, a knife appearing in the sorcerer's other fist. Vex drove the knife through Reagor's palm. He flinched, pulling his hand back as pain flared and the crowd gasped.

"What are you…" Reagor exclaimed as blood poured from his wounded hand.

"Watch!" Vex shouted.

From the hole in Reagor's palm came a light, expanding and swirling. Sparks emerged from the chests of the surrounding guards and the people in the crowd, all drawn toward the beam of light. As the sparks gathered, the light from Reagor's palm grew brighter and brighter. As rapidly as it had risen, the light withdrew into his hand and was gone.

Stunned, Reagor twisted his hand. There was no pain. The blood and wound were already gone, making him wonder if it had even been real.

Vex stood in front of him, a golden crown in his hand. He lifted it and placed it on Reagor's head. "I give you the GaLang Reagor, god and king of Ghealdor."

The crowd roared. Applause, cheers, and shouts came from all directions. Reagor raised his hands, holding his palms toward the audience, and slowly lowered them. The chant died, and the plaza fell quiet.

"Welcome, citizens of Fastella," his voice boomed, the volume startling him. "You may know of me from my days as a gladiator, fighting for my life in the Bowl of Oren. Years have passed since then...years I have spent here, in this city. Although I am a foreigner by birth, Fastella has come to be my home. I have grown to love this city and its people. However, I did not love the way you were treated. The wizards saw you only as a means to satisfy their own desires, by forcing your participation in Devotion or by levying taxes to fund their extravagant lifestyles. All the while, you toiled and struggled.

"But no more." His gaze swept across the crowd, all eyes focused on him in expectant silence. "As of today, the city of Fastella is free from wizard rule."

A cheer ran through the crowd, forcing Reagor to raise his arms to again silence them.

"Not one wizard remains in Fastella, and do not worry, for none will return. The queen is dead. The wizards in league with her are gone as well. From this day forward, Fastella will remain wizard-free. Any wizard who attempts to pass these walls will be considered a criminal. In addition, I am sending missives throughout Ghealdor, demanding all wizards leave our nation by Lunartide, thirty days from now. After that date, any wizard found within our borders will be arrested and tried unless they possess a warrant signed by me.

"Your taxes will now be used solely for the purposes of maintaining and defending Fastella and the rest of Ghealdor. Effective today, your tax rate will be half of what it was, giving you more coin to use for your own needs."

Another cheer rang out, fists pumping in the air as the crowd rejoiced. Reagor allowed them to savor the moment.

"Lastly are the former wizard estates. From this day forward, the portion of the city known as Wizard Hills will be called Liberty Hills. The buildings and possessions left behind by the wizards now belong to the people of Fastella."

The people cheered again, a chant rising, as they repeated his name again and again. Reagor accepted their ovation and stood proud, hoping to inspire his people. Inside, doubts twisted his stomach, and he felt uncertain about the future of Ghealdor.

39

CORONATION

With a confident, commanding stride, Montague marched down the palace corridor, bracketed by Tranadal and Vordan. A squad of six Midnight Guard led the way, another eight of his own soldiers from Lionne trailing at the rear. Dressed in a midnight blue robe with silver lightning bolts marking the hems at his wrists and ankles, he appeared every bit the ruler of Farrowen. *Soon, a crown will rest on my head, completing my ensemble.*

They reached an open hall, the high ceilings emblazoned with murals of past wizard lords. As the Midnight Guard led them toward another corridor, the hall doors opened and the distant roar of a crowd echoed in the chamber as a wizardess entered. She wore a black dress that hugged her curves and a gray stole over her bare shoulders. A female bodyguard walked at her side, and four personal guards trailed closely behind them.

"Montague!" Ydith Gurgan shouted.

Montague stopped, the rest of his retinue doing likewise, and they all turned to face the wizardess as she crossed the hall toward them. "Well, if it isn't the high wizardess of Eleighton." His tone was friendly, as was his smile. *Not even she could ruin this glorious day.* "I am short on time, so you must make it quick."

She stopped a few strides away, her bodyguard standing beside her. As before, the woman wore black leathers and a stern expression. Her steely gaze shifted to Tranadal and she nodded. Arching a brow, Montague watched the man for a response. If there was one, it was hidden within the shadows of his hood. *Does she know him?*

"This is an outrage!" Ydith bawled.

"To what do you refer?" Montague asked lightly.

"Your self-appointment to the throne...and so soon after the queen's death."

He held out his palms, his tone reassuring. "An empty throne is a danger to the citizens of Farrowen. The longer it remains so, the greater risk to our fair wizardom." Smiling, he tilted his head. "As for my self-appointment, who better? High Wizard Wrenthal is old and feeble. High Wizard Bordain is young and inexperienced...as are you."

She grimaced. "Neither Wrenthal nor Bordain are in Marquithe, so their claims, if they have any, go unheard. I, however, stand here to claim my right to wear the crown. My family has a long history of ruling in Eleighton. I have been trained to govern since I could walk. I have just as much right as you."

Montague smiled sadly and shook his head. "Have you not heard the crowd out there? They long to see their new king take his rightful place."

Surprisingly, Ydith smirked. "The people long for something, but it is not what you think."

Montague's expression darkened, his mood suddenly crushed. "My coronation *will* happen. You can join the crowd in the temple, or you can leave. Regardless, there is nothing you can do to stop it."

Face reddening, Ydith fumed as she turned to the woman beside her. "Can you take them, Tempest?"

The bodyguard stared at Montague with a hard expression, her eyes flicking to Tranadal. "Now is not the time, wizardess."

Balling her hands into fists, Ydith sneered. "I hope you choke on that crown. When you do, I'll be first in line to take it."

She spun around, her bodyguard and soldiers following as she stomped across the hall and out the door.

"Let's be off," Montague said with a gesture. "My people await."

The guards led him into the next corridor, past the quarters where the temple clerics lived, as far as the pair of heavy doors at the end of the hallway where four Midnight Guard were stationed. Opening the doors,

Montague, Tranadal, Vordan, and the escorting guards all entered an antechamber.

High Priestess Dianza stood ready, a tall female cleric at her side. Both women were dressed in dark blue robes. A white and silver stole rested over Dianza's shoulders, and she held her hands clasped at her waist. "Welcome, High Wizard."

Montague frowned, thinking that the high priestess's voice sounded younger than it had at the wedding a few days earlier. Perhaps it was the throne room acoustics. Dismissing the thought, he nodded. "Thank you, High Priestess."

"Are you ready?" she asked.

More than you could ever know. "I am. Do you have the crown?"

"It awaits upon the dais."

"Outstanding," he rubbed his palms together. "I am ready to receive what I am due."

"And you shall." Dianza smiled, her eyes sweeping Montague's retinue. "Everyone who wishes to witness the ceremony should now proceed to the temple. My cleric will show you to your seats." She turned back to Montague. "When the gong rings, you will make your appearance."

The high priestess and her cleric led the others down the corridor to the temple.

As the others walked away, Vordan turned to Montague. "Would you like me to remain?'

"No. The doors are guarded, so this room is safe. Go and find a seat. Enjoy this moment, it is as much yours as mine. After all, I will need a new captain of the Midnight Guard."

Vordan smiled, a rare occurrence. "Very well."

The man walked down the corridor, opened the door, and faded from view. As Montague stood alone in the quiet room, he heard the distant roar of thousands chanting, the words too muffled to distinguish. Surely, the citizens were cheering for him, longing for their new leader to take the throne. His heart swelled in anticipation. Unlike wizard lords of the past, he would not be raised by the hand of Farrow, but he would be king, nonetheless. As for Narine...she was born and raised a Ghealdan – she had never deserved the Farrowen throne. *Yes. I am a far more logical choice.*

The low boom of a gong rang out, its vibrations echoing in the antechamber. His heart racing and stomach bubbling in anticipation, Montague headed down the corridor, opened the door, and entered the palace temple.

A massive building, the temple was square with an arched roof. Through a circular window high on the far wall, the round moon was visible amid the pale blue daytime sky. In the center of the room, six feet above the floor, stood the square dais where Dianza, her cleric, and a trio of altars waited. Split by aisles at the corners, four sections of benches filled the building, all facing the center.

Montague strode down an aisle bracketed by two dozen Midnight Guard, his gaze sweeping the room. Seated at the front were Tranadal, Vordan, and the guards who had come with him from Lionne. Only two others were present, both seated in the shadowy back row, far across the room.

When he drew close to the dais, he spotted Captain Giralt sitting alone in the front row. Montague paused before the dais and leaned toward Giralt. "Where are the people?" he asked in a hushed voice.

"Outside," Giralt replied.

"Well, let them in!" Montague huffed.

The man shook his head. "They refuse to come in."

He blinked. "What? Why?"

Giralt shrugged.

Frowning, Montague climbed the dais stairs to meet the waiting priestess. Quietly, he asked, "Was the temple empty like this for Narine's coronation?"

The priestess smiled. "Not one seat was open. People stood in the aisles and along the back while more crowded the square, eager for a chance to see their new queen."

"I don't understand. Where are they?"

"Listen," Dianza said. "Hear that chanting?"

The low hum of thousands of voices carried through the walls. "Yes."

"Those are the citizens of Marquithe."

"Why won't they come witness my crowning?"

"Because," a male voice came from across the temple, "they are calling for your head since you murdered their beloved queen."

Montague turned as two shadowy hooded figures walked down the aisle, one a male of modest height, the other tall with broad shoulders and a barrel chest. They stepped into the light, the face of the shorter one becoming clear when he pulled his hood back. It was a face Montague knew well...and one he had thought to never see again.

"Landish!" Montague bellowed as Vordan leapt to his feet. "How? I saw your corpse."

Landish smiled. "Turns out, I am very much alive. Good thing, too, or you might have actually become king."

Montague laughed. "Your luck cannot save you this time, Landish." He spread his arms. "Look at this room. Vordan and my guards already outnumber you four to one. In addition, thirty Midnight Guard standready to protect their new king. And, do not forget." Montague flashed a menacing grin. "I am a high wizard, and you are nothing but a lowly thief with failed dreams to rise beyond his rightful place."

The thief stopped at the end of the aisle, his arms crossed over his chest. He glanced toward Vordan. "I see you are as ugly as ever, Captain. Perhaps it is time I separated that ugly head from your body, so it can finally have peace."

Vordan began to lunge toward Landish, but Tranadal gripped his wrist, stopping the other man short.

"Hello, Crusser," Tranadal said.

"Tranadal." The brawny man towering over Landish pulled his hood back to reveal a bald head and dark skin. "I forgot elven eyesight can see so keenly."

Montague frowned. *Did he say elven?*

Tranadal stood ready, the butt of his naginata on the floor as he gripped its shaft. "This man will be king, Crusser. Try anything and you will die. As it stands, the thief's life is forfeit."

Landish snorted. "Sorry to disappoint you, Tran-a-dumb, but I am incredibly stubborn when it comes to dying." He grinned. "Besides, Crusser and I are not alone. In fact, we outnumber you by a fair margin because Captain Giralt and the Midnight Guard remain loyal to Queen Narine."

Montague, Tranadal, and Vordan all turned toward the Midnight Guard.

Captain Giralt drew his sword, the two dozen guards along the aisle behind him mirroring the action. The guards posted at each entrance also drew their weapons and stood ready.

"Sheath your blades, for I am your new king," Montague snarled, "Why remain loyal to a dead woman when it will only bring you death?"

Landish said, "Did I forget to mention...Queen Narine is *not* dead."

Montague blinked. "Of course, she is. I saw her body myself."

"Wrong, Montague," Dianza said. "She is alive, and she is furious."

The images of the priestess and her cleric wavered, their faces, hair, and clothing shifting to something else. Suddenly, Narine Killarius and a tall brunette with a sabre stood before him.

Faced with a woman who had risen from the dead, Montague gaped in shock. *It cannot be!* He backed up a step, his foot finding only open air. Arms waving, he tried to catch his balance, but it was too late. A shriek slipped from his throat as he tumbled down the dais stairs.

Chaos erupted.

40

JUST DUE

Using a trickle of magic too slight to detect, Narine held the illusions of Dianza and her cleric in place. When the time came, she released the spell, the illusions fading to reveal her and Harlequin. Montague gaped in shock, stepped back, and fell down the dais stairs as the others in the room leapt into action.

Narine drew in her magic and cast an energy construct. Through it, she released a bolt of lightning as Montague rolled to his back at the bottom of the stairs. Ready, the wizard cast a shield of grounding. The bolt struck, electricity sizzling across the invisible shield to the temple floor, blasting the rock tiles in a spray of shards.

Still on the floor, the man formed a wedge of hardened air and blasted it toward Narine's lower legs. She leapt, but it was too late. The blast swept her feet from beneath her, and she fell forward on her chest, the air bursting from her lungs. Lifting her head, she saw Montague rising to his feet, ready to strike.

The moment Narine revealed herself, Jace drew both fulgur blades, expecting an attack. He had no idea it would come so swiftly.

Tranadal opened his mouth, emitting a horrible sound as he raised his naginata. The elf then leapt, took three steps along the back of a bench, and launched himself. Staff and blade spinning as he flipped, Tranadal landed before Jace and swung. The naginata flashed with terrifying speed, but Jace used his enchanted blades to parry it as he dove away. The elf then attacked Crusser, who blocked a strike with his sword. The butt of the elf's staff came around to thump the man's chest, launching him down the aisle.

Tranadal turned back toward Jace who was rising to his feet, his eyes wide as the elf burst forward. Jace held his blades ready, but feared the elf's superior speed. Rather than attack him, the elf darted along the dais stairs and leapt at Giralt as the lieutenant swung his longsword at Montague's back. The blow never landed, for Tranadal blocked it and countered with an upward strike, severing Giralt's sword arm from his body. Screaming, the man stumbled backward onto a bench, blood spurting from his wound.

As the other guards rushed in to attack, Tranadal emitted another horrible wail, darkness enveloping his blade. With incredible, inhuman speed, he burst forward and confronted the guards.

Jace, back on his feet, spotted Narine lying on the dais and began to move toward her when a sword came at him. Just in time, he swung his arm, sparks crackling when the fulgur blade deflected Vordan's strike.

On the dais stairs, Harlequin twisted her wrist, using her sabre to parry a blow from one of Montague's guards. Another guard came at her from the side. She twisted to avoid the lunge and then chopped down. Her blade struck the man's hand, severing several fingers and forcing him to drop his blade. The other guard swung at her legs and she leapt, landing a stair higher, but backing away as three guards advanced on her.

Her sabre slashing left and right, she blocked strike after strike, focused and intent on defending herself. Her back struck an altar. She blocked a high swing from the man on her right, while one on her left swiped at her legs. Leaping backward, she landed on the altar and rolled off, narrowly avoiding an overhand chop, the guard's sword clanging off the stone. She raised an arm and shied away as a bolt of wizard lighting struck the altar, cracking it and sending a spray of shards pummeling her arms and torso.

Panting, she lowered her arm to find the three guards rounding the altar, the first guard's sword coming at her.

On her knees at the top of the dais, Narine wove multiple shields, one of grounding, another against heat, a third against physical attacks, each to counter magical attacks intended to end her. Casting and holding multiple constructs required every bit of her concentration and magical strength, even when bolstered by her hand chain and anklet. Yet, Montague wove spell after spell, striking again and again, altering his attacks while others battled around him, none daring to get close.

Electricity, fire, and other forms of deadly magic deflected from her shields, burning and destroying the immediate surroundings. Two altars lay broken, the third cracked and scorched, and the nearby stairs fared no better. Narine worried that she might tire, since women were unsuited for energy constructs and those used for shielding. Her enchanted jewelry had allowed her to survive thus far, but could she outlast Montague's magic? Until the flurry of attacks slowed, she dared not attempt a counter attack and prayed for someone else, anyone else, to intervene.

However, wizard duels were the thing of legend. Infamous legend. And few were brave or foolish enough to attempt to enter the fray.

Crusser reclaimed his weapon and rose to his feet. His chest throbbed, sharp pain flaring across his right side with each movement. Trained to fight with either hand, he gripped the sword in his left and surveyed the scene.

At the far side of the dais, Narine and Montague were engaged in a battle of magic – light and fire flashing again and again. To one side, Jace fought against Vordan, the small thief holding his own. Harlequin stood between an altar and the dais stairs, facing three guards, two others lying dead at her feet. Her sabre flowed from one to another, blocking their advancing strikes, their backs to him as they slowly forced her to retreat toward the deadly wizard attacks.

Ignoring his pain, Crusser dashed down the aisle and struck, his sword slashing into the hamstring of the nearest guard. The man screamed and fell, his comrade turning toward Crusser, who kicked and drove a heel into the man's leg, forcing him to stumble into the third guard. Crusser swung again, the guard blocking his blade unaware of Harlequin's thrust until it slid into his armpit. With that opening, Crusser lunged past the man and drove his longsword into the exposed side of the last guard.

Jace dodged a thrust from Vordan. The bigger man snarled as he lifted his sword with two hands and chopped down, intending to cleave Jace in two. Before the blade could fall, Jace dove forward, twisting as he slid on his side, between the man's spread legs as Vordan's sword tip struck the floor, narrowly missing. As Jace slid along the marble, he slashed, the tip of his fulgur blade gouging through the man's inner thigh, severing his artery. Vordan screamed and collapsed. Jace rolled and rose to his feet in a flash, racing toward the dais.

Lightning flared from Montague's outstretched hands, sizzling across an invisible dome protecting Narine, who grimaced at the effort. Rather than avoid the deadly magic, Jace climbed the stairs, leapt, and intercepted it in mid-air. The thunderbolt struck Jace in the chest, his amulet growing so cold it burned, the magic fizzling away. The fierce expression on the wizard's face faded, his eyes widening as Jace came at him with a fulgur blade raised. Jace landed as the blade slammed into Montague's chest, buried to the hilt. The wizard staggered backward while blue sparks sizzled around his wound. He fell to his knees and gaped at Jace.

"For treason," Jace said as he gripped the hilt. "I sentence you to death."

He yanked his weapon free and the wizard fell over, sparkling, crimson blood running down his silver robes.

Jace turned to find Narine rising to her feet, focusing on something beyond where he stood. Spinning around, he looked past Montague's corpse and found a trail of bodies littering the aisle. Twenty-five Midnight Guard, all highly trained warriors, lay dead. At the far end of the room, Tranadal remained upright, the elf and his naginata moving at an impossible speed, leaving trails of darkness that faded from the air shortly after the blade swept past. In the span of a breath, the four remaining guards fell to his blade.

The Drow then turned toward the dais. His dark almond-shaped eyes scanned the carnage until they landed on the dead wizard at Jace's feet.

A grimace turned Tranadal's thin lips downward. "This is unfortunate."

Harlequin stopped beside Jace, holding her bloody sabre. "They are all dead, Tranadal. Montague is dead as well. Xavan's plan has failed."

Crusser stood beside her. "Come and face us, Drow. Let us see how you do against a wizard and three skilled opponents."

The dark elf stared for a long moment, seeming to consider the challenge. Finally, he said, "This is not over. Beware, for you are all doomed."

Lifting his hood, Tranadal opened the door and walked out, the chanting from the crowd growing louder for a moment before the door closed and the temple fell silent.

Jace and Narine waited in the antechamber, anxiously waiting for Harlequin and Crusser. Just one room away, the temple remained quiet, its aisles and dais still littered with corpses.

He turned toward Narine whose eyes were downcast. With a finger, he lifted her chin and turned her face toward him. In her eyes, he saw doubt and worry.

"Are you alright?"

She looked away. "I suppose."

"You do realize we won, right?"

"Yes…but it should have gone much better."

He shook his head. "Nobody could have guessed the Drow would destroy thirty Midnight Guard on his own. I don't know what magic Tranadal holds, but his speed…that was supernatural."

"It's not that," her voice filled with sadness.

Gently, he asked, "What then?"

Narine took a deep breath and exhaled slowly. "When I revealed myself to Montague, I reveled when I saw the shock in his eyes. As expected, it shook him to the bones. He even fell down the dais stairs." She looked Jace in the eye. "I had the advantage of surprise, but I selfishly savored the moment rather than striking immediately. When I finally attacked, I chose an energy spell, ill-suited for a woman. The delay allowed Montague to shield himself. By then, he had recovered and took the offensive." A tear trailed down her cheek, her voice a weak sob. "It took everything I had to protect myself."

He put his hand on her arm. "You did your best…"

"No!" she snapped. "I didn't. If I had, I would have used mental manipulation. Yes, wizards are resistant to it…" She lifted her fist, flashing the enchanted hand chain. "But with my boosted power and Montague caught off balance, I could have reached out, touched him, and attacked his mind. His involvement would have ended right there."

"Perhaps…" He did not like seeing her so upset. "Regardless, it worked out. Montague is dead, and he will cause no more problems."

"You heard Tranadal…"

"Yes. The Order will not stop with Montague."

"What will we do?"

Jace had already decided on a course of action, one he suspected Narine would resist. "We must remain dead."

As expected, she reacted poorly, her voice rising in tone and volume. "What?"

Placing his hand on her upper arm, he shook his head. Although emotional, Narine responded to logic once the facts were made clear. He hoped she would do so this time.

Jace explained, "Our funeral has passed. The world believes Narine Killarius and Jerrell Landish are dead. Those who knew of our survival now lie as corpses in the room next door…other than Tranadal. I think it is best we distance ourselves from Marquithe while we figure out what to do next. That means we leave the throne vacant and allow the Order to place another of their choosing upon it. If you are concerned for the people of Farrowen, we can best serve them by going after the Order and stopping them from achieving their end goal, whatever that may be. Think about it. If they will go to these lengths to place a pawn upon the Farrowen throne, what else do they have planned?"

She pressed her lips together and stared at him while he spoke, her expression slowly softening until the sadness returned to her gaze. "So, my reign has officially ended."

"I am afraid so."

The door opened. Crusser and Harlequin entered.

"It is done." Crusser said.

"Dianza and her cleric are freed?" Narine asked.

"Yes," Harlequin replied. "And we told them about Montague paying for his role in Narine's assassination. They went to gather more guards and will return to the temple soon. Neither knows anything about you two being alive or your involvement today."

"Good," Jace turned to Narine. "We are done here. Let's return to Kelmar."

With a nod, Narine turned toward the center of the room, furrowing her brow in concentration until a gateway appeared. The opening was only four feet in diameter, the top of it five feet off the floor. *She is tiring*, he thought, knowing how taxing the spell could be.

Crusser and Harlequin each ducked through the portal. Jace and Narine followed them, leaving Marquithe and their old lives behind.

41

DEPARTURE

T he city of Kelmar teemed with emotion ranging from anticipation and excitement to anxiety and sadness. At the top of the Temple of the Oracle stairs, Narine waited with Jace, while Harlequin and Crusser stood a few strides away, engaged in quiet conversation. Below them, Seers in white gathered, many accompanied by children – some holding babes in their arms, others with young children tugging at their skirts, and a few with visibly upset teenagers. Not one boy stood among them.

Far across the cavern, a steady stream of dwarfs in armor followed switchbacks up the cliffside before fading into a dark tunnel. Citizens of Kelmar, both dwarfs and the male Thrall, stood in the streets, appearing mesmerized.

The temple doors opened. Xionne stepped out, followed by Zhialta and a cluster of other Seers, all old enough to be grandmothers. The petite young Seer approached the top stair, her expression resolute as she looked down at the women and children.

In a loud voice, Xionne announced, "It is time to depart." She gestured toward the elder women behind her. "Rather than risk the journey, Zhialta and the other senior Seers will remain in Kelmar while we younger Seers seek a means to change the world."

Jace arched his brow. "Change the world?"

Narine elbowed him. "Hush."

He grimaced and rubbed his ribs but remained silent.

"The Guardians will escort us and keep us safe," Xionne announced. "Some citizens have decided to join us, but most will remain here in Kelmar. Their decision is understandable, for it has been the only home any of us has ever known."

Xionne raised her arms. "However, we Seers are strong. While our original purpose has been satisfied and the Dark Lord is no longer a threat to our world, the future is not secure. We have been watchers for millennia, but we can watch no longer. It is time for the Seers to become warriors who fight for the light, for if the world falls to darkness, everything we have done will have been for naught." She lowered her arms. "With determination in your heart, let us leave Kelmar and embrace the unknown."

Xionne descended the stairs, the crowd at the bottom parting as she passed through, followed the narrow walkway between the barracks, and headed into the city. The other women and children trailed behind in a long silent procession.

Narine glanced at Jace, who watched the Seers with a furrowed brow. "What's wrong?"

He shook his head. "I don't know. This just feels…strange. Like the beginning of the end of something. Maybe it's just because the Seers have lived here for so long, bound by a single purpose, and now, it's over."

She slipped her arm beneath his and pulled herself against him. "I know what you mean. It feels like a funeral."

Still watching the departing Seers, he nodded.

Harlequin stopped beside Jace. "Shouldn't we follow them?"

Jace exhaled and nodded. "In a moment."

He pulled away from Narine and approached Zhialta. The woman arched a brow, her mouth turned down in her usual scowl.

"I suspect we will never see each other again," Jace said.

"I suspect you are correct, thief."

"While we haven't really ever gotten along, I want you to know I respect what you have done for Xionne and the Seers. I know how difficult it is to keep everyone on task."

The woman blinked. "Why, thank you, Jerrell."

His mouth turned up in a smile. "Even if you are a bitter old hag."

The other women blanched, their eyes widening in shock.

Rather than scowl or snap back at him, Zhialta burst out laughing. Narine shot a questioning glance at Jace, who merely shrugged.

As her laughter simmered, Zhialta put a hand on Jace's shoulder. "For two decades, I have been waiting for someone to say as much."

"You aren't angry?"

"No," the woman shook her head. "In fact, I like you, Jerrell…even if you are a sneak, a liar, and a cheat of a thief."

He grinned at Narine. "See? Women cannot resist my charm."

Rolling her eyes, Narine said to Zhialta, "I fear you have further inflated his head. Now, Jace may be trapped in Kelmar forever, for how can he hope to fit it through the tunnels leading out of the city?"

The old woman laughed again. This time Harlequin, Crusser, and the other elder Seers joined her. Jace gave Narine a forced scowl but was unable to hold it, eventually chuckling along with everyone else. As their laughter calmed, Jace, Narine, Harlequin, and Crusser picked up their packs. Shouldering them, they waved goodbye and headed down the stairs.

The walk through the city was akin to floating through a dream, the streets lined with dwarfs, young and old, waving as they passed by. When they came to the Cup of Life, Arletta was waiting outside the tavern.

The dwarven barkeep lifted four steaming mugs off the front step and held them out. "I heated these for you as a farewell gift."

Grinning, Jace took one. "Thank you, Arletta." He glanced at Narine, who appeared hesitant. "It would be rude to not accept."

Narine picked up a mug and smiled, thanking the woman, Harlequin and Crusser doing the same.

The four of them sipped the heated drink as they walked through the remainder of the city. They reached a bridge over an underground stream and caught up with the Seers at the base of the cavern wall, a string of women climbing the angled path to the tunnels.

After just two sips, Narine's head began to buzz. Her mind wandered as she climbed.

So much had happened since she and her companions had first visited Kelmar over a year ago. She was suddenly struck by the gravity of the changes to the world. The gods' passing, the Dark Lord's defeat, and even the loss of wizard lords seemed inconsequential in comparison to this thing she was now part of – the Seers departing from Kelmar was, somehow, the most dramatic shift of them all.

Other than Xionne and a few dwarfs, none had ever emerged from their mountain home. The entire world would be foreign to them, filled with unknowns ranging from wondrous to terrifying. For them to venture out with the intent to never return meant the world had altered in a significant way. *But, what does it mean?*

She feared the answer would come soon.

EPILOGUE

Alone in an abandoned building, Tranadal sat in the dark, brooding. He had come so close to placing Montague upon the throne, the man set to become an unwitting pawn at the helm of Farrowen. *It was that blasted thief… Somehow, Harlequin had found him and alerted him to our plans.* The pirate woman's appearance in Marquithe had caught Tranadal off guard. The fact that she had escaped from the Valley of Sol and managed to avoid Order agents for so long was one thing, but travelling halfway across the realm only to turn up at the worst possible time…it was an odd twist of fate, one he dare not ignore.

After the confrontation, he gathered every Order agent in the city, twenty-six in total, and sent them to search for the queen, Landish, Harlequin, and Crusser. Four were posted in the palace itself, four more assigned to watch the perimeter, and the rest scoured every inn and tavern in the area. Two days later, the search had proven fruitless. *Somehow, they escaped the city.* Better to admit defeat than deny the truth.

He stood and approached the dormant fireplace stuffed with broken furniture – victims of a rare fit of rage. A thick layer of dust coated the mantle. The building had been unoccupied for years, perhaps since it was last purchased. The Order owned numerous buildings in every major city across the Eight Wizardoms, some going unused for decades while others were occupied on a regular basis. A few were among the most profitable businesses in the world.

From his pack, he removed a small vial. The stopper came free with a pop. He squatted and dribbled three drops of dark liquid onto the corpse of a chair. Capping and pocketing the vial, he rose, backed away, and gripped Ichor. He opened his mouth and called upon the spirits bound to the weapon. Power flooded through his veins, bolstered by thirty recently captured souls. A call came from his lips, shrill and terrifying, igniting the blade at the end of his naginata. He drove the flaming metal tip into the wooden debris, the fireplace bursting to life.

Closing his mouth, he released the magic, and the souls withdrew into the weapon. Again, he squatted, this time staring into the fire.

"Sister," he said. "Dai-Seryn, hear my call."

Flames licked the wood in the fireplace, flickering, dancing, and slowly shifting from orange to purple. An image coalesced into a familiar face.

"Tranadal, I hear you." Dai-Seryn's voice echoed in his head.

He was glad to see her but reluctant to voice his failure. Still, truth cannot be denied. "I have failed, sister. Queen Narine was to die and Montague to claim the throne, but Harlequin and Crusser alerted Landish and the Farrowen queen to my plans." He shook his head. "Montague is dead, Harlequin and her cohorts missing."

Dai-Seryn stared in silence, Tranadal assuming she was relaying his information to Xavan. After a moment, she asked, "Queen Narine has abandoned the throne?"

He frowned. "It appears so. In fact, none outside the Order know of her survival, for her funeral was held days ago."

"What of our alternative plan?"

"The Gurgan girl?" He considered their encounter prior to entering the temple, the wizardess demanding Montague forgo the coronation so she might pursue the crown. *Too bad you did not listen, Montague.* "She appears eager to claim the throne. Tempest has her ear and is in position to facilitate the Gurgan girl's rise."

Again, there was a pause before Dai-Seryn replied. "You are to approach the high wizard of Eleighton. Promise her the throne with the same terms given to Montague. We *will* control Farrowen."

"It will be done," he said.

"Xavan wishes to know about Andar. He has not contacted us or any of our agents in Orenth."

Andar…he had forgotten. "I am sorry, but Andar is dead. The entire crew of *Hassaka's Breath* was killed along with him."

"What happened?"

"There was an explosion that destroyed the ship and killed the men on board." He frowned, realizing something. "I believe Harlequin and Crusser were at fault." It made too much sense, for who else would have known that Andar was to lead the takeover in Orenth? He dismissed the thought, focusing on the future. "What of the others? Vex and Temmen departed from Antari when we did."

She responded, "Vex has proven victorious in overthrowing Queen Dalia. A man bonded to the sorcerer wears the crown of Ghealdor."

Tranadal nodded. "Very good. Hopefully, Temmen will have similar success in Pallanar."

Dai-Seryn said, "Arci-Aesha and I will soon depart from the Valley, for the next phase of our plan draws near."

He smiled. "We shall sow chaos like the wizardoms have never known."

As her flickering image faded, Dai-Seryn said. "And when we are finished, the Drow will rule over mankind."

The story continues in
Legend of the Sky Sword, Fall of Wizardoms Book Two

NOTE FROM THE AUTHOR

Thus **Fall of Wizardoms** has begun. You can expect five more novels in the series, all releasing in 2021.

To make sure you do not miss any updates or new release, join my author newsletter. As a gift for joining, you will receive Wizardoms companion novellas featuring Jace, Brogan, Narine, and even Tranadal.

If interested, proceed to www.JeffreyLKohanek.com.

Best Wishes,
Jeff

Follow me on:
Amazon
Bookbub

ALSO BY JEFFREY L. KOHANEK

Fate of Wizardoms

Book One: Eye of Obscurance

Book Two: Balance of Magic

Book Three: Temple of the Oracle

Book Four: Objects of Power

Book Five: Rise of a Wizard Queen

Book Six: A Contest of Gods

* * *

Warriors, Wizards, & Rogues (Fate of Wizardoms 0)

Fate of Wizardoms Boxed Set: Books 1-3

Fate of Wizardoms Box Set" Books 4-6

Fall of Wizardoms

God King Rising

Legend of the Sky Sword

Curse of the Elf Queen

Shadow of a Dragon Priest - Aug 2021

Book Five: TBD - Oct 2021

Book Six: TBD -Nov 2021

Runes of Issalia

The Buried Symbol: Runes of Issalia 1

The Emblem Throne: Runes of Issalia 2

An Empire in Runes: Runes of Issalia 3

Rogue Legacy: Runes of Issalia Prequel

* * *

Runes of Issalia Bonus Box

Wardens of Issalia

Made in the USA
Monee, IL
07 April 2023

31521551R00173